The Strange Story
of Linda Lee

As the creator of the Duke de Richleau, Gregory Sallust and Roger Brook, Dennis Wheatley has become world famous. Now he produces an entirely different rabbit out of his hat: the loves and adventures of a beautiful girl with all the odds against her.

> She was poor but she was honest, victim of a village crime
> For the squire's cruel passion robbed 'er of 'er 'onest nime.
> Then she went right up ter London, for to 'ide 'er grief and shime,
> There she met another squire, an' she lorst 'er nime again.
>> (Old drinking party song)

Except that Linda's first seducer was not a squire, the above gives a fair idea of the opening of this story. Actually, too, she ran away to London because life as 'a slave' in a market garden had become intolerable to her. Linda's exceptional vitality, good looks and eager inquiring mind led her second squire to act as a fairy godfather. He transformed her from an uncouth country wench into a cultured and elegant beauty, whom he could take with pride to de luxe restaurants, and to travel with him in Europe. But when he died, Linda was left in dire straits.

Linda was not a wicked girl, but to save herself she committed a crime, and to escape arrest had to flee the country. For many thousands of miles she is pursued by the police, backwards and forwards across Canada. In the United States she is faced with even more desperate situations. Time after time only her wits and courage save her. At last it is her own patriotism that brings her to book.

After nearly forty years of writing about espionage, battles, international intrigue and gun-fights, what a challenge it was to produce this kind of book! Who, other than the 'Prince of Story Tellers', could have done it? Again he gives us those graphic descriptions of far countries in which he has travelled, twist after twist in the plot, pages of agonising suspense and ever-rising excitement until it is not prison but death that stalks brave and lovely Linda—then a magnificent denouement.

BY DENNIS WHEATLEY

NOVELS

The Launching of Roger Brook
The Shadow of Tyburn Tree
The Rising Storm
The Man Who Killed the King
The Dark Secret of Josephine
The Rape of Venice
The Sultan's Daughter
The Wanton Princess
Evil in a Mask
The Ravishing of Lady Mary
  Ware

The Scarlet Impostor
Faked Passports
The Black Baroness
V for Vengeance
Come into my Parlour
Traitor's Gate
They Used Dark Forces

Black August
Contraband
The Island Where Time Stands
  Still
The White Witch of the South
  Seas

To the Devil—a Daughter
The Satanist

The Prisoner in the Mask
The Second Seal
Vendetta in Spain
Three Inquisitive People
The Forbidden Territory
The Devil Rides Out
The Golden Spaniard
Strange Conflict
Codeword—Golden Fleece
Gateway to Hell
Dangerous Inheritance

The Quest of Julian Day
The Sword of Fate
Bill for the Use of a Body

The Eunuch of Stamboul
The Secret War
The Fabulous Valley
Sixty Days to Live
Such Power is Dangerous
Uncharted Seas
The Man Who Missed the War
The Haunting of Toby Jugg
Star of Ill-Omen
They Found Atlantis
The Ka of Gifford Hillary
Curtain of Fear
Mayhem in Greece
Unholy Crusade

SHORT STORIES

Mediterranean Nights   Gunmen, Gallants and Ghosts

HISTORICAL

A Private Life of Charles II
(Illustrated by Frank C. Papé)
Red Eagle
(The Story of the Russian Revolution)

AUTOBIOGRAPHICAL

Stranger than Fiction
(War Papers for the Joint Planning Staff)
Saturdays with Bricks

A SERIOUS STUDY OF THE OCCULT

The Devil and all His Works
(With 215 illustrations in colour and black and white)

DENNIS WHEATLEY

The Strange Story
of Linda Lee

HUTCHINSON OF LONDON

HUTCHINSON & CO (*Publishers*) LTD
3 Fitzroy Square, London W1

London Melbourne Sydney Auckland
Wellington Johannesburg Cape Town
and agencies throughout the world

First published 1972

*This book has been set in Baskerville type, printed in Great
Britain on antique wove paper by Anchor Press, and
bound by Wm. Brendon, both of Tiptree, Essex*

ISBN 0 09 110330 4

DEDICATION

for

Jim and Helen Phillipson

At whose home, The Manor House, Everton,
the plot of this story was thought out early in
the mornings of a Saturday and a Sunday

NOTE

*

No character in this book is based on that of any living person, and their names were chosen by the author as those of people he had never met or even heard of.

Contents

8   CONTENTS

1

Escape

IT was early on the evening of the first Sunday in May 1970 that Linda stood on the platform of the little railway station at Market Rasen, in Lincolnshire.

She was a big girl: five feet eleven in height, broad-shouldered and strong-limbed. Her brown hair had golden lights in it and was short and springy; so that it stood up naturally in dozens of wavy curls, forming a bright aureole round her head. Although she was wearing her best coat and skirt, they were obviously of poor quality, and the shabby canvas suitcase beside her was bursting at the seams.

Except for herself and the solitary porter, the little station was deserted. As she stood, half-concealed, in the entrance of the waiting-room, she tapped one large foot impatiently and kept glancing nervously from side to side first in the direction from which the train would come then through the railings toward a road leading up to the station.

Her full-lipped mouth was tightly closed above her strong, aggressive chin, but she was praying silently, 'Don't let him come! Don't let him get here before the train! I'm over eighteen now, so I'm legally of age. He no longer has the right to stop me. But don't let him come! Oh, don't let him catch me!'

It was her father whom she feared might appear at any moment, for she was running away from home and had been caught in the act by her mother. She had chosen Sunday evening as the best time for getting clear away with a good start because, after his afternoon nap, her father always went down to the village pub, and her mother usually spent a couple of hours with friends who made up the Chapel sewing circle, while Linda watered the plants in the glasshouses that formed a part of her father's market garden, and prepared the Sunday supper.

That evening her mother had not felt well, so had left the sewing circle early. To her amazement, she had found Linda up in her room, wearing, instead of overalls, her best outfit, and on her bed was an open suitcase crammed with the contents of her scanty wardrobe.

No explanation, other than the truth, had been possible. In a spate of angry words, Linda had declared she would not stand the life she was leading a day longer, and meant to find a job in London. Her mother was well aware that she had ample cause for complaint, but endeavoured to persuade her to change her mind, promising that she would speak to 'Pa' about making things easier for her.

But Linda proved adamant. She knew Pa too well to believe that he would ever change. Bill Lee was a great, red-faced brute of a man, ignorant of everything except the soil from which he made his living. He was honest, God-fearing and worked exceptionally long hours without complaining of his lot. But he expected his wife and daughter to work as hard as he did himself, and woe betide them if they showed any slackness or wanted time off to go 'gallivanting', as he called it.

Most Saturday evenings he returned home a little drunk and, if put out, knocked his cowed wife about. From time to time Linda, too, received a hefty cuff. It was not to be wondered at that she had grown to hate the very sight of him. Mrs. Lee's tearful appeals to Linda, that they could not possibly run the place without her having been brushed angrily aside, she took a different tone and began to threaten. Turning toward the door, she cried:

'Very well then, you ungrateful girl. I'll go and fetch your Pa from the local. He'll soon learn you for this he will; yes, with his belt across your bottom.'

At that, Linda had become desperate. She was much bigger and stronger than her mother. Grabbing her by the arm, she had pulled her back and cried, 'No, you don't, Ma! I'm going to London and nothing ain't going to stop me!'

The struggle was brief. Mrs. Lee tripped on a mat and fell heavily on the far side of the bed. Linda seized the opportunity to snap to the locks of her suitcase and run out into the passage with it. Dropping it there, she turned, pulled the key from the lock of the door, pushed it in on the outside and, before her mother could stop her, had turned it. Three minutes later, she had lashed the suitcase on to the back of her bicycle and was pedalling with all the strength in her long legs from the outskirts of Willingham village, where they lived, to the railway station five miles away at Market Rasen.

Her mother's unexpected arrival on the scene had led to her starting at least ten minutes before she had intended, so she had arrived at the station nearly a quarter of an hour before the train was due. She had meant to have the bicycle labelled and put in the guard's van, then sell it in London. But panic had

decided her to hide as soon as possible, so she had left
the bike behind a shed in the station yard, bought her
ticket, hastily gone to ground in the ladies' lavatory and
emerged from it only when she saw from her wrist
watch that the train should arrive at any moment.

During that agonising wait she had weighed up the
chances of her father's catching her. Although she had
left her mother locked in, there would be little difficulty
in escaping from the bedroom. The small, ugly, late-
Victorian house was jerry-built, and the door of her
room was flimsy. If her mother threw her weight against
it, the lock would give. It would take her only five
minutes to cycle to the 'Dragon and Crumpet'. In
another ten minutes Pa should be back at the house and
in the station-wagon. If things had gone like that, it
would be a toss-up whether he or the train arrived first
at the station.

As she stood in the doorway of the waiting-room she
was straining her ears for the sound of a motor engine.
In the hush of this quiet Sunday evening, she could
have heard it while still half a mile away.

She caught a distant rumble. It increased. Then, to
her intense relief, the train appeared in the distance. It
was a 'slow' and even while moving seemed to crawl.
As Linda stepped out of the waiting-room, she looked
anxiously along the platform and through the railings
beyond it. Her heart missed a beat. The noise from the
engine had drowned that of the motor; but there was
her father's station-wagon no more than a few hundred
yards away, coming all-out up the road.

The leisurely train meandered to a halt. Linda made
a dash for the nearest carriage, praying as she ran
across the platform that her father's view of her was
blocked by some intervening buildings. But it was cer-

tain that he would describe her to the porter and learn that she was on the train. Her only hope now lay in his failing to find which carriage she had got into before the train moved off.

Seizing the handle of the carriage door she wrenched it open and pushed her suitcase in along the floor. As she did so she threw a glance over her shoulder. Her heart missed a beat. Her father had just come through the barrier, but he was looking in the opposite direction. Jumping into the carriage, she slammed the door behind her, heaved her suitcase up on to the rack, then flung herself down in the far corner. Huddling back into it, she prayed frantically for the train to start.

The only other occupant of the carriage was a rather plump man of medium height. He had neither beard nor whiskers, but smoothly-brushed greying hair, and was obviously of a much older generation.

Suddenly Linda caught the sound of pounding feet. Next moment her father appeared outside the carriage window. It flashed on her that he must have glimpsed her at the moment she had boarded the train. He was carrying his big blackthorn stick, that he always took with him when he went to the pub on Sundays. Purple in the face from rage, and his thirty-yard dash along the platform to catch her, he waved the stick and bellowed:

'Come art of there, you bitch! Tryin' ter do the dirty on me an' yer Ma! I'll learn yer! Come art, or I'll break me stick across yer bottom.'

Petrified, Linda crouched back in her corner. She knew that even if she obeyed him, when he got her back to the house, he would half-kill her. A whistle blew. Her father grabbed the handle of the carriage door to pull it open. Linda threw a despairing glance at the middle-aged man opposite her, wondering, if she appealed to him, whether he would intervene when her father started to drag her from the carriage. But he was not looking at her. When she jumped in he had been reading a book. Now he had laid it down and was staring out of the window at her father.

As Bill Lee was grasping his stick in his right hand, he had made the mistake of trying to open the door with his left. The handle was a little stiff and it failed to turn. With a curse, he transferred his stick from one hand to the other. At that moment the train began to move. With his right hand he again seized the handle. It turned but pulled him along with it. He began to run. The speed of the train increased, preventing him from pulling the door open. In the distance the angry shouts of the porter could be heard. Suddenly Bill Lee stumbled. The door handle was wrenched from his grasp. Another moment and he had disappeared from Linda's view. A great sigh of relief escaped her and, after a few minutes, the beating of her heart slowed down.

When she had sufficiently recovered to take stock of her companion, she put him down as about fifty. He had been studying her with interest out of kindly hazel eyes; but as soon as their glances met, he quickly looked away and resumed reading his book. The hand that held it was slim, long-fingered, pale pink and carefully manicured. Instinctively, Linda hid her own hands in her jacket pockets. They were not ugly, but rough from hard work, and, strive as she would, she could never quite succeed in getting all the dirt from under her nails. She had also taken in the fact that the man's clothes were unostentatious but of fine material and well cut.

Her nerves now at rest, and having no book to read, she amused herself by speculating about him. He had plump, slightly-reddish cheeks, which suggested a love of good living. His mouth was thin, but had laughter lines at the corners. His nose was on the small side and high-bridged. His most striking feature was his broad, smooth forehead, and it was that which made Linda think that he was probably a professor or an artist.

While she had been getting her breath back and settling down, he had had ample time to form an impression of her. Obviously a country girl, he decided. No make-up, other than a touch of lipstick, and healthy, rosy cheeks from leading an open-air life. A fine, Junoesque creature, who, given ample money for clothes and beauty treatments, could have made men's heads turn in any de luxe restaurant. The halo of curling bronze hair was a fine example of what has been termed 'woman's crowning glory'; the big golden-brown eyes, with very clear whites and long lashes under beautifully arched eyebrows, were truly splendid; and the firm mouth, with its very full underlip, indicated a forceful, determined personality. But the cheap clothes, scruffed shoes and awful bulging suitcase, all revealed that the girl came from a poor home; so she was probably lacking in all but a rudimentary education and had in her beautiful head only an apology for a brain. He had, for a few moments, been acutely interested in the attempt by the coarse-looking, red-faced man to get her to leave the train; but it was no affair of his. With that casual summary the gentleman sitting opposite Linda dismissed her from his mind and concentrated on his book.

For half an hour the train meandered on, stopping briefly at two stations. Then the door of the compartment was opened by the ticket collector, with the usual request.

Linda's companion produced his ticket and it was duly clipped. She opened her bag and handed the man hers. After a glance, he said, 'Sorry, Miss. This is a second, and you're travelling first.' Then he produced his pad and added, 'I'll have to charge you excess. One pound six shillings please.'

In her panic, Linda had not noticed the class of the carriage into which she had jumped. Now she had let herself in for spending money she could ill afford. On the previous morning she had drawn all her savings out of her Post Office account. They amounted to little more than thirty pounds; but she had decided that it would be ample to keep her in a modest boarding house in London until she found a job.

Diving again into her bag, she ignored her purse, knowing that after buying her ticket it contained only a few shillings. Quickly she hunted for the wallet she had bought to hold her savings. Next moment she was frantically turning the things in the bag over and over. But the wallet was not there.

Then the reason why it was missing came back to her. The wallet had been lying on her dressing table. She had been about to put it in her bag when her mother came into the room. In the scene that followed, she had forgotten all about it and, when dashing for the door, left it there.

Horrified, she realised the awful truth. She was on her way to London with barely enough money to buy herself a meal, let alone a bed.

2

The Third Alternative

LINDA's golden-brown eyes were wide with fright and apprehension. Her mouth dropped open, then she stammered, 'I . . . I'm sorry. I didn't mean ter travel first. Couldn't I move to a second-class compartment?'

The elderly collector shook his head. 'First-class coaches are clearly marked, Miss. You couldn't have failed to see the yellow line.'

'But I did. I promise. I was in an awful hurry.'

'That's as may be. But you're travelling first, and I 'ave ter abide by the rules. One pound six shillings please.'

Linda was almost in tears. In her ignorance she had awful visions of being sent to prison for defrauding British Railways. Miserably she burst out, 'But I can't pay. I haven't got the money. I left me notecase on the dressing table.'

The well-groomed, middle-aged man opposite her had put down his book. Taking his wallet from his pocket, he said, 'That is the sort of thing that might happen to anyone. You must allow me to lend you the excess fare.'

'That's terrible good of you.' Linda swallowed hard. 'But . . . but I may not be able to pay you back.'

Handing two notes to the collector, her rescuer gave a quiet laugh. 'What refreshing honesty. It is as good as a promise that you will when you can afford to, and I'm in no hurry for the money.'

The collector scribbled a receipt. Handing it to Linda, he closed the door and went off down the corridor. After a moment, she said, 'Thank you, Sir. I'm that grateful. Cross me heart, I am.'

Her companion smiled again, produced a visiting card and gave it to her. 'There's my name and address. When you are really in the money, you can send me a cheque.'

The card read, *Roland Frobisher, 103 Park Side West, London, N.W.1.*, and in the bottom right-hand corner, *St. James's.* The latter puzzled her, as she had no idea that it was the name of a club. Returning his smile, she said, 'More likely it'll be a postal order. Only businesses and rich people has bank accounts, an' there's not much chance of me becoming rich all of a sudden. When I get to London I haven't even got a job to go to.'

'No doubt you'll soon find one.'

'Hope ter goodness I do! By leaving me notecase behind I've landed meself in an awful mess.'

'Surely your—er—father or mother will post it on to you?'

Linda shook her head and again tears came into her eyes. 'Ma might,' she gulped. 'That's if she don't let on to Pa that I forgot it. If she does, he won't let her. That was him you saw tryin' to get the door open. He's mad as hell at me. You see, I've run away.'

A kindly smile again lit Frobisher's plump face. 'I guessed that might be the case. So you are going to the great, big, wicked city to make your fortune, eh?'

'Oh, go on! You're kidding,' Linda retorted. 'Dick

Whittington and them sort only happen in fairy-tales. All I'm after is a chance ter lead a happier life.'

At that moment a steward passed down the corridor, calling out, 'First service. First service.'

Frobisher stood up, put his book into his suitcase and said, 'Before starting on any adventure it is always wise to have a good, sustaining meal. You must be my guest for dinner.'

Linda hesitated only for a moment; but she had a hearty appetite and had left without cutting the sandwiches she had meant to bring with her. 'You are nice, you really are,' she said in a small voice, and, when he held the door open for her, preceded him to the restaurant car.

Although Frobisher was not a tall or impressive figure, he had the quiet, self-confident manner that always begets good service. The moment the head steward caught sight of him, he hurried forward, gave them a table for two and produced both the menu and the wine list.

'Sherry?' asked Linda's host, 'or something with gin in it?'

She shook her head. 'I never touch spirits. Fact is, I hardly ever drink at all. But I'd like a sherry. It'll cheer me up.'

'A dry sherry then, and a glass of hock to follow won't do you any harm.' Frobisher ordered ham and eggs for himself, and Linda said she would have the set meal. Then, to encourage her to talk about herself, he said:

'Now I'd better tell you a little about the kind of chap I am. I'm a scientist of sorts. I'm fortunate in having a certain amount of money and I don't like being tied down. By keeping my freedom, I can go abroad whenever I wish. But now and again the back-room boys call me in to help on special problems, and that suits me because I'd hate to lead an entirely idle life. I'm married, but my wife is no longer living with me. I have a stepdaughter who is also married, but no children of my own. I've a comfortable house overlooking Regent's Park, and I belong to a Club where I lunch fairly frequently, and another where I play bridge occasionally. So you see, although I don't lead an exciting life, it is a very pleasant one.'

'You're lucky,' Linda remarked seriously. 'Ever so lucky. They say one half of the world don't know how the other half lives, an' I'm sure that's true. A gentleman so fortunate as you just couldn't picture the God-awful sort of life I've led up to now.'

'Try me and see,' he smiled.

'Here goes, then. I haven't told you me name yet. It's Linda Lee; Pa is a market gardener. Not a grand one with acres of glass and half a dozen men workin' for him. He's what they call a smallholder. We've got three and a half acres. It's mostly tulips. They're our main crop, but we've two hothouses an' several rows of Dutch lights. In them we grow tomatoes, lettuces and bedding plants that we can sell local before the tulips come on. Pa works the place and takes the stuff to market. The only help he has is Ma and meself. But a good part of her time goes in shopping, cooking and keeping the house decent.

'When people eat vegetables and enjoy the flowers they buy they never think about the grind it is for other people to grow them. A market garden's not like a factory, where the workers get there at eight o'clock and knock off at five. There's no union hours and no weekends off either. Everything's got ter be watered, mostly twice a day. While each crop is growin', it has ter be hoed between the rows. Soon as it's over, the ground has to be dug afresh an' manured before the new crop's planted. The weather must be watched all the time and someone always there to open or shut the ventilation to the houses. The plants growin' in them must be sprayed. When they've finished bearing, the houses have ter be disinfected and all the pots washed so as they can be used again. It never stops, never. Diggin', to hoein', stakin', tyin'-in, prunin', waterin', pickin', packin', and bunchin' for market, day in day out, from dawn to dusk, with hardly an hour off to call your own. That's the life I've led ever since I was old enough ter be taken away from school.'

Frobisher shook his head sadly. 'You're right. In my time I must have spent hundreds of pounds on flowers, but the labour that goes into growing them has never once crossed my mind. You poor child. I don't wonder you have run away.'

'It weren't so much the work that got me down,' Linda went on. 'Pa hardly ever let me have an evening off, because there were always bills to be sent out, keepin' the books up-to-date, orderin' bulbs an' seeds, writin' labels and other chores to be done. I didn't have no chance to enjoy meself like other girls, and I thought meself lucky if I could get to a cinema or a village hop 'bout once in ten days. It weren't quite so bad when Sid was still at home, but since he 'opped it, often I've been so tired nights that on floppin' inter bed I could have slept the clock round.'

'Who was Sid?'

'My brother. Sid's six years older than me. He chucked his hand in a bit over five years ago. My! You should have seen the row there was when one evening

after supper he told Pa what he could do with his
something tulips. And that he was going ter emigrate to
Canada. There'd have been a stand-up fight if Ma
hadn't snatched up a broom and threatened to bash
whichever of them started it. How Sid had ever
managed ter save enough fer his fare none of us could
think. Not till afterwards. Then it came out. He'd
collected some of the market-garden accounts owing to
Pa, on the q.t. I suppose that's why he never let us
know what become of him. He cleared out next day
and not a word have we heard from him since.'

'From what you've told me of your father, one can
hardly blame your brother. But about yourself. What
sort of job do you hope to get in London?'

'I'd like to be a secretary, a private secretary to a
gentleman like you. That would be much nicer than
workin' in some office.'

'You can type and take shorthand then?' Frobisher
asked with surprise.

'I can type. I typed all our accounts and business
letters. Can't do shorthand, though. I meant to take a
course.'

Frobisher looked a little dubious. 'To get a really
pleasant private post one needs quite a bit more than
being just a shorthand typist. I think you'll find that
you will have to do a year or two in an office first.'

Tears came to Linda's eyes. 'I said I *meant* to take a
course. But . . . but how can I, now I've lost me
money?'

'Surely you can borrow enough from relatives or
friends with whom you are going to stay?'

She shook her head. 'I'm not. I don't know no-one
in London.'

'Good Lord alive!' Frobisher exclaimed. 'What on

earth do you mean to do, then? How can you possibly get along with not a soul to turn to and only the few shillings in your purse?'

'You're askin'! Heaven knows, I don't. Leavin' that thirty quid was cruel luck. Still, I'll manage somehow. On all the big stations there's always do-gooders who look after people in trouble; so I bin told. Maybe they'd get me a bed fer the night at a welfare centre. Come morning I'll find a Labour Exchange an' take the first job that offers.'

'But you wouldn't be paid till the end of the week. How could you live in the meantime?'

'I've got a little brooch what my grandmother left me. I could pawn that and my wrist watch for a few quid.'

Frobisher shook his head. 'My dear girl, I don't think you realise what you would be up against. You would find being alone in London and living on a shoestring even worse than the life you have been leading with your parents. I know it's a bitter pill to swallow, but I really think it would be best for you to go back to them. I'll let you have some more money so that you can get a room in a respectable hotel for the night and buy a return ticket tomorrow.'

'No, thanks all the same. You're kind, you are. I never met anyone so kind before. I'm not goin' back, though. Pa would give me a real belting. But it's not just my backside. If I crawled back now, I'd lose me self-respect.'

They had finished dinner. Taking a long cigar from his case, Frobisher lit it, exhaled the first draw of fragrant smoke, then said:

'Big cities are very cruel places to people who have no friends in them. You will have to take a job that you'll probably dislike, and the rates of pay are based on the fact that most young women either live at home or share a flat with several others. On your own, you'll find it difficult to make both ends meet. You won't be able to afford anything better than a back room in a third-rate boarding house, and the ill-cooked food they dish up in such places. You're going to hate that after the plentiful, honest country fare you must have been used to at home. You'll have little money to spare for cinemas or jaunts into the country on Sundays; and when winter comes, you will have to choose whether you save your shillings to keep yourself decently clothed or to push into the gas meter in your room to keep yourself from shivering under scanty bedclothes. I suggest that you postpone a decision till tomorrow. I'll give you the money for a couple of nights at a hotel and my phone number. Then, when you've thought it over, you can ring me up; and, if you've decided to go home, I'll send you the cash for your ticket.'

Linda tossed off the last of her hock, and set the glass down with a thump. 'No!' she said firmly. 'You may be right about me jumpin' out of the fryin' pan into the fire. But me mind's made up. So 'elp me God, I'll never handle a spade, a hoe or a trowel again. I'd rather throw meself into the Thames.'

Frobisher took another long pull on his cigar. Then he looked straight into her eyes and said with a quiet smile, 'There is another alternative. As I have told you, I have a very pleasant house. You could come and live there with me.'

3

The Transformation of Linda

LINDA stared at the smallish, rather plump man sitting opposite her. 'Come and live with you?' she repeated.

He nodded. 'That is what I said. And, of course, I would provide the money for you to take a secretarial course. Then, if you did well enough, you wouldn't have to take just any job that offered. You could bide your time until something that really appealed to you turned up.'

'But . . . but,' she stammered. 'You tol' me that though you're married, your wife isn't livin' with you.'

'That's so. We used to have a country cottage down near Haslemere. One night, about two years ago, she had a terrible motoring accident. At the time I was up at Harwell, the nuclear experimental station near Oxford, so I was not with her. She had been out to dinner with some neighbours. Celia had always liked her tipple, and I fear the truth is that she had had one over the odds. Anyhow, poor woman, coming out of a lane to turn on to the high road, she was careless and ran full tilt into a lorry. As she had forgotten to fasten her seat belt, her head went clean through the windscreen. Her skull was so badly fractured that she was lucky to escape with her life. Or perhaps, in one way, it would have been better if she had died. She was trepanned and, of course, everything possible was done for her; but her brain was so badly injured that she went out of her mind. Ever since, she's been well cared for in a mental home; but there's been no improvement in her condition, and the doctors say now that there never will be.'

'Cor! What an awful thing ter happen.'

'Yes. Of course, she doesn't remember anything about it, or about our marriage. As soon as she was physically well enough, I tried to tell her, but she couldn't take it in. Life as she knew it before the accident is a complete blank to her, and nothing now remains in her mind for very long. When I go to see her, after a few minutes she recognizes me as an occasional visitor and, for some strange reason, she believes I am her uncle. You see, her mind has become again that of a little child. Physically now she's very well, and she seems quite happy playing the childish games her nurse provides for her.'

Frobisher paused for a minute, then went on: 'Apart from the pain she suffered after the operations it hit me worse than it did her. She was a wonderful companion: gay, *chic*, attractive. I was devoted to her; so for months afterwards I missed her terribly. I still do.'

'Is that why you want me ter come an' live with you?'

'I suppose subconsciously that is what prompted me to suggest it. Of course, I have my Clubs, and now and then I have friends to dinner or go out to them. But, at times, living alone can be very depressing.'

Linda shook her head. 'Thanks for the offer; but I don't think I could. I know that these days most girls are willin' ter sleep with any fellow who comes along. That is, after they've been about with him a bit. And, well . . . no offence meant, but you're old enough ter be my father. So if I did, in a way I'd be acting like a tart, wouldn't I?'

'Oh, bless you!' Frobisher suddenly sat back and laughed. 'I must have put my suggestion very badly for you to get that idea. It never entered my head. I wouldn't lay a finger on you, I assure you.'

'You . . . you really mean that?' Linda stared at him doubtfully. 'You really mean you'd give me a home and not expect me to act as though I was your missus?'

'Yes. I ask nothing except your company. To have a young person living in my house would make a new life for me; so really you would be doing me a favour.'

Linda still looked a little dubious. 'It's all very well for you ter say that; but how do I know that I can trust you? You may be middle-aged, but you're no old dodderer. How do I know that when you get me all alone in that house of yours, you won't start something?'

He laughed again. 'I promise you your suspicions are quite unjustified. Since I've told you so much about myself, I won't disguise from you the fact that, at times, I still enjoy jumping into bed with a pretty girl. In fact I spend the night with one now and again. But, honestly, I'm not the sort of man who would take advantage of a girl in your situation. Perhaps, too, I ought to have mentioned that I have an Italian couple living in; so you could scream for help if I attempted to molest you.'

'Molest?' Linda laughed suddenly. 'What a funny way of putting it. And you've made me feel a bit badly now about doubtin' you. But at first I just couldn't believe you was on the level and really meant to act so decent to me.'

'It's a deal then?'

She nodded. 'Yes. And thank you, Mr. Frobisher. Or

would you rather, now, that I called you Mr. Roland?'

'My friends call me Rowley, so I'd like you to drop
the Mister and call me that. Now, how about a liqueur
to drink to our arrangement? Or would that revive
your suspicions and give you the idea that I'm trying
to make you tight in order to seduce you?'

'Seein' I'm not used to drinking, I didn't ought to
have any more. But just to show I do trust you now, I
will. And I've never had a liqueur, so I'd love ter try
one.'

He ordered a Cointreau for her and a brandy for
himself. When they returned to their carriage, her eyes
were shining and she felt a little unsteady on her feet,
but cheerfully confident that, by a miracle, an exciting
future now lay ahead of her.

At Liverpool Street they took a taxi for the long drive
up to Regent's Park. As it ran through the well-lit
streets of the almost deserted city, he pointed out to her
the Mansion House, the Bank of England and St. Paul's
and, later, the B.B.C. building. She was thrilled by her
first sight of the capital and, never having been in a
city larger than Lincoln, she was amazed at the size of
the mansions and blocks of flats in Portland Place.

When they reached Park Side West, Linda found
that the terrace of pleasant, early-Victorian houses
overlooked the south side of Regent's Park. Rowley let
himself in with his key, but also rang the bell, which
brought his Italian couple up from the basement. He
simply said to them, 'This is Miss Lee. She will be
staying with us for a while. I am sure you will make her
comfortable.' But he proffered no particulars about her
or explanation of her visit.

The couple were middle-aged: the woman short,
plump and dark, the man tall, wavy-haired and with a

slight cast in his left eye. As they studied Linda with polite interest Rowley smiled at them and said to her, 'Bella and Stefano Lucheni have been with me for eight years. She is an excellent cook, and he is a most willing fellow.'

Picking up Linda's suitcase, he added, 'Stefano will take up my cases, but I will take yours, and we'll go straight up to your room, as after your long day you must be very tired.'

On the second floor, he threw open a door, switched on the lights and ushered her into a room with twin beds. Dumping her suitcase on a chair, he turned on the electric fire, although it was not a cold night, then opened another door on the far side of the beds and said:

'Here is your bathroom. Mine is on the first floor, so this is your private domain. I do hope you will be happy here.' Turning, he smiled. 'Get to bed now, my dear, and we'll talk about your future in the morning.'

Linda returned his smile and wished him good night. As he closed the door behind him, she looked round the room, but took in only the fact that it was the sort of room she had seen only on television and never before been in. She was a little tight and suddenly felt desperately tired. Getting out of her clothes, she let them fall to the floor, undid her suitcase only to get out a nightdress, went to the bathroom, then wriggled into the nearer bed, and switched off the light. After her own thin mattress, the one on which she stretched out her long limbs was unbelievably soft and comfortable. Two minutes later she was sound asleep.

When she woke, sunshine was coming through a chink in the curtains. For a moment, finding herself in a strange bed in a strange room, she thought she must be

dreaming. Then the events of the previous evening
came back to her.

Getting out of bed, she drew back the curtains,
fingering the rich brocade with awe, then looked round
the room. The furniture was not a suite, as she had
expected it to be, but individual pieces, mostly maho-
gany, and obviously old. On the dressing table there
was a large, gilt-framed mirror; on a small desk pens,
ink, writing paper and cigarettes; on the mantelpiece
an ormolu and tortoiseshell clock, and some lovely
pieces of china.

Next she explored the bathroom. Into her mind
came the one at home: the stained walls and faded
curtain, the old iron bath with splayed feet from which
the paint had long since peeled, and the two lines of
assorted washing that always hung over it. By compari-
son this was palatial. It had a low, blue china bath, tiles
with coloured fish on them, gleaming glass shelves on
which stood a powder bowl, bath salts and scent. The
bath towel on a hot rail was blue, to match the bath,
and huge; there were others of fine linen. And Rowley
—yes, he'd said to call him Rowley—had told her that
she could have it all to herself.

Returning to the bedroom, she began to unpack her
things and, suddenly becoming conscious of their cheap-
ness, wondered unhappily what the Italian servants
would say to each other about them. She had barely
finished when there came a soft knock on the door.
Thinking that it might be Frobisher, before calling
'Come in', she scrambled quickly back into bed and
drew the bedclothes up to her chin.

But it was Bella, carrying a heavily-loaded tray. As
she set it down, she said, 'Good morning, Miss. Mr.
Frobisher, 'e say you was used to 'ave breakfas' early,

so I bring it at eight o'clock, not nine like other visitor. 'E say, too, please to join 'im in 'is study, back of 'ouse on ground floor at eleven o'clock.'

Again Linda thought she must be dreaming. Never before, except when ill with childish ailments, had she had breakfast brought to her in bed. It was an un-dreamed-of luxury. The moment Bella had left the room, Linda examined the things on the tray with delight. Under a cover there were fried bacon and eggs, hot toast concealed in a napkin; the teapot was encased in quilted satin, flanked by dishes of marmalade and butter, and a big goblet filled with slices of orange and grapefruit. Enjoying every morsel, she demolished the lot.

The bathroom provided another treat. Instead of the trickle that came from the rusty geezer at home, gallons of hot water gushed from the tap. She made lavish use of the bath salts and luxuriated in the warm water for a good twenty minutes. Having dried herself on the huge towel, she powdered and scented herself, then spent a long time trying to improve the appearance of her hands and nails.

At eleven o'clock, having made herself as attractive as she could, she went downstairs to the library. It was a comfortable, book-lined room, looking out on to a small, well-kept garden. Rowley was working at his desk in an open-necked shirt, over which he had on a loose, silk jacket caught in by a sash round the waist. She had knocked on the door, and he had called, 'Come in.' As she entered the room, he pushed aside his papers, swivelled round in his chair, smiled at her and said:

'When you are living in a house, knock on bedroom doors, but never that of a living-room.'

A little surprised by this greeting, she returned his smile and replied, 'I'm sorry. I didn't know.'

Waving her to a chair, he asked her how she had slept and when she had replied, 'Like a top, thanks,' he went on:

'My dear, from your background, I imagine there are a great many things you don't know. But if you really want to become a private secretary to a man of some importance you will have to learn many things in addition to typing and shorthand. How did you do at school?'

'Not too good,' she admitted. 'From the time I was a kid Pa made me do odd jobs evenings and weekends, so I was always gettin' bad marks for me prep. Then, as soon as I was old enough to work full time, he took me away from school, so I never had no chance to study for A Levels.'

'Have you ever read any serious books?'

'I like reading, but I didn't get much time for it. Only authors I ever read are them what writes lovely romances.'

'I imagine you have never been out of England; but where did you go for your holidays?'

Linda gave a bitter little laugh. 'People what run market gardens don't go for holidays. Even a couple of days away could mean losin' a crop.'

'Yes, I suppose so. Now, we'll just see how well equipped you are with general knowledge. Where is Montevideo?'

'Italy,' Linda hazarded.

Rowley shook his head. 'You're guessing. It's in South America, the capital of Uruguay. Who did the Finns fight in the Second World War?'

'How should I know? I wasn't even born then.'

'No. Perhaps that was unfair. How far off is the moon?'

'Millions of miles.'

'No, only two hundred and forty thousand. Have you ever read any books by Thackeray, Dickens or Scott?'

'Yes, Dickens's *Tale of Two Cities*. We took it for literature one term at school.'

'What else did he write?'

' 'Fraid I don't know.'

'How many dollars can you get for a pound?'

'Four, I think.'

'You are guessing again. Where does the extra day in Leap Years fall?'

'I've never thought about that.'

'What colours make up green?'

She smiled. 'Come orf it. Green's a colour in itself.'

'No. There are only three primary colours: red, blue and yellow. Green is a mixture of the last two. What king succeeded Queen Elizabeth I?'

'Henry VIII.'

'Wrong again. He was her father. Who wrote the Ninth Symphony?'

'Never heard of it.'

'What was the date of Waterloo?'

'That was where Wellington defeated Napoleon, but I've forgotten the year.'

'Well, here's a simple one. Who was Prime Minister before Harold Wilson?'

'Mr. Macmillan.'

'No, Alec Douglas-Home.' Rowley sighed and shook his head. 'I'm afraid you are not exactly up to running for academic honours. As I thought probable, if you're ever to make anything of yourself, I'll have to send you back to school.'

Linda was almost in tears at the ignorance she had been forced to display. 'School!' she echoed miserably. 'Oh, have a heart! Not at my age, please.'

B

'It wouldn't be school as you remember it, but a series of night classes. As you did your father's accounts, we can assume that you have enough knowledge of elementary maths to get by. But you must take courses in history, literature and geography, in addition to attending a secretarial college in the daytime. I think, too, we must improve you in various other ways that will make you more socially acceptable.'

Linda bridled. 'You mean I'm not good enough for people like you?'

'That's right,' he replied with disarming frankness. 'You don't speak with a Cockney accent, but some elocution lessons would do you no harm, and there are certain expressions that upper-class people rarely use. For example, they usually refer to their parents as "my father and mother" not as "Pa and Ma".'

'So you think me common.' Linda tossed her head resentfully. 'Well, maybe I am. That's going ter make it awkward for you when your smart friends come to the house. Be best I think if I went to live with me own sort in cheap lodgings.'

Ignoring her last remark, he replied, 'You are right again. It would be embarrassing for both you and my friends if I introduced you to them. The great Duke of Wellington's dictum, *Never explain*, was a very sound one. To the servants I don't need to, and I have no intention of hatching up some cock-and-bull story to account to my friends for your presence. For the time being, at least, you will not meet them. I don't entertain a great deal, but when I do your meals will be brought to you here, in this room.'

'Why not tell the truth about me? It does you credit, and there wouldn't be no awkwardness on either side.'

Rowley shook his head. 'No, my dear. You must be

aware that you are a very lovely girl. They would at once assume that I had made it all up about our meeting on the train, and my having rescued you from a life of poverty and peril on your own in London. They'd think I have installed you here as my mistress. In due course you are certain to meet a pleasant young man who will want to marry you and you him; but he might think twice about it if someone told him that I was your lover.'

'I see. Yes. That's very considerate of you.'

'No. It is just sound planning for my own selfish ends. For all practical purposes, I am adopting you. That is, if you agree to stay on my terms. If not, you can leave as soon as you have found a job and I'll give you enough money to see you through for a month or two. But, if you do stay, I want to make you a ward that I can be proud of, and one who will repay me by sincere affection. Now, which is it to be?'

Linda did not hesitate. 'You bet I'll stay. I'd be crazy not to. And thanks; thanks ever so.'

'Good. I'm glad. Then I must tell you about the running of the house. The Luchenis—Stefano and Bella—had already been with us for over six years when my wife had her accident, so they had only to carry on as they had before it happened. However, they naturally have their limitations. I have no sisters or other close relatives, but Celia had a daughter by a previous marriage. Her name is Elsie Spilkin. She and her husband Arthur, who is a lawyer, live at Haslemere. Naturally, after the accident it was to Elsie that I turned, and I gratefully accepted her offer to take charge here. She comes up only on Tuesdays, arranges with Bella my meals for the week and deals with anything else that requires attention. Most Tuesdays her husband joins her in the evening and they stay on for dinner.

'Elsie is a good, conscientious girl—or woman, I should say, as she is now just over thirty. But she is old-fashioned in some ways: very strait-laced and a pillar of her local church. For that reason I am particularly anxious that, for the present, she should not know that you are living here. To avoid that, on Tuesdays I want you to have your dinner, as well as lunch, out and go to the cinema or something; so that you don't come home before ten o'clock. They always leave before ten; so, if you do as I suggest, there will be no chance of your running into her.'

'How about Bella and Stefano, though?' Linda enquired. 'Surely they'll let on 'bout me being here?'

'I shall use the infallible method of the carrot and the stick with them. I'll put their wages up two pounds a week for doing your room, cleaning your shoes and doing the odd bit of washing and ironing for you and . . .'

'Fer me?' Linda's big eyes popped. 'D'you really mean Bella's going to act like a maid ter me?'

'Certainly. She has ample time, and I want you to spend as much of yours as possible on your studies. I shall also warn them gently but firmly that, should Elsie learn that you are living here, they will find themselves looking for another job. On Tuesdays, when Bella has done your room, she will lock the door and bring the key to me. Then, should Elsie take it into her head to go upstairs to see that the rooms are clean and tidy, I shall tell her I am storing some of my papers there, and she knows that much of my work is highly secret.

'The only other person who comes here regularly is a Miss Adams. She works for a secretarial agency and comes to me three mornings a week: Mondays,

Wednesdays and Fridays. She would be here this morning, but I phoned and put her off. I have a typewriter here on which she does my letters, and she takes away with her to type in her office the essays I write for scientific magazines and other non-secret documents. She also does the household accounts for me. But we needn't bother about her, because when she is here you will be out.'

During the next few days they worked out Linda's curriculum. Rowley arranged for her to go to a secretarial college, to attend evening courses at the Polytechnic, to have elocution lessons, and also took her shopping to buy a by no means extravagant but much superior wardrobe to the scanty one she had brought with her.

Very soon Linda had settled into her new and happy life. Two days after arriving in London she wrote to her mother to say that she was safe and well, but giving no address. Then she put all thoughts of her former harsh existence out of her mind. She revelled in her new comfort, smarter clothes and the good dinners which, most nights of the week, she took with Rowley. The better he got to know her, the more reason he had to congratulate himself on having befriended her. His gloomy loneliness was a thing of the past, for she proved a most cheerful companion and, when at home, was always singing about the house. Out of the allowance he made her she often bought him little presents, and took over from Bella various odd jobs such as doing the flowers.

The servants had been her only worry. It was not that she minded what they might suppose her relationship to Rowley to be, but she was acutely conscious that they must regard her as a lower-class girl, so resent having to wait on her. But Linda was shrewd as well as kind. She had noticed that there were never any flowers in the kitchen. So, out of the first week's allowance that Rowley made her, she bought a bunch of roses and took them down to Bella. She also bought a bottle of Italian wine for Stefano, and told them that she meant to do so every week. They were surprised and effusive in their thanks. From then on they were all smiles and could not do enough for her.

At first, after the quiet of the open country in which she had always lived, she was a little frightened of the congested traffic of the London streets, the crowded pavements and the ceaseless noise; but she soon got used to them and could find her way about the West End.

While attending her various classes, she made many acquaintances, but no friends, because she became so utterly absorbed in her work. Several of the men students asked her to go to the cinema or have meals with them; but, although she thought two of them quite attractive, she refused all invitations in order to have more time for her books, and she always took something with her to study while she lunched at a nearby café. She found shorthand much more difficult than she had expected, and the knack of it seemed to elude her, but in all other subjects she made rapid progress and, being determined above all to learn to speak like a lady, she never tired of practising the cultivation of her normally pleasant, slightly husky voice.

On Saturdays or Sundays she and Rowley often went on expeditions. He did not keep a car, but hired one whenever he was going any distance, or out for the evening. They drove out to Kew, Richmond, Greenwich and sometimes down into the country to lunch at a Thames-side inn. At other times he took her to

the Tower of London, St. Paul's, the Zoo, museums and
picture galleries. She was fascinated by it all, and
proved a quick learner; so it was a great joy to him to
take her to these places and tell her about art and
history. On her free evenings she avidly devoured the
good novels that Rowley suggested she should read.

June and July went by and, by the end of the latter
month, her mind and personality had developed out of
all recognition. During the three months that she had
lived in Rowley's house, on eleven occasions he had
spent a night away from home at the scientific development centre at Shrivenham; or, as she suspected,
perhaps with his girl friend. As she had always welcomed him joyously on his return he was greatly
surprised when he got back from one of these absences
early in August to find her gloomy and depressed.

After they had dined he asked her gently what was
troubling her, upon which she suddenly burst into
tears. Getting up, he came round the table, patted her
on the shoulder and said:

'Come, come, my dear. Whatever is the matter?
What is it that has upset you so? You know that you can
tell me anything.'

'It . . . it's my shorthand,' she sobbed. 'Oh, I hate it!
And I've let you down terribly. I've never been able to
pluck up the courage to tell you, but I think I suffer
from a sort of time-lag in my hearing. I simply can't get
the beastly stuff down quickly enough. I've taken test
after test and a hundred a minute is the very best I
can manage. That's no earthly good for the sort of job
I hoped to get. I failed . . . failed miserably. I . . .
I'll never make a really competent secretary.'

'There, there!' He patted her shoulder again. 'It's not
the end of the world. There are lots of other jobs.'

'I . . . I suppose I could become a shop assistant.'

'Lord preserve us, no! I haven't spent the past three months turning you into an educated young lady for you to serve behind a counter. How about becoming a model? Your height and looks qualify you for that.'

'No they wouldn't. Models have to be slim. My figure is all right, but I'm much too big all over. Besides, fashion houses require their girls to have lovely hands and feet. My hands are square, instead of being long and graceful, and my feet are enormous.'

'A hotel receptionist, then. Or you might get a job in a travel agency.'

'Oh, I don't know. I'll have to think. Nearly everything that is worth while would need months' more training, and I can't live on you for ever.'

Rowley looked at her steadily for a moment, then he said, 'You could, you know. So don't let that worry you. Anyway, we'll talk it over in the morning.'

Next morning he gave her a cheque for fifty pounds to cash at the bank, and said with a smile, 'You need cheering up, so I'm going to take you out to dinner. I've been waiting to do that until . . . well, until you finished your schooling. Get yourself a pretty dress and shoes, and we'll dine at the Savoy.'

That evening when she came downstairs, dressed to go out, he smiled his approval. 'Linda, you've turned yourself into a pin-up girl overnight. I'll be proud to be seen with you. So would any man. But there is one thing needed to complete the picture.'

They were in his study. Going to the safe, he turned the combination lock to and fro several times, opened the safe and took from it a number of leather jewel cases. As he put them on his desk, he said, 'These belonged to my mother. Normally I keep them in

Harrods' safe-deposit which enormously reduces the insurance premium, but this morning I got some of them out. Poor Celia will never wear them again, but I should like you to wear some of them tonight.'

As he spoke he was opening the cases. There were a rope of pearls, bracelets, brooches and rings. Diamonds, rubies, emeralds and sapphires glittered and scintillated in the light of the desk lamp. Linda, her mouth a little open, stared in amazement at the dazzling display. Tentatively she fingered the rope of pearls, then shook her head:

'No, I wouldn't dare to. They must be terribly valuable, and if I lost one I'd never forgive myself.'

'Don't let that worry you. I telephoned my insurance company this afternoon and arranged cover to take out seven thousand pounds' worth.' Taking the pearls from her he clasped them round her neck.

Her cheeks flushed, her eyes glowing, Linda selected some of the other things: a diamond and ruby clip, a two-inch-deep bracelet to match and a big diamond solitaire ring. She picked up another ring, but he gently took it from her and put it back. 'No, my dear; that's enough. I want you to look like a Duchess, not Mrs. Public House.'

'Very well then.' She transferred the diamond solitaire from her right hand to the engagement finger of her left. When she had, with some difficulty, managed to wriggle it on, she smiled at him, 'Just for tonight we'll pretend that I am your fiancée.'

The evening was a great success. It was the first time Linda had ever dined in a famous restaurant or seen a cabaret, and she enjoyed every moment of it. Rowley was enchanted, not only by her appearance but also by the way she talked and behaved. No-one would ever have guessed that, little more than three months ago, she had been an ignorant and uncouth girl, digging for her bread and butter in a market garden.

It was two o'clock before they got home. Neither of them was tired, and they had had just enough drink to make them gay without being tight. When Rowley suggested they should have a night-cap before going to bed, Linda laughed and cried, 'Yes, let's! I'd love another glass of champagne.'

Rowley was very fond of champagne and always kept a bottle in the refrigerator. When he had fetched it, poured it out and they had toasted each other, there fell a short, pleasant silence; then he said:

'Linda I want to ask you a question. You've no need to answer it if you'd rather not. But I'd like to know. Are you a virgin?'

4

Sex Rears its Ugly Head

LINDA's golden-brown eyes opened wide, then she laughed. 'Since you want to know, I'm not. I was raped soon after I was sixteen.'

'Oh, my dear, how awful for you. But no girl can really be raped if she's determined not to be.'

'I don't agree. Not if the man is much stronger than she is.'

'It doesn't matter how strong he is, she has only to stretch out her hand, grab his testicles and squeeze them for all she is worth. It sends an excruciating pain through him right up to his heart, rendering him as helpless as an infant. All she need do then is to push him off her and take to her heels.'

'Really? I didn't know that. I'll remember it in case sometime in the future a man I don't like gets me in a corner and becomes really difficult.'

After a moment, Linda went on: 'Perhaps, though, rape is not quite the right description of what happened to me. I ceased to resist, mainly owing to a threat, but partly from curiosity. I was rather advanced for my age, and had already experienced sexual excitement. I imagine that at most schools girls talk to one a'other about that sort of thing. We did, and a few of the older girls had let fellows go the whole way with them.

Opinions differed about what it was like, but one girl I knew enjoyed doing it with her boy friend regularly; and I suppose both mentally and physically I was ripe for the picking.

'The man was a junior master. It was my last term, and I went to the end-of-term hop. He singled me out and danced with me several times. Naturally, I was flattered, as there were a number of older girls there who were staying on in the hope of making university. A brother and sister who lived near me had taken me in to the dance in their family car, and were going to give me a lift home. But this fellow suggested taking me for a spin on the back of his motor bike, then dropping me off. Like a little fool, I agreed, and left the dance early with him.

'We started out on the right road, but he soon turned off on to another. When we had run on for about five miles, I became a bit worried and shouted in his ear, "We had better turn back now, or I'll be late in and get in trouble with my Pa."

'He only laughed and shouted back, "Don't worry. The dance can't have finished yet, and I'll get you home in good time." After we had covered about another mile, he pulled up opposite a haystack which had been cut into, and said, "This will do, sweetie."

'Of course, I had expected that there would be a little petting party and goodnight kisses when he dropped me off at the house, so I made no objection when he led me over to the stack. He pulled some more hay out of it and made a place for us to sit down. I didn't like him overmuch; but, as I've said, I was flattered by receiving the attentions of a grown-up man, so I let him kiss me all he wanted.

'That worked me up a bit, so I didn't protest very

hard when he started fumbling, as I'd already let two or three boys do that. His hand excited me still more, but after a few moments he unbuttoned his trousers and, at that, I did draw the line.

'But he was determined to have me and told me so. I refused to play and tried to throw him off. Finding that he couldn't persuade me, he became angry and panted, "You silly little bitch, if you don't let me, I'll leave you here and you can damn' well walk home." '

'The swine!' Rowley exclaimed with a sudden frown.

'He was; and his threat scared me stiff. I would have had to walk six miles, and it would have been close on two in the morning before I got in. My father would have believed the worst and given me a proper belting. All the excitement which had been aroused in me drained away. I burst into tears and went limp with fright.

' "That's better," he muttered, and got me the way he wanted.

'I began to fight again, but not very vigorously. For a long time I'd been curious to know what it really felt like, and now I was faced with the choice of finding out or walking home to the worst leathering I had ever had. By then he had partly entered me. Next moment he thrust hard, and I screamed with pain. The pain went on to the very end. I hated every second of it. And afterwards he hadn't even the decency to try to comfort me. He never spoke a word to me all the way home. For couple of weeks I was absolutely petrified by the thought that he might have put me in the family way. But, thank God, I was at least spared that. So there you are. That was my first experience of sex with a man.'

'You say your "first",' Rowley commented. 'Does that mean that you've had others?'

'Yes, but not until a few months before I left home. That first time had been so awful that, for a long time afterwards, I never let myself get into a situation where I might be taken advantage of again.

'Jim and another fellow picked up me and the girl I was with one night in the cinema. He was a fine, strapping fellow with dark, curly hair and a ready laugh. Afterwards he and his pal took us for coffee and cakes to a café. He asked me to go to the pictures again with him the following week, and I agreed. He saw me home and we had a petting party in the barn before I went in. During the month that followed we had three other meetings, and each time things became a bit warmer. Then one night he asked me to let him. I wasn't afraid of Jim, because he was so gentle. And by then I was getting pretty steamed up, so I was in half a mind to; but I was scared that he'd put me in the family way.

'He got over that hurdle by telling me that his married sister used the Pill, and he'd get some from her for me. He did, then on our next evening together we made love properly. It was utterly different from the first time. In fact, I thoroughly enjoyed it. So after that we did it regularly every time I could get an evening off.'

Rowley nodded. 'I imagine he was frightfully upset when you told him that you meant to run away to London.'

'I didn't, although I felt terribly bad about it. I was afraid that if I did, he would persuade me not to.'

When Rowley had refilled their glasses, he said with a smile, 'When we first met, I told you that I had no intention of trying to seduce you, and I meant it. I also told you that I was still virile and had a girl with whom

I spent a night now and again. A month after you came to live here I stopped going to see her. The reason was that I'd fallen head over heels in love with you.'

Linda started to say something, but he held up his hand to check her. 'Please let me finish. You said last night that you couldn't live on me for ever. I replied that you could, and you can. Half a loaf is far better than no bread, and I'd be utterly miserable if you left me. So, if you are against the suggestion I'm going to make, we'll simply forget that we have ever had this conversation.

'I know only too well that a man like myself can't possibly be physically attractive to a girl like you; so I'm going to be quite unscrupulous and attempt to off-set my age by dangling temptations before you.

'It is impossible for me to ask you to marry me, as long as Celia is alive. But, apart from the legal tie, I want you in all other respects to become my wife. You'd have a handsome allowance to buy lovely clothes, and could wear my mother's jewels whenever you wished. I normally spend several months of the year abroad. In September I always go to Venice and stay at Cipriani's. It is one of the most comfortable hotels in Europe, and you would love its beautiul swimming pool. We'd go to the South of France in January, and Paris in the spring. I'd take you to Greece, the Rhine and Spain. There is so much to see in these places, and I'd love to show them to you. Whenever we travelled, you would stay in luxury hotels and all the year round live a life of leisure. Now, what do you say?'

There were tears in Linda's eyes. Getting up, she went over to him, stooped, and kissed his rosy cheek. 'Oh, Rowley,' her voice quavered, 'you needn't have mentioned the clothes, jewels and travel. Your age and figure—they don't really count. It's yourself that matters, and you're the most lovable person I've ever met. Anyway, if after all you've done for me I didn't let you have your wish, I'd be the meanest girl in the world. Come, darling. Let's go up to bed.'

After that night Linda's life entered a new and still happier phase. She no longer had to struggle five days a week with that baffling shorthand and she had acquired a great deal of useful knowledge from her special classes. These, combined with all that Rowley had taught her on their visits to museums and galleries, had given her as good a background in history, literature and art as is acquired by most girls who have been sent to expensive schools.

Now that all this was behind her, Rowley said that the time had come for her to assume a definite position in the household and act as his hostess. Then, a few evenings later, he told her that he had invited their first guest to dinner.

This was a Wing Commander Eric Dutton. Rowley said that they had met in the latter part of the war, when he had been the Meteorological Officer at an R.A.F. station, and Dutton, a very young fighter pilot who, during the Normandy landings and the last year of the conflict, had so distinguished himself that he had been awarded both a D.S.O. and a D.F.C. After the war he had left the R.A.F., entered the Foreign Service and served in several Embassies abroad as Cultural Attaché. For the past two years he had been *en poste* in Persia, and had only recently returned, to be given a job at a scientific establishment.

'Why would they want a Cultural Attaché at such a place?' Linda enquired innocently.

Rowley gave her a slight smile. 'The term covers a multitude of activities, my dear, particularly where a knowledge of aircraft is concerned. Security is one of them, but we needn't go into that. Anyhow, now he is back in England we shall be seeing quite a lot of him, as whenever he's had a job in this country and comes to London for a night or two, I've always put him up.'

He then told her why, on this occasion, Dutton was to be their only guest. It was to prepare the way for her meeting with Elsie and Arthur Spilkin. At his Club that day Rowley had given Dutton lunch, and confided to him his true relationship to Linda; but he alone was to be made privy to this secret. They had then hatched a pretty little plot. Linda was to be passed off to the Spilkins and other acquaintances of Rowley's as Dutton's cousin; and, when he came to dinner, they would work out the details of this deception which would give her a respectable background.

That afternoon Rowley set the ball rolling by writing to Elsie to make certain that she and Arthur would be staying to dinner on the following Tuesday, thanked her for all she had done for him since her mother's accident, and explained that new work he had undertaken now made it essential for him to have a full-time secretary, who would also in future save her the bother of supervising his household. He added that he had been most fortunate in finding just the type of young woman he needed, in a relative of his old friend, Eric Dutton. He felt sure Elsie would like her and, naturally, he expected Elsie and Arthur to continue to dine with him on Tuesdays whenever they were not otherwise engaged.

Linda felt it was one thing for a girl to have an affair with a man near her own age, and quite another for her to be kept by a middle-aged gentleman; so, although she appreciated the soundness of Rowley's plan, she was none too happy about being produced as his mistress to the gallant Wing Commander. But her fears that he had agreed to accept her nominally as a relation only out of friendship for Rowley and might scarcely bother to hide a low opinion of her, proved groundless. When, two evenings later, they were introduced, he promptly kissed her on the cheek, then turned to Rowley with a laugh and cried:

'By Jove, you old devil! How dare you keep it from me all these years that I had such a lovely cousin! She's a corker!'

Eric Dutton was in his early forties, so was ten years younger than Rowley. He was a tall, wiry, pale-faced man, with dark hair and 'side-burns' that came half-way down his cheeks. His swift speech frequently included the type of slang that had been popular with the Royal Air Force during the war, which rather intrigued Linda, as she had never met anyone like him. Dutton's eyes were bright blue, and she sensed that even when he appeared to be disinterested, they missed nothing. His ready laugh and the easy way in which he talked to her as if he had known her for years she found very attractive.

After dinner they had quite a little fun, making up the story that they would tell Elsie and Arthur Spilkin. Dutton opened the discussion by saying to Linda, 'Look, coz. The first principle in putting over a deception is to stick as near the truth as possible, so you'd better put me in the picture about yourself.'

When Linda had given a *précis* of her life before she had run away, he said, 'My sister, Daphne Chatterton, and her husband, Ralph, have an igloo in Cheshire, and quite a sizable farm. The Spilkins have never met them and are unlikely to, so we had better transfer the Chattertons' place to Lincolnshire, because you know the gen about those parts. Daphne's older than I am. She's hitting forty-eight by now, and her better half is a good bit longer in the tooth than she is. He was a Tank Corps wallah in the war, and got himself gonged with an M.C. In view of their age, you'd better be their daughter. That will make you my niece instead of my cousin. I've got photographs of them both I'll let you have. All nice gels tote about the physogs of their parents and you can stick 'em up on your dressing table.'

'Then in future she'll be Linda Chatterton,' Rowley commented. 'What shall we say about her education?'

'I leave that to you, chum. You could look up a school guide and pick some respectable but not too posh place in Lincolnshire. As Linda is only eighteen, she wouldn't have got off the hockey field until fairly recently; only long enough to take a course in bashing the old typewriter and mastering the pothooks and hangers.'

'I've been able to bash for quite a while,' Linda told him, 'but shorthand proved beyond me.'

'No need to let on about that. In fact, the less you say about yourself, the less likely you are to be shot down. Now, how about hols? As you have never been abroad, you'd better have dipped in the briny at somewhere like Scarborough. You could say that your papa has a bungalow there, and that you went there every summer. Get all the leaflets about Scarborough that you can, and do a recce on them.'

'Her parents would have had a car,' said Rowley. 'I suggest a Jaguar.'

Eric nodded. 'What did she do in her spare time?'

'Reading,' said Linda. 'I've read scores of books in the past three months.'

'Not enough for an Amazon like you, duckie.'

She laughed. 'You can add gardening. God knows I've done enough of that—and flower arrangements. I've never done much arranging, but I know a lot about flowers.'

'Right. Now, why did you come to the great big wicked city?'

'To get a job.'

'No dice, chum. You could have got one nearer home. Tell you what, though. A broken romance. The feller jilted you. And, if I may say so, the more fool him.'

For another half-hour they talked on, settling other details about Linda's supposed past. Then, before Dutton left, he said to her, 'I'll jot down all the gen I can think of on the Chattertons and let you have it with the photographs. If you learn it all parrot fashion, there won't be much risk of you landing in the drink.'

Turning to Rowley he added with a grin: 'When I got back from Persia, I asked you to put me up for a couple of nights, and you made an excuse not to. I've a hunch that Linda's being here was the reason. Now the cards are all on the table, how about the future?'

Rowley laughed. 'Of course, my dear chap. Linda now has the best spare room, but you can have the smaller one at the back on the first floor, and share my bathroom. We'll be delighted to see you.'

'Thanks, chum.' Dutton winked a merry blue eye. ' "Roger" to that.'

When Linda went to bed that night her mind was entirely occupied by Eric. He was so obviously a man of the world: elegantly but not ostentatiously dressed, completely at his ease and sure of himself, with charming manners, a delightful sense of humour and knowledgeable on every subject they had talked about. She had never before met anyone remotely like him.

For the greater part of the past twenty years Eric had lived in British Embassies or Consulates, with the constant companionship of widely-travelled, university-educated men, and had enjoyed the friendship of diplomats of other nations and upper-class families in the countries in which he had been stationed. Rowley alone, of all the people to whom Linda had ever talked, equalled Eric mentally; physically, of course, poor Rowley could not be compared to his younger friend.

It remained only for Linda to have a word next day with the Luchenis. At Rowley's suggestion she told them that she had inherited some money from an uncle on condition that she changed her name to Chatterton. Accepting her statement without question, they smilingly congratulated her.

The following Tuesday evening proved by no means so enjoyable. Although smooth politeness was maintained throughout, Linda was conscious that beneath the surface lay troubled waters. Elsie Spilkin was a short, stout woman, with small, pale-blue eyes and reddish hair. Her husband, Arthur, was considerably older. His dark hair was thinning and long strands of it were brushed sideways across a balding scalp. His eyes were black and slightly hooded, but his most remarkable feature was his nose. It was a veritable beak: arched, and so thin that it ended in a downward-curving point. Linda was so intrigued that she could hardly keep her eyes off it.

She was feeling decidedly nervous and was comforted only by the knowledge that she had learned by heart the particulars about the Chattertons that Eric had sent her, so was equipped as well as possible for her role as his niece.

The Spilkins greeted her pleasantly enough, and asked her only a few casual questions about herself, which she had no difficulty in answering. But almost from the beginning the conversation was stilted. Rowley was also evidently nervous. Having welcomed the couple effusively and gone into an unnecessarily long explanation as to why he now needed a living-in secretary, he seemed to become almost tongue-tied. Frequently there fell brief, awkward silences, and how they would have got through the evening Linda could not think, had not Eric adroitly produced new topics of conversation.

Toward the end of dinner, Elsie said to Linda with a patronising air, 'I would not dream of questioning your abilities as a secretary, Miss Chatterton; but I imagine you have had little experience of housekeeping. So it might be best if I continued to come up every Tuesday to arrange about the meals and so on.'

Linda took this fast ball admirably. 'It's most kind of you to suggest doing that, Mrs. Spilkin; but it really isn't necessary. My mother always hated housekeeping, so she made me take a cookery course and, as soon as I left school, turned the running of the house over to me. So I've had quite a bit of experience.'

'Oh well, in that case . . .' Elsie gave a little shrug of evident annoyance. Then Rowley broke in quickly:

'You really needn't worry, Elsie dear. Owing to your admirable training, Bella has become quite competent as a Number Two, and she will brief Linda on my likes and dislikes. But, of course, I should be most distressed if you and Arthur stopped coming to see me on Tuesdays.'

When the Spilkins took their departure there were mutual expressions of goodwill, but Linda felt certain that Elsie intensely resented her having come to live in Rowley's house.

Once they had gone the atmosphere became distinctly more cheerful. Both Eric and Rowley congratulated Linda on the way she had played her role, and the latter declared with delight that no-one could now possibly guess that she was not a member of a county family.

During the few days between Eric's first meeting with Linda and his second, she had not thought much about him, because her mind had been mainly pre-occupied with apprehension about meeting the Spilkins; but, on the night they had come to dinner, she had been much impressed by the skill with which, using apparently casual remarks, he had given her leads that had enabled her to pose convincingly as his niece, and his urbane cheerfulness that had saved the party from becoming remarkably frigid.

She felt, too, that there was something about Eric that not only made him an unusually pleasant companion, but also stimulated her in a way that brought out the most attractive side of her own personality; so, now that he was stationed in London, she hoped they would see a lot of him.

When Rowley was in bed with her, two nights after the Spilkins' visit, he produced a letter from Elsie over which they laughed a lot. It was a delightful demonstration of his stepdaughter's prudish mind. She said she thought Linda charming, but went on to ask if he was really wise to have engaged such a young and attractive girl as a living-in secretary. She, of course, would not dream of doubting Rowley's faithfulness to her poor mother, but other people might jump to most distressing conclusions, and that would be painful to him, Arthur and herself. Surely, if he had to have a secretary living in his house, it should be someone much older and less likely to provide cause for gossip? Arthur would be able to find such a woman for him without difficulty.

Bubbling with merriment, they decided that the reply should be that, while Rowley saw the good sense of her suggestion, he could not now make a change without giving serious offence to Linda's uncle, his dear friend the Wing Commander.

Linda was strong, abundantly healthy, passionate by nature and, that spring, had been fully aroused by Jim. During the past three months she had missed being made love to; so, on the first night that Rowley had gone to bed with her, she had felt no reluctance in giving herself to him. When younger he had had his full share of affairs, so, although he was now a 'once-a-night' man, he was a sufficiently accomplished lover to ensure that she enjoyed it. As with Jim it had never been more than once at the end of each meeting, she had expected no more from Rowley. Moreover, he came to her two or three nights a week, which was much more frequently than she and Jim had been able to meet, so, physically, her new sex life satisfied her completely.

Yet there developed an aesthetic side to the affaire. On the first few occasions Rowley put the light out before taking off his dressing gown, and she was too keyed up with anticipation deliberately to visualise him in the nude. But there soon came a time when he wanted to add to his enjoyment by contemplating her beautiful figure, then leave the light on during their passionate embrace. To her dismay, she found the sight of his squat body, bulging tummy, lean shanks and knobbly knees, as he stripped before getting into bed with her, distinctly off-putting, and was vaguely repelled until her sensations enabled her to forget his defects.

It was, therefore, not altogether surprising that, to hide from him the lack of desire that seized her when she saw him naked, she took to shutting her eyes and making herself imagine that she was about to be made love to by Eric, to whom she had become so strongly attracted.

5

Disaster

A FEW days after the Spilkins had dined with them,
Rowley told Linda that he had opened an account for
her, as Linda Chatterton, at his bank, and paid into it
the first quarter of an allowance which was four times
the amount he had previously been giving her to cover
her lunches and other minor expenses. She was greatly
touched by his generosity and, never before having had
anything like so much money in her life, was more than
ever happy.

Since writing her mother a brief note shortly after
arriving in London, Linda had not written again. She
had then determined to regard her grim past as though
it had been a bad dream from which she had woken to
her real and promising new life; and she had since been
so fully occupied that memories of it came to her only
infrequently. But now she was able to look back on it
dispassionately, and realise that there had been at least
some bright spots in her otherwise hateful existence.

Apart from her affair with Jim during her last few
months at home, those few bright spots had been
almost entirely due to her mother, who had skimped to
buy her a new frock or a pair of nylons now and then.
She had been as good a parent as she could be under
the circumstances and must, Linda felt sure, have been

greatly worried at the thought of her being on her own in London.

In consequence, she decided that she ought both to reassure her mother about her well-being, and make some gesture to show her appreciation of the love she had received from her.

This resulted in her writing a letter to say that she had been very fortunate in getting a job as a companion— although, naturally, she did not disclose the sex of her employer—and that she lived in a very pleasant house where she was well fed and well cared for. Then, knowing how terribly short of money her mother always was, she enclosed in the letter five one-pound notes and said that, as long as her good luck lasted, she hoped to send a similar sum every month or six weeks. Against the rather remote possibility that, if she gave her address, her mother or Jim might come up to London to see her—which was the last thing she wanted —she said that any reply should be sent *poste restante* to the Great Portland Street Post Office.

A week later she went there and collected a reply. It proved a strange mixture of relief, gratitude for the money and bitter reproaches. Pa had been furious about her running away, got drunk and taken it out of her mother by beating her and blacking an eye. Jim had come to the house, told them that he had been 'walking out' with Linda, and been terribly cut up at her having left home without a word to him. He was a fine young man, earning good money in a steady job, and as nice a fellow as any girl could wish for. He was willing to make an honest woman of her, so why couldn't she come back and marry him? If she remained in London, she might meet some city slicker who would get her into trouble. The letter went on:

What have I done to deserve all this? First Sid clears out.
He writes now and then, though your Pa don't know that. He's
married and has two little ones, both girls. He's in a good job,
to do with the City authorities in Montreal. But he don't send
me any money, or his address. And now you. Two children that
I've slaved to bring up decent, and neither of them here to be a
bit of comfort as I get old. It's enough to give you the heart-
break. If you are going with a fellow on your evenings off, do
watch your periods, dear. And write again soon.

Up in her bedroom, Linda laughed herself silly over
the expression 'city slicker'. Her mother must have
picked it up in her girlhood when reading some cheap
novelette. Then it occurred to Linda that she had met
one, or at least, if her mother knew about dear, plump,
rosy-cheeked Rowley, she would regard him in that
light. But 'trouble'—no. Linda had no intention of
letting him put her in the family way. By now she
knew quite well how to look after herself.

About brother Sid having also withheld his address
she was not at all surprised. After all, he had made off
with the best part of two hundred pounds of Pa's
money. And Pa could be vicious mentally as well as
physically. He might quite well have demanded it back
and, if Sid failed to pay up, put the police on to him.
She wondered what sort of job Sid could have got with
the Municipality of Montreal. It sounded quite important, which was surprising, as his education had been
no better than her own. Still, he had a streak of their
father's hard forcefulness in him, and he might have
struck lucky.

As for 'writing again soon'—definitely not. She
could tell her mother nothing about the life she was
really leading, so what was there to write about? She
would send her another five pounds now and again, in

a plain envelope, but she had no intention whatsoever of entering on even an occasional exchange of letters.

Within a fortnight Linda had both taken over the household and had insisted on being run in by Miss Adams, to replace her as Rowley's secretary. Although she had failed to master shorthand, she was a competent touch-typist, and took his letters straight on to the machine. Naturally, the strange symbols and fantastic calculations Rowley used to work out his problems on nuclear energy were as meaningless to her as they had been to Miss Adams; but she typed out very neatly the essays he wrote in longhand, and filed all his papers efficiently.

During August Rowley gave several small dinner parties to introduce Linda to his friends. She slipped easily into her new role as his hostess and they all soon accepted her as a pleasant new acquaintance.

Eric twice stayed the night and plainly showed his liking for his new 'niece'. Each time he came he brought her flowers and gave her an avuncular kiss on the cheek. The more she saw of him the more attracted to him she became, and there were times when she had difficulty in putting out of her mind that it was of him she thought every time Rowley made love to her. Several times she decided that she must try to break herself of this habit; but by then it had become such an essential part to her giving herself unrestrainedly to Rowley that she found she could not do so without imagining herself to be in the younger man's arms.

In September Rowley took her to Venice. For Linda their stay at Cipriani's was another revelation. They spent their mornings either in or by the splendid swimming pool, and lunched and dined on the garden terrace looking out toward the Lido. In the afternoons they went ashore to visit the galleries and the many beautiful churches, then listened to the bands in St. Mark's Square, outside Florian's and Quardi's, while drinking Camparis before returning for dinner.

In January they went for three weeks to Nice, where Rowley hired a car to take them for expeditions up to St. Paul de Vence or to Cannes, Beaulieu, St. Tropez and Monte Carlo. Walking along the Promenade des Anglais in the winter sunshine, she became more radiant than ever, and wherever they went heads turned to look at her.

In May they went to Paris. The chestnut trees were in blossom, the girls gay in their new summer dresses. They lunched and dined in the best restaurants, went to night clubs, visited the Louvre, Notre-Dame, the Conciergerie, where Marie Antoinette had been imprisoned, the Sacré Cœur, the Invalides, and drove out to Versailles and Fontainebleau.

Between their stays on the Continent, their life in London continued happily. They regularly gave little dinner parties and were asked back in return. Rowley's friends became hers too, and now and then she went shopping or to a cinema with their wives.

The only jarring note in their existence was Tuesday nights when the Spilkins still always came to dinner. As Elsie had lived in the house most of the years while she had been growing up, Rowley still behaved like a father to her. For his sake Linda endeavoured to get closer to her, but in vain. They had nothing whatever in common; Linda was a born enjoyer, Elsie a dyed-in-the-wool do-gooder. Her husband was obviously subservient to her and eagerly endorsed all her opinions.

Eric continued to come to the house on average about twice a month, to dine and sleep. Sometimes there were other people dining, but more frequently

Rowley and Linda were alone with him. Owing to these evenings, when the two men talked of old times, she had long since come to know all about Eric's past.

She learned from Rowley that Eric had lost his parents tragically while still in his teens. They had both been burned to death in a fire and he had no other relative than the sister whose daughter Linda was supposed to be. The shock of his parents' death had caused him to have fits of depression, to become introspective and unable to make friends easily. It was on account of his being such a lonely young man that Rowley had taken him under his wing and acted as an affectionate older brother to him.

A few years after the war he had made an unfortunate marriage. He had learned too late that the girl was hopelessly unstable. She drank too much and then proved easy game for any man she fancied. When Eric had told her that he meant to divorce her, she had threatened to commit suicide. He had not believed her, but she had carried out her threat, after drinking nearly a bottle of whisky, by driving her car over a cliff near Beachy Head.

All this added to the fascination he had for Linda. Not having been born until after the Second World War, none of her contemporaries had been in it and decorated for bravery; so, from the beginning, she had regarded Eric as an almost mythical figure, and endowed him with a halo. That he should have overcome his early inability to mix happily with others and turned himself into a model of self-assured lightheartedness was, she felt, an equally courageous feat of a different kind. The knowledge of his spoiled youth and tragic marriage aroused in her the motherly feelings that play so large a part in woman's nature. These, combined with the physical attraction he had for her, resulted in his never being far from her thoughts, and she was convinced that she would never meet another man who so completely fulfilled her ideal of what a man should be.

That second summer, on two occasions, first in June and again in August, when Eric proposed himself for the night, the dates happened to coincide with those when Rowley was going on one of his trips to Shrivenham. But he insisted that that made no difference—Eric must come just the same.

On both occasions Linda and he sat up till the small hours, replenishing their drinks from time to time and deep in conversation. They were evenings of perfect companionship and when they said good night after their first long session together, he said:

'Linda, you're a girl in a million. Old Rowley was damn' lucky to have met you that night on the train. You've made a new man of him.'

On the second occasion he actually took her in his arms and kissed her on a small mole she had under her left ear, not passionately but very gently and reverently, as though she were something sacred. She let him do so without protest, and when she got up to her room she found that she was trembling. She now had no doubt at all that Eric was in love with her, and she had known for a long time that she was desperately in love with him.

The happiness of that knowledge was mingled with a sadness that nothing could come of their love, for she had no intention of being unfaithful to Rowley, and felt quite certain that Eric would not make things difficult for her by trying to take advantage of the fact that she was obviously attracted to him.

In September she and Rowley again went to Venice. It was on their fourth day there that, while swimming in the pool, he had his first heart attack. Two other men fished him out, and a doctor who happened to be present dealt with the situation. Rowley was put to bed, and Linda, seized with terrible distress and anxiety, did everything possible for him. For a week she nursed him devotedly, then he was declared fit to travel and, to her immense relief, she got him safely back to England.

He was soon fully recovered, but from then on had to be careful not to exert himself. His doctor warned him that in future sexual intercourse might prove very dangerous to him. When Rowley told Linda this, she said at once that he must not come to her room any more.

With considerable diffidence she took the opportunity to broach a subject that had been worrying her ever since he had had his coronary, and said:

'Darling, I hate even to think of such a possibility, but if you had died in the pool, or do so from another attack, I'll be back where I was eighteen months ago, when you took pity on me in the train. Even worse off, in fact, because apart from the terrible grief I'd feel at losing you, having been so wonderfully spoilt by you I'd be even less capable of making both ends meet in an ill-paid job, and I wouldn't have a penny.'

He pressed her hand. 'Don't worry, my sweet. For months past I have been meaning to make a new will, to ensure that you are well provided for. I'll put it off no longer, and see to it next week. And I'm sure you know that although we can no longer sleep together I love you as fondly as ever.'

Nevertheless by early December he felt so much like

C

his old self that he asked her to let him. She was very loath to agree, but she had become so accustomed to enjoying his caresses that, during the past ten weeks, she had sadly missed them; so, with considerable anxiety, she gave way.

They were both very careful not to let themselves become over-excited, and no harm resulted. But they decided that it would be wise to restrain themselves to once every few weeks.

In February they went to the south of Spain and, after a fortnight idling in the sun, went on to Madrid, Seville, then Granada. There Rowley had his second attack. It was due to their having failed to get a taxi down in the city, so they had walked back up the long, steep hill to the Granada Palace Hotel, with its marvellous view over the valley.

Again Linda suffered torments of anxiety, but again Rowley recovered and she got him home safely. After a few weeks he was once more as spry as ever. But now they took a firm line. Visits to Linda's bedroom had become too great a risk, and they resigned themselves to agreeing that these should take place no more.

March, April, May and June of 1971 went by, for Linda with a growing sense of frustration. During the first thirteen months that she had been Rowley's mistress, in spite of his age he had, owing to his experience as a lover, not only satisfied her but, as she thought of Eric, aroused her passions to a pitch that she had never known during her brief encounters in the barn with Jim.

Throughout the autumn that followed Rowley's first coronary, she had sadly missed the revels in which they had indulged at least once a week. Then, from December until February, there had at least been their

monthly sessions to look forward to. The two months of
continence during the autumn had been bad enough;
but now it was over four months since she had known
the delights of being made love to.

She was now over twenty, fully grown and strongly
sexed. Every week that passed made her more unhappy
about this aspect of her life, to which it now seemed she
was condemned for an indefinite period. Angrily she
endeavoured to put thoughts of sex out of her mind, but
in bed every night, and sometimes during the day, they
tormented her.

It was on the last day of June that Eric again came
to stay while Rowley was absent at Shrivenham. As on
previous occasions she saw to it that they had an
excellent dinner. Afterwards they sat in the cosy study,
talking happily until past one o'clock in the morning.
Before they went up to bed, Eric kissed her tenderly
on her little mole, then playfully ruffled her hair and
gave her a slap on the bottom.

During the long evening they had had quite a lot to
drink and, as she bent down to peel off her stockings,
she staggered slightly. Then, having put on her nightdress, instead of getting into bed she sat on the edge of
it, her mind in a turmoil.

That Eric wanted her she had no doubt at all.
And she wanted him. If Rowley had been competent
she knew that, after all he had done for her, she would
have resisted the temptation to be unfaithful to him;
but he was not. And if she were unfaithful, he would not
be hurt, for he would never know. Damn it, why not?
These were the best years of her life, and she needed to
be made love to; needed it desperately.

For close on two years she had been in love with
Eric. Almost from the beginning of her liaison with

Rowley she had used him as a substitute for Eric, by shutting her eyes and concentrating her thoughts on him. She had not let Rowley down, for he could not possibly have known that the ardour with which she gave herself to him was inspired by the mental image of another man. No woman could have given Rowley more enjoyment than she had, and she had never shown the least interest in any other man during the times when they had been abroad together; so she had been completely fair to him.

But now that, for his own sake, she no longer dared let him make love to her, matters were different—very different. For months past she had been tormented by the natural cravings of her body. Why should she continue to deny herself to a man who obviously wanted her? And what bliss it would be, not merely to imagine that Eric was holding her in his arms, but to know it to be the real thing—to be able to keep her eyes open and smile up into his.

With sudden resolution she stood up, put on her dressing gown and went out into the passage. There she paused, not from irresolution, but owing to the sudden thought that Eric might think less of her if she just walked into his room and brazenly offered herself to him. She must have some excuse, then let him make the running.

After a moment a pretext came to her, and she walked on down to the first floor. A light was showing beneath his door. She knocked, and he called, 'Come in.' With her heart beating like a sledge-hammer, she entered the room.

He was sitting up in bed, reading. Laying down the book, he said, 'Hullo, chum. Something wrong? Not feeling dicky I hope?'

Her mouth felt dry. With difficulty she got out the words, 'No . . . no. I wanted to ask your advice. I meant to earlier this evening, but somehow I never got round to it.'

'Never too late,' he smiled, then patted the side of his bed. 'Come and sit here and brief your Uncle Eric.'

Sitting down on the bed, she said, 'It's about Rowley. Since his last attack we haven't risked sleeping together and . . .' She paused, hoping that she had given him a good opening.

He nodded. 'And as a healthy young woman, you're feeling your oats, eh?'

'Well, yes,' she admitted. 'It has been rather frustrating. But I'm more worried about him than about myself.'

'Why?'

'It's like this. About two months after his first attack, we did start again, limiting ourselves to once a month, and no harm came of it. Now he is fully recovered from his second attack he's been pressing me to let him have his fun again.'

'And naturally you want him to.'

'Yes, but it seems such an awful risk to take.'

'I agree. Personally, I don't think you ought to.'

Linda appeared to consider this, but she made no move to get off the bed. After a moment, she said, 'I suppose you're right. But it's very hard on both of us.'

He gave her an appraising look and nodded. A pregnant silence followed. She broke it by saying, 'I owe so much to Rowley that I don't want to be unfaithful to him. But having to give it up altogether . . . well, there are times when I can't help thinking about it. Would you . . . would you think me very awful if I did it with someone else? After all, Rowley would never know.'

'Not if you were careful. Is some young spark chasing you?'

'No; oh no!' She leaned forward a little, so that her dressing gown fell slightly open, giving him a glimpse of one of her breasts under her chiffon nightie. 'But I thought perhaps . . .'

'What did you think?'

'Well,' she hedged. 'I was thinking that . . . that if I'm as lovely as you say I am, I shouldn't have much difficulty in finding a lover.'

'No, you weren't,' he suddenly snapped at her. 'You were thinking of me!'

Leaning forward, his chin jutting out and his blue eyes blazing, he went on angrily, 'You slut! How you have the gall to come to my room half naked and try your wiles on me passes my comprehension. Damn it, I'm Rowley's best friend! He's been much more than a brother to me. Is it likely that I'd take his girl behind his back? If you want it that much, find yourself a boy friend. There are plenty of guys who'd be delighted to jump into bed with you; but it won't be me. Now get to hell out of here.'

Linda was utterly devastated by his outburst. Tears welled up into her big eyes. Giving a little, strangled cry, she slid off the bed and ran toward the door.

In a flash he was out of bed and after her. Grabbing her by the arm, he pulled her back, swung her round and threw her down in the armchair. For a moment he stared down at her, then he spoke hoarsely:

'I'm sorry, Linda. Of course you're not a slut, and I should never have said you were. I should have thought you would know that I wouldn't *trompé*

Rowley. But I suppose a lot of fellows would have, and you must have realised for months that I'm in love with you.'

She had buried her face in her hands and was weeping bitterly. At his last words, she looked up and sobbed. 'I . . . I know. And I am with you. It . . . it wasn't only . . . just needing a man. Although I do . . . desperately at times.'

'You poor darling.' He laid a hand gently on her hair. 'How I wish to God it could be me. But it can't. I'd never be able to look old Rowley in the face again.'

She nodded. 'I understand. Of course I understand. I should have realised how you would feel about us both deceiving him. I should never have come here. It was wicked of me.'

'No. The devil of it is though that the damage is done now.'

'But it's not!' She looked at him in surprise and moved to stand up. 'You haven't succumbed to wanting me, and I'm going back to my room.'

'My dear, it is done.' He shook his head unhappily. 'As long as we only knew that we loved each other and kept it to ourselves, everything was "Roger". But now we've told each other so, things can never be the same again. How can I possibly continue to come here, knowing that you're mine for the asking? I simply couldn't bear it. I'll have to take off for some place abroad.'

'Oh, no!' The cry came from Linda's heart. 'Without being able to look forward to seeing you now and again, I'd be utterly miserable. And Rowley! Think of Rowley! He'd miss your visits terribly. I'd have it on my conscience that I'd broken up your friendship with him.'

'I realise all that. God knows, I'll miss you, too. But what's the alternative? There are some emotions one can't hide all the time. From now on, unless I bow out, just the way we look at each other will give it away to Rowley that we're in love. And what then? First suspicion, then certainty, will eat like a cancer into his happiness. A time will come when he'll be able to hide his feelings no longer, and he'll charge us with it. No amount of lying on our parts would convince him that he was wrong. Then, being the generous pal he is, he will probably offer to let you go, so that you could marry me. But I couldn't. How could I possibly rob him of the thing he cherishes more than his life?'

'No,' Linda choked out. 'And I wouldn't marry you even if you wanted me to. Not like that. I simply couldn't bring myself to leave Rowley after all he's done for me.'

'Then you see why I'll have to fade out. And soon too.'

Linda stood up. 'I know you are old-fashioned. You have proved that tonight by your loyalty to Rowley. But I wouldn't have you any other way. I love you for it, and always shall.'

As she spoke, she moved toward the door. He made no attempt to stop her. Both of them knew that to risk a last kiss would be too dangerous. Two minutes later she was back in her room. Now completely sober, chastened and drained of energy, she lay for a while reproaching herself bitterly for having made such a mess of things. Then she cried herself to sleep.

Rowley had already made arrangements for them to go again to Venice in September, and Linda was counting the days until their departure. London was hot and oppressive. She knew that her affair with

Eric was now a closed chapter of her life, so was doing her best to put him out of her mind. But the scene in his bedroom continued to haunt her, and she felt that only by getting away from the house to Venice would she be able gradually to rid herself of thoughts of him.

In the latter half of August he rang up Rowley to say that he had been appointed to a new job and that he would be leaving the country very shortly because he was wanted at his new post urgently; so he could only manage a lunch to say good-bye.

The meal went off quite smoothly, but when asked to what country he was going, he shook his head and replied, 'Sorry, chums, but for the present, for security reasons, I'm not allowed to say.'

Afterwards, fighting down tears, Linda stood on the doorstep beside Rowley and, smiling bravely, waved her love away.

What she had told Eric about Rowley's pressing her to let him resume sleeping with her was only partly true. During the summer he had on three occasions asked her to; but, in spite of her own cravings, she had firmly refused, and he had not pursued the matter.

Eric's departure for an indefinite period had left Rowley very low; so, two nights later, to cheer up both him and herself, she suggested that they went out to dinner.

They dined well at the Connaught, sank two champagne cocktails apiece, a bottle of hock between them and topped off with liqueurs; so, when they got home at about half past eleven they were both much more cheerful and slightly mellow. Rowley suggested fetching a bottle of champagne from the fridge. Seeing the red light, Linda would not let him; but he insisted on mixing them both brandies and soda as nightcaps.

Her foreboding proved right. Having taken a good swig at his drink, Rowley said that the evening would not be complete unless it finished up in her room. She promptly replied that they had been into the matter before, and she did not mean to change her mind. This time he would not take 'no' for an answer, and declared that it could not possibly do him any harm. She remained firm in her refusal and for a quarter of an hour or so they continued to wrangle. Eventually she told him that it was useless to keep on repeating himself, and went up to bed, leaving him there.

His raising the subject and talking about it for so long had again aroused her own frustration. Striving to rid her thoughts of sex, she undressed, got into bed and put out the light; but she could not get to sleep.

For over an hour she tossed and turned. Then she heard the door open. A moment later Rowley was leaning over her, breathing heavily. From his breath she guessed that, for the past hour, he must have remained downstairs drinking brandy. Shaking her by the shoulder, he said hoarsely:

'Linda, I've got to. It's six months since we did, and I . . . I can't bear it any longer.'

Sitting up, she pushed him back. 'No, darling, no! Please! I want to, too, but I'm not going to let you.'

Bursting into tears, he knelt down beside the bed, grabbing feebly at her with his hands and sobbing, 'Linda, my love; please, please! You must, or I'll go out of my mind.'

For how long he pleaded with her she could not afterwards remember; but his sobbing tore at her heart-strings as nothing else could have done. Meanwhile she was thinking, 'We waited for only ten weeks after his first attack, and he is as fit now as he was then. To let him once a month, as we did in the winter, can't seriously harm him; and if I have that to look forward to, it will free my mind of this awful obsession. He's right, too, about it being cruel of me to refuse him. After all, if he does have an attack, I know how to deal with it, and could get the doctor here quite quickly.' So, at length, overcome by compassion for him, she surrendered and said:

'All right then, darling; but for God's sake, don't let yourself become too excited.'

In a moment he had pulled down the sheets and was in bed beside her. Wasting no time in preliminaries, he embraced her and rolled her over on to her back. After that, everything happened very quickly. His breathing had hardly begun to quicken as a result of his amorous assault when, suddenly, he made a choking sound, reared up on her and gave a strangled cry. Then he collapsed and went rigid.

In awful terror, she called his name, 'Rowley! Rowley!' But she already sensed the appalling truth. His body weighed twice as much as it had before. She had a dead man lying on top of her.

6

Night of Horror

FOR a few moments Linda lay still, positively paralysed by horror. She knew that she ought to have thought of the possibility of this happening, to have visualised herself in her present terrible situation. But she had not. She had thought that, at worst, Rowley would be stricken with another attack, that he would go purple in the face and become unconscious just as he had in Venice and Granada. But she had long since learned the first-aid treatment for a coronary. She had only to force him to swallow a couple of the pills the doctor had prescribed for such an emergency, and the worst would be over. Then she would telephone the doctor to come at once. For a few days Rowley would have to remain in bed, and then there would be another period of convalescence. When he had fully recovered, she would make him swear never, never to come to her room again.

But he was not going to recover. He was dead. She was positive of it.

Taking Rowley by the shoulders, she exerted all her strength, heaved his heavy body sideways, stretched out an arm and switched on the bedside light. Both their heads were still on the pillow. His face was within six inches of hers and, as the light went on, she found herself looking straight at it.

Her hand flew up to her mouth to stifle a scream. The face was Rowley's, but hardly recognisable. It had turned purple, the mouth hung open and seemed to have been wrenched down at one side, the eyes were wide open, bulging and staring straight into hers. Their expression seemed to her to be one of malevolent accusation.

Closing her eyes to shut out that fearsome sight, she gave a little whimper and began babbling to herself:

'It wasn't my fault! I didn't want to. Oh, but I did, and that's why I gave way. If only Eric hadn't been so loyal to him this wouldn't have happened. I'd not have been so weak. No, that's not true. He wouldn't have known that I was deceiving him, and would have come up here tonight just the same. And even if Eric had been with me only the night before, I'd have given way. How could I have helped doing so? I let him because I was so sorry for him. That's the truth. Oh, dear God, believe me! That is the truth, the truth.'

Suddenly a new thought came to her. Perhaps Rowley was not quite dead. It might be possible to revive him, and she was losing precious moments. Her legs were still entangled with his. Jerking up her knees, she knocked his legs away, rolled over and fell out of bed on to the floor. As she turned over to get up, she saw that one of his naked feet, grotesquely twisted, was hanging over the side of the bed.

Scrambling to her feet, she staggered over to her dressing table and wrenched open a drawer. When he had again started to come up to her room the previous December, she had made him give her a bottle of his pills to keep there in case he had an attack. Though it had never crossed her mind that it would be an attack such as this.

Grabbing the bottle, she ran back with it, unscrewed the top and shook two of the pills out into her hand. Rowley's accusing eyes stared up at her, making her feel sick and faint. One of her handkerchiefs lay on the bedside table. With her free hand she snatched it up and draped it over those awful, protruding orbs. Then she pushed the pills into his twisted mouth. But his tongue was terribly swollen. When she felt its slime on her fingers as she tried to force the pills past it and down his throat, her flesh crept. It was no good. One of them got lodged up in his cheek, the other slipped out.

For a moment she wondered if she could bring herself to give him the kiss of life. Then she realised that her breath would not get past his tongue. Perhaps, though, through his nose? Nothing, nothing that might revive him must be left untried.

Tears were streaming down her cheeks. She was trembling in every limb. But she steeled herself to the grim task. Stooping over him, she put her hands on his shoulders and her mouth to his nostrils. For over a minute, with rising nausea, she kept it glued there and strove to force her breath into him. His body did not respond by the faintest twitch of a muscle. Suddenly her own body revolted. Jerking away her head, she swivelled round on her knees, her stomach heaved and she was violently sick on the carpet.

It took her several minutes to recover. Rowley lay sprawled on his back on the bed. Tentatively she put out a hand and placed it over his heart, to make certain that he was really dead. After a moment she became conscious of a faint beating. New hope flamed in her.

Frantically she began to massage his chest and ribs. The violence of her actions jerked the handkerchief from his eyes. As she knelt above him, his glassy, accusing eyes again stared into hers, but they showed no flicker of intelligence. Nevertheless she continued to work on him until sweat was mingling with the drying tears on her face, and her arms felt as though they would drop out of their sockets. Breathless, she stopped and again laid a hand over his heart. The beating was still faint, but much faster. The devastating explanation for the beating flashed upon her, her face crumpled and tears again sprang to her eyes. It had not been Rowley's heart that she had felt, but her own racing pulse.

Brushing aside her tears, she went over to her dressing table again and came back carrying her hand-mirror. As a final test she held it for a full minute over Rowley's mouth. When she looked at it, there was not a trace of mist. He was dead beyond all question. No longer Rowley, but an ugly corpse.

Although their doctor could do nothing, she must telephone him. But not yet. Rowley had had many friends who respected him. She owed it to him that they should respect his memory. Some of them might suspect that she had been his mistress, but she could not possibly allow them to think of him as an old lecher who had died in the act of making love to a girl young enough to be his daughter. Doctors did not gossip about their patients, but the body would have to be moved. As far as she knew, if Stefano and Bella believed Rowley to have been her lover they had, from fear of dismissal, kept it to themselves; and she was on excellent terms with both of them. But now that Rowley was dead, they might feel free to talk. Somehow she must get his body down to his own room.

Having wriggled into her dressing gown and opened the door, she put her arms round the body and tried to lift it from the bed. It was far heavier than she had expected, and seemed to weigh a ton. Strong as she was, she realised that she had not the strength to carry it. For some minutes she stared at it in dismay. Then an idea came to her. Kneeling down beside the bed, she drew one of the limp arms across her shoulders and round the back of her neck. Exerting all her strength, she levered herself up with the corpse on her back in a fireman's lift. Clutching the dangling legs to her with her free hand, she staggered out into the passage. Half-way down it, her burden proved too heavy for her; she sank to her knees and let it slide to the floor.

When she recovered from her effort, she again attempted to get the body across her shoulders, but could not manage it. She began to weep, but now from anger. In desperation, regardless of treating the corpse with indignity, she took it by the ankles and drew it in jerks along the passage.

When she had hauled it some way she stepped back on to one of the Persian rugs that partially covered the polished parquet floor. As she pulled hard again, the rug slid from beneath her feet and she went over backward, coming down with a resounding thud.

For a few moments she remained where she had fallen, now petrified by a new fear. Stefano and Bella slept on the floor above. If either of them chanced to be awake, he or she must have heard the noise of her heavy fall, and wondered what had caused it. Holding her breath, she listened for the door of their bedroom to open, dreading that, within a minute, one of them would have switched on the light and be peering over the banister, to see her crouching there beside Rowley's sprawling, naked body.

When she could hold her breath no longer, she let it

rush from her lungs, by then reassured that the servants must be fast asleep. Her heart still beating furiously, she got to her feet, again grasped Rowley's ankles and dragged him to the head of the stairs. Having straightened the rug, she returned to the corpse and, going down the stairs in front of it, alternately pulled at and checked it until she had it lying on the third step from the bottom. Now, kneeling down, she was able to get it on her back once more.

Staggering drunkenly under its weight, she carried it to the door of Rowley's room. Fortunately the door was ajar. Kicking it open, with a gasp of relief, she dropped the body inside, then switched on the light.

Rowley's bed not not been slept in. Going to it, she rumpled the pillows and pulled down the sheets until they were in disarray. She had intended to get the body up on to the bed, but decided that, when discovered, it would look more realistic if it appeared that he had fallen out; so she dragged it to a position alongside the bed. As she arranged the limbs suitably, nausea welled up in her again. But she knew that she must not be sick in that room, and fought it down. Her grim and grisly task completed, she switched off the light and hurried out into the passage.

Instead of returning to her bedroom, she went down to the study. The glasses they had drunk from earlier in the night were on a small table with the bottle of brandy. It had been nearly full, but was now two-thirds empty; so, to get up his courage, Rowley must have consumed over half the bottle before going up to her.

Picking up the bottle, she sloshed a good portion into a tumbler, then splashed in a little soda and drank it straight down. The potent draught took her breath away, but it warmed her inside and made her feel better. Her hand reached out for the bottle again, but she drew it back. In her present state, if she drank what remained, it might make her tight, and that would be fatal. To play this grim game out, she must keep all her wits about her.

Five minutes later she was back in her bedroom. There could be no question of ringing up the doctor now. She was not supposed to know about Rowley's death, and must appear not to until Stefano found his body and came to tell her in the morning.

To her surprise and distress she saw from the French clock on the mantelpiece that it was not yet a quarter to two. It seemed impossible that so much had happened in so short a time. But they had been home by half past eleven, and it could not have been much more than an hour and a quarter later that Rowley had come up to her room. So all this ghastly business had taken place in less than an hour.

That meant that she had over six hours to wait until the next act in the drama. Stefano called Rowley with a cup of China tea at eight o'clock, so it would be a few minutes after that when he would come up to tell her of his master's death. Six hours seemed an eternity. How she was going to get through them she could not think.

She remade the bed after clearing up the mess she had made beside it, then decided to have a bath. The beautiful bathroom had long ceased to be a marvel to her. But as she ran the bath she did wonder how long it would remain hers.

From the moment of Rowley's seizure, her mind had been so occupied that this was the first time a thought about her future had entered it. As she got into the bath and lay down to relax in the warm water, she began to ponder the possibilities. She thought it unlikely that

Rowley had left her the house and its contents, because quite a lot of the furniture had belonged to his wife, so would go to Elsie; but she felt sure that he had made ample provison for herself.

She would have to start a new life, and she would miss Rowley terribly. But after a while she would get over her loss. He had made her life what it was, taken her from poverty and uncertainty to affluence and security, so she would always think of him with the deepest gratitude. But now that he was gone, she was free to marry; so it was doubly infuriating that, before going abroad, Eric had refused to let them know to which Embassy he had been posted. His real reason, she felt sure, had been to prevent her writing, and so continuing to think about him. But perhaps she could find out from the Foreign Office where he had gone. Somehow she must do so. But what evil luck that, by her own folly, she had driven him abroad and now needed him so badly to lean upon!

When she had got out of the bath and dried herself it was still only three o'clock. Half the night still lay before her, so she took two sleeping pills. But they did not work. Again and again, as she was about to doze off, she roused with a shudder of terror, having seen Rowley's bloated face only a few feet away, standing out against the surrounding darkness like a ghastly, purplish balloon. The protruding eyes were no longer accusing, but leered at her, and the twisted mouth now seemed to bear a malicious grin as though the animating spirit of this horror wished her ill and knew some secret that would bring about her ruin. Yet she could not believe for one moment that Rowley's spirit wished her harm. Not only had he always been most kind and generous, but he owed it to her that the last two years of his life had been extremely happy ones. She knew that the hostility she saw in the distorted face was purely imaginary and due to her nerves having been stretched almost to breaking point.

All the same, when another vision of this revolting face again caused her to start up from a doze, she felt that she could bear it no longer. Switching on the light, she got out of bed to fetch her library book which she had left with her handbag on the writing table. As she came back with it, her glance fell on Rowley's dressing gown. Having taken it off in the dark, he had thrown it aside and it had fallen behind a small armchair that stood against the wall between the bed and the door.

As she picked it up, she groaned. She dared not keep it in her room, and the thought of having to take it down to his filled her with new dread. The travesty of his face that had haunted her for the past two hours or more must surely emanate from his dead body. If she took the dressing gown to his room, she could not just open the door and throw it inside. She would have to switch on the light and lay the gown in some appropriate place. That meant that she could not avoid seeing Rowley's twisted corpse again.

Yet she knew there was no escape from this new ordeal. Steeling herself to face it, she crept downstairs, but paused before Rowley's door for a full minute. With her nightmare visions still fresh in her mind, she was gripped by the fear that when she opened the door some awful thing would seize and drag her in. At length, summoning all her resolution, she threw the dressing gown over her shoulders, so as to have both hands free. With one, she grasped the handle, turned it and flung the door wide open; with the other, almost simultaneously, she found the light switch and snapped it down.

The room was exactly as she had left it and immediately all fear of the supernatural left her. Rowley's
sprawled body lay face upward beside the bed, and she
found herself looking down on it quite calmly. The
suffused face was an unpleasant sight, but the eyes
now seemed blank, and held no trace of either
accusation or malice. Unhurriedly she dropped the
dressing gown over the back of a chair at the foot of
the bed, turned out the light and closed the door
behind her.

Relieved though she was, reaction swiftly set in. Her
head ached and her mouth felt parched. She would
have given anything for a large cup of strong coffee, and
thought of going down to to the kitchen to make herself
one; but decided that it would be wiser not to, as dawn
had come. Daylight was seeping through the gaps
between the curtains and soon the servants would be
getting up.

Instead, she went down to the study and finished the
bottle of brandy. Stefano would know that the previous
evening it had been a nearly full one, and the more
Rowley was believed to have drunk, the better that
would account for his seizure. That thought gave her
an idea. Picking up the empty bottle and Rowley's
glass, she went back to his room, set the bottle on his
bedside table and laid the glass on the floor a foot
away from his outflung hand.

As she was going upstairs, she heard a door on the top
floor open and close. Her heart missed a beat. In
another moment the Luchenis would be coming down.
In an agony of apprehension she ran lightly up the last
few stairs then, hugging the wall of the passage, tiptoed
along to her room. As she closed the door noiselessly
behind her, she found that sweat had broken out on her

forehead and that her hands were damp. Closing her
eyes, she thanked God for her narrow escape.

As soon as she had recovered, she went to the window
and drew the curtains. In the early-morning light, the
outlook over Regent's Park was as lovely as ever. For
nearly two and a half years she had enjoyed that vista.
Soon now she would be deprived of it, and never see it
again. It was only one of the many things she owed to
Rowley and must lose by his death. Sadly she redrew
the curtains and got into bed. The servants would make
their own breakfast and tidy up downstairs before
Stefano brought Rowley his morning tea, so she must
resign herself to another hour of waiting, for there was
no hope of her dropping off to sleep.

Nevertheless, exhausted by her ghastly night, she did
fall into a doze, so sooner than she expected there came
a quick knocking on the door. Her impulse was to sit
up, but she restrained it, turned over so that her back
was to the door, and called, 'Come in.'

Normally Bella came to wake her; but, as she had
expected, it was Stefano's agitated voice that cried,
'The Master! I take up his tea. He is not in bed but on
floor. Taken ill in night. Very ill. I fear dead.'

Instantly she reacted appropriately. Jerking herself
erect, she stared at him wide-eyed and gasped, 'No!
No!' Then she jumped out of bed, grabbed her dressing
gown and, while still struggling with it, pushed past him
to run downstairs.

Stefano followed and entered Rowley's room on her
heels. It was exactly as she had last seen it. With a wail
of woe she threw herself down beside the body, put her
hands on its shoulders and cried, 'Rowley! Rowley! Oh,
this is too awful.'

Turning to Stefano, she said quickly, 'Telephone

for Dr. Mead. No, I'd better do that. Where's Bella?'

At the sound of the commotion Bella had come upstairs. She was standing just outside the door and had burst into tears. As Linda made to leave the room she added, 'While I telephone, between you get Mr. Frobisher into his bed.'

Running down to the study, she rang up the doctor. As it was only a little after eight o'clock, he had not yet gone out on his rounds, and promised to come at once. Stefano and Bella had just come out of Rowley's room and closed the door behind them. As though in a daze, she accompanied them downstairs to the kitchen. She knew that she ought to be crying but, having wept so much during the night, she could not now squeeze out a single tear. It struck her then that they might wonder why her eyes were so red, so she pretended to collapse in a chair and covered her face with her hands.

The Italians fussed about her. They were obviously most distressed at losing their kind master and kept making doleful exclamations in their own language. Then, with the practical good sense of her race, Bella boiled up the kettle and made Linda a big cup of instant coffee. She drank it gratefully.

Dr. Mead lived only a few streets away. She had just finished the coffee when the front-door bell rang and Stefano hurried off to let the doctor in. Linda accompanied him to Rowley's room. No explanations were necessary. The empty brandy bottle was enough to tell the tale. Having drawn the sheet up over Rowley's face, the doctor turned to her and said with a shake of his head:

'I feared this would happen before very long, since he refused to heed my warning about limiting himself to only an occasional glass of spirits. It must have been a terrible shock to you, Miss Chatterton. I'll sign the necessary certificate and get in touch with an undertaker for you. You'll inform his relatives, of course, and when you've done that you'd better go back to bed. I'll leave you a sedative.'

When he had gone, Linda shut herself in the study and rang up Elsie. Rowley's stepdaughter received the news without apparent emotion. Having said, 'How terrible,' she expressed no sympathy for Linda, only added: 'Hold the line while I tell Arthur.'

Some minutes later, she came on again and said, 'We are coming up to London and should be with you at about eleven o'clock. In the meantime, of course, you will remove nothing from the house.'

'Why should I?' Linda enquired in surprise.

'I'm only warning you because it and its contents are now mine. Arthur drew up Rowley's last will and, apart from a few legacies, he left everything to me.'

'I see,' Linda murmured. 'But the legacies. I take it he has left me enough to live on?'

'No. You are not mentioned in it.' Elsie did not attempt to disguise her satisfaction as she added, 'You don't get a penny. Not one penny.'

7

A Thief in the Morning

LINDA was still holding the receiver to her ear. 'Hello!' she cried. 'Hello!' and jiggled the receiver cradle agitatedly. But Elsie had hung up; the line was dead. She, too, hung up. Then, dazed with shock, she remained for several minutes looking out of the window with unseeing eyes at the small back garden.

Gradually her brain took in the full implications of what Elsie had said. Rowley had not made a new will, as he had told her he would, soon after he had recovered from his first heart attack. To ask a man how he meant to leave his money, when one hoped to inherit a share of it, was a very awkward thing to do. Linda had brought herself to raise the matter only with great diffidence and, having received Rowley's assurance that he would provide adequately for her, had never again mentioned his possible death. Like many scientists he was, at times, apt to be absent-minded about practical matters; evidently it had slipped his mind again.

She felt certain that the last thing he had meant to do was to leave her high and dry: but the fact remained that he had. The thought appalled her. Most of the handsome allowance he had made her had gone on clothes, presents and sending periodical 'fivers' to her mother, so in her bank she had only about one hundred and eighty pounds. That was all that now stood between her and starvation.

It should keep her long enough to get a job. But what sort of a job? Owing to her inability to learn shorthand, it could be only a job in a typists' pool, as a sales girl, or possibly a receptionist. She would be very lucky if she could earn as much as twenty pounds a week.

She was well stocked up with clothes, but she would have to feed herself. With such a wage, and constantly rising prices, she would have to live in some cheap boarding house or share a flat with several other girls, and with a television set permanently blaring, which would prevent her from the reading she had come to love.

The prospect filled her with dismay. Memories of the Ritz in Paris, the Reserve in Beaulieu, the sunny garden terrace and swimming pool at Cipriani's, the many happy hours visiting castles, cathedrals, museums, old galleries, all came back to her. She had become used to drinking champagne, château clarets and *auslese* hocks, to eating caviare, foie gras, smoked salmon and the rich dishes that Rowley had ordered for them at first-class restaurants. Yesterday all these joys had been within her normal orbit; this morning, in one brief moment, they had been snatched from her for ever.

Never, never again was she to enjoy such things. Instead, some dreary, monotonous job from nine to five, a fortnight's holiday a year at Brighton or Margate, snack lunches in tea shops, a cut off the joint and two veg. for her evening meal, and a glass or two of cheap wine occasionally as a treat. After the life she had been leading, it was worse than a prison sentence. She almost wished she were dead.

She would not submit to it, not without a struggle. Somehow Elsie must be made to do something for her. She could not bring an action. Legally she had not a leg to stand on. But morally, she was entitled to a pension of sorts. Had she never met Rowley, by now she would at least be earning her living, have made a few friends of her own class and settled down reasonably contented with her lot. Her looks would certainly have secured boy friends for her, and quite probably she would by now be married to some decent, steady fellow. But Rowley had spoilt any chance she had ever had of that.

She must put her case to Elsie and enlist Arthur's help. He wasn't a bad fellow, although he was so subservient to his wife. Rowley had been rich, so they would now have a big income. A few hundred a year would mean little to them, but make all the difference to her. If need be, she would swallow her pride and plead with Elsie.

But Elsie was as hard as nails and had never disguised the fact that she disliked her. They had not a thing in common, and to assert that she had given Rowley the happiest years of his life would not help. To reveal that she had been his mistress would only make things worse, and arouse all Elsie's puritanical prejudices. No, for all Elsie's self-righteous, charitable works, there was little hope that she would loosen her purse-strings for her stepfather's 'secretary'.

Then a sudden inspiration came to Linda. Elsie had made a special point of telling her that she must take nothing from the house. At the time she had been vaguely puzzled, because it had not seemed to her that there was anything of much value that she would be likely to take. But now the thought flashed upon her. There were Rowley's mother's jewels.

Being honest by nature, for a few minutes she balked at the idea. Had she been able to get in touch with Eric, she would not have dreamed of taking them. But it might be months before she could trace him. She might even fail altogether, and this was a case of 'now or never'. Rowley, she was convinced, would have approved her making good in this way his own forget-fulness and neglect. Reason told her too that it was foolish to be deterred by scruples. Those jewels could prove a life-raft in a stormy sea. She could live in comfort for several years on the money they would fetch. She would be crazy to go out into the world alone and almost penniless when a fortune lay close to hand for the taking.

Stepping quickly over to the door, she transferred the key to the inside and locked it, then knelt down beside the safe. Ever since she had become Rowley's mistress, he had let her wear any of the jewels she liked and, so that she could get them out whenever she wanted without bothering him, he had given her the combina-tion. Swiftly she twirled the knob to and fro, then swung the heavy door open.

The lower shelves held Rowley's papers, with their secret nuclear calculations; the upper the pile of small, leather cases, the valuable contents of each of which she knew well. Sweeping them out, she stuffed them into a large manilla envelope and on top of them her passport, then closed the door of the safe and, twirling the knob, relocked it.

The jewels Rowley's mother had left were, she knew, worth about twenty-five thousand pounds, but only a part of them was here. To keep the insurance premium down to a reasonable figure, the most valuable items were lodged in Harrods' safe deposit. But, as she dealt with Rowley's insurances, she was aware that the haul she had made was worth about seven thousand pounds. If she could dispose of them, that would enable her to weather the storm for a long time to come.

Unlocking the door of the room, she peered cautiously out. Neither of the servants was to be seen. With trembling fingers she put the key back in the outside of the door, then ran lightly up to her bedroom. There she transferred the jewel cases to her largest handbag.

By this time it was just after nine o'clock, so there were nearly two hours to go before Elsie and Arthur could be expected; ample time for her to make herself respectable. When she looked in the bathroom mirror she was shocked by her haggard appearance, but her eyes were now shining with excitement. Another bath refreshed her; then she did her face and hair and put on a grey coat and skirt, which was the nearest thing she had to mourning.

Having locked in a drawer the bag in which she had put the jewels, she went downstairs to the kitchen. Normally she had her breakfast brought up to her at half past eight, and it was now a few minutes past ten; so, in spite of her disturbed state of mind, she was hungry. The Luchenis were making no attempt to get on with the housework, but talking together in low voices. As she walked in they both stood up and gravely expressed their sympathy for her. She told them that Mr. and Mrs. Spilkin would be arriving shortly and would most probably stay to lunch. Bella said that there were in the fridge both cold vichyoisse and a lemon sponge she had made, and that for a main course she would slip out and get a leg of lamb. Linda nodded agreement, then, having asked Bella to make her an omelette and more coffee, she went to the dining-room.

As she sat there waiting for her belated breakfast and while she ate it, she knew that she ought to be grieving for Rowley. She would have been had not Elsie's bombshell suddenly made her future so uncertain; and it was on that her mind was working overtime.

The odds against Rowley's having told Elsie the combination to open the safe were very long; so a man from Chubb's would have to be sent for, and it was unlikely that one would be available until the following morning at the earliest. Even so, that gave her a safety margin of only twenty-four hours. During that time she must dispose of the jewels and get herself lost without trace.

That brought her face to face with the fact that she had become a criminal and, if found out, might be sent to prison. She blanched at the thought, and for some moments considered putting the jewels back while there was still time. But again there loomed up in her mind swift visions of being pushed around by some slave-driving employer, or pestered by some unpleasant boss who wanted to sleep with her, of doing her own washing, of dreary Sundays when she would be unable to afford to go out of London to lunch at some old country inn, and the smell of stale cabbage coming up from the kitchen of a cheap boarding house. No, she decided. She could not face it. Prison could hardly be much worse.

Elsie would, no doubt, expect her to move out within the next few days. But she would have to any-way, now that she had taken the jewels. Would they insist on searching her luggage, to make sure that she had not packed among her things some of the silver, or half a dozen of Rowley's collection of valuable snuff-boxes? Well, they could search her luggage if they liked.

But what about her handbag? Suppose they suspected that she might be making off with the jewels? If she refused to let them look in her bag, that would be as good as a confession of guilt. They would detain her forcibly and send for the police. Then she would have 'had it'.

In sudden panic she choked on a piece of toast and marmalade. Pushing back her chair, she stood up. There was only one way in which to make certain of escaping such a catastrophe. She must leave with the jewels before they arrived. But if, when they reached the house, they found her gone, they would immediately jump to it that she had stolen something. She would not be in the clear even for twenty-four hours. On some excuse they would start a hue and cry after her, perhaps say that, as she had left all her clothes behind, they feared that Rowley's death had sent her out of her mind.

No. She must get the jewels out of the house and be back there before they turned up. But how in the very brief time now left at her disposal could she deposit the jewels in some safe place from which she could afterwards collect them? Her quick mind swiftly produced an answer. She could rush along to the Post Office, put them in a large, registered envelope and address them to herself at some hotel. Any hotel would do. Leaving the table she ran upstairs to get the bag with its precious contents. She had unlocked the drawer and snatched up the bag when the front-door bell rang. Momentarily the shock paralysed her. She found herself looking at the clock. The hands stood at ten to eleven. She must have spent more time over breakfast than she had thought, for she had believed it to be not much after half past ten. The bell that had rung must be the Spilkins. She had left it too late. With a little groan she dropped the bag back into the drawer and relocked it.

Suddenly it occurred to her that they would not expect to find her dressed and self-possessed, but prostrate with grief. Quickly she slipped off her coat, skirt and shoes, put on her dressing gown and lay down on the bed.

A few minutes later there came a peremptory knock on the door and, without waiting for an answer, Elsie walked in. Linda felt a strong aversion to the short, plump figure, the little, piggy eyes and the fleshy chin, but she forced herself not to show it, gave a faint smile and said in a low voice, 'I'm glad you've come.'

Elsie surveyed her critically and replied, 'Naturally we've come. The sooner we get everything settled, the better. Rowley's death must have been a most unpleasant shock for you. But I trust you are not too laid out to put on some things and come downstairs to talk matters over with me and Arthur.'

'No,' Linda murmured, sitting up. 'I'll be down in about ten minutes. And I'll be glad to have your advice about my future.'

A brief nod was Elsie's only reply before leaving the room and closing the door none too softly behind her.

Ten minutes later Linda joined the Spilkins in the study. They were busily employed going through such papers as Rowley had left in his desk. Arthur greeted Linda politely and his eyes expressed the sympathy that he evidently feared to voice in the presence of his dominating wife.

Elsie opened matters by saying, 'You know the combination of the safe, of course. Be good enough to open it.'

Sitting down on a chair, Linda shook her head. 'I'm sorry, but I don't know it. Rowley kept all his secret calculations in it, and he never told me the combination.'

With a shrug of annoyance Elsie said, 'In that case, we'll get a lock man along as soon as we can. Now, about yourself. Naturally, we've no wish to hurry you unduly, but how soon can you get packed up and find somewhere else to live?'

The realisation that she had already become a thief filled Linda with dismay. So she had decided that, if she could persuade Elsie to give her even a modest allowance, she would take the first opportunity of putting the jewels back in the safe. Hesitantly she replied:

'I . . . I hardly know. This was so terribly unexpected. I . . . I wanted to consult you about my future.'

'Well, what about it?'

'You told me that I'm not mentioned in Rowley's will. That came as an awful shock, because after his first heart attack he promised to have a new will drawn up, in which he would provide for me.'

'Maybe. But he didn't. On our way here we called at Arthur's office and collected a copy of Rowley's last will.' Turning to her husband, she added: 'Arthur, show it to her.'

Arthur produced a long, folded paper from his brief-case and gave it to Linda. Glancing at it, she saw that it was dated April 17th, 1968. That would have been some weeks after Rowley's wife had had her near-fatal accident. Handing the document back, she said:

'There is no point in my reading it through, since you say that I am not mentioned. Evidently Rowley forgot his promise to look after me.'

D

'That is so,' Arthur agreed, running a finger down his long, needle-point nose. 'I'm sorry, but there it is. However, you can return to your parents in Lincolnshire. I recall being told that they are quite well off, so are in a position to take care of you.'

Temporarily Linda had forgotten that they believed her to be Eric Dutton's niece and Colonel Chatterton's daughter. Taken completely by surprise she was at a loss how to reply. To hide her expression and gain a few moments in which to think, she buried her face in her hands. Her mind worked swiftly. While they stared at her in silence for a full minute, she thought up a story, gave a muffled sob, then took her hands from her face and said:

'I thought you knew. Daddy died last winter. When . . . when Rowley and I were in Spain. No-one suspected it until he was dead, but he had behaved very badly. Racing was an obsession with him. He ruined himself backing horses. The place was mortgaged up to the hilt, and had to be sold. My poor mother was left terribly badly off. She went to Spain to live with a friend, because it's so much cheaper there and . . . and she couldn't possibly afford to support me.'

The Spilkins swallowed this tissue of lies, and both of them expressed conventional sympathy for Linda's 'mother'. Guilty as Linda felt at having slandered the Colonel, she also felt that having done so had improved her own case; so, with all the pathos she could muster, she went on:

'Yes, it was too awful. And I'm left high and dry. Really, it isn't fair. I haven't a bean, and life with Rowley has completely unfitted me for the only sort of jobs that I'm capable of doing.' She turned to Elsie. 'Rowley was rich. You must have come into a fortune.

Couldn't you possibly spare me a few hundred a year, to ante up the miserable sort of wage I'll be earning?'

'I could, but I see no reason why I should. Most girls would count themselves lucky to have led the sort of life you've had for the past two and a half years: travelling, staying in luxury hotels and dining in the best restaurants. It is obvious from the way you dress, too, that Rowley must have paid you very handsomely for your services—far more than is earned by an ordinary secretary. If you had really worked to make a career for yourself from the beginning, you would be qualified to take a well-paid job by now. That you elected instead to batten on Rowley is not my affair. Your job here, like any other, has come to an end; that's all there is to it.'

'Of course I've had a good time,' Linda admitted. 'But it was Rowley's wish that I should, and I was very much more than a secretary. I didn't only run the house and keep his papers in order. He owed his happiness these last years to me, and I looked after him like a mother.'

'A mother indeed!' Elsie snapped. 'I've never heard it called that before. I'm not quite such a fool as to suppose that my stepfather treated you as he did, letting you wear his family jewels and buying you expensive presents like your mink coat, because you "mothered" him.'

Her words dashed Linda's last hopes of assistance. She had thought that if the myth that had been built up about her position in the household was accepted by Elsie, there was just a chance that she might do something for her; but since she realised the true situation she would not part with a penny.

Linda's blue eyes flashed and she declared angrily, 'Very well, then! I was his mistress! So what?'

'So you admit it,' Elsie retorted. 'Irreligious as you are, no doubt you've heard of "the wages of sin". I consider that by being deprived of your jam and having to live on bread and scrape in the future you are getting off lightly.'

'You sanctimonious prude!' Linda cried.

Elsie gave an unpleasant little laugh. 'Hard words break no bones, my dear. I was wrong just now, though. With your looks you don't need to look for a job. You can get plenty of jam simply by becoming a professional. You won't have to walk the streets for long.'

Infuriated by the insult, Linda jumped to her feet, turned toward the door and flung over her shoulder, 'If I don't leave this room, I'll hit you.'

'You can get out of the house, too,' Elsie retorted. 'And the sooner the better. You can stay overnight if you like, to pack your things. But not in your room. Except for Rowley's, it's the only room in the house which has two beds, so I want it for myself and Arthur.'

Linda thought swiftly. There could be no question of returning the jewels now, and she must endeavour, somehow, to dispose of them before their loss was discovered. Every moment was precious. Pausing in the doorway, she said bitterly:

'I wouldn't sleep in the same house with you if you paid me. I'll go right away and get myself a room at an hotel. But I'll have to collect my clothes. I'll come for them tomorrow.'

'That is an excellent idea,' Elsie agreed briskly, as, slamming the door behind her, Linda ran upstairs.

Within ten minutes she had crammed into a suitcase

all she would need for the night. Then, with the bag containing the jewels hanging from her free arm, she carried them downstairs. As she reached the first-floor landing, Arthur called to her from the library:

'Linda. Would you come here for a moment, please?'

Setting down the suitcase, she joined him and, her eyes hard, asked, 'Well, what is it?'

'The safe,' he said, a little unhappily. 'Are you sure that you don't know the combination? I mean, perhaps you misunderstood Elsie when she asked you about it a little time ago.'

Linda shook her head. 'As I told you, Rowley kept his secret papers in it, and he never told anyone the combination. I'm sure it wasn't because he didn't trust me, but out of habit I suppose.'

'But, er . . . Linda. The jewels will be in it, too. You have often worn some of them. Surely he didn't get them out himself each time for you?'

Linda felt herself colouring and had difficulty in keeping her voice steady. 'He did. He always chose what he wished me to wear, according to where we were going or if it was for a dinner party here, and locked them away again afterwards.'

'I see. Well, in that case we'll have to send for a man from Chubb's to open it. I'll get on the telephone to them now.' Arthur paused for a moment, then added:

'I'm sorry about all this, Linda. But please don't think too hardly about Elsie. Before you came Rowley relied on her for so many things and, having no children of his own, used to make quite a fuss of her. Not unnaturally, she was jealous of all the things he did for you, and the sight of you wearing the jewels her mother used to wear made her furious.'

Raising a faint smile, Linda said, 'It's true that she

has no cause to love me, although I've always done my best to be nice to her. Anyhow, thanks for your sympathy.'

Turning on her heel, she collected her suitcase and went out into the hall. Every moment she expected Elsie to emerge from one of the rooms to challenge her about the contents of her handbag. With her heart in her mouth, she tiptoed along to the front door and let herself out.

With a sigh of relief she ran down the steps and set off at a quick walk, looking for a taxi. She had got away with it. Elsie could not stop and challenge her now. But, by this time, Arthur was ringing up Chubb's. It was only just on midday, so they might send a man that afternoon.

She was now a thief, a criminal. She was still free, but how long would she be able to keep her freedom? Within twenty-four hours, perhaps less, the police would be after her.

8

On the Run

IN the Euston Road Linda picked up a taxi. It was on the tip of her tongue to ask the driver to take her to a small, respectable hotel. Just in time it flashed upon her that, as soon as the police were asked to trace her, her description would be circulated to all taxi garages. The man might well remember her and supply the name of the hotel to which he had taken her. After a moment's thought it struck her that first things should come first and, Bond Street being her all-important objective, she told him to drive her to the Westbury.

Rowley had taken her to dine at several of London's best hotels, but never there; so there was no risk of her being recognised. As the commissionaire took her suitcase, she told him that she wanted to leave it in the cloakroom while she did some shopping, tipped him well but not extravagantly and put the cloakroom ticket in her purse.

It was only a minute's walk round the corner to Cabouchon's. She had been into the famous jeweller's on a number of occasions. Twice Rowley had agreed to her having the stones of old-fashioned pieces reset in a more modern style, twice she had had the pearls of the smaller necklace restrung, and once a stone in an earring had been lost and had had to be replaced.

From the first she had realised that she could not possibly hope to dispose of all the jewels in one transaction and, whenever she had had a moment, had been badgering her wits about how to turn even a few of them into ready money. But on the way down in the taxi inspiration had come to her and, on entering the shop, she knew exactly how she meant to proceed.

Looking round, she was glad to see that the nice old gentleman who usually looked after her was behind his counter. Greeting him with her sunniest smile, she said, 'I've wonderful news, Mr. Smithers. I'm going to be married.'

He returned her smile. 'Indeed, Miss Chatterton. Your fiancé is to be congratulated. May I enquire . . .'

'Oh, to Mr. Frobisher. I expect you know that Mrs. Frobisher has been—er—in a home for a long time past. She died quite suddenly, on Sunday. I felt that we really ought to wait, but Mr. Frobisher wouldn't hear of it, so we are being married by special licence on Friday.'

Mr. Smithers smiled again. 'How exciting for you. I hope you will be very happy.'

'Thank you. I'm sure we shall. Now I must tell you what I've come to see you about. Mr. Frobisher has given me a most wonderful wedding present: his mother's jewels. Not the very valuable pieces that are in Harrods' safe deposit. He promised his wife that he would leave those to her daughter, Mrs. Spilkin, but all the lesser pieces that we keep at home, and he's let me wear during the past two years.'

'I see. And in what way can I be of help to you?'

'I want to sell one or two of them. Not for money to spend on myself, of course. It is to buy Mr. Frobisher a really nice wedding present. He loves Georgian furniture, but he has never bothered to get himself a genuine desk, and I've seen just the very thing in Partridge's. It's Regency, and the price is five hundred and twenty guineas. I couldn't possibly afford such a sum, and I had this wonderful idea of parting with some of the rings. There are more of them than I shall ever want to wear, and some of them are not particularly beautiful. The diamond cluster, for example, and the marquise ring—that's very old-fashioned.'

In the taxi Linda had sorted out her haul and put two of the rings into a separate compartment of her bag. She now produced them and laid them on the counter.

Mr. Smithers screwed his magnifying glass into his eye and examined the rings in turn. But only cursorily, as he had revalued them only the previous year, to bring Rowley's insurance on the jewels up to date; so he already knew approximately what they were worth.

'I think we could give you three-fifty on the cluster,' he said, 'and two-twenty on the marquise. That would leave you twenty-four pounds in hand.'

Linda was tempted to jump at the offer; but she knew that the rings were worth considerably more, so felt bound to say, 'That is more than I need, but surely it's not a very good price. And wouldn't there be about fifty over?'

Mr Smithers smiled his benign smile. 'No, Madam. You spoke of the price of the desk in guineas, and I was quoting for the rings in pounds.'

'I see. Well, could you make it guineas?'

Turning the rings over with his long fingers, Mr. Smithers considered for a moment, then he said, 'I think I could, Madam, if you were willing to spend the extra fifty with us. The desk will be a most handsome gift, but perhaps you might also like to make Mr.

Frobisher a more personal present, something he could wear?'

Linda would have much preferred the extra fifty pounds, but she had yet to get over the really big fence of asking the jeweller, without arousing suspicion, to pay her on the spot; so she agreed to his idea and said she would like to spend the extra money on a pair of cuff-links.

Compelling herself not to hurry over her choice, she selected a pair of white gold and mother of pearl, with tiny sapphires in the centre. Picking up the links, Mr. Smithers said, 'No doubt you would like to take these with you, Madam. I'll find a case for them and pack them up. Our cashier will post the cheque on to you.'

'Oh, no!' Linda exclaimed, having expected this. 'That would never do. As I told you, we're being married on Friday and we leave for the Continent that afternoon. It would spoil everything if the desk was not delivered until we got back. I want to give it to Mr. Frobisher tomorrow, Thursday. And, as I've never bought anything from Partridge's, I can't ask them to send it unless I give them my cheque; so I must have one from you to pay into my bank this afternoon.'

'I see; I see.' Mr Smithers suddenly became thoughtful. 'Yes, I see. Well, if you'll excuse me for a few minutes, Madam, I will try and arrange matters.'

To Linda those few minutes seemed never-ending. She was gripped with the awful fear that Mr. Smithers would ring up Rowley to get confirmation that the transaction was in order. Then, when he learned that Rowley was dead, the fat would be in the fire with a vengeance. Having made his first call, Mr. Smithers would then make another—to the police.

The temptation to cut and run while the going was

good was almost irresistible. Yet, so far, things could not have gone better. Her story that she was about to marry Rowley and that he had given her the jewels was perfectly plausible. There was no reason whatever why they should suspect her; whereas, if she tried to sell the jewels anywhere else it was certain that she would be asked all sorts of questions and required to supply evidence that they were her property—which she could not possibly do.

No. She must sit tight. Her whole future was at stake. This was her one and only chance of getting hold of enough money to leave the country and have enough to live on until she could sell some of the other jewels. If she abandoned it at this last moment, her entire plan collapsed. There would be no alternative but to throw in her hand. If she returned the jewels at once, no charge would be brought against her. But she would have condemned herself to hardship and misery.

Taking a cigarette from her case, she lit and pulled upon it avidly, while keeping her eyes riveted on the glass-panelled door at the back of the shop, through which Mr. Smithers had gone. At last he reappeared. He held something in his hand; but it was not a cheque. Her heart sank.

He laid the thing he had been carrying on the counter. It was the pair of links, now done up in a neat parcel. Then he said, 'I'm terribly sorry, Madam, but there has been a slight difficulty.'

'What! You . . . you can't let me have a cheque?' Linda stammered.

'Not for the moment, Madam. You see. . . .'

'But why? Why not?' She could not keep a quiver out of her voice. 'It . . . it's very disappointing. I was counting on it. Surely you can arrange something?'

'Please, Madam.' Mr. Smithers sought to reassure her. 'There is no cause for your distress. It is simply that all our cheques have to be signed by two partners. There is only one here at the moment. The others have gone out to lunch.'

Looking down to hide her intense relief, Linda stubbed out her cigarette. 'Oh, I see. Yes, of course I understand. When will one of them be back?'

'If you look in about three o'clock, Madam, I'll have the cheque ready for you.'

'Thank you. Thank you very much. I'll do that.' She gave Mr. Smithers a bright smile, put the links in her bag and turned away. He hurried round the counter to open the door for her, and bowed her out into Bond Street.

She was still free, and unsuspected. But she had not got the money.

The moment she had left Park Side West she had temporarily put aside her bitterness against Elsie for the more urgent matter of thinking up this plausible story by which she might turn some of the jewels into money. While doing so, it had come into her quick mind that, now she was fully committed, she might as well be hung for a sheep as a lamb. So, on leaving Cabouchon's, she took a taxi down to Harrods.

There she went first to the leather department and bought a brief-case, which would easily hold all the jewels and could be locked. As it was an expensive item, she had to wait some time while they checked her signature, but putting it down to the joint account that she ran with Rowley tickled her sense of humour, as Elsie would now have to pay for it.

She then went down to the safe deposit in the basement. As she rang the bell outside the iron-barred gate, she felt no qualms of apprehension, as Harrods could not possibly yet know that Rowley was dead. She had been down there before, several times, to take out or return some of the more valuable pieces, as Rowley had liked her to wear fine jewels when he took her to City dinners, receptions given by the Royal Society and similar functions. Her Junoesque good looks had registered with the young man who unlocked the gate, and he greeted her with a smiling 'Good morning'.

At the reception desk she gave the password, 'To Hell with Harold', that Rowley had chosen some years before, and handed over the key to his locker. The attendant fetched the box, put it on the wide shelf of one of the booths and closed the door behind her. With the smaller key she unlocked the box, then transferred the leather cases in it to the brief-case. Beneath them, at the bottom of the box, there was a long, fat envelope.

As she saw it, her heart gave a bound of joy. She had forgotten it was there, but knew what it contained. Like many people who were law-abiding in other respects, Rowley had resented being dictated to by the Labour Government on how he should spend his money. In those days, holiday-makers had been restricted to taking thirty pounds out of the country, and when abroad he normally spent that amount in a couple of days. In consequence, he had acquired a fat wad of Swiss francs, and whenever he left England used to take several hundred pounds' worth with him. Since the restriction had been lifted, four years previously, he had had no need to draw on this nest-egg.

The notes were all of high denominations and, with eager fingers, Linda totted up their value. At a rough calculation, she found to her delight that they were worth well over one thousand pounds.

It was more than enough to get her out of the country and keep her for quite a time; so, had she remembered this hoard, she need not have risked endeavouring to sell some of the jewels while still in England. But it was too late to job backward now, and she could certainly count herself lucky in making this unexpected find.

Having put the envelope with the jewels in the brief-case and locked it, she relocked the now empty tin box, gave it back to the young man outside and, with a light heart, heard the iron gate of the vault clang to behind her.

It was now past her usual lunchtime, but she still had a lot to do, so resisted the temptation to go up and have a snack in the restaurant, and took a taxi to her bank in Baker Street.

She had there something over one hundred and eighty pounds. To have left it there would have been greatly against the instinct she had acquired when she had worked in her father's market garden, and every penny counted. But she knew that she must proceed with caution. It was just possible that Arthur might already have notified the bank of Rowley's death, in case they had a joint account and she might be tempted to draw on it.

Actually they had not, but now, her mind a prey to every form of apprehension, she feared that if the people at the bank did know of Rowley's death and she failed to mention it, they would think it very strange and perhaps ask her awkward questions which might result in her being caught out in a lie.

The attitude of the cashier would, she decided, be the acid test. If he condoled with her, that would be that. If not, she would be in the clear. As she walked up to

the counter, she saw that the cashier on duty was a
young, coloured girl who had cashed her cheques on
several occasions. The girl smiled at her politely and
said only, 'Good morning, Miss Chatterton. I hope
you're well.'

Thanking her, Linda asked for her balances. They
proved to be one hundred and eighty pounds on
deposit and eight pounds fifty-three pence on current
account. Feeling that it would be less likely to arouse
comment if she sacrificed the lesser sum, she said, 'I
want to draw out one hundred and eighty.'

'Certainly, Miss Chatterton,' the girl smiled. 'It's
quite a sum, isn't it? You must be going on a real
spending spree.'

Linda returned the smile. 'As a matter of fact, I am.
I'm getting married on Friday to Mr. Frobisher, and
I want to buy him a really nice present.'

'Oh, how lovely. Congratulations. I'm sure our
manager will want to congratulate you, too. Mr. Coxon
is in his office. I'll let him know.'

Only then did Linda realise that she had been
extremely stupid. To get her own money out of the
bank it had been quite unnecessary to tell the lie she
had used at Cabouchon's. She had spoken without
thinking. And now, the moment the girl left the
counter, she was seized by a new fear. Mr. Coxon
might know of Rowley's death, but not have told the
cashier about it.

A minute later, the girl came back. 'Mr. Coxon
would very much like to have a word with you, Miss
Chatterton. But he's got someone with him at the
moment. He'll come out to you as soon as he is free.'

It seemed to Linda that the girl was no longer
smiling. With a lump in her throat, she said, 'I . . . I'm

in rather a hurry; and I'd like the money in tenners please.'

The girl waved aside her protest. 'Oh, he won't be long, I'm sure. And there has been quite a run on ten-pound notes this morning, so I'm getting short. While you are waiting I'll send down to the vaults for more.'

Most reluctantly Linda took a chair at a small table, as she wondered if the cashier was lying in order to detain her while Mr. Coxon rang up Arthur to tell him that she was saying she was engaged to a dead man. Still, they could not refuse to let her have her own money. But what if Chubb's had already sent a man to open the safe? If so, she had cooked her own goose. Arthur would ask the manager to send for the police.

Her mouth had gone dry again from nervous strain, and her hands were clenched tight under cover of the table. Again she was tempted to run for it. She would have to sacrifice the one hundred and eighty pounds, but she had the Swiss francs.

With her eyes fixed on the clock on the opposite wall, she counted the agonising minutes—five, six, seven, eight, nine. At last, bald-headed little Mr. Coxon came bustling out of his office, and he was smiling. Taking both Linda's hands, he wrung them heartily and cried:

'My dear young lady, I am delighted; delighted. Mr. Frobisher is one of our oldest clients. I do congratulate you, and also him. He is a very lucky man. It is a pleasure to wish you both every possible happiness.'

Five minutes later Linda had cashed her cheque, stuffed the wad of crisp, new notes into her handbag and was out in the street.

Glancing at her wrist watch, she saw that it was half past two, so her next hurdle was to collect the cheque from Cabouchon's. A taxi got her to Bond Street in ten minutes. It was close on three hours since her previous visit. In that time much might have happened. Chubb's men might have opened the safe. Arthur might have telephoned the jeweller and learned that she had attempted to sell two of the rings. If so, there was probably a detective in the shop, waiting to arrest her when she returned there.

As it was still well before three o'clock, Linda made that an excuse to herself for not yet going in. For ten minutes she loitered from one shop window to another, apparently studying the goods in them, but without her brain registering what they were or their prices. A smartly-dressed grey-haired man, wearing a curly-brimmed bowler, attempted to pick her up. For a moment she did not take in the remark he had made to her; then she sharply brushed him off, turned and walked quickly away.

Finding that she was going toward Cabouchon's she rallied her courage. Then, telling herself that the odds against the safe having yet been opened were a hundred to one, she pushed open the door and went in.

Mr. Smithers was not at his counter. A young man whom she did not know came forward and enquired politely what he could do for her. She asked for Mr. Smithers, but he had unexpectedly had to go out, and the young man knew nothing about her arrangement with him that morning. Much irritated, she told him about the rings that she had sold from the Frobisher collection. Asking her to take a chair, he disappeared into an inner office. He was absent for several minutes, while Linda tapped her foot impatiently. Presently he emerged, smiling and holding the cheque. Standing up, she took it from him and was about to put it into her bag when she caught sight of the last half of the name written on it. Instead of to herself, it had been made out to *Roland Frobisher, Esq.*

Her nerves taut to breaking point, it was on the tip of her tongue to scream at him, 'Damn you for a bloody fool!' but she checked herself in time. Whatever happened, she must not make a scene. Choking down her fury, she pointed out the error and gave him back the cheque.

Apologising, he again went into the office. Linda endured another wait of several minutes. Then the young man returned, accompanied by an older man who introduced himself as Mr. Bendon, and told her that he was one of the partners. Holding the same cheque in his hand, he said:

'I understand that you are Miss Chatterton, a friend of Mr. Frobisher. In fact, I've seen you in here once or twice when designs were being submitted to you for re-setting some of his jewels. But the jewels belong to Mr. Frobisher; so, naturally, we made out our cheque to him.'

Calling up the last dregs of her patience, Linda told him the same story as she had Mr. Smithers. He listened, unsmiling, to the end, then made a little bow:

'It is a pleasure, Madam, to wish you every happiness in your forthcoming marriage; and I hope you will continue to give us your patronage. But—er—I trust you will forgive me for pointing out that this transaction is a little irregular. I mean, without a written authority from Mr. Frobisher, I hardly like to buy from you jewels which, as far as we know, are his property.'

Linda felt a chill run down her spine. She was not, after all, going to get the cheque. She had been through all this agonising business for nothing. But there was one last chance, although it was a desperate one. She could try a bluff.

Drawing herself up to her full, splendid height, she said haughtily, 'I am not accustomed to having my word doubted. If you don't believe that I am engaged to Mr. Frobisher and that he has given me his jewels to do with as I wish, I'll have to explain to him why I wanted to sell the two rings. That will ruin the surprise I planned for him; so it will be the last time I shall ever enter this shop.'

Mr. Brendon gave her an unhappy look, bowed and walked toward his office. The second his back was turned, Linda would have given anything to take back her words. They had been incredibly rash. She had virtually invited him to ring up Rowley. Elsie or Arthur would take the call, and be told what she had done. And that, when she already had in her bag over twelve hundred pounds. Why, in God's name, had she been so greedy, instead of sensibly sacrificing the money for these accursed jewels? Now she had burnt her boats with a vengeance. After Mr. Bendon had telephoned, he would invite her into his office and keep her there until the police came.

He was away only a few minutes. When he returned, he was still holding a cheque in his hand. Forcing a smile, he handed it to her and said, 'Madam, I apologise for having upset you; but we do have to take every possible precaution, in the interests of our clients as well as ourselves.'

A quick glance at the cheque showed her that it was another and made out to her. 'Thank you,' she murmured. 'I'm afraid I was rather hasty. But—er—of course I do understand. I'll be coming in to see you when I return from my honeymoon.' Then she picked up her bag, and they bowed her out.

At a quick walk she went round to the Westbury; but

not to collect her suitcase. In the writing-room she wrote a brief note to Mr. Coxon, asking him to pay the cheque into her current account, enclosed the cheque with it, bought a stamp at the office and popped it into the post-box.

On leaving the hotel, she decided that for her next business it would be quicker to walk than take a taxi; so, at a good pace, she went up Conduit Street and down Regent Street to the B.O.A.C. offices. She would have preferred to get her ticket through Milbanke Travel in Bond Street, as the manager there, Mr. Unger, had always, with admirable efficiency, made the arrangements for her travels abroad with Rowley. But to use Milbanke would almost certainly lead to the Spilkins learning where she had gone.

She had decided to escape to Canada, her choice possibly having been subconsciously influenced by the fact that her brother, Sid, had gone there. But she had no intention of trying to seek him out, as he had a streak of his father in him and had often bullied her into doing jobs that he should have done himself; so she felt no affection for him. Canada's main appeal to her as a country in which to start a new life was an assumption that life there could not be very different from what it was in England.

At the B.O.A.C. offices, she asked for a seat on the next day's aircraft to Montreal, only to learn to her dismay that every seat was already booked. It was imperative that she be out of England by the following night, so she enquired if there were any planes flying to other Canadian cities. There proved to be an Air Canada flight direct to Edmonton. A glance at the map showed her that Edmonton was in the far west, just this side of the Rockies. With the thought that the further she was from England the better, she decided that she would get on it if she could; so, leaving the B.O.A.C. office, she walked quickly up Regent Street to that of Air Canada. There her luck was in, as several seats on the flight were still available.

Her original object in selling the two rings had been to get enough money to pay her fare, and she had meant to take the cheque straight to her bank and cash it. On learning that she would not receive the cheque until too late to bank it that day, she had hoped that B.O.A.C. would accept a cheque on her own account, otherwise she would have to use her deposit money for her fare and arrive in Canada with very little cash. That would have meant selling more of the jewels almost at once to a jeweller to whom she could give no references. But within an hour she had been relieved of that worry by the unexpected help of Swiss francs; and would not have risked returning to collect the Cabouchon cheque had she not feared that if she failed to do so the jewellers would ring up to find out why she had not, which would prematurely alert the Spilkins to the fact that she had made off with the jewels.

Now that she had posted the cheque she was able to use one of her own to pay for her ticket: much relieved by the knowledge that it would not bounce and lead to Air Canada putting the police on to her a day or two after her arrival at Edmonton.

The thought that she must leave the greater part of the money she had received for the rings untouched in her bank annoyed her. But there was one consolation. She felt no qualms about paying the much more expensive first-class fare, and signed a cheque for two hundred and four pounds. A further comfort was that she would not have to wait in agonised suspense all next day right up till the evening, as the Edmonton flight took off at five past two in the afternoon. Even so, if the Chubb man got through his rounds quickly there was still a nasty risk that the Spilkins might get on to the police in time to have her arrested at the airport.

The girl at the desk had just handed Linda her ticket when her mind was suddenly distracted from the risk she must run next day by a terrible shock. Her precious brief-case was not on the floor beside her. The upset at Cabouchon's had taken her mind off it, and she must have left it there.

The blood draining from her cheeks, she ran out to get a taxi. But all those in sight were occupied. For the best part of ten minutes, she stood fuming on the kerb, watching the stream of traffic alternately halt in a solid block, then run on. At length one drew up in front of the Air Canada office. Without waiting until the passenger had paid the driver, she jumped inside and shouted to him to take her to the jeweller's as quickly as possible.

On the way she had frightful misgivings. The best part of three-quarters of an hour must have passed since she had left Cabouchon's. Perhaps during that time Mr. Bendon had decided that, after all, he ought to telephone Rowley, and had got on to Elsie or Arthur. If so, she was deliberately walking back into the trap she had set for herself but had been lucky enough to escape. Dare she risk it? She must. It was no longer a question of getting hold of five hundred-odd pounds, or even of retrieving the jewels she had stolen from the safe. The big stuff from Harrods' safe deposit and the Swiss francs were also in the brief-case—the whole fortune she had been counting on to keep her in comfort for years to come.

In London it was the height of the tourist season. The West End streets were a seething mass of traffic, its free flow hampered by motor coaches and enormously long lorries, which brought everything else to a halt as they manœuvred their way round corners. Owing to the one-way street regulations, the taxi had to cover twice the distance and Linda felt that it would never get there.

At last it pulled up. On getting out, her mind occupied to the exclusion of all else with what would happen in the next five minutes, she forgot to pay the driver. The man called after her, 'Can't wait here, Miss!'

Turning back, she fumbled in her purse, found she had not enough small silver, thrust a fifty-pence piece into his hand and said, 'Keep the change.'

Grinning, he cried as she crossed the pavement, 'Thanks, ducks. Good luck to you.'

His shout put new heart into her as, for the third time that day, she pushed open the door of Cabouchon's. A moment later she knew that things were all right. The young man who had attended to her on her second visit gave her a welcoming smile, emerged from behind his counter with the brief-case, and said:

'I see that you remembered where you left this, Madam. We were afraid you had forgotten. When you came in I was thinking of telephoning your home to let you know we had it and would send it to you by messenger.'

Raising a smile, she thanked him, took the brief-case and again walked out into Bond Street. Another reprieve. She sighed with relief. Had she returned ten minutes later the brief-case would have been on its way up to Park Side West. As it was locked they would not have known what was in it; but the fact that it had been sent from Cabouchon's would have been certain to arouse their suspicions. She would never have had the nerve to face Elsie and reclaim it.

At a bag shop not far down the street she bought a satin pochette and the largest size in waist belts made of strong satin. Then she walked round the corner to the Westbury and got her suitcase out of the cloakroom. The hall porter shook his head over the taxi situation, but a few minutes later an American couple drove up in one.

She had at first intended to lie low in a small hotel somewhere south of Kensington Gardens, where no-one was likely to know her by sight. But further thought had decided her that it would be safer to go to a large place, where people were constantly coming and going, and she would not be remembered by the staff.

As she got into the taxi, for the benefit of the hall porter she told the man to take her to Charing Cross Station; but when they reached Piccadilly Circus she tapped on the window and shouted to him that she had changed her mind and would travel from Victoria. There, having paid the man, she waited until he had driven off, then told a porter to take her suitcase across the station to the Grosvenor Hotel.

The initials L.C. were on her case, but she might have borrowed it, and she booked herself in as Mrs. Ronald Smith of 109 Burnside, Newcastle-on-Tyne. It was the first name and address she could think of and she had no idea if such a street as Burnside existed in Newcastle; but the odds against the receptionist's checking up were astronomical. A bell-hop showed her up to a lofty, comfortably-furnished bedroom. As soon as he had closed the door behind him, she kicked off her shoes and sank into the armchair.

She was so exhausted from continuous strain that, for a while, her brain refused to function further. Gradually the tension eased, and episodes from her long day began to drift through her mind. With a shudder she recalled the eyes in Rowley's dead face staring up at her from her bed. Had that been two, three or four nights ago? No, it had been only the previous night. Barely fifteen hours had passed since he had died in her arms. It seemed impossible that so much could have happened in so short a time.

Since breakfast, just before the Spilkins arrived, she had had nothing to eat or drink, yet she was no longer really hungry. But she must keep her strength up. In a station hotel the restaurant would be open at all hours. She would go downstairs and have a meal. Better not, though. She must show herself in public as little as possible. Heaving herself to her feet, she rang for the floor waiter.

When he arrived with the menu, she ordered a grilled sole, pineapple with Kirsch and a bottle of Rowley's favourite champagne—Louis Roederer Crystal. Almost imperceptibly the waiter raised his eyebrows:

'A whole bottle, Madam?'

She had felt that she needed more than a pint, so she nodded. Too late she realised that she had been rash. The man would remember a single woman ordering a quart, and the most expensive wine on the list at that.

As he had said the sole would take half an hour, when he had gone she locked the door, unpacked her things, undressed and had a bath. When he returned she was in her dressing gown, but she had tidied her hair and was considerably freshened up. He seemed to take an age laying the small table, transferring the dishes from the trolley, and opening the wine. She tipped him, but not too lavishly, and, immediately he had bowed himself out, she drank her first glass of champagne straight off. With the sole she had another glass, and after the pineapple a third. By then she was feeling slightly light-headed.

Lighting a cigarette, she rang for the waiter to clear away and carried the last glass of champagne over to the bedside table. As he wheeled out the trolley, she hung the *Do Not Disturb* notice outside the door, locked it and, although it was still full daylight, drew the curtains.

Having stowed the precious brief-case under the bed, she got between the sheets, drank the rest of the wine and lay back on the pillows. As always happened when she got a little tight, she was filled with goodwill toward all the world. It had been an extraordinary day, but a marvellously successful one. Under the bed she had a fortune. If only her luck held. But why shouldn't it? Filled with optimism, she drifted off to sleep.

Linda had been awake for the whole of the preceding day and night, so it was close on thirty-five hours since she had slept. In consequence she slept the clock round, but it was still early when she woke. Dimly, by the light coming between the curtains, she saw the furniture of the room. For a moment she wondered where she was. Then the horror of Rowley's death and all that had followed it flooded back to her.

At the realisation of what she had done, remorse and fear gripped her. She had stolen twenty-five thousand pounds' worth of jewels. She must have been mad. How could she possibly have allowed herself to do such a thing? Never in her life before had she stolen even as much as a postage stamp. Now, overnight, she had become a criminal. Within a few hours the police would be after her. If they caught her Elsie would show no mercy. She visualised herself being tried and found guilty. Rowley's friends—who had been hers too—would come to the court out of curiosity and witness her shame.

Forcing such thoughts from her mind, she managed to fight down her sense of guilt and look on the brighter side. She had covered her tracks so efficiently that no-one could possibly trace her. She had her ticket for Canada. She had enough money in cash to keep her comfortably for a long while. All the odds were that the safe had not yet been opened. She had only to get through the next eight hours and she would be out of the country.

She remembered then that she had arranged with Elsie to return and pack her belongings that morning. But, as there was just a chance that the robbery had been discovered, she dared not. To have to leave behind all her lovely clothes and, above all, the mink coat that Rowley had given her the previous Christmas, was infuriating. What a fool she had been not to have taken it with her. As it was still summer and she had left in such a hurry, to get it out of its bag and put it on had not occurred to her.

Ever since she had forgotten her brief-case and left it at Cabouchon's the previous afternoon she had been worried by the possibility that she might again forget it somewhere, or have it stolen from her and again find herself nearly penniless. It was for this reason that she had bought the satin pouch.

Getting out of bed, she threaded the satin belt through the flap of the pouch, then adjusted the belt round her waist so that the pouch hung down just below her pubic hair, then she put into it the Swiss francs and ten of the 'tenners' she had drawn from her bank. Satisfied that being so flat it would not show under her dress, she washed her teeth, put on her dressing gown, unlocked the door and telephoned down for breakfast.

By the time she had eaten it, had her bath and dressed, it was half past eight. As she was wondering how she could pass the morning, an inspiration came to her. Taking the brief-case, she went down in the lift and to the manager's office. There, loath as she was to part with the jewels, she asked for it to be put in the safe. It was taken away and she was given a receipt for it.

Walking through to the station, she mingled with the hundreds of men and women who had just come off the trains from the suburbs, and were hurrying to their offices. Many of them, doubtless going to uncongenial jobs, looked peaky and worried. Pity for them mingled in her mind with the thought of the good fortune that would be her own lot if all went well; for it struck her that, had she not stolen the jewels, she would have become one of them, perhaps for life.

At a bookstall she bought a copy of *The Times*, and quickly looked down the deaths reported. Rowley's was not among them, so evidently Arthur had not been in time the previous day to get it in. A glance at the big clock told her that it was still only ten minutes to nine. She would have to wait until nine o'clock at least before she could put through the telephone call she had been inspired to make. Sitting on a bench she tried to read the main news in the paper, but found that she could not concentrate. Impatiently she watched the clock until five past nine, then she went into a telephone booth and rang up Chubb's.

Having told the man who answered that she was Mr. Frobisher's secretary, she asked, 'When are you going to send a man to open his safe?'

'Hold the line a minute,' replied the man. After several minutes, he came back and said, 'We received a call from you yesterday, Madam, but as you were informed then, only a specialist can open one of our safes without knowing the combination. Our man has several calls to make today; but he may get round to you by this afternoon.'

Linda smiled seraphically. She was still in the clear, at least until after lunch. A man waiting his turn to go into the next box thought she had smiled at him. He returned the smile rather weakly; then, as she stepped out of her box, plucked up the courage to raise his hat and say, 'I felt sure we had met before. How nice . . .'

Staring at him in blank surprise, she turned and walked quickly away.

Outside the station she got a taxi. Instead of telling the man to drive her to Park Side West, she told him to take her to Selfridges. There, as at Harrods, she could sign on Rowley's account and she could not get all her things into the four suitcases she owned. At the store, she bought two of the most expensive air-travel cases they stocked and, as she signed for them, laughed to herself at the thought that, later, Elsie would again have to pay.

When she arrived in another taxi at Park Side West, Bella let her in. The small, stout Italian woman was evidently aware of the way Linda had been treated for, in a low voice but volubly, she began to express her sympathy.

Linda told her that she was going back to her old

home for a while and then would have no great difficulty in finding a job; so she was not to worry.

At that moment Elsie came out of the study. Her little piggy eyes were hard and accusing. Fear suddenly gripped Linda. From that baleful glance she felt certain that Elsie knew. Something unexpected had happened. Somehow she had been found out. Perhaps, after all, Mr. Bendon had telephoned, or Mr. Coxon called up to congratulate Rowley on having become engaged to her. She had been mad to risk coming back. Elsie would shout for Arthur. Between them they would hang on to her, push her into a room and lock her up there until the police came. Panic seized her. She must get out before they could make her a prisoner. Even a call to 999 would not bring the police on the scene in less than ten minutes. She would still have a chance if she ran for it.

She gave a quick look over her shoulder. The front door was closed. She was impeded by the two suitcases she was carrying and Bella blocked the narrow passage between her and the door. Elsie's voice came, bleak and sarcastic, but not in denunciation.

'So you've come for your loot. When you've packed, let Stefano know, and he'll get you a taxi.'

In her relief, Linda nearly gave vent to hysterical laughter. It was only her guilty conscience that had led her to imagine that Elsie was about to accuse her. She was wildly tempted to shout back, 'You mean, sanctimonious bitch! I've got most of it already.'

Instead, controlling herself, she muttered, 'Thanks. Yes . . . yes, I will.' Then, refusing Bella's offer of help, she carried the two suitcases upstairs.

Habitually she was careful about her clothes, but now her one thought was to get out of the house as quickly

as she could. Frantically, she emptied drawers and cupboards, folded the clothes with little thought about
creases, forcing them down into her four cases and the
two new ones until none of the six would hold any more.
There were still quite a number of things over, but she
would give those to Bella.

The job had taken her half an hour. As soon as she
had finished, she went to the top of the stairs and
shouted for the Luchenis. They both came up. Stefano
now said how grieved he was for her, and how much
they would miss her. Bella thanked her for the clothes,
but was near to tears and completely broke down when
Linda kissed her.

Between them they carried the suitcases down to the
hall. While Stefano was telephoning for a taxi Elsie
again came out of the drawing-room and asked,
'Where do you wish me to forward any letters that
come for you?'

Taken by surprise, Linda hesitated a moment, then
she said, 'To my aunt's place, please. She lives in
Lincolnshire, and I shall be staying with her for a
while.' Taking her diary from her bag, she wrote her
mother's address on one of the blank leaves and gave it
to Elsie. It was the only address she could think of from
which letters could be forwarded to her if she asked for
them, and she felt sure that Eric would write to her
when he heard about Rowley's death. For the moment
she had forgotten that when he did hear he would also
learn that she had stolen the jewels, be horrified, and
not wish to have anything more to do with her.

By five minutes past ten she was in a taxi. For Elsie's
benefit she told the man to take her to Liverpool Street
Station. When they arrived she had a porter put her
cases into the left-luggage office. As soon as his back

was turned she got another porter to get her luggage
out again and took another taxi back to Victoria.

The morning's effort had played havoc with her
nerves again and, as the day was warm, she was pers-
piring in the mink coat she had had to wear. Going up
to her room, she ordered a pint of champagne.

As she gratefully drank the iced wine, she reviewed
her situation. Everything had gone well—extra-
ordinarily well. She had now only one more hurdle to
take—getting away from Heathrow that afternoon. If
the man from Chubb's did arrive earlier than expected,
Elsie would not lose a moment in informing the police
about the jewels. The description of the suspected thief
would be sent out immediately, and the airport police
would be scrutinising every passenger.

Linda's passport had been secured for her by
Eric, as his position enabled him to get one for her
without any references, other than his own, and he had
had it made out in her real name, Linda Lee. That was
now most fortunate, as the police would be looking for
a girl carrying one in the name of Linda Chatterton.

But what was not so fortunate was Linda's outstanding, tall figure and good looks. Her description
coupled with her first name, Linda, and the initials
L.C. on her suitcases, might lead to her being detained,
and prove her undoing. Could she disguise herself in
any way? Yes, to some extent. She could shave off the
corners of her eyebrows, lipstick her mouth into a
squarer shape and do something about her hair.

At first she thought of having it dyed, then a better
idea came to her. She had read in a women's magazine
that just as a permanent wave could make straight hair
curly so a reversal of the process could make curly hair
straight, and that in the United States coloured women

frequently resorted to this method of giving themselves
a less negroid appearance. No passport officer would
question a girl having changed her hair style, yet if she
could flatten out her halo of wavy hair, it would make
a big difference to the description of her that might be
issued.

But had she time? Glancing at her watch, she saw
that it was a quarter past eleven. The aircraft took off
at five minutes past two, but she was due to report at
the Cromwell Road Terminal at twelve-twenty. By
taking a taxi instead of the bus, she could save half an
hour. As long as she got there in time to catch the plane,
that was all that mattered. The less time she spent
waiting at the airport, the less chance there would be
of her being spotted. If she hurried, she might just do it.

Running into the bathroom, she doctored her face,
then shoved her things into the suitcase she had brought
with her the previous night. Downstairs, as she enquired
for the nearest hairdresser's, a clock struck the half-
hour; but her luck was still in. There was one in the
basement. Again fortune favoured her, the solitary hairdresser was sitting doing nothing. Producing two pounds
from her bag, she said:

'I have to catch an aircraft at two o'clock, so I
haven't much time to spare. But I've just had an idea.
I want to give my husband a surprise when he meets
me at the other end; so I want you to take all the kinks
out of my hair, then I'll be able to wear it hanging
down over my shoulders.'

The man grinned at her. 'Very well, lady. To make
it really straight will take a bit of time, but I'll do the
best I can.'

Systematically he adjusted the apparatus and went
to work. Linda thought he would never be done. But by

E

twenty-five past twelve, he had finished; she paid him and gave him the handsome tip.

Dashing up to the ground floor, she asked for her luggage to be brought down, paid her bill and retrieved the precious brief-case. To her fury another quarter of an hour went by before her luggage appeared in the hall. One of the suitcases she had collected that morning was missing. The porter went back upstairs. He was away ten minutes. She had just made up her mind that she must abandon the missing case when he returned with it. By the time all her things had been loaded on to a taxi it was five past one. She promised the man double fare if he could get her to Heathrow by a quarter to two. As he snapped down his flag, he replied laconically:

'Depends on the state of the traffic; but I doubt it.'

Her heart sank. If she missed the plane, it would be all up with her. Within two or three hours the police would be circulating her description. She would not dare attempt to get on another plane the next day. Where could she go into hiding? Within a week or two, some sharp-eyed policeman would recognise her from the photographs of wanted people that they pinned up in all police stations. Arrest would follow, the shame of a trial, then prison. She could now only hope against hope.

The drive seemed interminable. It seemed that every light was against them. Just past South Kensington Station a lorry was delivering coal, so narrowed the way to single-line traffic. In Barons Court, opposite the old playing fields of St. Paul's School, the road was up for a hundred yards—single line again, so another delay. Fidgeting in her seat, Linda thought they would never make it, but at last they were out on the broad motorway and the driver got her to the airport by ten minutes to two.

She paid him double fare, her luggage was piled on a trolley. Glancing at the cases, she suddenly realised that she had forgotten to label them. But at the desk everyone was most helpful. Her ticket was checked, the luggage labelled and weighed. To her distress she had to pay out seventy-two pounds seventy-five pence excess, but it was no time to worry about the amount. She dared not ask them to take a cheque, as she would have had to sign it Chatterton. Hurriedly fumbling under her skirt she produced the money from her pochette. Her well-tipped porter ran alongside her to show her the right barrier.

Holding her breath, she gave her passport to the immigration official. He only glanced at it, waved her through and said, 'You'll have to hurry, Miss. The aircraft is just about due to take off.'

Clutching her handbag in one hand and the brief-case in the other, she raced down the long, enclosed passage, with its side-ports for boarding. At last she reached the one with a sign up reading AC.853, and turned into it. Breathlessly she boarded the plane. The steward gave her a quick grin and closed the door behind her. A hostess led her to her seat. She had only just taken it when the plane began to taxi out. After going no more than a hundred yards, it stopped. She seemed to freeze where she sat. The police had caught up with her after all! With closed eyes, for five minutes she sat in mental agony. Then the aircraft began to move again, and she realised that the delay had been caused by putting her luggage on board.

Lying back, she closed her eyes and breathed again. She had made it. She was still free and they were off.

She had crossed the last hurdle, and got away with a fortune.

The hostess made the usual speech over the loudspeaker to the passengers. The aircraft reached the end of the runway and halted. Its jets roared. Linda thought complacently, 'They may have opened that accursed safe by now. Anyway they will have within an hour or two. When Elsie finds it empty she'll telephone Cabouchon's, on the off chance that Rowley had placed the jewels with them for safe-keeping. They will tell her at once about my having sold them the two rings. So she'll know then, without a doubt, that it was I who cleared the safe before I left. But they can't get me now. It's too late. So what the hell do I care?'

Then she was seized with sudden consternation. Another thought had struck her. She had not, after all, yet crossed the last hurdle. The first criminals ever caught by a wireless message had been Dr. Crippen with Miss le Neve. Since then hundreds of others had been caught by the same means. There were nearly nine hours to go before she landed at Edmonton. Would the police be waiting for her there?

9
Unhappy Exile

ON the Saturday morning Linda awoke in an eighth-floor bedroom of the Hotel Sheraton Summit in Calgary. It was a curiously-shaped room, for the hotel was a large, round tower, so all its rooms formed segments of a great circle.

When Linda realised where she was, she stretched luxuriously, smiled and gave a sigh of happiness. She had pulled it off. The likelihood of her now being traced was comparatively remote, and she had got away with a fortune. Her mind ran back over the journey of the preceding day.

Extraordinary as it seemed, she had left Heathrow at five minutes past two in the afternoon and had been carried the thousands of miles over Scotland, Greenland, Baffin Island and five-sixths of the vast territory of Canada to arrive at Edmonton only forty minutes later according to local time. In fact, however, the flight had actually taken nearly nine hours. Owing to her fear of being arrested at the other end, those hours had seemed interminable, the more so on account of the unvarying daylight as the aircraft virtually kept pace with the apparently western-travelling sun. In a vague way she had realised that Air Canada provided excellent service and tempting food, but worry had prevented her from enjoying them.

At Edmonton she nerved herself to face the worst, but no official accosted her as she left the aircraft and reached the Immigration desk. On entering the Customs hall she almost choked with fear. Ladies do not often travel with twenty-five thousand pounds' worth of jewels in their luggage. The officer might well have been warned to look out for such a hoard. In any event it seemed certain that he would question her and make notes describing the most valuable pieces.

Asked if she had anything to declare, she replied, 'No, I've come to Canada only for a holiday,' and, her heart beating wildly, unlocked the brief-case.

The officer barely glanced at the toilet things under which lay the tissue-paper-wrapped jewel cases. Smiling at her, he said, 'You've brought a lot of luggage for a vacation,' and told her to open two of her suitcases. Finding only clothes in them, he chalked all her baggage, wished her a happy time and turned away.

It was through a remark made by a man nearby she learned that the plane, after refuelling, was flying on to Calgary. That offered a chance to cover her tracks still further, so she bought a ticket for the onward flight, had her luggage relabelled and went back on board. Soon after seven o'clock a Calgary taxi-driver set her down at the Sheraton Summit. She had booked in there as Miss Lily Carter, then, too exhausted by the strain of the past day to face a meal, gone straight to bed.

Getting up, she drew back the curtains sufficiently to see the view from the window. At least half the area she could see consisted of several vast car parks. Later she learned that Calgary was said to have more cars per head of population than any other city in Canada. Here and there, among the car parks, there rose sky-scrapers, but few other buildings.

While breakfasting in bed, she thought over her next move. By now the police in London would be looking for Linda Chatterton. She had arrived in Edmonton as Linda Lee and in Calgary as Lily Carter. But to be on the safe side she must move again as quickly as possible, and take yet another name. Having flown over the endless wheat-fields of Alberta the previous afternoon, she could imagine nothing more dreary than starting a new life in such surroundings. Besides, a newcomer in any of its scattered towns was much more likely to arouse unwelcome interest than a solitary woman in a big city. To go still further west to Vancouver therefore seemed the obvious choice. That also offered the fascinating prospect of a journey through the Rockies.

She had awoken early, so by nine o'clock she had bathed, dressed and was down in the hotel lobby. There she learned that the daily train for Vancouver left Calgary at 1.40 that afternoon. Having booked a drawing-room on it, she went to a nearby bank where she exchanged enough Swiss francs to pay for her ticket, her bill and leave her nine hundred Canadian dollars over. Returning to the hotel, in the ladies' room she stuffed eight hundred dollars into her pochette, then decided that the best way to kill the morning was to go for a drive round the city.

The hall porter produced a car with a pleasant, talkative young driver, who pointed out to her the sights of Calgary, such as they were: the tall Husky tower topped by its radio mast, the big Hudsons' Bay Company store and the best shops that were on Seventh and Eighth Avenues. Within half a mile of them the streets grew strangely ragged. Occasional modern blocks stood with large vacant lots on either side of them or dilapidated-looking private houses with small gardens, evidently built forty or fifty years before. They then drove through tree-lined streets of suburbs, with much more pleasant homes, to a high ridge on which stood a fine group of buildings housing the university. From the ridge there was an excellent view of the Bow River which, hundreds of miles distant, flows into the Mississippi.

Back at the hotel Linda had an early lunch in the Casa Lounge. It was a lofty, curved room, with dim lights and red walls, which gave it the atmosphere of a warm cave. The list of drinks produced by a pretty waitress surprised Linda by its size and variety. Among the recommended cocktails were El Toro, Brown Bull and Lady of Spain, all previously unheard of by her. She chose the last, which was one ounce of vodka, half an ounce of blackberry brandy, a dash of orange juice, a dash of Grenadine and a maraschino cherry. While it was being brought she wondered if the names of these strange drinks had been selected on account of the annual rodeo, for which Calgary was famous, in which tough cowboys seized young bulls by the horns and threw them on their backs.

By a quarter past one she was standing on one of the long, windy, seatless platforms of the railway station. The train was late, but at last it arrived and she clambered up into it. The drawing-room she had booked came as a pleasant surprise. It had a wardrobe next to a private washroom and, in addition to the two bunks which made up into a comfortable sofa during daytime, it had two large armchairs.

Soon after leaving the city the train went round a long curve, and she was able to appreciate its make-up. The chain of long coaches seemed endless and above several of them there were large glass domes from which passengers could get an uninterrupted view of the scenery. As for some while it remained flattish and uninteresting, she did not bother to go along to one of them. But after about two hours they stopped at Banff, in the foothills of the Rockies, so she walked down the corridor to the nearest observation car, and went upstairs.

It was the slowest train she had ever travelled in. She assumed this was because of the gradients it had to mount, but its snail's pace gave ample opportunity, as it crawled round curve after curve, to take in each new vista. Except for the angle from which they were seen, the views had little variety. They consisted of lakes and creeks surrounded by rising ground densely covered with Canadian pines. Each scene provided a perfect setting for befeathered Indians paddling canoes; but not a human being or an animal, let alone a Redskin, was to be seen.

Linda sat under the transparent, inverted bowl that covered the long omnibus-like coach until it was time for dinner, then she went down to the restaurant car, enjoyed an excellent meal, and went early to bed.

After breakfast next morning, she went up again. The sun was shining on a rushing river far below, to the left in a deep gorge through which the train was winding. Again the scene consisted of endless slopes of pine trees, broken only occasionally by a smallish drift of snow on the higher peaks. After a while Linda decided that the Alps were incomparably grander and went down to get her things together. Soon after ten o'clock the train pulled into Vancouver Station.

Having for so long been used to travelling de luxe with Rowley she had so far denied herself nothing and had instinctively engaged a private drawing-room on the train. But it suddenly struck her that, although she had

a large sum in cash, she might find it difficult to dispose
of more of the jewels, so she ought not to fritter away
money by staying at one of the big hotels.

Outside the station, when her luggage was brought
out, she ripped off the labels while the porter was
getting her a taxi. Then she said to the driver of the
taxi, 'I am a stranger to Vancouver and know no-one
here. Can you take me to a hotel that is not too expensive? Quite a small one would do, provided it's respectable and has passably good food.'

The man glanced at her smart suitcases, hesitated,
then replied, 'My sister runs a place, the Astley it's
called, down on the bay. But it's on the modest side.
Might not be grand enough for a lady like you.'

Linda smiled. 'I'd be happy to try it, so please take
me there.'

As she had supposed, Vancouver was very different
from Calgary. There were no vacant lots or decayed-
looking houses in the streets through which she was
driven, but block after block of good shops, restaurants
and offices. Beach Avenue proved to be not much over
a mile from the centre of the city. Most of the buildings
there were old-fashioned, two-storied, clapboard houses,
but a few were larger, with three stucco-covered storeys,
and the Hotel Astley was one of these.

The taxi-driver took her in and introduced her to his
sister, Mrs. Burnaby, a plumpish, pleasant-faced
woman with greying hair whose husband, it transpired,
had once been a chef at the Ritz in Boston. Linda now
decided to ignore the second initial on her suitcases, and
said her name was Lucille Harrison, and that she had
come up from Los Angeles where she had been for some
time playing small parts in films. The lie was designed
to allay any suspicion Mrs. Burnaby might have about

the initial, because film actresses often married but retained their maiden names. Linda added that she had recently been ill, so wanted somewhere that was very quiet where she could rest for a few weeks. Her face and figure amply supported her statement that she was a starlet and she refrained from saying whether she was British or American, hoping that in spite of her lack of accent Mrs. Burnaby would assume anyhow that she had lived in the States for several years.

They then discussed terms. Mrs. Burnaby said the only single room she had free was on the top floor at the back of the house, but it overlooked the bay, and Linda could have it for forty-five dollars a week, which would include full board; so Linda said she would like to see the room. It proved to be small and had a sloping roof, and she would have to go along the passage to a communal bathroom, to which she had long been unaccustomed. But the bedroom was quite pleasantly furnished. She was then shown two rooms on the ground floor. Both ran the full depth of the house. One, a lounge, had a reasonable number of easy chairs in it; the other, which was a dining-room, had one long table in the centre and six small ones along the sides. Linda guessed that, had she not so stupidly said she was a film actress, she could have got such accommodation for forty dollars or less, but staying at a good hotel would have cost her at the very least three times as much; so, having stipulated that she should be given one of the small tables in the dining-room to herself, she said that she would move in.

Mrs. Burnaby's brother obligingly carried up the seven suitcases. Linda tipped him handsomely and, having shaken hands with her, he went off grinning. The luggage almost filled the small bedroom, but the landlady said there was an attic along the corridor that Linda could have the use of to hang up some of her clothes and store the empty cases; then she left Linda to unpack.

For a few minutes Linda gazed out across the beach at the Pacific. It was not blue, as she had hoped, but there were several ships in the distance and, nearer the shore, four small yachts, which gave the view a pleasant animation. She had only freshened herself up with a wash, redone her hair and unpacked her overnight bag when a gong sounded downstairs, evidently indicating lunch.

In the dining-room there were two elderly couples and one middle-aged pair, seated at small tables, and two Chinese men at the larger one. They all eyed Linda with interest as she was shown to her table by a pert, teenage waitress; but she gave only the slightest of bows on passing the nearest couple, then settled herself to read the menu. It was handwritten and offered no choice, simply stating: *Cauliflower Soup, Macaroni Cheese, Strawberry Ice.* When the waitress brought the soup, Linda asked for the list of drinks. The girl's eyebrows shot up.

'Drink list! We don't have them sort o' things here. No licence. But you can bring in yer own if you like. I could do you a Coke, though, or a Seven-Up.'

A shade ruefully Linda settled for a Coke. While she was eating the meal, which proved quite passable, two ladies, who looked like spinsters, and a bald man with a limp came in and took separate places at the big table. Linda had, in any case, decided to keep herself to herself as much as possible, and what she had so far seen of her fellow guests strengthened her determination.

Having been up so early, by the time she had finished

lunch she felt very tired, so she went up to her room and lay down on the bed to sleep. When she woke it was close on five o'clock. Although she did not feel like going out, to drink cocktails and wine had become such a habit with her that she could not face the prospect of a drinkless evening, so she dressed for the street and went in search of a wine merchant's. Failing to find one in the neighbourhood, she enquired of a policeman, to learn to her dismay that in Canada there were none. One could buy liquor only from the State stores, and these shut at five-thirty.

A little further back she had passed a quite large hotel, so she retraced her steps, went in, settled herself in the lounge and beckoned over a waiter.

Smiling, he shook his head. 'No drinks served here, Miss, nor in the rooms. The only parts of an hotel like this that are licensed are the dining-room and the bar downstairs.' Marvelling at this evidence of barbarity in an otherwise civilised country, she made her way down to the bar. There were only a few people there, so she took one of the unoccupied tables and ordered a White Lady. As she drank it, a man nearby started to ogle her. Looking straight through him, she froze him with her stare, then ordered another cocktail. As she lingered over the second, she was beginning to wonder if she had been wise to choose Canada as her place of exile. For a single woman, and a very attractive one, who could get a drink only by going into bars where she was likely to be pestered by men, life there did not promise to be very pleasant.

By the time she got back to the Astley she found that she was late for the evening meal. The dining-room was now nearly full, but the guests she had not previously seen appeared to be as dull as those who had been there for lunch. Again, although there was no choice on the menu, the meal proved quite good, and she noted with relief that on several tables there were bottles of wine, so she would not be remarked on if she brought her own in. Afterwards she felt that she could not face the lounge, so went straight up to her room and read a paperback until she became drowsy enough to go to sleep.

The following morning she unpacked two of her suit-cases but left the rest untouched, taking them along to the attic to get them out of the way; because as yet she was by no means certain that she would stay on at the Astley. Her trouble was that, for about the same money, she would encounter similar conditions in any other small hotel, and she was reluctant to make serious inroads into her capital by staying for any length of time at a big one. For the same reason she resisted the temptation to go out and lunch at a good restaurant, instead of eating the unexciting but adequate meal she was already paying for, because that might become a habit.

But immediately after lunch she telephoned for a taxi and when it arrived, taking with her the brief-case in which she kept the precious jewels, she asked the driver to take her to one of the banks in the centre of the city. He set her down at the Bank of Montreal, and there she arranged to hire a safe-deposit box. Into it she put the jewels, except for a few minor pieces to wear if the occasion arose, and the rest of her Swiss francs.

After that she had a hair-do, which made her feel much more cheerful; then, having spent an hour window-gazing in Grenville and West Georgia Streets, she went into the big Hudson's Bay Company store, where she bought chocolates, fudge, butterscotch, sweet biscuits and several paperbacks.

Her last visit was to a State liquor store. To her great annoyance she found the price of French champagne prohibitive and even European still wines were very expensive. Mistrusting the wines with names unknown to her, she bought two bottles of rum, two of gin and one each of sweet vermouth, brandy, Cointreau and Benedictine. With the rum she could spike Cokes to drink with her meals and the other half-dozen bottles she reckoned would keep her going for quite a time with a variety of cocktails which she would mix in her room.

As she returned to the hotel in a taxi with her purchases it occurred to her that, although she had become a criminal, she could at least console herself with the thought that, had she not become one, she would now be living in a London boarding house which would be less comfortable than her quarters at the Astley, and leave her next to nothing to spend on such luxuries as books, drink and chocolates.

During the day the thought that had worried her most was that she would have to spend her evenings in the lounge with her unattractive fellow guests; but a way had occurred to her of avoiding boring conversations.

That evening at dinner when the little waitress asked her a question, she pretended not to hear it clearly. The girl repeated it louder and added: 'Didn't know you was deaf.'

'Unfortunately, I am; rather,' Linda replied.

Later, in the lounge, when the bald man with a limp came up and introduced himself, she again pretended that she found difficulty in catching what he said. After a few minutes he gave up and, with a little smile, bowed himself away to look at the television programme which was operating on a low key at the far end of the long room. Shortly afterwards the two ladies whom Linda had judged to be spinsters came up and spoke to her. By the same tactics she soon got rid of them and was able to settle to her book.

At the far end of the street lay the entrance to Stanley Park, so next morning she went for a walk there. The park covered the whole of a great irregular, club-shaped peninsula that jutted out between English Bay, on which Beach Avenue stood, and Burrard Narrows, in the broad inland bight off which lay Vancouver harbour. The park was a thousand acres in extent and Linda thought it the loveliest she had ever seen. Near its entrance nearly every form of sport imaginable was catered for, and further on there was a large, boat-studded lake with a lovely fountain in the centre; also great areas preserved as primeval forest in which rose towering Hemlocks, Douglas Firs and Redwoods, one of the latter bearing a plaque stating that it was estimated to be two thousand years old. At the Tea House on Ferguson Point she had a light lunch, then continued to wander about in the beautiful woods for a good part of the afternoon.

She spent the next morning in the town and in the afternoon went to see a film. The following day she again spent in the park, this time exploring the eastern side, where there were two zoos, one specially for children, and an aquarium in which there were sharks, dolphins, turtles and even a whale. There were also a miniature railway, a rose garden with one bed in which both red and yellow roses were blossoming on every bush, and another garden which had in it every tree, bush and flower mentioned in Shakespeare's plays.

These expeditions served to while away the days, but

the meals and evenings in the lounge at the Astley
were already proving tedious. An alternative was to let
herself be picked up. On numerous occasions in London
men had endeavoured to accost her and here, while
walking in the city, several had given her more than a
passing glance. But if she allowed a man to dine and
wine her more than a few times he would naturally
expect her to go to bed with him, and that she was not
prepared to do.

For her to get a job of any kind was out of the
question, because she had no work permit, and to
obtain one she would have to produce her passport to
the Canadian authorities. They would then register her
as Linda Lee and, by now, Interpol might be aware
that Linda Lee and Linda Chatterton were one and the
same person; so such a step could prove her undoing.

To move on to another city was no solution, and
Vancouver at least had museums, art galleries and
other attractions which would provide her with things
to occupy her for a while. But she could not escape the
fact that she had saved herself from poverty only to face
a bleak and lonely future.

On her fifth morning in Vancouver, after her bath
Linda sat for some minutes looking in her dressing-
table mirror at the face she knew so well. The golden
brown eyes with their exceptionally clear whites under
the high arched eyebrows were undeniably beautiful; so
was the mouth, with its full inviting underlip and
perfect teeth. The oval face made an admirable setting
for the features but they had been even more striking
when crowned with the halo of springy curls.

Her brown hair, with its golden lights, was now parted
in the middle and hung down on either side of her face.
But, after nearly a week, it had become slightly wavy

and showed a distinct crinkle where it had grown a trifle above her forehead. To keep it straight it would soon need another treatment. It then occurred to her that this partial disguise was now pointless, and that to restore it to its pristine glory she need not wait for it to become naturally curly again. She could have a permanent wave.

In consequence she spent the better part of the afternoon at one of the best hairdressers in the city; and during the long session she had ample time to again contemplate the situation in which she had landed herself. She had beauty, intelligence and plenty of money; but of what use were these to her if she must continue to lead this dreary, solitary existence? Too late she saw that she had acted like a fool. She now felt no remorse for having robbed Elsie of the jewels, as she had not done so from greed, but on a stupid impulse to which she had been driven from fear of poverty.

If only she had had more time in which to think she would have realised that her own one hundred and eighty pounds, plus the pay from any typing job, would have enabled her to live without real hardship for several months. That would have been ample time for her to trace Eric and get in touch with him. Even had she failed in that, it was certain that within a few weeks he would have learned of Rowley's death and written to her care of her mother, whose address she had left with Elsie. In either case his response, she felt certain, would have been immediate. He would have rescued her from poverty and with him she would have found security and happiness. Whereas, in a moment of madness she had cut herself off from him by becoming a criminal and was now faced with a miserable, joyless future.

10

A Lucky Break

NEXT morning, now listlessly, with not the faintest premonition that fate had in store for her a drastic new turn in her affairs, Linda once more went for a walk in the park. This time she took the main road that ran through it up to Prospect Point at its northern end.

She had covered about half the distance when she started to cross the road to get a closer look at a rare species of tree that she had never before seen. Just there the road curved and, as she stepped out from behind a clump of tall bushes, a car came round the corner. Before she could draw back it ran past, narrowly missing her. But one of the door handles caught the handle of her bag. It was jerked from her hand and the sharp pull on it flung her sideways to the ground. Her forehead struck the exposed root of a tall tree, and she was knocked out.

Linda remained unconscious for barely a minute. She was lying face down, with her forehead on the tree root. She heard running feet, then strong hands grasped her shoulders and turned her over. As she opened her eyes she found herself staring up into the anxious face of a brown-complexioned man with a high-bridged nose, black eyes and smartly-trimmed black hair.

When he realised that she was not seriously injured,

his big, generous mouth relaxed into a wide smile; then he exclaimed, 'Praises be! I feared I'd smashed you up real bad.'

Sitting up, she put a hand to her aching head. 'No, no. I'll be all right in a minute. And it was my fault. I shouldn't have stepped out from behind those bushes without making certain that nothing was coming.'

He grinned. 'I'm at least half to blame. Shouldn't have taken that corner so quickly in a park like this where kids are always chasing one another. I'm terribly sorry.'

Having helped her to her feet, he turned away to collect the scattered oddments that had dropped out of her bag, while she brushed the fallen leaves and dust from her skirt. He had pulled up his car about thirty yards away. As he rejoined her, he pointed to it and said:

'Least I can do is to give you a lift home, or to wherever you were going.'

'I was only going for a walk, up to Prospect Point. I haven't been that far yet.'

'You a stranger here, then?'

'Yes. I'm from England.' Linda was still a little dazed and the admission slipped out before she had fully recovered her wits.

'Are you now? Well, I'm a stranger in these parts too. I come from Montreal and as I'd never been out west I thought I'd take my vacation here. Friends told me this park was well worth seeing, so I was just driving around. What say I run you up to Prospect Point and we take a look at the view together?'

Linda did not hesitate. She thought the tall, broad-shouldered, black-haired man who was smiling at her decidedly attractive. Returning his smile, she replied, 'Why not? I'd like to do that.'

Two minutes later they were in his Cadillac. As he let in the clutch, he said, 'My name's Big Bear Orson. What's yours?'

'Lucille Harrison. But surely your Christian name isn't really Big Bear?'

'It sure is. Thought you would have guessed from the tint of my skin and my beak of a nose that I've got Indian blood. The rest of my family are as white as you; but I'm a throwback. I was christened Isaiah. But I didn't like it, so when I was a kid, and we used to play Injuns and Cowboys, I gave myself the name of a chief who was my ancestor, and somehow it's stuck to me.'

When they reached the Point they sat in the car for a few minutes admiring the great Lion Gate suspension bridge that spans the narrows of Burrard Inlet, and the mile-long line of wharves along the shore of North Vancouver. Then, turning his head in the other direction, he said:

'That's a coffee joint back there. You must need a little something after your fall. Let's go over.'

In the ladies' room of the little restaurant Linda re-did her face. Her headache was already subsiding and she had suffered no damage except a slight abrasion on the forehead, which she was able to powder over.

When they were seated at one of the little tables, he asked her how she liked Canada.

'This part of it is lovely,' she replied, 'and Vancouver is a splendid city. But I wouldn't like to live in the wheat belt or one of the smaller towns, like Calgary. The people are nice. I mean the taxi-drivers, waiters, shop assistants and so on. They couldn't be more friendly and helpful. But the licensing laws are suitable only for children, and I find that very surprising, seeing that Canada has such strong connections with France.

Even here all the signs are dual-language, and while one would have expected that in Quebec, it's strange to find it in the far west.'

'There's no great number of French in Alberta or B.C., but plenty of French-Canadians come here from the east, and some of them speak only French. That's why in these parts they have "*Messieurs*" as well as "*Gents*'" written up on the johns. You're right about the liquor laws, though. Place like this ought to be a proper café.'

Linda smiled. 'I wish it were. I don't usually drink anything until the evening, unless I'm lunching in a restaurant, but after my fall I could have done with something stronger than coffee.'

'Fair enough, and that's given me an idea. It's close on midday. How say we beat it back to the city? Let me give you lunch, and everything that goes with it.'

'Well, that's very nice of you.' Linda hesitated only so as not to appear too eager. 'Yes, why not? I'd like to do that.'

On their way back through the park they passed some gaily painted Indian totem poles and Big Bear told Linda that they were not just a form of idol. The eagle represented the genius of air, the wolf that of land, the whale that of the sea and the frog the link between earth and water.

They lunched in the Timber Room at the Vancouver Hotel. Big Bear said he was staying at the hotel because it was the best in the city. Over an excellent meal he told her about himself. He was the managing director of one of the biggest advertising agencies in Canada. He enjoyed his work because it meant always being right on the ball. Constantly to produce new ideas that would boost his clients' sales entailed a knowledge of every public activity and new trend that developed in fashion, food, entertainment and general behaviour. When he asked her what she did, she shrugged.

'I'm afraid I'm just a drone.'

At that he gave her a speculative look. She laughed and shook her head. 'No, I'm not a *poule de luxe,* as the French call it. I'm quite respectable, but I've never earned my living.'

He glanced at her hand. 'It's rare these days to meet an unmarried girl who doesn't do some kind of job.'

On the way from the park and while he was parking his car Linda had had sufficient time to think out what she would tell him about herself, and she said, 'I am married—in a way. But I've left my husband. The last time I saw him we had a blinding row and I flung my wedding ring at him.'

'Then you're by way of getting divorced?'

'Yes, but how long it will take I don't know. We had been married only a few months, so it would be the best part of three years before we could get a decree for incompatibility; and I've no evidence against him or he against me, so it's stalemate. His parents are very rich and he is dependent on them. They have never liked me, and are anxious to have me out of his life so that he can marry again. But they are old-fashioned in their views about divorce, and feel that it would be a stigma against him if he gave me grounds and became the guilty party. Their hope is that I will get tired of being on my own, so take a boy friend, and I discovered that they had engaged detectives to watch me. That meant that I couldn't even have a drink in a man's flat without becoming compromised. Being tailed everywhere made me feel so awful that I decided to leave England and come to Canada.'

'They could employ a "private eye" to keep tags on you here.'

Linda shook her head. 'No. The only address they have is a bank to which my husband sends me a monthly allowance. And I'm living under another name in quite an obscure hotel not far from the park. But what about you? Are you married?'

'No, no,' he grinned. 'I love 'em all a little bit.'

'You obviously have plenty of money, so I suppose you have pleasant bachelor quarters.'

'The best ever. I've a suite in Montreal's Ritz-Carlton Hotel.'

'That must cost you a pretty penny.'

'It's not cheap, but it pays off in the long run. Time is money in my game, and I have to do a lot of entertaining anyway. If I had an apartment I'd have to have a housekeeper, tell her what I wanted for meals, fend for myself when she had her day off, use part of my secretary's time checking up on dozens of bills and making phone calls about one thing and another. As it is, I'm on the spot when I ask people to lunch or dinner, take my pick of a first-class menu, have myself valeted and my washing done, never have to bother with plumbers, electricians or garbage disposal, get day and night service all the week through and, at the end of it, pay for the whole shooting match with one cheque. Added to that, as a permanent resident I get special terms.'

'Then you're certainly getting value for your money,' Linda agreed. 'How long are you here on holiday?'

'Another eight days. How long do you figure to stay?'

'I've no plans at all at the moment.'

'Then how about seeing something of each other? I've no friends here 'cept our Vancouver agent, Dave Kane, and his wife Judith. They're a grand couple and have a nice home up in the Shaughnessy district. I've been out there twice to dinner and had them here; and Judith's twice taken me for drives round about. But I can't live in their pockets. What say to your taking pity on a poor, lone Redskin brave?'

Linda laughed. 'What nonsense. You are no more a Redskin than an Englishman would be if he had spent a few weeks sunbathing in the West Indies, and plenty of Romans had noses as big and curved as yours. But I know nobody here either, except the people in my hotel. They are dreary beyond belief, and I go out of my way to avoid them.'

'Dinner tonight then, eh? We'll dine up in the roof restaurant here. The view is quite something. I'll run you back to your hotel now and call for you round seven o'clock. O.K.?'

'That would be lovely. It will be my first evening out since I arrived in Canada. When you call for me, remember my name is Harrison.'

'I sure will, Lucille, and my lucky star was certainly in the ascendant when I went driving through the park this morning.'

Linda spent the rest of the afternoon lying on her bed, thinking about her new acquaintance. She felt that her lucky star also had been in the ascendant that day. Apart from the fact that she might have been killed or injured, the chances against her being knocked down by a youngish man—she judged Big Bear to be in his early thirties—who was not only good-looking, amusing and rich, but also on holiday and obviously attracted to her, were thousands to one against. What fun it would be to dine with him and once more enjoy the best of everything.

The evening proved fully up to Linda's expectations. She had put on one of her best dresses for the occasion, and Big Bear caught his breath in admiration when he saw her. The Vancouver roof restaurant consisted of a very long bar on one side and a much wider restaurant on the other. From a window table they had a wonderful view of the lights of the city, and the cuisine proved excellent. As a main dish her host suggested Alaska crab, which she had never before eaten. It proved to be a number of giant crab legs which the waiter cracked at the table, then poured hot butter on them.

Linda found them absolutely delicious, but was surprised that Big Bear should have ordered a Canadian white wine to drink with them, as for lunch with their tournedos he had given her an excellent French claret. As it was poured, she said:

'I didn't know that any wines were grown so far north as Canada, and I've been told that there is very little good wine made in the United States except in California.'

He smiled. 'Over lunch I tumbled to it that you were quite a connoisseur. That's why I'd like to know what you think of this. It's our Domain St. Martin and comes from the north side of Niagara Falls.'

It had been well iced and she found it to resemble a fine, medium-dry Sauterne, but it had the added attraction of a faint bouquet of violets. Linda raised her well-arched eyebrows:

'But it's real nectar. Why ever don't we have it in England?'

'I wouldn't know. Maybe duties and freight make it too expensive; but it's reasonable enough here.'

Afterwards he took her to the Gold Room, downstairs in the New Penthouse Night Club. There was a very good cabaret and she found him an excellent dancer. So much so that she completely forgot the time until she happened to glance at her watch and found it was getting on for two o'clock.

In sudden panic she said she must go home at once, as she felt sure that a small hotel like the Astley normally closed at midnight, and she would have to knock someone up to let her in.

'Oh, come!' Big Bear protested. 'This joint stays open until four. If someone has got to get out of bed to let you in anyhow, what does another hour or two matter?' But Linda insisted on leaving at once.

When he drew up in front of the Astley, all the lights in the hotel were out. As she thanked him for a lovely evening he drew her to him and kissed her. She willingly opened her mouth, but when he tried to go further she broke the kiss, pushed his hand away and said firmly, 'No! That's enough for now,' and scrambled out of the car.

As she ran across the pavement he called after her, 'See you tomorrow. Pick you up round about midday.'

She had to ring the bell three times before a light appeared. A few minutes later Mr. Burnaby opened the front door. As Big Bear was still outside in his car waiting to see her safely inside, it was obvious that her lateness had not been caused by an accident, so to her apology he replied only with a surly, 'Fine time o' night to come in.'

The following morning Linda slept late and at eleven o'clock, while she was doing her hair, there came a knock at her door. On her calling 'Come in,' the

usually pleasant Mrs. Burnaby came in and said
dourly:

'Miss Harrison, our custom here is to lock up at
eleven o'clock. That is quite late enough for respectable
people, except on special occasions, and then I am
quite willing to lend permanent residents a key. But you
do not qualify for that yet. Another thing. We expect
our guests to be out of their rooms at the latest by ten
o'clock, in order that my two women can do the beds.
Unless you are prepared to conform, I shall have to ask
you to find other accommodation.'

Linda said she was deeply sorry to have got Mr.
Burnaby out of bed, and left it at that, reluctantly
realising that if she was to continue going out with Big
Bear she would have to move to a bigger hotel with a
night porter, which would be much more expensive.

At midday Big Bear picked her up and took her
across the peninsula to Cardero Street, at the end of
which lay the s.s. *Princess Louise II*, originally the
passenger ship *Lady Alexander* that, at the cost of a
million dollars, had been converted into a floating
restaurant. From the restaurant there was a fine view
of Vancouver harbour and, beyond it, the mountains on
the western skyline.

Over baked clams and abalone they got to know still
more about each other. Big Bear's favourite sport was
skiing and the first winter that he could afford to take
sufficient time off to make it worth while he meant to
go to Switzerland. As he had never been to Europe,
Linda told him about London, Paris, Venice, Spain and
the South of France. Having told him the previous day
that she had been married only a few months, she had
to say that she had been with her parents. When he
asked about them she again used the story she had given

Elsie, that her father had owned an estate in Lincoln-shire, but had recently died, leaving her mother very badly off.

He then said, 'Don't tell me if you'd rather not, but I'm mighty curious to know why you left your husband.'

Stubbing out her cigarette, Linda kept her eyes lowered and invented a plausible story. 'I'm not a prude. In fact before I married I had an affair with a man with whom I was in love. It lasted for eighteen months and I thoroughly enjoyed all the usual games. But—er—Alistair, that is my husband, wanted me to do things that I wasn't willing to. In fact, I found them utterly disgusting. And it was when he tried to force me that I pulled off my wedding ring and threw it at him. Next morning I walked out.'

Big Bear's black eyes narrowed. 'The dirty bastard! You were dead right to quit. I'd like the chance to use a stock-whip on him for being so foul with a sweet kid like you.'

For dinner he took her to the Jester's Room at the Ritz, which she found very English. Afterwards they strolled round the corner to Oil Can Harry's—an extraordinary contrast. It was the largest night haunt in the city, and could hold a thousand people. There were several rooms: Dirty Sal's, where couples could lounge and drink or eat at dimly-lit tables; the Back Room, decorated with gangster posters, in which films of the 'Roaring Twenties' were shown; the longest bar in Canada and a sunken dance floor.

Linda said how clever Big Bear was to find such a variety of places to take her. He shrugged. 'I owe that to Dave Kane. He put me wise about this city. And talk of variety! There are at least a score of night spots in Vancouver. We've yet to try the Down Under,

Diamond Jim's, Pharaoh's Retreat, the Red Garter,
Your Father's Mustache and a whole lot more.'

'That would be fun.' Linda made a grimace. 'But if
we're to do that I'll have to change my hotel. The
woman who runs it gave me a rocket this morning.
Normally they lock up at eleven o'clock.'

'Snakes alive!' he exclaimed. 'It's just on that now.'

'I know. I'm terribly sorry, but we will have to leave
soon after half past. I'm prepared to keep them up till
twelve, but it wouldn't be fair to get the old boy out of
bed again. I'll look round tomorrow for a place that
has a night porter.'

For a moment he was silent, then he laid his hand
over hers and said earnestly, 'Look, honey. After a week
in Vancouver I'd planned to spend a week in Victoria
Island. I'm booked in at the Empress, and they say it's
a real grand hotel. Having fallen flat on my face for you
I meant to call them tomorrow, cancel and stay on here.
But we could play it another way. From what you told
me lunchtime, it wouldn't be cradle-snatching. How
about my calling the Empress in the morning, and
telling them that I'm bringing my wife along?'

Linda threw back her head and laughed. 'Really! As
girls said of proposals in the old-fashioned novels, "This
is so sudden". After all, we haven't yet known each
other for forty-eight hours.'

'What in heck has that to do with it? I'm quite a
connoisseur of dames, yet I've never played round with
one who could hold a candle to you. And you're not far
off hooked on me. You showed it in that kiss you gave
me last night. Come, now. We're not children. Why not
let's grab a real fine time together?'

'I don't know.' Linda fiddled with her champagne
glass nervously. 'You must give me time to think. Let's

dance again before we go. I'll let you know tomorrow.'

A little before twelve o'clock, as he brought his car to a stop in front of the Astley, he did not attempt to kiss her, but said, 'It's the better part of an hour's drive to the ferry, so if we go I ought to pick you up sharp at eleven o'clock. I'll call you early, to give you plenty of time to pack.'

Linda took his hand and pressed it. 'Don't think too badly of me, darling, if my answer is "no". I do like you a lot; but I've known only two men that way before, so it would be quite a step. I do promise, though, to think it over really seriously.' Then, giving him a swift kiss on the cheek, she slipped out of the car.

11

A Joyous Interlude

FOR Linda it was a big decision to make, and for the past hour she had been turning it over in her mind. Apart from being raped when she was sixteen, she had so far had only two lovers: Jim and Rowley. Jim had been gentle, but not very expert. Poor dear Rowley had roused her fully, but only because when he made love to her she had always thought of Eric.

She still thought of Eric now and again, although ever since he had left London she had done her best to put him out of her mind. She felt certain that he would always be the love of her life; but, after she had stolen the jewels, she realised that her act had put an end to all hope of being happily united to him. Not only was he thousands of miles away but, as he was such an upright man, she felt sure that if they ever did chance to meet he would not, now that he must have learned that she was a criminal, want to have anything to do with her, let alone marry her.

Although she was not in love with Big Bear she recognised that he was as attractive a man as any girl could wish for in a lover. And, after all, she had never been in love with poor dear Rowley; yet she had been his mistress for close on two years.

Against that, she was just a little frightened of going

to bed with Big Bear. Mentally he did not appear to differ at all from a well-educated Englishman or American, but he had that dash of Red Indian blood and, according to tradition, the Indians were very cruel. He was, too, a very powerfully-built man, so if he did have a cruel streak in him she might be letting herself in for a very unpleasant time.

A few lights were still on in the hotel, and it was Mrs. Burnaby who opened the front door. 'Late again,' she said sharply; then, in a very loud voice, in the belief that Linda was deaf, 'Really, Miss Harrison, I can't have this. I told you that we lock up at eleven.'

Subconsciously Linda must have already made up her mind. Spontaneously she replied, 'I'm awfully sorry, Mrs. Burnaby, but I have been making fresh arrangements. I am going away for a week, but I'd like to keep on my room at the price we agreed, although I shan't be here for meals; and when I get back I shall be going out very little in the evenings. Will that be all right with you?'

The normally good-natured woman smiled. 'Certainly, my dear. Having lived in Hollywood, I appreciate that you are not used to the early hours we keep here. We'll be glad to have you back.'

Next morning Linda rose early and packed, then Big Bear called for her. Bursting with high spirits he drove her out through the city and over the two arms of the Fraser river across flattish country to Tsawwassen. The ferry steamer there was the largest she had ever seen. Its centre was a huge tunnel into which streams of cars, coaches and lorries disappeared. The deck above consisted of glassed-in lounges and a large self-service restaurant.

While they ate a picnic lunch at a corner table near

F

a window, they enjoyed the view of calm waters on which yachts were sailing, and a group of islands ahead. All of them were densely covered with pine trees but, as in the Rockies, few of the trees were more than twenty feet in height. When she remarked on that, Big Bear told her that it was because the soil was so poor and the trees were so close together.

Presently they passed between two of the islands and shortly afterwards docked in Swartz Bay. From there they drove another twenty miles through pleasant, undulating country, with occasional pine woods and, between them, many pleasant houses of clapboard or brick in an acre or more of ground. For the last mile and a half they were on the main street of Victoria City and found the Empress Hotel to be nearly at its far end.

The hotel resembled a huge, nineteenth-century French château. They entered it through a conservatory which gave on to a spacious lounge in which there were numerous shops, and other big rooms opening off it. Big Bear had asked for a room overlooking the sea. He need not have bothered, as the hotel was on a narrow isthmus and at both back and front there were harbours with many small craft either moored or moving to and fro, and several large ships anchored further out.

As soon as their luggage had been brought up Big Bear took Linda into a truly bear-like hug. She let him kiss her for a few minutes, but then pulled away her head and said, 'No, no! Don't let's spoil things by rushing them. It will be much more fun after dinner and champagne, with all night before us and no need to dress again.'

After pressing her hard to let him have his way with her there and then, he reluctantly let her go. Highly conscious of the frustration he was feeling now he had her on her own, she took a long time unpacking, then persuaded him to go down with her and explore the hotel. They looked in at the restaurant, a handsome room having, in addition to many tables in the centre, others on a low gallery running round it. For a while she lingered, commenting on the contents of the numerous shops. To avoid going up with him again to their room she asked a porter if there was a coffee shop. There was, on the floor below the lounge, at the end of a long corridor, the walls of which were lined with paintings of Victorian royalties. On returning to the lounge floor they learned that the bar was now open, and Linda gave a silent sigh of relief.

With a view to fortifying herself against the uncertainties of the coming night, she made a start by putting away two large Bacardis. By then it was time for them to go up and change for dinner. On the way up in the lift she wondered anxiously what might happen when he saw her with her clothes off. As a precaution she took the dress she was going to wear into the bathroom, and began to change there. She thought of locking the door, but decided that would be going too far and might quite possibly enrage him.

Her fears that he would come in and again attempt her were soon realised. No sooner had she pulled the dress she was wearing over her head and taken her bra off than he came striding in, gave a hearty laugh, grabbed her, pushed her down on to the floor and began to pull down her briefs. Struggling beneath him she gasped:

'Stop it! Stop it, damn you! I said I preferred to wait until bedtime. If you force me I won't play. I'll go as limp as a corpse and that won't be much fun for you.'

'Have a heart, honey,' he panted, pressing his mouth hard against her neck. 'You're angelic. The sight of you in your undies just drove me crazy. I've got to have you.'

'Not like this,' she shot back. 'You may be a barbarian, but I'm not. Civilised people don't make love on the floor.'

Her taunt did it. He loosed his arms from round her, knelt up, stooped again to kiss one of her nipples, then said angrily, 'O.K., have it your way. But you agreed to come here, and I'm not used to dames saying "no" to me at any time I feel like laying them. If you don't give me a good time tonight, I'll beat the living daylights out of you.'

After he had left her, slamming the door behind him, she spent some time in the bathroom. When she went into the bedroom to do her hair, he was lying on his bed staring at the ceiling. A few minutes later he got up and, without a word, walked past her to shave and wash. Returning, he dressed, maintaining a sulky silence.

Linda was hard put to it to conceal her nervousness. If she allowed the present atmosphere to continue, it boded ill for the hours to come. When they were ready to go downstairs, she made an attempt to change it by smiling at him and saying, 'Did the wicked lady spoil the little boy's fun, then? Perhaps he'll feel better when a kind waiter has given him a lollipop.'

At that he suddenly roared with laughter. 'You win, kid. Maybe I am a barbarian where sex is concerned. But you've said it. Let's go eat, and plenty. You'll need all your energy before we're through.'

Although his good humour was restored, that did not sound particularly reassuring and, since he had threatened to beat her if she didn't prove as eager as himself, she wondered nervously if he took pleasure in beating girls, so might do so to her just to get a kick.

They were given a table on the gallery in the dining-room, and the dinner proved excellent. He talked as amusingly as usual all through it and, somehow, she managed to keep her end up. But all the time her thoughts were not far from the bedroom, and the fear that she might be in tears in a hour or so. His appetite, as she already knew, was gargantuan, and she was unable to do full justice to all the food he had ordered; but she did her share in emptying a magnum of champagne. She was in half a mind to top off with a liqueur but refused one fearing that it would make her really drunk. He had a double brandy and drank it off in a couple of gulps, then signed the check.

In the lift on the way upstairs, again Linda silently upbraided herself as an utter fool for having agreed to come on this jaunt with a man she hardly knew. But there was no escaping whatever might happen now. She could only thank God that she was three parts tight, which would help her to go through with her part in the affair.

Up in the bedroom he almost tore off his clothes, and threw them on the floor. She also undressed quickly, anxious now both not to anger him by delay and to get her coming ordeal over. When she came out of the bathroom in her dressing gown, he was standing stark naked, a splendid figure of a man. The sight of him sent a shiver of excitement through her and made her suddenly conscious of her womanhood.

Next moment he had stripped her of her dressing gown and, big as she was, picked her up in his arms as easily as if she were a child, then flung her on the bed.

In little more than a minute it was all over. He left her gasping, yet unsatisfied.

But not for long. His virility reasserted itself so swiftly that she was amazed. That second time she gave herself until she was near delirium.

As the streaks of early-morning light showed between the curtains, she was lying in his arms, her head pillowed on his broad, hairy chest. Vaguely she tried to count up how many times it had been, but she could not clearly remember. Never had she known anything like it, or imagined that any man could be capable of such frequently-renewed vigour. She felt exhausted, yet completely relaxed and happy. Her last waking thought was how stupid she would have been had she refused to come to Victoria with Big Bear, and so missed this wonderful experience. Then she drifted off into a heavy, dreamless sleep.

They both slept late, made love again on waking, then rang for the waiter and ordered an enormous breakfast.

For Linda the next six days were like a honeymoon. Some days they went for runs in the car, taking a picnic lunch with them to eat in the pine woods. Learning that she had never driven a car, he decided to teach her.

As the roads a few miles outside the city had little traffic on them, the island was an excellent place to learn and, although she was at first a little nervous, she soon got the hang of it. On other days Big Bear hired a motor launch that took them out to the islands. Usually on their return they strolled up the long main street to drink in restaurants, and on one occasion they visited the floodlit Butchart Gardens, said to be the most flower-covered thirty acres in the world. But they always dined at the Empress and were in bed making love by half past ten.

Yet, happy as Linda was, every now and again she was momentarily cast down by the thought that, all too soon, she would lose this gay and handsome lover whose companionship, both in bed and out of it, she found so stimulating. Then she would be back at the Astley, again a lonely exile. Another thought occurred to her. Although she still had plenty of cash, sooner or later she would have to dispose of some of the jewels. That might prove difficult and even dangerous if she was unable to give as a reference some solid citizen who knew her; so she would be missing a good opportunity if she neglected to sell some of them before Big Bear left her.

As a result of her cogitations, on the fifth morning of their stay at the Empress, while she was doing her hair she said:

'Darling, I need some money.'

In the mirror she saw his expression of sudden, shocked surprise, as he said, 'I thought . . .' then broke off and added in a toneless voice: 'O.K. sweetie. I've plenty, and I certainly owe you a good fat wad for the fun you've given me.'

Turning round, she blew him a kiss. 'Thanks a lot for that generous answer. But, as I told you, I'm not a tart, and I'm enjoying our little jaunt every bit as much as you are. My trouble is that my husband is letting me down about the monthly allowance he agreed to make me. It was already three weeks overdue when we met, and after I had my hairdo downstairs yesterday, I phoned the bank in Vancouver. It still hasn't come in.'

'The dirty bastard! But don't worry, honey. I'll give you ample to tide you over.'

'Thanks again, darling. But that won't be necessary. My aunt on my father's side was very rich and she left me all her jewellery. I brought it with me from England, and put it in the bank. I won't miss a few pieces, but I don't know anyone in Vancouver who could see to it that I got a fair deal from a jeweller.'

'That's easy. Dave Kane will know for sure who you'd best go to. As I've told you, I'm already committed to lunch with him and his wife on the last day of my vacation. I'll call him, say I'm bringing you along, and fix with him to take us to his jeweller's.'

On the Saturday morning, instead of taking the ferry back to Vancouver, Big Bear turned in at a local garage the car he had hired for his holiday, and engaged a taxi to take them to Swartz airfield. A twenty-minute flight took them to the international airport on Sea Island, a few miles south of Vancouver City. They booked in at the airport hotel for the night, then drove in to the bank where Linda had lodged her jewels. When her box was brought to her she selected from her hoard a diamond-cluster brooch, which was one of the better pieces, to sell; and, on second thoughts, a valuable square-cut emerald ring and a diamond bracelet to wear should the Kanes prove friendly and, later, ask her to a smart party.

By twelve o'clock, in the lounge of the Vancouver Hotel, Big Bear was introducing Linda to his friend Dave, a short, tubby, genial little Jew who looked about forty.

Dave took them along to Robson Street where there was a jeweller from whom he had bought several presents for his wife. One of the partners examined the diamond cluster and offered Linda two thousand dollars for it.

'Come now, Mr Bowerman,' Dave said, with a quick

shake of his head. 'It's a lovely thing, and worth more than that. I'd give two grand for it myself.'

The jeweller smiled and spread out his hands. 'Business is business, Mr. Kane. But, seeing the lady's a friend of yours, I'll make it two-two-fifty. That really is the very best I can do.'

Linda accepted the offer and, as it was such a large sum, asked Big Bear to put the notes in his wallet, in case she had her bag snatched. As he took them he laughed and said:

'Where do you think you are, honey—New York or London? We don't allow bag-snatching in Canada. You could walk on your own round the old French quarter in Montreal at midnight without the least fear of being robbed. People don't steal cars, either. Our courts believe in protecting law-abiding people, and the penalties they inflict for theft are so heavy that crime simply does not pay.'

When they had left the shop Linda thanked Dave for having got her an extra two hundred and fifty dollars. She still had nearly eight hundred from the Swiss francs she had exchanged at Calgary, so now she had over a thousand pounds which would keep her going for a long time, without having to make further inroads into the jewels or the francs. Feeling that it was too large a sum to keep with her, she said she would like to put some of it in the bank. While Dave went to fetch his car, Big Bear accompanied her back to the bank, where they willingly opened an account for her and she put the two thousand dollars on deposit.

Dave collected them and drove them up Grenville Street to his home, which lay in one of the avenues off Osler Crescent, all lined with fine houses standing back from the road in well-kept gardens.

Judith Kane, a dark, elegant woman, looked considerably younger than her husband. She welcomed Linda cordially and they were soon all chatting cheerfully over cocktails. After an enjoyable lunch, Judith said to Linda, 'Dave told me he has a lot of business to talk over with Big Bear, so I thought I might take you for a drive and show you some bits of Vancouver that maybe you haven't yet seen.'

For the better part of two hours Judith then took her guest on a tour of South Vancouver, which included the Fraserview Golf Course, which ran down to the river, Renfrew Heights and, on the way back, Queen Elizabeth Park, where they got out and walked for a while.

That morning Linda had been saddened by the knowledge that she was soon to lose Big Bear, but the afternoon drive consoled her a little, as she had got on excellently with Judith, and hoped that she would now have at least one friend in Vancouver. Her hopes were confirmed when, after tea, Dave was about to drive Big Bear and herself to the airport hotel, and Judith said:

'You must come to see us again. Call me some time and we'll make a date to go shopping, then come back here for lunch.'

That evening she dined with Big Bear in the airport's Sea Island restaurant, then went early to bed; but, much to her surprise, he refused to make love to her more than once, on the grounds that they would have to be up early next morning, as reporting time for his flight was 8.15.

They breakfasted in bed at seven o'clock, and soon after eight were packed and dressed. Now that the time to part had come, Linda felt very low. He took her in his arms and kissed her. Then he put his big hands on her shoulders and held her a little away from him. There were tears in her eyes as he said, 'Seems you're sorry to have me go.'

She nodded dumbly and the tears flowed over. 'Maybe too,' he went on, 'you're wondering why I didn't make the most of our last night together?'

Again she nodded.

Releasing her, he took his air ticket from his breast pocket, opened it and said, as though in surprise, 'Now, just look at that! I must have been real crazy yesterday. There are two tickets here.' With a wide grin he held them out. 'I'm taking you to Montreal with me, honey.'

Flinging her arms round his neck, she cried, 'Oh, darling! How marvellous! What a wonderful surprise.'

It was a long flight and after six o'clock when they landed at the airport outside Montreal. There was a chauffeur-driven car to meet Big Bear, and at the Ritz-Carlton she found that he had telegraphed the day before to get her a room on the same floor and in the same corridor as his suite. They dined down in the beautiful, oval restaurant, but he told her that he rarely ate there, preferring the Maritime Room on the lower floor, or had something sent up to his sitting-room. Later, when he had joined her in her big, comfortable bedroom, he told her that he would be out most days on business, but she was to order anything she wanted, as he had told the cashier that she was his guest, so whatever she signed for would go on his bill. While dropping off to sleep in his arms she felt that she was one of the luckiest girls in the world to have found such a devoted and generous lover.

Next morning, it being Monday, he was off to his office at half past eight, and he did not get back until six o'clock. That, except for weekends, became the pattern of their days. If he was entertaining a small party that included women executives or the wives of clients, he always asked her to join them; but more often than not he gave lunch only to men, or had it out, and every few days he had to attend convention rallies in the evenings, so Linda was much alone.

But she found Montreal, with its broad streets and massive skyscrapers, a beautiful city. Peel, Metcalfe, La Montagne and St. Catherine Streets were all soon familiar to her. She visited the Cathedral, 'Basilica of Mary, Queen of the World', on tree-filled Dominion Square, and the Arts Museum where, to her, the outstanding exhibit was the collection of beautiful figures of people and animals carved in stone by Eskimos. Another wonder was the Central Metro Station. It consisted of an enormous underground area having several levels, the sides of which were all lined with a great variety of shops. There were scores and scores of them, so that they formed a city centre in themselves, and a perfect place to make one's purchases during Montreal's bitter winters.

One day she took a taxi up to Mount Royal Park, where, from the balustrade high up on the south side, there was a wonderful view over the city and Montreal Island. On another occasion she went to the Botanical Gardens, with its acres of glass houses, and on yet another day had herself driven from the island across one of the bridges that spanned the St. Lawrence, to see the intriguing variety of buildings, dominated by a lofty, aluminium pyramid, that had been erected for Expo '67.

Linda soon realised that the population of Montreal was mainly French and that the good service she enjoyed at the Ritz-Carlton was largely due to the majority of the servants being French-Canadians. The names over a good half of the shops were French, and she constantly heard that language spoken.

She thought, too, that the most fascinating part of Montreal was the old French quarter, with its narrow streets and many small restaurants. One evening Big Bear took her to dine there at the *Filles du Roi*. It consisted of a bar and several small rooms, with stout, wooden tables under low ceilings supported by big, rough-hewn beams. All the waitresses wore little white caps, ample petticoats and white aprons, that having been the uniform of the original Filles du Roi—orphan girls provided with a dowry by King Louis XIV and sent out in the charge of nuns as wives for his soldiers in Canada.

Much as Linda enjoyed Big Bear's company, she was not unduly bored in the evenings when he could not be with her because, from the time she had first known Rowley, reading had been one of her greatest pleasures, and she became a frequent visitor to the book counters in Eaton's great department store.

Sometimes, when Big Bear entertained, he told her afterwards that she had been a big help in sweetening his prospective clients; and more than once he had declared that, if only she were free, he would marry her. Although she had scotched that possibility by her own story that she was tied to a husband in England who would not give her grounds to divorce him, there were times when she was tempted to tell Big Bear that, without naming him, she had written to her mythical husband admitting adultery, so that he would be able to use her letter to set them both free. But each time the thought crossed her mind, she put it from her because she knew that nothing could now alter the fact that she was a criminal, and that one day she might be traced and arrested. She had even had qualms about involving Big Bear and Dave Kane in helping her to sell the diamond cluster, then reassured herself with the fact that, since they were innocent parties to the transaction, they could not later be held accountable for having taken part in it. But to saddle Big Bear with a wife who was a crook was a very different matter.

Linda had been in Montreal for close on a fortnight and on the second Friday a couple she had met twice at parties given by Big Bear had asked them both to lunch at the Hôtel Champlain. At a quarter to one, he picked her up in his car and drove her the half-mile to the great thirty-seven-storey hotel that filled one end of Dominion Square.

They had drinks and lunch up in the roof restaurant, and Linda found that the meal was in keeping with this ultra-modern hotel de luxe, which differed in so many ways from the quiet, gracious, old-fashioned Ritz-Carlton. There was no menu, but a large, semicircular table stood against the inner wall of the room. On it was a splendid variety of dishes, both hot and cold, from which chefs served patrons with their choice of food.

Afterwards Big Bear dropped Linda in St. Catherine's Street so that she could go into Dionne's—the Fortnum of Montreal—and buy some pâté de foie gras for them to eat up in his suite. Having bought the pâté and a few other things, Linda walked up Peel Street on her way back to the Ritz.

The hotel formed a block in itself. Behind it there was a narrow alley in which were the service entrances. As Linda was passing one end of the alley, she noticed that it was almost blocked by a big waste-disposal van.

Standing behind the van, with an empty trash can over his shoulder, was a tall, sour-faced man. He was no more than six feet from Linda, and she happened to glance at him. Instantly she recognised him. He was her brother Sid.

At the same instant his pale eyes boggled. He dropped the trash can and exclaimed, 'Swelp me Gawd! If it ain't our Linda!'

12
Nemesis

IN a matter of seconds several thoughts raced through Linda's mind. So this was the fine job with the Municipality of Montreal that Sid had said he had got in a letter to Ma—a dustman! What ghastly luck to have run into him like this. How ashamed she would have been if Big Bear had been with her. Must she acknowledge him? If she did, it was certain that he would make a nuisance of himself. Why should she? She owed him nothing. In the old days, before he had stolen the money to go off to Canada, he had followed Pa's example and often bullied her. Many a time when she was only a kid at school, he had made her do dirty jobs he should have done himself.

The blood had drained from her face. But her eyes flickered only for an instant before she turned them away. Exerting all her will-power, she kept her expression unchanged and walked on without increasing her pace.

'Linda!' cried the man, hurrying after her. 'Yer can't not know me, yer brother Sid.'

She turned round then, stared at him and said coldly, 'I thought you were calling out to that woman who just went past. Why you should imagine that I am your sister I cannot think.'

'You are,' he insisted, walking beside her as she

moved on. 'You're Linda Lee or I'm a Dutchman.'

'I am not,' she snapped. 'My name is Harrison, and I never had a brother. Be good enough to go back to your work.'

'Stop foxing, Linda,' he said, angrily now. 'For all yer fine clothes an' hoity-toity airs, I'd know you anywheres.'

By then they had reached the corner. Halting, she faced him, drew a quick breath, then declared firmly, 'I may resemble your sister, but I am not. Now if you pester me any further I'll call a policeman.'

To her intense relief that silenced him. She covered the fifty paces to the entrance of the hotel and did not look back until the porter touched his cap and gently pushed the revolving door for her. From that one swift glance she had seen that Sid was still standing on the corner, staring after her, with an expression of puzzled anger.

Although she had had plenty to drink at lunch, the shock had so shaken her that, as soon as she was upstairs in Big Bear's sitting-room, she poured herself a stiff brandy and soda. When she had taken a big gulp she sat down with the glass in her hand and stared out of the window.

Again her thoughts were racing. Had she got rid of Sid for good, or would he make an attempt to force himself on her? For a month now, Linda Chatterton's name must have been on Interpol's list of wanted criminals, and no doubt, by questioning the Lucheni couple, they had learned soon after she had got away from England that Linda Chatterton had come to Park Side West as Linda Lee. She had therefore been doubly right in refusing to recognise Sid, and so give away her alias as Lucille Harrison. If he did succeed in seeing her again, she must stick it out and swear black and blue that she was not his sister.

On further consideration she persuaded herself that he was unlikely to try. All he could have heard about her from Ma was that she had gone to London and got a job as a companion, presumably to an old lady. Had that really been the case, although she might have improved herself from the down-at-heel teenager she had been when he last saw her, it was most improbable that she would have acquired an impeccable, upper-class accent and become an elegantly-dressed woman wearing expensive furs and jewels. She might, of course, have married. But the odds would be long against an old lady's companion meeting the sort of man who could afford to give his wife a mink coat and take her travelling de luxe in Canada. She had grown a lot and was now a mature woman, six feet in height. Only her face had remained unchanged. Surely, after the firmness with which she had denied her true identity, he could not continue to believe that the lady he had accosted was the same person whom he had known as a schoolgirl?

Through the rest of the afternoon she continued to be upset and worried; but that evening Big Bear was giving a party to celebrate the silver wedding of one of his best customers, and that took her mind off the matter. Nevertheless, on the Saturday morning she decided not to go out, in case Sid was lurking somewhere in the neighbourhood of the hotel on the chance of being able to confront her again. That afternoon Big Bear took her to the Blue Bonnets race-course, where she had the good luck to back three winners. As he worked so hard all the week, he liked to do nothing on Sundays, and they spent the whole day in dressing gowns up in his suite.

Although she had her own bedroom further along the corridor, she had at first feared there might be embarrassing complaints owing to his making no attempt to conceal the fact that they were living together; but his lavish tips ensured that the staff continued to treat her with respect; and luxury hotels do not usually regard themselves as responsible for the morals of their best customers, provided that in public their behaviour is discreet. Her Sundays in Montreal, when she had Big Bear to herself, had therefore been among her happiest days; and by Monday morning she had almost forgotten her encounter with Sid.

It was recalled to her most unpleasantly when the *femme de chambre* brought in her breakfast tray. There was a letter on it. No-one she had met in Montreal was likely to write to her and, although she did not recognise the writing, the sight of the untidy scrawl and cheap paper made her sit up with a jerk. Ripping open the envelope, she saw at a glance that her worst fears were realised. Although it was addressed to Mrs. Harrison, it began *Dear Linda,* and went on:

For all your new finery it isn't no good you pretending you're not who you are. Just as you walked off from me on Friday with your head in the air I catched sight of that little mole you got behind your ear. Identified you as good as a set of fingerprints it did. But I didn't chase you because I don't want to make no trouble. Saturday I got the lowdown though from a pal of mine what is one of the hotel cleaners. You've struck it lucky and no mistake. Nearer the mark though to say you've learnt to lay on your back and open them fine legs of yours to the right kind of gent. No sleezy back rooms for you, old girl, eh? Mrs. Harrison, with her own fine bedroom. Living respectable, I don't think. Whole staff knows you're the fancy bird for mister moneybags Orson along the corridor.

Well, ducks, that's all right by me. Good luck to you I say.
If he thinks you are the daughter of a Duke, I'm not telling him
different. But it ain't right to high hat your own brother.
Blood's thicker than water, ain't it? All I want is a friendly
chat about old times. That won't cost you nothing and we'll
meet in a place where poor old Sid won't disgrace you. Wear
me best suit I will and we'll have a cuppa in Marcel's café on
the Rue Notre-Dame. It's a decent middle-class joint and only
Frenchies go there. I'll be waiting for you at five o'clock. If
you're tied up Monday I'll be there again same time Tuesday.
Looking forward to seeing you, lovie. Your affec. brother, Sid.

Linda's hand was shaking, and she had skimmed
through the letter, so absorbed only the main points.
Re-reading it carefully, she tried to assess what really
lay in the writer's mind. Although that damnable little
mole behind her left ear had given her away, he had not
followed her into the hotel and made a scene. He had
found out that Big Bear was her lover, but said that he
had no intention of embarrassing her with him. All he
asked for was a chat about old times. Although they had
never had any affection for each other they had, after
all, been brought up together; so the request did not
seem unreasonable, particularly as he had spent the past
six years as an exile.

Although she was most loath to meet him, she
realised that if she refused his request he might change
his mind about not making trouble. Big Bear was quite
capable of throwing him downstairs and, no doubt,
would think no worse of her for having been told that
she came of a poor family. But that might not be the
end of the matter. It would come out that she was, or
anyway had been, Linda Lee, and that might lead to
her ending up in prison.

Clearly she must see Sid and the sooner she got it over

the better. Although he had not asked for money she thought it certain that he would expect her to give him some, and she decided that it would be better to do so freely, otherwise there was the unpleasant possibility that he might resort to blackmail. So that afternoon, when she made her way to the Café Marcel, dressed in a skirt, high-necked sweater, and wearing a cloth coat instead of her mink, she had in her bag an envelope with two one-hundred-dollar bills in it.

The place was half-empty and Sid was sitting at a table at the far end of the room. He did not get up as she approached him, but gave her a cheerful wave and said, 'Well, ducks, nice to see yer. Take a pew and tell us how yer come to strike so lucky.'

He was now dressed in a shiny blue suit, a pale yellow shirt and a flamboyant tie that had evidently seen a considerable amount of wear. Although only six years her senior he looked a lot older than twenty-six, and reminded her uncomfortably of her father. He had the same mop of coarse black hair and pale, slightly protruding eyes. His face was lean, and his mouth bitter. Obviously fate had not been very kind to Sid.

She waited until he had ordered tea and cakes for them both, then shrugged and, in an endeavour to keep the conversation on a light note, said, 'It's the old story—just like the song. *"She was poor but she was honest, victim of a rich man's crime. 'Twas the Squire's cruel passion robbed her of her honest nime. Then she went right up to London for to hide her grief and shime. There she met another Squire, an' she lorst 'er nime again."* '

Sid's thin lips broke into a grin. 'Ma writes me now and then. Over two years ago she wrote me that yer'd hooked it on yer own to London and got a job as companion to a rich old woman.'

'I never told her that; she just jumped to that conclusion—as I meant her to. Actually it was with a very nice middle-aged man who picked me up on the train. He died some months ago, and left me enough money to travel. I thought I'd like to see Canada, and after I'd been here for a while I met Mr. Orson. As I am free, and liked him very much, I saw no reason why I should not "lose my name again".'

'Gawd; if only I could lose my name for the pickin's you're gettin'. 'E's the big shot in advertising in these parts, ain't 'e?'

'Yes. But that's enough about me. How have you been doing, Sid? I heard from Ma a long time ago that you'd married and had two children.'

'Yes, that's right. An' more bloody fool me. With that lot to feed and clothe, what chance has a feller got to save enough to set up for 'isself or buy a share in a promisin' little business? Bein' a refuse collector, as the sods who pay me call it, is one hell of a life; but I don't see no way ter get nothing better.'

Linda nodded, and produced the envelope from her bag. 'You've had rotten luck, Sid. Now, look. My old friend did not leave me a fortune, only just enough to see something of the world in a modest way. And I wouldn't be staying at the Ritz-Carlton if it were not for Mr. Orson. But, believe me or not as you like, he doesn't give me any money, because we are really very fond of each other, and that would spoil our relationship. All he does is to buy me presents and pay my bill at the hotel. I refused to recognise you the other day because, to be honest, I didn't want it known that my brother was a dustman. But I felt very sorry for you. So I went to the Bank of Montreal this morning and used my letter of credit to get these two hundred dollars for you.'

'Strewth, Lindy!' he exclaimed. 'You're a real brick, you are. I'm ever so grateful. Why, with that I'll be able to buy meself a motor bike an' sidecar, an' take my old woman an' the kids out for runs in the country when it comes spring again.'

As he eagerly pocketed the money, she asked if he had heard from their mother lately.

He nodded. ' 'Bout a coupla months ago. Things ain't no better than they was when we lived at 'ome. Pa's as big a slave-driver as ever, and 'as a skinful regular Saturday nights. The old girl is still sore about yer goin' off on yer own an' never even droppin' 'er a line. But she did say in one of 'er letters as 'ow you send 'er a few quid to help out now an' then. That's decent of yer, Lindy. You always was a good kid. 'Fraid I didn't make things any too easy fer yer. But you must blame Pa fer that. He used to work me something chronic, an' at times I got so mad I used ter take it out on yer.'

For a while they talked of the way they had slaved in the market garden, and of people they had known in the neighbourhood. Then Linda stubbed out her cigarette and said, 'Well, it's nice to have had our chat, Sid, but I must be getting back now.'

As he produced some loose change to pay the bill, he gave her an earnest look, and spoke in a humble voice. 'Lindy, it's darned good of yer to give me this money; but there's just one other thing I wish you'd do. I'd like yer to meet my missis an' the kids. 'Ow about coming along one evening and having a bite of supper?'

Imperceptibly Linda stiffened. 'No, Sid. I don't think that would be a good idea. We've agreed that it is better that we should go our separate ways.'

'Oh, come on na. Don't yer want to see yer little nieces? It would make 'em no end proud to know that their auntie is a fine lady like you, and put my stock up with Doris inter the bargain.'

The last thing that Linda wanted to do was to meet Sid's family, and she shook her head. 'No, really. If you introduce me to your wife, she will probably ask me to come again, and expect me to take the children to a movie, or something.'

'No, she won't. I'll see to that. And this means a lot to me. Doris's father is a builder. In a small way, but quite well off. 'E bought us the 'ouse we live in, an' she's always gettin' at me about me not earnin' better money, an' 'ow superior her family are to the people I come from. You comin' along in your mink and sparklers would put an end to that line o' gab and teach 'er better. Come on, Lindy. Be a sport. It'ud be only for once, 'cause I'll tell 'er that you're off back to England in a couple of days' time.'

Put that way it was a request that Linda found it impossible to refuse, and Big Bear had to attend a conference on the coming Wednesday evening, so she agreed to Sid's plea. With a stub of pencil he wrote down his address for her and said, 'There yer are. It's quite a way out, but it won't break yer ter take a taxi. Thanks, ducks; you've proved a real pal.'

After they had parted, she felt that Sid was not such a bad fellow after all, and that things had gone off well —except for this new commitment. That evening and all through Tuesday, the thought that complications might arise from it worried her; but she endeavoured to comfort herself with Sid's promise that after this one visit he and his would once more disappear out of her life.

On the Wednesday morning, feeling that she ought to take some presents with her, she went out and bought

for Doris a quite expensive costume-jewellery brooch
and for the two girls dolls that could be dressed up in a
variety of clothes, and large boxes of candy.

At six o'clock that evening, loaded with her parcels,
she took a taxi out to the address Sid had given her. It
was, as she had expected, in a poor district, but she
was a little taken aback by the appearance of the house.
That it was only a two up, two down did not surprise
her, but the little garden in front was a tangle of weeds,
the woodwork had not had a coat of paint for a generation and the window curtains were faded brown repp,
one of them torn at the top.

Sid had been watching for the taxi to drive up, and
let her in. He greeted her with exuberance, took her
coat and led her into the front room. It was shoddily
furnished in appalling taste. On the walls there were
several coloured lithographs of sacred subjects, from
which Linda guessed that Doris was a Roman Catholic.
She was making up the fire as Linda came in. Turning,
she showed good teeth in a nervous smile, then instinctively ran her hands down her front, as though wiping
them on an apron, before shaking hands with Linda.
Doris had once been pretty in a flashy way, but looked
older than Sid or, perhaps, was prematurely aged by
work and worry. Linda's experienced eye took in the
fact that the gold of her hair had come out of a bottle
and her blue dress was of artificial silk.

The two little girls, aged four and three, were seated
on the edge of the sofa. One was named Angélique and
the other Bernadine, but it soon transpired that they
were called Ang and Ber. The hair of both had obviously been crimped for the occasion and was kept in
place by none-too-clean ribbons. Their clothes had been
freshly ironed, but the frock of the younger one was so

old that the colours had faded and the shoes of both were scruffy. Out of pinched little faces their big eyes were riveted on the visitor as though she were a being from another world.

Sid had carried in Linda's parcels for her and she now distributed them with smiles. Doris gawped at the piece of costume jewellery and exclaimed, 'Oh, my! Ain't that just too lovely. To bring me that was ever so kind.' The children tore their parcels open, stared at the dolls for a moment then put them quickly aside and fell upon the candies like two small, famished wolves. They had devoured several while their mother was admiring her brooch. When she saw what they were doing she snapped at them:

'Stop that, you two, or you'll be sick. And I've no mind to clean up after you. Now thank your kind auntie, and behave proper.'

Sid produced a bottle of Canadian red wine and, when he had filled three glasses, started on what amounted almost to a monologue. To Linda's embarrassment, it consisted of a tissue of lies about a fine home in which he and she were supposed to have been brought up, designed to lead Doris to believe that they came of an upper-class family from which he had become an outcast owing to a quarrel with their father. At times he asked Linda questions about nonexistent rich relatives and, greatly as she disliked doing so, she felt bound to play up to him.

How, with his awful speech, he could have the nerve to such pretensions, Linda could not imagine; but Doris, who remained almost silent, appeared to accept them. Her voice showed that she was better educated than he was, but that was the only evidence to suggest that she considered herself superior to her husband.

Most of the time she sat there like a frightened hen and, as she said not a word about her own family, Linda decided that Sid's statement that she was the daughter of a prosperous middle-class builder was a lie.

To Linda's added discomfort the crowded little parlour brought back to her an unpleasantness of which she had been unconscious before she left home, but had soon afterwards come to regard with aversion—the smell of warm, rarely-bathed bodies. To her relief, after about twenty minutes, Sid said:

'We eat early, Linda ducks. 'Ave to because of the nippers. Sorry we ain't grand enough ter give yer supper in a dinin'-room, but the eats taste just as good in the kitchen. Doris 'as it all ready, so let's go feed our faces.'

They then all trooped into the back room. There the kitchen table was already laid for five, and an attempt made to give it a festive air by arranging brightly-coloured paper serviettes so that they protruded like fans from the glasses. While Sid opened another bottle of the red wine, Doris took from the oven a big casserole that proved to contain an Irish stew plentifully laced with onions. Sid's table manners were no better than Linda remembered them to have been at home, but Doris's were genteel. She helped herself only to a small portion and used her knife and fork with her little fingers stuck out sideways. Ang and Ber laboured awkwardly with spoons, receiving a sharp rebuke from their mother each time they spilt food on their bibs or on the red-checked table cloth. The stew was followed by a blancmange highly flavoured with vanilla. When the last of it had been demolished by the two children, Sid said to his wife:

'While yer put the kids to bed an' wash up, Lindy and I'll have a cosy 'eart-to-'eart in the parlour.' Linda

dutifully kissed Ang and Ber good night, then followed
Sid into the other room.

As soon as he had shut the door behind them, he said
in a tone from which all the joviality had disappeared,
'When I said you an' I would 'ave a 'eart-to-'eart I
weren't joking. You'll have guessed by now that Doris
don't come of a family any better than ours, but it were
a good excuse ter get yer on yer own here to 'ave a
showdown. I didn't want no scene in a public place like
that café; much less the Ritz where they would 'ave
thrown me out on me arse.'

Linda's heart missed a beat. Staring at him in consternation, she stammered, 'Showdown; what . . . what
do you mean?'

He gave a nasty laugh. 'Yer must be dumber than
yer seem not to have tumbled to it that I know all
about yer making off with them jewels.'

The blood drained from Linda's face. 'How . . . how
could you?' she gasped.

'Why, from Ma, of course.'

'But . . . she knew nothing about it.'

'Be yer age, girl. When that there Mrs. Spilkin what
yer robbed askt yer fer an address to forward yer mail,
yer give her Ma's, tellin' 'er that she was yer aunt and
yer was goin' back north ter live with 'er.'

Linda then saw the awful blunder she had made.
Caught off her guard by Elsie, she had given Ma's
address as the only one she could think of from which
a letter from Eric could be forwarded on to her,
failing to realise at the time that when Eric knew
what she had done he would not write to her and that,
even if he did, she would not dare to let Ma know where
she had gone, so that a letter could be forwarded to her.

Meanwhile Sid was going on: 'It follows, don't it,

that when the police was put on to yer, Mrs. Spilkin
gives them Ma's address. Ma couldn't 'elp the 'tecs
when they questioned 'er, but she learns from them
about the sort of life you been livin' as an old buffer's
doxy, an' 'ow 'im forgetting you in 'is will, yer makes
off wi' all them jewels. Twenty-five thousand smackers'
worth, so they say, an' a month or more back Ma writes
me all about it. Strewth! What a lucky day it was for
yours truly when I runs into yer.'

'Why?' Linda demanded tersely. 'What I've done is
no affair of yours. But you were lucky in that I've given
you two hundred dollars.'

'Come orf it! That ain't no more than two hundred
dimes to yer now. I want a proper cut. An' I'm goin'
ter have it, if yer want me ter keep me trap shut.'

Linda looked at him aghast. 'D'you mean . . . d'you
really mean that you would split on me to the police?'

'You've said it! There never was much love lost
'tween us. Wouldn't cause me a wink o' sleep if they
put yer in the can. Fer years past you've been 'aving a
high old time as a gilded whore, while I've been livin'
like a rat. Fer me this is the chance of a lifetime. You're
goin' ter set me up in a nice little garage. Cost abart
thirty thousand dollars, I reckon. That's less than half
what you got. Added to that yer can go on selling the
goods yer peddle fer plenty more.'

'I won't get thirty thousand dollars, or anything like
it,' Linda protested. 'I sold only a few of the jewels in
London and . . . Anyhow, the greater part of them is in
a bank.'

'Where?'

'I'm not telling you.'

'Well, get 'em out, and sell some more.'

'Don't be a fool. No-one could sell stolen jewels to

raise the amount of money you are demanding without exciting the jeweller's suspicions that they might not have been come by honestly.'

That made Sid think. For a moment he stared morosely at her, then he snarled:

'Maybe yer right. But turned out posh, like you are, an' 'avin' thought out a good story about how yer come by the stuff, the risk wouldn't be great. Anyways, I want my cut; so it's a risk you gotta take.'

'I won't,' she flared. 'I'm damned if I will! It would be as good as handing myself straight over to the police.'

'You got no choice,' he muttered.

'I have. I'd prefer to walk out of here now. And if you are such a swine as to inform on me, may you rot in hell. Anyhow, if you do, you won't get a penny.'

Scowling, Sid considered this. He knew of old how pig-headed Linda could be, and decided that her threat was not an empty one. During the past few days he had been having marvellous visions of himself, dressed in a loud checked suit, lounging about as a garage proprietor, while his mechanics did the work. Now this 'castle in Spain' was rapidly vanishing. Then a new light came into his pale eyes, and he suddenly exclaimed:

'All right, you bloody tart. Go if yer like; but you're leavin' yer sparklers behind yer.'

Linda's face paled and she took a quick step away from him, but not quickly enough to place the small table between them. His teeth bared in an ugly grin, he grabbed her arm with one hand and snatched at her pearl necklace with the other. The string broke and most of the pearls cascaded on to the floor. Instead of attempting to retrieve them, he wrenched off her brooch, then seized one of her hands to pull off her wrist watch, rings and a bracelet. As he bent his head, she

jerked hers forward and savagely bit him in the ear. He
managed only partially to repress a cry of agony.
Furiously angry, he hit her hard in the stomach. The
blow knocked all the breath out of her. Gasping, she
doubled up. By the time she was able to come upright
again, he had stripped her hands and wrist and was
stuffing a handful of gems into his trousers pockets.

Livid with rage, she swore at him, using all the filthy
words she had picked up during her teens. He only
laughed, jerked his thumb in the direction of the door
and cried:

'Now get out if yer like, an' go back to yer whoring.'

Tears were streaming down Linda's face. Choking
back her sobs, in two strides she reached the door and
wrenched it open. Her mink hung on a peg in the hall.
Snatching it down, she flung it round her shoulders. As
she did so, Sid suddenly shouted from the parlour:

'Hey! 'Alf a mo'. You ain't goin' ter get away with
that. I can flog it for three thousand bucks.'

As he ran forward, she braced herself, her big eyes
blazing, and kicked out with all her strength. The toe of
her shoe caught him right in the groin. His eyes nearly
popped out of his head. He screeched like a scalded cat,
pitched forward on to the floor, and writhed there,
groaning.

Without losing a second, Linda had the front door
open and, still sobbing, dashed out into the street. It
was only dimly lit and few people were about, none of
whom took any notice of her. As she struggled into her
coat, she realised with relief that she had instinctively
snatched up her bag before rushing from the parlour.
But the loss she had sustained was enormous.

Normally she wore only her single string of pearls—
the very valuable triple rope was in the bank at

Vancouver—a brooch and one good diamond solitaire. But she had brought several other items with her to Montreal, which she wore when Big Bear had her with him at parties and that evening, to conform to Sid's wish that she should impress his wife, she had put them all on. The most precious was a square emerald that had been valued at two thousand five hundred pounds. In addition to that and the solitaire, he had robbed her of a beautifully-cut jade ring, her diamond wrist watch, and a heavy diamond bracelet. With the pearls and the brooch, she estimated that her meeting with him had cost her the better part of a fifth of her stolen fortune.

It seemed to her that she walked miles before she found a taxi; but fortunately, when she left Sid's house, she had turned in the right direction. As she entered the hotel she was surprised to see that it was only half past eight. She thanked her gods for that, as Big Bear would not be back from his convention rally before ten o'clock at the earliest. Hours seemed to have elapsed since she had left the hotel, and she had dreaded the possibility of running into him before she could get to her room, because her face must be in a shocking state; far worse, the left shoulder of her dress had been torn right open when Sid ripped her brooch from it, and that would have been far from easy to explain.

When she reached her room and looked in the mirror, as she had feared her tears had caused her make-up to run. While she repaired the damage, she hoped that none of the staff had noticed the state she had been in and, later, when Big Bear was with her, ask if she had been involved in an accident. Hurrying out of her clothes, she hid the torn dress in a bottom drawer, in case the *femme de chambre* should see it, then lay for a while in a hot bath before getting into bed.

At about half past ten, Big Bear came in to her. She knew that she must positively reek of onions, which normally neither of them ate in quantity; so, holding her breath, she let him kiss her, then turned away her face and said, 'I can't let you make love to me tonight, because my curse has just come on.'

Actually it was nearly due, but she had thought up the excuse while in the bath, since she felt so shattered that she could not have made love with anyone that night—not even with her beloved Eric if she had suddenly found him in bed with her.

For about ten minutes Big Bear remained there, telling her about his evening and asking about hers. She said that she had had a light dinner down in the coffee shop, then, the curse having made her feel rotten, gone early to bed. Again she held her breath as he kissed her good night. Relieved by his departure, she was free to think miserably about the future.

Heavy as her loss to Sid had been, it was not catastrophic. In the bank at Vancouver she still had jewels valued at about seventeen thousand pounds, six hundred pounds in Swiss francs and another two thousand dollars on deposit; added to which, allowing for what she had spent in Montreal and the two hundred dollars she had given Sid, she still had between five and six hundred dollars out of the thousand odd she had brought with her from Vancouver. So, theoretically at least, she still had assets worth nearly nineteen thousand pounds.

Her immediate worry was how to account to Big Bear for all the jewels she had had with her. All she could do was to go out first thing in the morning, buy herself some junk jewellery resembling as nearly as possible the pieces she had lost, and hope that he would not notice the difference.

G

On the Thursday she spent all the morning and a good part of the afternoon hunting for suitable items. A string of false pearls, and an imitation diamond solitaire ring were easy; but it took her a long time to find a brooch at all similar to the one of which she had been robbed, and she could not find anywhere a ring that might have passed for the square emerald; so, if Big Bear asked about it, she decided to tell him that she thought it too precious to wear and had put it in one of the hotel safe-deposit boxes. Fortunately she had a second wrist watch. It was not so valuable as the one she had lost, but would serve.

All through Friday she felt extremely sore about the way in which Sid had lured her to his house on a false pretext, then treated her so damnably. It consoled her a little to think that the kick she had landed on his private parts might have caused him a permanent injury or would at least have laid him low for a day or two. So far Big Bear had not noticed the change in design of her brooch, or that the clasp of her pearl necklace was no longer a jewelled one.

By Saturday she had become more or less resigned to her loss and was looking forward to a party that Big Bear was giving that evening. After lunch, as usual, she had a lie-down on her bed. Soon after three o'clock the telephone rang. As she picked up the receiver she expected her caller to be one of the many people to whom Big Bear had introduced her while she had been in Montreal. But it was Sid's voice, low and urgent:

'Spot of trouble, Lindy. Thought I ought ter warn yer, spite of that bloody kick you give me. Tried to hock a ring this mornin'. The one wi' the big green stone. Chap said it were worth a packet, but 'e'd see what 'e could do about it an' let me know. Then 'e askt me name an' address, an' I give it. 'Twas only arter that 'e showed suspicious. Wanted to know where I got it. I wasn't sayin', so 'e says then I must give its description to the police so they can check it's not listed as stolen property. That means the 'tecs may be comin' round ter my plice termorrer. I won't giv' yer away. But Doris may. When I let out that yell she came tumblin' downstairs, found the scattered pearls an' all, an' I 'ad ter tell 'er what I'd done.'

Before Linda had time to speak, he rang off. As she hung up, all the frightful implications resulting from Sid's stupidity in trying to sell her big emerald without most careful precautions rushed through her mind. The fool had been trapped into giving his address. It was certain that the police would question him; certain, too, that he would not let himself be sent to prison to save her. Through him they would learn that Lucille Harrison was Linda Lee. If she was not already on the files of the Canadian police as a wanted criminal under that name, she would be as soon as they had radioed Scotland Yard. Sid had said he would not give her away, although Doris would, but that seemed to Linda a despicable invention. That poor creature would do whatever Sid told her. It was he who would tell to save his own skin, and he would tell everything except that he had robbed her of the jewels. He would say that she told him she had inherited them and had given them to him to dispose of for her.

In an agony of fury and despair she slumped into the chair beside the table on which the telephone stood, clenched her hands until the nails bit into her palms, then hammered with both fists on the table.

'The fool! The brainless idiot! The swine!' For him, an illiterate dustman, to walk into a jeweller's or a pawnbroker's and expect to sell an emerald worth two thousand five hundred pounds without being questioned! A teenage hippy would have had more sense. And what a ghastly mess his impatient greed had landed her in.

Panic seized her. Visions of prison again took possession of her mind. She must get out, and at once. But how, and where? Vancouver seemed the obvious answer. She must get the rest of the jewels and her money out of the bank there, with the minimum of delay, and start a new life under yet another name.

At the thought tears sprang to her eyes. That meant leaving Big Bear, and she loved him in a way. Not as she had loved Eric. She would never really love anyone but him; but Big Bear was kind, generous and a delightful companion. Never had she experienced such transports of passion as she enjoyed with him, and he had created for her a new, happy life, meeting pleasant people.

She glanced at her watch. It was a quarter past three. That afternoon he was out, taking an American client on a tour of the sights of Montreal. For that she thanked her gods; for, had he been in she would have been with him in his sitting-room, and Sid's call would have been put through to her there; so she could not have left without giving him some explanation, and what possible explanation could she give? But he would be back about five o'clock, so she had not a moment to lose.

Frantically she began to dress, choosing a serviceable tweed suit. As she pulled it on, she realised that she would have to abandon nearly all her other clothes. Even if she could have left the hotel with all her suitcases without arousing comment, there was no time to pack them. Angrily she thrust into her overnight bag the things that were most necessary to her.

As she did so, she thought of writing a farewell note to leave in Big Bear's sitting-room. But what could she say in it, except that circumstances compelled her to leave him; and time was passing with terrible rapidity.

It was twenty to five when she left her room, wearing her mink, a fur toque she had bought in Montreal now that the weather was becoming so much colder, and carrying the small suitcase. Out in the corridor and in the lobby downstairs, she was a prey to awful apprehension that Big Bear would return early and that she would run into him. She was spared that, but spent a desperately anxious five minutes while the hall porter got her a taxi.

Jumping in she told the driver to take her to the big new Queen Elizabeth Hotel on the Place Vieille Marie. There she spent a few minutes in the crowded lounge, then took another taxi out to the airport.

At the enquiry desk she learned to her consternation that the next flight to Vancouver did not leave until the following morning. As the jeweller's report about the emerald was only a routine enquiry, particulars of it would probably not reach the police until that evening, so the odds were that they would not go to Sid's house and question him that night. But they might; so she dared not risk remaining in Montreal until the morning, in case the airport people had by then been alerted to keep a look-out for her. Yet it was imperative that she should go to Vancouver and draw funds from the bank, because, after buying her junk jewellery, she now had only something under six hundred dollars in cash. Impelled by the necessity of getting out of Montreal within the next few hours, she decided to try the railway station but, before leaving the airport, she sent Big Bear a telegram which read:

*Have left you with deepest regret but compelled to do so stop
You will soon learn reason stop Please don't think too badly of
me stop Thank you for everything Fondest love Lucille.*

At the railway station she was more fortunate. A
train was leaving for Vancouver in an hour and three-
quarters. Realising that until she could get more money
she must now watch every dollar, she took a second-
class ticket instead of a drawing-room.

Her companion in the two-berth compartment she
found to be a cheerful, talkative, middle-aged woman.
In her still agitated state of mind, the last thing Linda
wished to do was to gossip, so she resorted to her old
trick of pretending to be deaf and said that her hearing
aid had suddenly gone out of order.

From Montreal to Vancouver by train took the
better part of three days and nights, so Linda had ample
time to think over her new and far from happy situation. It was a certainty that, to protect himself, Sid
would disclose her real name and that she had been
staying at the Ritz-Carlton as Mrs. Harrison, and it
seemed equally certain that the Canadian police,
having communicated with Scotland Yard, would soon
be hunting for her. Their next move would be to find
out all they could about her at the hotel. Inevitably
they would question Big Bear. Greatly as he cared for
her, he could not afford to have it said that he had
knowingly been associating with a jewel thief; so, to
protect his business interests, he would have at least to
tell the police that he had picked her up in Vancouver
and that she had then been staying at the Astley.

On arriving in Montreal she had sent a cheque on
the Vancouver bank to pay for the room that had been
kept for her during the week she had been on Victoria
Island; but Mrs. Burnaby could tell the police little

more than how long she had stayed, the date of her arrival, and that she had said she had come from Los Angeles.

But, as she was drifting off to sleep on the second night on the train, an awful thought struck her. She had counted on Big Bear being sufficiently in love with her to hope that she would not be caught and, knowing that to keep on the run she would need more money than she had with her, keeping it to himself that she had opened a bank account in Vancouver. But what of that accursed cheque she had sent Mrs. Burnaby?

That would give away the place in which she had cached her stolen fortune. Dared she now go there? If only she had taken the risk of remaining in Montreal until the Saturday morning and gone to Vancouver by air, she would have been able to collect her hoard first thing on Monday, before enquiries about her in Vancouver had begun. But now she would not reach Vancouver until Monday afternoon, and too late to go to the bank that day. That loss of twenty-four hours could make all the difference. By Monday the police in Vancouver would have been alerted and, that day, make their enquiries at the Astley. As soon as they learned about her cheque they would instruct the bank to detain her if she went there. So, on Tuesday morning, she would walk straight into a trap.

Bitterly she realised that her whole future was in jeopardy. The remaining nineteen thousand pounds were now as lost to her as though Sid had robbed her of the lot. After paying her fare she was down to four hundred dollars in the pouch under her skirt, enough to meet immediate expenses in her bag, and some pieces of imitation jewellery. For a long time she lay

awake, wondering what would happen to her. At length
she cried herself to sleep.

On the Sunday morning, as she again thought over
the desperate situation in which Sid had landed her,
another danger occurred to her. She had spent eight
days in Vancouver. She was known by sight to all the
people at the Astley. Many others had obviously
noticed her beauty in the restaurants and night spots
to which Big Bear had taken her; in addition there were
the Kanes, the jeweller to whom she had sold the
diamond cluster, and the staff at the bank. If a description of her was put in the papers by the police, any of
those people might recognise her and so bring about her
arrest. She dared not go to Vancouver.

In the early afternoon, when the train stopped at
Banff in the eastern foothills of the Rockies, she got off.
Up there in the Rockies winter was setting in and light
snow falling. A hire car was standing outside the little
station and she asked the driver to take her to an hotel.
Scenting money, on observing her mink coat, he said:

'Château Lake Louise is the place for you, lady.
Jump in.'

She was a little surprised when he drove her out of
the small town, but made no comment until they had
covered several miles through pine woods. Only then
she learned to her annoyance that Lake Louise was
thirty miles from Banff. When they arrived she found
that the hotel was an enormous place, overlooking a
beautiful lake with mountains reflected in its still
waters. On asking for a room she was further dismayed
to learn that the end of the season was at hand, and the
hotel closing in three days' time. The driver must have
known that. He could have taken her to another great
C.P.R. hotel just outside Banff; but, to earn a big fare

which she could ill afford, he had literally 'taken her for a ride'.

She booked in as Mary Watson, then found that the huge hotel was crammed with people making the best of the last days of the season. It was as crowded as Waterloo Station in a rush hour, and she had to join a queue before she could eat a very expensive dinner. She found too that, having had one drink with it, the licensing laws prevented her having another, either in the vast lounge or up in her room. Weary and dispirited, she went to bed, having decided to get out of the Château Lake Louise as soon as possible.

Next morning she sought the Social Director. He proved to be a charming man and most helpful. Only a quarter of a mile away there was a much smaller hotel, The Fisherman's Paradise, which remained open all through the year. He telephoned there for her. The only room available was on the ground floor, but she took it, and he had a car take her there without any charge.

She found The Fisherman's Paradise unpretentious but comfortable, and much more within her means. Even so, she knew that she could not afford to stay there for long. She must make for a city and somehow earn some money. But at least she could afford a week or so to recover from the frightful shock of finding herself again so badly off, and decide which city to go to.

There was nothing to do, but the scenery was beautiful and, although it snowed now and then, she went every morning for long walks along tracks through the forest.

It was now becoming dark quite early and, as she found it wearisome constantly to have to lie about herself when mingling with the other guests, instead of spending the long evenings in the lounge she stayed for most of the time in her room and amused hereslf by starting to write a novel.

The saying that everyone has one good story in him is true enough, so it was natural that Linda's plot should be based in the main on her own experiences, with certain imaginary alterations. She made her heroine a factory girl in a northern town, with whom one of the directors of the firm fell in love. He was married, but she duly became his mistress and, as he often had to go overseas on business, he took her with him to all sorts of exciting places. Like Rowley, he had a couple of heart attacks but promised to see that she was well provided for in his will. Then he died unexpectedly, and it transpired that he had left everything to his wife. But his wife was away from home at the time, and the girl knew that he kept several thousand pounds' worth of bearer bonds in his safe; so she took his keys, got into his house at night and stole them. All sorts of adventures were to follow and eventually the girl was caught; but, at the last moment, it was found that her late lover's solicitor, who was the wife's brother, had deliberately suppressed a last will, in which the bearer bonds had been left to the girl.

It was on the third morning of her stay at The Fisherman's Paradise that she returned from a long walk, during which she had been thinking out the details of the second chapter of her romance, and found two men waiting for her in the warm little lounge. The taller produced a pasteboard from his waistcoat pocket, showed it to her and said:

'Mary Watson, alias Lucille Harrison, alias Linda Chatterton, alias Linda Lee, we want a word with you.'

13

Ordeal

LINDA stood rooted to the spot. The muscles of her throat tightened, her tongue clove to the roof of her mouth, her big eyes were wide with apprehension and her hands began to tremble.

The man jerked his head in the direction of the manager's office. 'Mr. Philson has placed his room at our disposal. We'd best go in there to say what has to be said.'

Still tongue-tied, Linda turned and led the way into the room. They followed and the shorter, younger man, who had a face like a friendly bulldog, closed the door behind them. His senior spoke again:

'You'll not deny that you are Linda Lee?'

From the string of aliases he had rattled off in the hall it was obvious to Linda that they knew all about her, so she shook her head. Then she found her voice and asked, 'How . . . how did you manage to trace me?'

The tall man shrugged. 'With an organisation like Interpol it wasn't difficult. In London you gave a cheque on your bank to Canadian Air Lines. Scotland Yard asked us to keep a look-out for you in this country and sent a list of the jewels you had stolen. The man your brother tried to flog the emerald ring to reported it; then your brother put us on to Mr. Orson. Incidentally, we have pulled your brother in for being in possession of stolen goods. We saw Mr. Orson at the Ritz-Carlton and he wasn't any too helpful. But when it was pointed out to him that unless he talked he was liable to get involved in a nasty scandal, he told us that he'd picked you up in Vancouver and that you had then been staying at the Hotel Astley. The woman there said you had sent her a cheque on the Bank of Montreal in that city. From them we learned that you'd lodged the jewels in their safe deposit. Seeing that you would have to have funds, it seemed a good bet that you had headed back there. We checked with the railway people and learned that a woman answering to your description had taken a ticket to Vancouver but got off the train at Banff. The rest was easy. And now we are taking you into custody, pending the arrival of an extradition warrant from England.'

Linda gave an apology for a smile. 'I see. Well, I suppose it was too much to hope that I could get away for good. I left nearly all my things in Montreal, so I've got only an overnight case here. It won't take me long to pack.'

The young, bulldog-faced detective gave her an admiring glance, grinned and said, 'Take your time, Miss. We'll catch a drink in the bar.'

As Linda walked down the passage to her room at the back of the hotel, her thoughts were chaotic. She had reached the end of the road. For a week or so she would probably be held in Canada, then be flown back to England with a policewoman who had been sent to fetch her. In London she would have to suffer the disgrace and misery of a trial. She had no defence. Not a leg to stand on. Not a friend to turn to. It would come out that she had been Rowley's mistress and, as he had been so much older than herself, she could expect little sympathy from the jury—particularly from any women who were on it. They would regard her as a gold-digging whore who had sold her young body for a lazy life of ease and plenty, then unscrupulously robbed her benefactor's legitimate heir.

By the time she had shut the door of her room and was packing her small case, she was feeling intensely angry with herself. What a fool she had been to imagine that she could escape for more than a few months from the long arm of the law. To have stolen the jewels had been a weak and cowardly thing to do. She should have had the courage to face hardship for a while. All the odds were against it lasting for long. Even if she had failed to find out where Eric had gone, he would have sought her out when he learned of Rowley's death, rescued her from poverty and, most probably, married her. In the very worst event of fate preventing their coming together again, with her face and figure she need not have feared being condemned for long to a miserable, cheese-paring existence. Some other man would have come into her life whom she might not have loved but found very attractive, as she had Big Bear. Nothing would have induced her to become a professional prostitute; but she had already been the mistress of three men, none of whom she had found repulsive. Even with Rowley she had enjoyed the sexual act by shutting her eyes and thinking of Eric. And this had become such a fixation with her that she had done the same with Big Bear and could do it again if she let other likeable men make love to her. In time she would have found one whom she liked enough to marry.

But it was too late to think of that now. Calamity had come upon her so suddenly after that terrible night when Rowley had died that her mind had then been incapable of assessing her situation calmly. She had been overwhelmed with the thought of facing immediate poverty. Inspired by the idea that she might escape from it by stealing the jewels, she had given way to that stupid impulse. Now she must face the penalty.

As she automatically packed her few things in the case, the full horror of the future she must face was borne in upon her. She visualised herself in prison: the coarse garments, the colourless surroundings, the limited baths without scent and only skimpy towels on which to dry oneself, the enforced work upon dreary tasks, the grim washrooms and cell-like lavatories, the carpetless corridors, the hard beds and rough sheets, the unappetising food, not a cocktail or a glass of wine, the lack of privacy, for companions only women who were vicious and depraved, the terrible monotony for month after month, perhaps for years.

She could not bear it. She would rather die. As she stared out of the window, she saw that it was snowing again. But no matter. There lay freedom, or at least a chance of it. Next moment her mind was made up. The younger of the two plain-clothes men had said that she need not hurry, and barely five minutes had elapsed since she had left them. She would cheat them yet. Running to the door, she locked it. When their patience wore thin and they came for her, they would have to break it down. That would give her several minutes' extra start. Having just returned from a walk, she still had on her fur coat and was wearing the fur toque, a woollen muffler and wool-lined boots which she had bought in Montreal against the approaching winter. Grabbing her case, she crossed to the window and forced it open. A blast of cold air struck her in the face, causing her to catch her breath. With her free hand, she snatched her handbag from the nearby dressing table, then flung one long leg over the window-sill. The ground was less than five feet below it. One swift wriggle and she was sitting on the sill. Letting her case drop, she jumped after it, stumbled, fell to her knees, then hastily picked herself up. Again seizing her case, she set off at a run.

The snow was only about an inch deep, so did not impede her progress, and the fact that it was snowing increased her hope of getting away before they could catch her. The drifting flakes were large and she was soon powdered with them, so she hoped that in a quarter of an hour at most they would cover her tracks. Heedless of direction, she plunged in among the pine trees.

The ground sloped up, but not very steeply. She ran until she was breathless, and reached the top of the rise. The trees were so dense that, as she lurched down the far side of the slope, she could not see more than thirty or forty feet ahead of her. Another ten minutes and she came to the bottom of a valley. Along it ran a stream. For a moment she halted in consternation. It was too broad for her to jump, and she dared not turn back. She would have to wade across.

To have got her wool-lined boots wet would have been fatal, for in that low temperature they would have frozen on her feet. Sitting down, she took them and her stockings off and tied them round her neck. By then she had got her breath back and nerved herself to make the crossing.

Fortunately the stream was only a few inches deep and about ten feet wide, but the water was icy. When she was half-way over, a memory came back to her

from a book she had once read. In it an escaper had
waded some distance down just such a stream to cause
the bloodhounds used by his pursuers to lose the scent
of his track. She had been counting on the falling snow
to cover her footprints, but in so short a time it might
not. Turning, she waded down the stream.

The water was well above her ankles. The pain in her
feet became excruciating and an awful chill ran up
from them all through her body; but she staggered on
until she could bear it not a moment longer. Then,
sobbing with agony, she crawled up the opposite
bank.

For a few minutes she sat there, weeping almost
hysterically, then she pulled herself together, dried her
aching feet on her woollen muffler and put on her
stockings and boots. She had managed to cling on to her
case, but that had left her only the hand from the wrist
of which hung her bag to hold up her coat, so splashes
had made its skirt sodden. As best she could, she wrung
it out, while stamping her feet to restore their circulation. When she set off again, up another slope, she felt
that the stream had been a blessing in disguise, as she
was now confident that she had thrown off the men
who must by this time be coming after her.

At a steady walk she trudged up the slope through
the same monotonous forest of Canadian pines. They
averaged only about twenty feet in height, and she
recalled Big Bear's having told her that they never
grew much taller, owing to the poverty of the soil. Often
they were so close together that she could not walk
through them in a straight line and had to make small
detours. Enough snow had not yet fallen to load the
branches down, but sufficient to powder them with
white crystals, making them a lovely sight, particularly

when she came into a small clearing from which there was a vista, as by then it had stopped snowing.

After a while she came to a large lake, so had to decide whether to turn left or right along the bank. So far, her mind had been so fully occupied with escaping and watching her step so that she should not trip on protruding roots or small boulders hidden under the thin crust of snow, that she had given no thought to the direction in which she was heading. Now from the position of the sun she judged that she had been going roughly north. To turn left would carry her deeper into the Rockies and so further from even scattered habitations. For her to find shelter was imperative, so she turned right and, where the edge of the lake curved away, she came upon a track which led through a valley to the east.

She followed the track for the better part of an hour until she came to a bridge across a deep ravine, at the bottom of which ran a narrow, rushing river. The bridge was partially broken and some of the remaining tree-trunks still spanning the chasm looked rotten; so she did not dare attempt to cross it.

Turning aside, she walked along the cliff until at last she came to a place where it was low enough for her to get down to a narrow strip of beach. The river was still foaming over partly-concealed rocks, and she could not judge its depth, but it was not much more than five feet across. For several minutes she hesitated. So far she had not encountered a single person or come upon any building, and she felt that only by continuing to move eastward was there any chance of her doing so. Summoning all her resolution, she threw her case over, bent her knees, then sprang forward and landed sprawling, but softly, beside her case on the opposite bank.

Her next intent was to get back to the track, but in attempting to do so she made a grave error. Instead of again following the course of the river, since it had made a considerable bend she took what she thought would be a short cut. It brought her to another, smaller lake and, by the time she had made her way round it, she had lost her sense of direction. On and on she trudged through the silent, snow-bound forest, up a steep slope and down the far side; but there was still no sign of the track or any human habitation.

Linda was strong and healthy, her small case contained nothing heavy so did not prove a burden, and the going was not difficult. Spurred on by determination to escape, she had covered many miles since leaving the hotel, with only a few, brief halts. But now the sun had gone behind a mountain and dusk was falling, so even her courage was beginning to fail her.

It started to snow again, softly but persistently, drifting down to sprinkle her toque, shoulders and coat. It chilled her cheeks and now and then she had to brush it from her long eyelashes. Dusk merged into darkness overhead, but the snow-covered ground enabled her to continue to see her way between the slender tree-trunks.

So far the denseness of the forest had protected her from any wind there was. But soon the drifting snow began to fall faster and at a sharper angle. The wind got up and made a weird whistling. It came in fierce gusts, whirling the snow about, driving it from the branches of the trees and bending their slender tops under its pressure. Visibility ahead was reduced to a few yards and, in near despair, she realised that she had been caught in a blizzard.

Still she pressed on, but she was now tired. Before

making her break for freedom she had already walked several miles that morning. The calves of her long legs were aching and the little case seemed to have become much heavier. She had missed her lunch, so was hungry. Visions of a roaring log fire and big bowls of hot soup began to haunt her. The undulating slopes of pines seemed never-ending. Several times, as the only alternative to proceeding up steep gradients which she feared led up to mountains, she had had to change her direction. She recalled hearing it said that people lost in the Australian bush sometimes walked round and round in circles.

At last, overcome with fatigue, she tripped and fell. The carpet of snow was thicker now, so she did not hurt herself. But, as she struggled to her feet, she brought herself to face the awful fact that she could go no further and was utterly lost in this vast wilderness of snow-decked trees.

Gazing desperately round the limited distance she could see, she realised that no one spot was better than another in which to pass the night—that was if she could live through it. Many travellers who had lost their way and had to sleep in the snow had, she knew, never woken up again.

Sitting down with her back to the tree nearest where she had fallen, she undid her case. Now at last she could bless the Canadian liquor laws. In order to be able to have a drink in her bedroom when she felt like one, she had bought a pint flagon of rum, with which to spike Coca-Colas. While hurriedly packing she had thrust it into her case, together with part of a slab of chocolate and the remains of a packet of biscuits.

The flask was three parts full. Avidly she took a long pull at the contents. The neat spirit made her gasp, but sent a lovely glow through her chilled body. She was terribly tempted to eat all the chocolate and biscuits, but forced herself to put by half of them against the morning. After another drink from the flask she made her preparations for the night, using every item in the case which might help to keep her from freezing.

Opening her coat and taking off her skirt, she drew on her spare pair of knickers. By the time she got her skirt on again, her teeth were chattering and tears seeping from her eyes. One pair of stockings she wrapped round her neck and another pair round her calves. Her silk nightdress she wound round her face, then turned up the collar of her fur. Using the soft-topped case for a pillow, she clasped her gloved hands round her body under her coat, turned on her side and settled down.

The soft cushion of snow on which she lay saved her from the hard, frozen ground, so she was not uncomfortable. Dreamily, scenes from her past drifted through her mind: the sunshine of Nice on the Promenade des Anglais; a wonderful dinner which she had had with Rowley at the Tour d'Argent in Paris; his first heart attack in the swimming pool at Venice; that awful wait she had had on the railway station when she had run away from home, fearing every moment that Pa would catch her; that fantastic night at the Empress on Victoria Island when Big Bear had shown her how a strong man could really satisfy a woman; and Eric, dear Eric. If only he had not proved so honourable when she had tempted him. At least for once in her life she would have known perfect happiness.

The blizzard had ceased. The wind no longer howled through the trees. The gently-falling snow had covered her, so that anyone passing by would now have seen her as only a mound in the carpet of whiteness. She made no attempt to throw the snow off. She felt warm, comfortable and not unhappy. At length she drifted off to sleep.

During the day her fears had spurred her on to exertions that would have tried even a strong man, so when she did drop off it was into the deep sleep of exhaustion, and she did not wake until full daylight had come. It was not snowing and above the glistening white tree tops the sky was a cloudless blue.

She did not feel cold, but was conscious of a pleasant numbness in her legs and arms. It made her reluctant to move, and for several minutes she was tempted to doze off again. But suddenly the realisation that she was lying under a pall of snow rang an alarm bell in her brain. It must be such mental apathy which led to people who slept in the snow never rousing properly, and dying where they lay.

Hurriedly she sat up, shook her shoulders and kicked until she had cast off the white shroud that encased her. Opening her case, she took out the flagon of rum and gulped down several mouthfuls. The strong spirit swiftly brought feeling back to her throat, chest and stomach, but her limbs remained heavy and there seemed no response when she flexed her toes. Seized by panic that her feet might have become frozen, she grasped the nearby tree-trunk and pulled herself up by it. As she let go, she staggered, but managed to recover her balance; then for some minutes stamped about and flailed her arms until pins and needles in her feet told her that the circulation was restored.

Sitting down again she hungrily demolished what remained of the chocolate and biscuits, took another swig of rum and repacked in the case the extra garments she had used through the night to help protect her from the cold, but keeping on her spare pair of briefs.

As she rewound her wrist watch, she saw that it was a little after nine o'clock. Fearfully she wondered what the day would bring. It was over twenty-four hours since she had had a proper meal, and then only an egg, toast and marmalade for her breakfast, so she felt half famished and badly needed hot food to keep up her strength. If she failed to get it within the next few hours she might feel unable to go any further, and another night in this accursed forest would prove the end of her. She could only pray that another blizzard would not blow up and impede her progress. The sun again gave her roughly the direction of the east. Resolved to make the best of the going while it was good, she picked up her case and set off.

Her long sleep had restored her normal buoyant energy. For two hours, with only three short rests, she kept up a steady pace. Striking another river which was too broad to cross, she followed its course until it flowed into a large lake. On the far side there was an opening in the trees with, beyond it, another tree-covered slope. As she halted for a moment on the shore of the lake, to her unbounded joy she saw a car driven at high speed pass across the further shore. It instantly told her that there must be a road between the lake and the distant slope.

Exultantly, her hunger and the police momentarily forgotten, she clapped her gloved hands and laughed aloud. Another quarter of an hour, striding over the crisp crust of snow round the lake shore, and she reached the road. It was broad and macadamed, so must be a main highway. Impatiently she waited at the side until a vehicle came along that would give her a lift. But

twenty minutes elapsed before one came in sight. It was
a six-ton lorry. She waved, and the driver brought it to
a halt within a few yards of her.

As he leaned from his cab, his face showed astonish-
ment as he took in her mink coat and toque, her lovely
face, fine, tall figure and the obvious fact that she was
a lady; then he grinned, showing an ugly gap in his
front teeth, and asked, 'Want a lift, Missy?'

She smiled. 'Please. I got lost in the forest. If you
could drop me off at the first town you get to, I'd be
grateful.'

His grin broadened, 'For nowt, or you goin' ter pay
me?'

'Oh, I'm quite willing to pay,' she replied promptly.

'Give us yer bag an' hop in then.'

Two minutes later she was sitting beside him in the
cab, and the lorry was on the move again. He was
wearing a bearskin cap, from under the rim of which
protruded a ragged fringe of yellow hair. His face was
lean, with a big, flattish nose and a long, unshaven
chin. She judged him to be about forty. After a few
minutes he asked:

'How come you got yourself lost?'

While waiting at the roadside she had got a story
ready. 'I came up here with a friend who has a chalet
for fishing. We had a violent quarrel and this morning
I walked out on him.'

She had decided against saying that it was a husband
she had walked out on, as this would hardly have
sounded plausible. However violent their quarrel, it
was unlikely that a wife would have left a husband to
go off into the forest. She would have waited until they
had got back to their home, and she could leave with
all her things.

The driver considered that for a while, then said, 'Surprisin' that a feller shouldn't have treated a pretty girl like you decent. Guess yer must 'ave played 'im up mighty bad fer 'im ter let yer go off on yer own in this sorta country, with snow on the ground an' all.'

She shrugged. 'I was a fool to let him bring me up here, but he told me there would be other people staying. There weren't, and I wasn't standing for the sort of thing that happened last night. That's why I left. He wouldn't have let me if he'd known I meant to. I cleared out this morning early, while he was still asleep. I had to go without breakfast, so I'm terribly hungry. Have you got anything to eat?'

'Yes, plenty. But yer'll have to wait a while till we can find a place where I can light a fire. Got to heat the vittles up.'

For eight or ten miles they drove on in silence, only occasionally passing or being passed by other vehicles. Then he spotted a broken-down shack not far from the road, beside a small lake, and pulled the lorry up on the snow-covered grass at the edge of the forest.

From under the driver's seat he got out a rusty tin box and, with her walking beside him, carried it to the abandoned shack. About a third of the roof had fallen in, but the earth floor in the larger part was free of snow and at the far end there was a fireplace.

She now saw that he was a tall, powerful man with gangling limbs. Opening the box he took from it a frying pan, a saucepan and several packages of food. With the dexterity of long practice, he smashed up some pieces of wood that had fallen from the roof, pushed two paraffin firelighters under them and soon had a good fire going. Having crammed the saucepan

full of snow, he put it on the fire to melt, then asked:
'What's yer choice: cod or tripe?'

When she said she preferred fish, he unwrapped a
large cod steak, then took from other packages onions,
potatoes and a loaf of bread. As he put the fish and
vegetables in the saucepan, he said, 'I don't go fer char,
but I can do yer a beer.'

'Thanks, I'd like one,' she replied. She did not much
care for beer—the only form of it she had drunk for
years had been Black Velvet—stout mixed with champagne—but at that moment any drink was welcome,
and she was so famished that she could hardly keep her
eyes off the bubbling pot.

He opened two cans and they settled themselves on
rotting logs in front of the fire. Now that he no longer
had to keep his mind on driving he became more talkative, and in answer to his questions she made up a story
about herself. Having already indicated that she was
not married, it would hardly have been plausible to
account for her expensive clothes by telling him that she
lived at home, as it was unlikely that rich parents would
have allowed their daughter to go off to the Rockies
alone with a man; so she said she was an actress and
had just finished a tour with a company in Vancouver.

When the meal was cooked, she opened the tin box
expecting to find plates, but there were none, and only
a single knife, fork and spoon. Picking up the frying pan,
he poured some of the hot water from the saucepan
into it, then spooned out half the fish and vegetables and
set it down in front of her, remarking: 'Yer can 'ave
the cutlery. I use 'em only fer cutting up meat an' such.
Fingers is good enough fer me.' And the moment the
water had cooled sufficiently he began to cram chunks
of the food into his ugly mouth. Hunger drove her to

eat her share of the mess almost as quickly as he did. Even the unpeeled potatoes tasted good, and she followed his example in mopping up the fishy, onion-flavoured water with chunks of bread.

When they had finished, he gave a loud belch, sat back, regarded her critically for a few moments, then said: 'Now, what about the payment wot yer promised me?'

Opening her bag, she took out a small roll of dollar bills, smiled and asked, 'How much are you going to charge me for the ride?'

His small, greenish, heavily-lidded eyes ran over her from her now tousled, light bronze, curly hair, good bust and hips under the fur coat that she had tightly round her, down to the shapely legs that protruded beneath it. Then they came back to her face: the big eyes with their long lashes, fine straight nose and wide, beautifully-shaped mouth. Displaying the ugly gap in his front teeth, he gave a great guffaw and cried:

'Be yer age, girl! It ain't dollars I want. Yer old enough ter know that. Yer got other goods yer goin' ter pay me with.'

14

The Price of a Lift

LINDA's eyes widened in sudden fear. For a moment she could hardly credit that she had heard aright. Back in that now misty past, when she had sweated in her father's market garden, she had heard it said by her older school friends that their still older sisters thumbed lifts and paid for them with kisses; or, if they liked the man and by habit had already become permissive, let him go the whole way in some secluded spot.

But that this unwashed human animal should have thought for one moment that she would submit to his caresses seemed to her almost unbelievable. Revolted as she was at the very idea, and not a little scared by the knowledge that probably no other human beings were within miles of them, she managed to keep her voice level, as she said:

'If you mean what I think you mean, I'm afraid you're going to be disappointed. I'm not that sort of a girl.'

'Come orf it!' he retorted with a frown. 'Maybe I ain't the class of gent yer used ter going with. But I'm as good a stallion as they come. Plenty of girls 'ave tol' me that. It's the one thing women really care about in a man. An' don't give me no gup about yer 'avin' yer monthlies.'

'I tell you I'm not the sort of girl you think,' Linda retorted with disgust.

'Yer kiddin'. You're an actress, ain't yer? All them girls in shows is tarts, or good as. Leastways they 'as to up with their 'eels any time the manager feels like 'avin' a bit, else they'd lose their jobs. My young sister is in cabaret an' she tol' me so.'

'That may be true about girls in night spots, but it's not about girls on the stage. Not now, anyway. These days even in musical comedy most of the chorus girls come from respectable families, and would never allow themselves to be blackmailed into sleeping with men they didn't like.'

'Oh, I ain't sayin' you wasn't brought up respectable. Anyone could see you got class. But that don't mean nothin'. 'Ow about the gent yer was shackin' up with till lars' night? You says yer walked out on 'im. It don't stand to reason any woman the likes of you would set off ter 'itch-'ike through the forest with it under snow. It's my guess that yer gent's old woman turned up unexpected an' threw yer out on yer arse.'

Linda had gone very pale, and her heart was hammering rapidly. With a steady stare her big brown eyes were fixed on those of her companion. Every moment she found his thatch of yellow hair, loose, gap-toothed mouth and long chin covered with stubbly bristles more repulsive. Only one car had passed along the road while they had been eating. Even if another came along within the next few minutes, the odds were all against its occupants hearing her shout for help. The memory of the night she had been raped by the young schoolmaster came back to her. This would be far worse. If she continued to refuse him, she felt certain that he would force her. Yet nothing—nothing—would induce her to submit.

Could she possibly escape? If she could evade the clutch he would make at her, there was a good chance of her getting through the door. But he would be after her in a flash. Strong and long-legged as she was, his legs were longer. He would catch her before she had covered a dozen yards, and haul her back.

Taking her silence for indecision, he suddenly grinned and said, 'I know what's bitin' yer. You're pernickety, that's what. Dames like you are used ter feather beds. Don't like the idea of yer bum on this 'ere earth floor. Well, maybe you'll find it a bit 'ard with me on top of yer. But you'll soon ferget abart that. 'Sight better than a springy mattress fer the game we're goin' ter play. Soon as I've 'ad yer you'll be askin' fer more.'

'Perhaps you are right,' she said quietly. 'But first I'd like another beer.'

He grinned again. 'That's better, kiddo. Glad yer've got sense enough ter take it willin'. The big one I've got 'ull make you 'it the roof. Pity it's so cold. I'd like ter have 'ad yer naked. That figure you got gave me 'ot pants the moment I saw yer. But we'll 'ave ter make do with yer jus' takin' orf yer drawers.'

As he was speaking he turned round to get another can of beer from the tin box behind him. Jumping to her feet, Linda sprang past him and dashed out of the door. Yelling an oath, he swung round, dropped the can and bounded after her. With every ounce of speed she could muster, she raced through the trees toward the road. Half crazy with fear she heard him pounding in pursuit. In little more than a minute he grabbed her by the arm and swung her round. His small green eyes were blazing with anger and he snarled:

'So yer'd bilk me, would yer? You bloody stuck-up bitch. I'll larn yer fer tryin' ter trick me. Just see if I don't. You got it comin' ter yer, an' no mistake. Said I'd like to 'ave yer naked, didn't I? Well, so I will. Strip yer of every rag an 'ave yer do a dance fer me, till yer teeth chatters in yer 'ead.'

As they glared at each other, the icy air turned their breath to steam and, although she had eaten onions herself, they were evidently his regular diet, for he stank of them. Pulling back her head, she gasped, 'Let me go! Let me go, you brute!' But, with a spate of curses, he began to pull her back to the shack.

She cursed, screamed and pleaded, all in vain. Linda was strong for a woman, but he was much stronger. Finding resistance useless, she fell to her knees in an attempt to check him. He gave a harsh laugh and, seizing one of her wrists in a huge, knobbly hand, dragged her behind him through the snow. She strove to bite the hand that held her, but could not reach it.

Once inside the shack, he let go. As she staggered to her feet, he slapped her hard across the face and said with a leer, 'Now fer it. I'll 'ave yer first while you're good an' warm, then we'll 'ave them fine togs off an' yer'll do a jig fer me. Lie dahn on the floor an' get yer drawers orf.'

Hysterically she screamed at him, 'I won't! I won't! I'll kill you first.'

With an ugly laugh, he grasped her shoulders, kicked her legs from under her and threw her on the floor. Next moment he was on top of her.

For a moment the impact of his heavy body drove the breath out of her. As she lay supine, his face came down on hers. The bristles on his chin rasped her skin. He glued his mouth to hers, licking at it avidly. She grabbed a handful of his coarse yellow hair and forced his head away. He shook it free, buried his face in her neck, sucked it then bit her. As she screamed he jerked his head around and his wet lips slobbered over her mouth again. The stench of the sweat on his unwashed body was so repulsive that her stomach heaved. Frantically she clawed with her fingers at his face. He seized her hands, forced them together to one side of her head, then imprisoned them both in his left hand. She strove desperately to free them, but his grip on two of her fingers and one thumb was too strong. Lowering his free right hand, he thrust it up under her skirt and grabbed a fistful of her knickers, trying to pull them down. Moaning, she squirmed under him. With a sudden wrench he tore part of the silk away, but she was still wearing the extra pair she had put on before going to sleep in the snow. When his hand came up against them, he cursed again, clutched the second pair and tore them open.

With all her remaining strength she pressed her thighs together, and his fumbling hand could make no further progress. Withdrawing it, he knelt up and hit her hard in the stomach with his fist. Winded once more, she gasped and lay still. His hand went under her skirt again, and this time he reached his target. Roughly, he jabbed his fingers at it. Having explored her for a few moments, he drew his hand away, grunted with satisfaction and began to fumble with the buttons of his breeches.

She was still lying limp, with her eyes closed, getting back her breath. As he was having difficulty in undoing the buttons with one hand, and thought she had either fainted or ceased to resist, he released her hands. Her head was turned sideways, and she opened her eyes.

They were lying within two feet of the still glowing fire. Her glance lit on a half-burned piece of wood protruding from the embers. Next moment she had seized it and, as he knelt over her, thrust the burning end into his face. She got him in the left eye. With a scream of agony, he fell back off her.

Kicking her legs free, she got to her feet. He was crouched on the floor, moaning. Snatching up her bag, she shot out of the door as swiftly as though she had been thrown out, stumbled, fell, picked herself up and ran toward the road. Her struggles during the past terrible ten minutes had taken a lot out of her, but fear lent her wings. Fear of death, for she knew that it was no longer only a question of being brutally raped; if he caught her he would kill her.

The type of man he had shown himself to be would not hesitate to choke her to death once he had satisfied his lust on her. What had he to fear? Nothing. She had told him that she was running away from a man with whom she had come to the Rockies, and had lost her way. She might easily have failed to find the road, wandered about in the forest until nightfall, and died sleeping in the snow. It was a miracle she had not died that way the previous night. He had only to carry her body a few hundred yards further in among the trees, put it in a ditch and pile snow over it. No-one had seen them together, so he stood no risk of being connected with her death. The snow would not melt until spring, so her body would not be found until then even if, in this wild country, it ever was.

When she was half-way to the road she threw a swift glance over her shoulder. He had come out of the shack and was after her. Sheer terror gripped her heart. She raced on, now sobbing for breath, the skirt of her coat flapping round her long legs. No moving vehicle was within sight or sound. There was nowhere she could hide. He would run her down, stun her if need be, and carry her back to as awful a death as she could imagine.

She looked back again. He had one hand over his injured eye, but was coming on through the trees at a stumbling run, moving nearly as fast as she was. For her to keep up her present pace she knew to be impossible. But he might. With such powerful limbs he would. He would run her down, batter her face with his great, knobbly fists and drag or carry her, bleeding, back to a vile and agonising end.

As she reached his lorry, she looked first one way then the other, praying desperately that help would reach her in time. But for half a mile or more on either side the road was empty. Suddenly his voice came, shouting obscenities and, as she had feared, that he meant to kill her. Then still worse:

'You bloody bitch! Yer done me eye in. I'll larn yer to play with fire! I'll shove a burnin' faggot up yer. Yes, up yer as far as it'll go.'

Terror gave her an inspiration. The lorry! Could she get away in it? She had driven Big Bear's car only a dozen times. With him beside her she had found it easy. But to handle a six-ton lorry? It was her only chance. Wrenching open the door of the cab, she hauled herself up, grabbed the wheel and stared helplessly for a moment at the dashboard.

He was only thirty paces off. She jabbed her thumb on the starter. Nothing happened. Again she pressed it, this time keeping her thumb hard down. The engine came to life. She knew she must let it run for a minute, otherwise it would stall. Still yelling at her, he put on a spurt. Almost fainting she forced herself to wait until he

H

was within six feet of the lorry, then she gently let in the clutch.

The lorry began to run forward. He bounded up to it and grabbed the still-open door of the cab. Wild-eyed, she stared at him. His closed left eye and cheek were smeared with ash, and flaming red. Just as he was about to pull himself up, she kicked him hard full in his ugly mouth. His eyes boggled, he lost his grip and rolled away into the ditch.

Next second she was seized with a new fear. The lorry had been parked at an angle. It was running across the road and about to be brought to a halt by a steep bank. Her heart lurched. If it did, he would get her yet. With all her strength she wrenched round the wheel. Missing the bank by inches, the lorry careered toward the other side of the road. Heaving again on the wheel, she was just in time to check it.

Another minute and she had it more or less under control. But the heavy lorry proved infinitely more difficult to handle than had Big Bear's car. All her efforts failed to keep it on the right side of the road. She was terrified that at any moment a vehicle might approach and she would collide head on with it. Yet she dared not stop and leave the lorry before she had put several miles between herself and that devilish man who had yelled that he meant to torture and murder her in such a fiendish manner.

Somehow she got the lorry round the first bend. That gave her more confidence. A long, straight stretch lay ahead, so she risked putting the engine into second, then top gear. On one side of the road there was a bank and the ground sloped steeply upward; on the other it descended to a valley, at times becoming a precipice.

A hundred yards before the next bend she meant to

slow down, but she had left it too late to brake hard without risking disaster. To her horror a station-wagon suddenly emerged from round the corner, coming straight at her. She missed it by inches, then had to wrench the wheel right over to prevent the lorry from hurtling down into the valley. It again charged toward the bank, but she slowed it just in time. Ahead there proved to be a succession of bends. They came so closely one after another that she dared not take a hand off the wheel, even for a moment. The next ten minutes proved a positive nightmare. The lorry swerved wildly from one side of the road to the other. At every curve she expected to meet another vehicle and be unable to prevent the lorry from crashing into it. Entering another straight stretch gave her a temporary respite. But it did not last for more than two minutes. Concentrating entirely on keeping the lorry on the road, she had not even glanced in the mirror. Now, an insistent hooting from behind brought home the fact that someone was trying to pass her. She pulled in, but too quickly, so had to pull out again. The driver of the car in her rear could not possibly have anticipated this dangerous zig-zag. As he shot past, she caught the sound of rending steel. The sides of the two vehicles had scraped harshly together. The impact threw the car out of direction. It shot toward the valley side of the road, crossed a ditch and, its speed checked by a steep bank on the far side, came to rest with the bonnet against a tree-trunk. In passing, Linda glimpsed enough to be sure that neither the driver nor the woman with him was seriously injured. She was sorry for them, but had far too many anxieties of her own even to think of them for more than a few minutes. She still had all her work cut out to prevent the lorry from running off the road.

When the vehicle was running along straight stretches, her mind reverted momentarily to the desperate situation in which the arrival of the police at The Fisherman's Paradise had placed her.

By suffering the most ghastly experiences during the past twenty-odd hours, she had so far managed to evade them; but how long could she continue to do so? She had no idea where she was, except that she could not be very many miles from The Fisherman's Paradise. The police in every town round about would have been warned to keep a look-out for her; so, at the very first place she entered, she might be hauled off to gaol.

While wandering in the forest the previous afternoon, she had thought a lot about possible ways of escaping capture, and had decided that her best plan would be to try to cross the border into the United States.

When she had been in Vancouver she had learned that it lay only a few miles north of the United States frontier, and that the big town of Seattle could be reached by ferry from Victoria Island. While she was there, she had had no reason at all to wish to leave Canada. Recent events had altered the whole picture. The principal difficulty of carrying out the plan was that from Montreal she had come only to the eastern side of the Rockies. Even so, she felt that the frontier running through them was so long that no place on it could be frequently patrolled by the Mounties and American frontier guards; so, by working her way from valley to valley, she should be able to cross it. But she had not then realised how desolate the country was, and how slender her chance of securing food and shelter during a tramp that must take several days. Now, after she had spent many hours in the forest, nothing would have induced her to enter it again.

A mile or so further on from the scene of the accident,
a single-line railway track emerged from a tunnel on
the side of the road away from the valley. Only a few
minutes before, a train had come out of the tunnel.
Linda could see it snaking away round a curve lower
down in the distance. From experience she knew how
slowly the trains meandered along through the Rockies.
Suddenly it occurred to her that, if she could catch up
with, then pass it, she might be able to board it at
the next stop, and so get clear away from this district
where it was certain that the police were hunting for
her.

She had just topped a rise and was about to run down
a long, straight slope. Daringly she put her foot on the
accelerator. The lorry increased speed to sixty miles an
hour. Half-way down the hill she became frightened
and fought desperately to check its headlong rush. The
weight behind her was so great that at such a speed the
brakes had little effect. A screen of trees on the corner
ahead loomed up with terrifying rapidity. She could not
have escaped running into them had she not had the
presence of mind to throw the engine into second gear.
Just in time she wrenched round the wheel. The lorry
tilted at an angle, then righted itself. She was safely
round the bend and her spurt had brought her to
within a hundred yards of the last wagon of the train.

Sweat was streaming down her face, but she felt that
she could do it now. Five minutes later she was level
with the engine. Another car came rushing toward her.
By a nerve-racking swerve she managed to avoid it.
Subconsciously she noticed that she was passing a few
scattered clapboard houses. Quite suddenly the lorry
entered a wide space, on the left-hand side of which
was a small railway station.

To her horror she recognised it at once. It was the whistle-stop halt for Château Lake Louise, where she could have got off on her journey from Montreal, instead of at Banff, which was thirty miles further east along the line. During the past few days she had several times walked down to the little station, in order to buy biscuits and sweets at the small general shop only a hundred yards or so away from it.

Dare she pull up and take a ticket there? Knowing that she could not get far on foot, it was very likely that the police would think it probable that she would make for it, and have a man in the little booking office waiting for her. Yet what was the alternative? In the past twenty minutes she had narrowly escaped death or serious injury half a dozen times. If she drove on, it was as good as certain that before she was an hour older she would either have a crash or go over a precipice. Even if she survived the hour, by then the hateful lorry-driver would have got a lift to a place with a telephone, reported the theft of his vehicle and given its number, so the police would be on the look-out for it.

The train was slowly clanking into the station. The sight of it decided her to risk arrest now sooner than later. In his vile fumbling to get his hand between her thighs, her attacker had not come upon the flat silk wallet suspended a little higher up round her waist. Thanking her gods for that, she brought the lorry to a halt a little way beyond the station, then fished out from the wallet a twenty-dollar bill, grabbed her night case and jumped down from the cab.

Before entering the booking office she gave a fearful peep inside. It was deserted, and no-one was about. Slipping through the doorway, she took off her toque. Her hair was already in shocking disarray. Now she pulled it right down, shook it out over her shoulders and replaced the toque low down, so that it almost hid her eyes. Stepping over to the *guichet,* she thrust the bill in and, without looking at the man behind it, asked for a second-class return ticket to Calgary. Scooping it up with her change she ran out on to the platform. A number of hampers and boxes were still being loaded on to the train. Clambering up into it she found that there were very few passengers, so she was able to get a carriage to herself. Huddled in the corner furthest from the station building, she waited impatiently for the train to move out. At last it did. Heaving a sigh of relief, she relaxed.

She had taken a return ticket to Calgary, with the idea that when the police learned that a young woman had got on the train at Banff, they should not associate her with their quarry, as anyone seeking to escape from the district would not be thinking of returning to it. When the conductor came along, she asked how long the train would stop at Calgary and, as she had intended to travel much further east, learned to her annoyance that, being a local, Calgary was the terminus.

Exhausted by her twenty-four hours of fear, strain, terror and spent energy, she soon fell asleep, and so soundly that when the train reached Calgary she had to be wakened by an attendant. From the long, bleak, naked platform she went down to the underground booking hall and enquired about trains going eastward. The next was not due in for two and a half hours. For the greater part of the journey it remained one train. At Winnipeg a portion was detached that went to Quebec and at Sudbury Junction another portion went south to Toronto, while the greater part of the coaches went on to Ottawa and Montreal.

Linda had again become very hungry, so she went into the station restaurant and ordered a substantial meal. While she ate it she thought over her next step. Now that the Canadian police were in full cry after her, she felt again that her best hope of escaping capture was to cross into the United States. The border between the two countries ran for so many hundreds of miles that she felt it should not be too difficult to get across it undetected, and that, after all, the most promising place to make the attempt might be in a well-populated area where numbers of people were moving about; so she decided to go to Toronto.

Having taken her ticket she was careful to avoid coming face to face with the two policemen who, side by side, were patrolling the booking hall; then she quickly went up in the lift. Twenty minutes later she was installed in a second-class sleeper and happy to find that she had it to herself. Still very tired from her recent ordeals, she asked the attendant to make her berth up right away, and told him that she had some sandwiches with her so would not go along to the restaurant car for dinner.

After several hours' sleep she woke in a sweat from a ghastly nightmare, in which she had again been struggling with the lorry-driver. The memory kept her awake for a long time, but eventually she drifted off into another lengthy sleep.

Next day, at Winnipeg, a girl of about eighteen was put in with her. She was going to the University of Toronto to study electronics. It was the first time she had left her native city, and she was thrilled with the idea of seeing something of the world. After breakfasting that morning, Linda had tried to read a paperback which she had bought in Calgary, but found that

she could not concentrate, so she was glad to listen to
the girl's pleasant chatter, and to have her as a companion at meals in the restaurant car.

When the train at last reached Toronto the girl went
off to get her heavy luggage from the van. Linda had
none, so made straight for the exit from the platform.
As she did so she was alarmed to see two policemen
scanning the people descending from the train. Swiftly
she mingled with the little crowd round the entrance,
but kept an anxious eye on them. Just as she was about
to pass the ticket collector, one of the policemen turned,
caught sight of her, grabbed the other by the arm, and
pointed. Instantly she knew that from her description
she had been recognised.

15

Sir Colin Galahad

LINDA caught her breath, swallowed and felt her heart begin to hammer. All her striving, her fortitude, her endurance, had been in vain. She had been spotted and in another few moments would be arrested. Visions of prison—bad smells, indifferent food, awful monotony, evil companions—again coursed through her mind in a matter of seconds. During her long journey across Canada her mind had never been free from anxiety that she would be traced. She had hoped that the booking clerk at Banff had caught only a glimpse of her and that the police would not connect the lone woman who had taken a return ticket to Calgary with herself, but would believe that she had become lost and frozen to death in the snow. Now, the terrible ordeal she had gone through that night, and her still more awful encounter with the bestial lorry-driver, had been suffered for nothing. Had she surrendered to the police at Lake Louise, she could have saved herself from both.

But to surrender was not in Linda's nature. Without losing a second, even while these thoughts came and went like flashes of lightning through her brain, she was forcing her way through the crowd at the exit from the platform. She was big, strong and, in her near despair, ruthless. Seizing a fat woman in front of her by the arm, she pulled her back. Dropping her night case, with her other hand she pushed aside a well-grown boy. Only two men now stood between her and the exit. With a swift 'Excuse me,' she thrust her way between them, dashed aside the outstretched hand of the ticket collector and, next moment, was outside.

Wildly her eyes sought the quickest way to get out of the station yard. They fell upon a car at the edge of the pavement. It was a long, low, open, bright red sports car. At the wheel sat a well-dressed young man. The other seat was unoccupied. The engine was ticking over. As her gaze took it in, he put his foot on the accelerator, and the car began to move. Dashing forward she flung herself flat on the long boot, grasped the back of the empty seat and began to pull herself over.

Taken completely by surprise the young man turned his head, his mouth agape. 'What the . . .' he began.

'Drive on!' she gasped, cutting him short, her big eyes imploring. 'For God's sake save me! I'm in deadly peril!'

In one glance he had taken in her lovely face, the fact that she was wearing a mink hat and toque, though both were soiled and rumpled; then, as she scrambled over the back of the seat, her long and shapely legs.

Recovering, he reacted swiftly. The car shot forward. She threw a quick glance behind her. A score of people, forgetful of all else, now stood blocking the entrance to the station. Some were staring after the car in amazement, others were laughing, no doubt having assumed that they had witnessed a scene in a lovers' quarrel, in which a determined young woman had risked injury rather than allow herself to be abandoned by her boy friend. As the car swung round the corner, the two policemen had still not succeeded in forcing their way through the crowd on the far side of the barrier.

The young man turned to look at Linda. 'What a cheek,' he began; but his words were accompanied by a smile, and he went on, 'So I'm cast for the role of a Galahad, eh? Called on to rescue beauty in distress. Well, where do you want me to take you?'

She returned his smile, showing her perfect teeth. 'Anywhere; anywhere, that is, where I can lie low for a day or two.'

He considered for a moment. 'The only place I can suggest is my apartment. But, I warn you, I live alone.'

'There's no fate worse than death,' she countered with a little laugh. 'But I should warn you that I'm not prepared to pay for my lodging. So if, after you know me better, you no longer feel inclined to play Galahad, you can always throw me to the wolves.'

'You've got me there,' he replied with a rueful grin. '*Noblesse oblige* and all that, eh? O.K. I'll take you to my apartment.'

For some twenty minutes they ran through the streets of the city, with their lofty buildings and fine shops, then out into the suburbs. During the drive they had spoken little, both being busy with their own thoughts. When he asked where she had come from, knowing that he could not know at which platform she had arrived she told him Montreal; because, having lived there for a fortnight, if they later talked of that city he would not be able to fault her. She then gave her name as Camilla Grey.

He said his was Colin Granard and they laughed about having the same initials. She was enjoying the view of the waterfront on Lake Ontario when he pulled up before a tall block of luxury flats. As they got out, the porter touched his gold-braided cap and said cheerfully:

'Nice afternoon, Mr. Granard, but chilly. Looks as if we'll be having our first snow soon.'

With an aplomb that Linda greatly admired, Colin replied:

'You're right, Briggs. I don't think you've met my sister. She's had lousy luck today. Smashed herself up in her car and had to abandon all her luggage. Couldn't very well go to an hotel without it, so she's going to picnic here with me for a day or two.'

While in the train Linda had done her best to make herself presentable; but her coat was torn and the bruise still showed on her cheek, where the lorry-driver had hit her. Colin had most skilfully accounted for her dishevelled appearance, and his assertion that she was his sister was plausible, because it was hardly likely that he would have brought a girl who was not a relative, in such a state and without even a toothbrush, to sleep in his flat.

The porter looked his sympathy at Linda and said, 'Glad to meet you, Miss. Bad luck about your car, but if it was real smashed up, you're lucky to have got off with only a bruised face.'

They went up in the lift to the eighth floor and Colin ushered her into his flat. The main feature was a huge, well-furnished room, with one twenty-foot-long window giving a beautiful view over the lake. There was a comfortable bedroom, a gaily-tiled bathroom and a kitchenette at the back. As he showed her the bedroom, with its wide but single bed, he saw her dubious look and grinned at her:

'Don't worry; this will be yours while you're with me. I can quite well sleep on the sofa in the sitting-room. I often have before, when putting friends up for the night, and it's very comfortable.'

While smiling her thanks, she surveyed him more carefully than she had previously had a chance to do. He was slim and tall, but a little less than her six feet. His hair was only a shade lighter than hers, their faces had the same oval shape, and their noses were somewhat similar. After a moment she said:

'How clever of you to have spun that yarn to the porter. Our eyes and mouths are quite different, but our faces do have a certain likeness, so we could pass at a push for brother and sister.'

'That's partly because you are so tall, and have a man's firm features,' he commented. 'Now, what about a drink?'

'I'd love one,' she said as they returned to the big sitting-room. One end of it was a solid wall of books, except for a central cupboard dividing the three lowest shelves. Opening it he revealed a well-stocked bar and asked, 'What's it to be?'

'Rum on the rocks, please. I need warming up. Another thing I need is a bath. I never feel clean after a train journey until I've had one.'

'That's easy. There are other things you need, too, as you bolted from the station without waiting for your luggage.'

'I know. I haven't even a toothbrush or brush and comb, and only the clothes I stand up in.'

'Tell you what. If I go out right away I'll have plenty of time to make a good round of the stores before they close. While you're having your bath, I'll slip out and get some things for you.'

Linda gave him her sweetest smile. 'You're awfully kind. And, of course, I'll pay for them. Get me toilet things, a nightie, a dressing gown, a pair of nylons and a pair of slippers, in the largest sizes they stock, and a small case for me to take them away in. But nothing too expensive, please, because I haven't very much money with me.'

They finished their drinks and, having provided her with a clean bath towel, he hurried off. She was glad of the respite, for, as yet, she had had no opportunity to think up a suitable story about herself to tell this charming young man by whom she had had the good fortune to be rescued.

While undressing, and afterwards relaxing in the warm water, she thought hard about it, but for a time inspiration failed her. Being by nature honest, she felt that, in fairness to him, she must admit that she was wanted by the police, and so give him the opportunity to get rid of her before the police came to the flat and charged him with harbouring her, as they would do should anyone have chanced to take the number of his car. But she could not bring herself to confess that she was a thief. Then, after a quarter of an hour, an idea came to her. By the time she had dried and dressed herself, she had thought out the details.

The better part of two hours elapsed before Colin returned and he was carrying not only a handsome pig-skin case, but also a load of parcels. With happy eagerness to show her his purchases, he undid them. There were brushes, powder, lipstick, scent, a padded silk dressing gown with bedroom slippers to match, a black chiffon nightie trimmed with lace, handkerchiefs, and not one but half a dozen pairs of nylons.

Linda looked at them with delight but consternation and before he had unpacked half the things exclaimed, 'They are lovely! But I told you I hadn't much money with me. I can't possibly pay for all this.'

He laughed. 'You're not going to. I'll not take a cent. It isn't every day that adventure comes my way. And you are my guest, remember. I want to make your stay here something you'll look back on with pleasure.'

'That's very sweet of you,' she smiled. 'But that nightie alone must have cost a packet. Can you really afford to spoil me in this way?'

'Sure I can. My old man brews beer. Thousands of gallons of it, and he gives me a mighty fine allowance, on top of what I earn as a science graduate in his laboratory.'

As Colin spoke, he was undoing other parcels, containing a large lobster, a tin of foie gras, hot-house grapes, a carton of ice-cream, cocktail nuts and bottles of hock and champagne. When he had done, he said, 'I'd have liked to take you out; but if someone is after you, even for you to be seen down in the restaurant on the ground floor might be dangerous, so I thought we'd feed up here.'

'How right you were. And, anyway, I'd like it better. I'm hungry, too, so we can have an early dinner. I only wish I had a pretty frock to change into, to be worthy of the occasion.'

He glanced at the now sadly crumpled tweed coat and skirt she had been wearing ever since she had escaped from The Fisherman's Paradise. 'Forget it, please. If only I'd known a bit about the size you take and your taste, I'd have bought you something. But you look fine just as you are. You'd look lovely in anything.'

'You flatter as well as spoil me. But . . . well, how would it be if I wore that beautiful dressing gown you bought me?'

'That would be fine,' he grinned. 'I'll change into a

dressing gown, too. And why should we wait? Let's get going. I'll fetch my things from the bedroom, then it's all yours.'

Three-quarters of an hour later, Linda had done her face and hair, admired herself in her new finery in the mirror and made the toast for the foie gras, and they were seated opposite each other at a table in the sitting-room. They had already had two glasses of champagne apiece and, with young, healthy appetites, now did full justice to the feast Colin had provided. During the meal, with a tact that she greatly appreciated, he did not ask her a single question about herself, but told her gaily about his life in Toronto, and the fun he had had a few years earlier when his father had sent him for six months to Europe. He said that he was twenty-five, that his major fun was fishing from a motor launch he owned, skiing in the winter, and girls. As she looked across at his slightly wavy hair, merry brown eyes and strong face, she felt sure that he had no difficulty in finding plenty of pretty girls to fall for him.

At length, when they were replete, she insisted on clearing the table and washing up the dishes, while he dried them. Returning to the sitting-room, he produced a bottle of Benedictine and filled two glasses. When they had settled themselves comfortably on the big sofa, she said:

'Now I think it's quite time I told you my awful story and gave you a chance to throw me out. I'm wanted by the police.'

'That's bad,' he said with a sudden frown. 'I imagined you were just getting away from some chap who had been horrid to you.' Then, on a lighter note, he added, 'What have you done, robbed a bank or hijacked an aircraft?'

'No. But I may be sent to prison if they get me. I suppose you've never heard my name before?'

'I can't say I have.'

'That's not surprising, as I'm not yet very well known; but I'm a concert pianist. Incidentally, although I was brought up in England I've since become an American. But for the past year I've lived in Montreal. When I first went there from the States, I was given introductions to several members of the Musical Society at McGill; so naturally they became my social circle. Another bond with many of the students at the University who are French is that I am quite a polyglot. My grandmother was French.'

Colin gave her a sudden stare. 'Are you mixed up with the F.L.Q.?'

She nodded. 'That's it. As you are so obviously British, I suppose you're very anti?'

'By God, I am! But it's not a matter of my being of English descent. Canada is now a great nation in its own right, and I'm one hundred per cent Canadian. If those bloody fools had their way, they'd split the country into two nations, cause hopeless confusion in industry, finance, legal rights, education and Lord knows what else. It would bring ruin to thousands and eventually probably lead to civil war, with close relations fighting one another. If I'd had my way, I'd have shot that egomaniac, de Gaulle, for the speech he made a few years back, encouraging the French-Canadians to strive for Quebec Province to be given independence.'

Secretly Linda was in entire agreement. Before knowing Rowley, she had thought little about such matters, but he had been a diehard Imperialist, who never tired of proclaiming the greatness of the British Empire and the immense amount it had done to bring

health, education, prosperity, law and order to millions
of its subject peoples who had, since independence, died
by the tens of thousands as victims in civil wars or now
lived in police states. She recalled Rowley's indignation
when Horrible Harold—as he termed the then Prime
Minister of Britain—had met Mr. Ian Smith for a
conference in a cruiser and was reported to have
deliberately sought to humiliate the leading representative of the Rhodesian people by consigning him to a
third-rate cabin without even a telephone. But, greatly
as it went against the grain, she had now to maintain
the part she had decided to play; so, with a sigh, she
replied:

'You may be right, but people's views differ according to their circumstances. Most young people know
little about practical considerations, and are idealists.
They feel that every minority should be given independence and have the right to make its own laws. That
goes for Americans, too.'

Colin gave a sardonic laugh. 'Don't I know it! I have
a lot of American friends. They are the kindest and most
generous people one could meet. But about this thing
they are a bunch of unconscious hypocrites. In the
early stages of the last war they nearly bankrupted
Britain in exchange for arms to defend the world from
Nazi terrorism. Then they took advantage of her
indebtedness to bully her into prematurely surrendering
her Empire to people mostly unfitted to govern themselves. But what about America's own huge population
of Negroes, and the Red Indians from whom they stole
their country? Do you think they will ever give them
States of their own? Not on your life! And they'd be
damn' fools if they did.'

'I know. But while I lived in the States I imbibed a

lot of the ideas that they have inherited from their own revolution, and my natural sympathies are with the French. Surely you can understand how I came to see eye to eye with the powerful group of students at the University who would like to see Quebec Province independent?'

He shrugged. 'I suppose so. Anyhow, you became committed to the F.L.Q. What have you done? Why are the police after you?'

'The F.L.Q. have difficulty in printing their propaganda pamphlets in Canada, so they had a big quantity done in the States. Their problem was to get them across the frontier; so they asked me to import a piano, in which thousands of these pamphlets, printed on thin paper, could be concealed. As I am a concert pianist, there was no reason to suppose my sending for a grand piano from my own country would arouse suspicion, so I agreed.'

'But the Customs rumbled you after all, eh?'

'No. I cleared it all right and had it brought to my own apartment. It was the following night that things blew up. One of my group phoned to tell me that someone had squealed on us, and that it was not pamphlets that were concealed in the piano, but three machine guns.'

'My God! Then you were properly in the soup!'

'Yes. My friend told me to get out at once. I did, but only as the police were coming in at the front door. I hadn't time even to pack a night bag. But I got away through the garden. It was in getting over the wall that I tore my coat.'

'You poor little devil—though you're hardly little.' Colin's tone was more sympathetic. 'Then you're more of an idiot than a dangerous criminal. Those rotten

maniacs took advantage of you, then one of them sold
you out, regardless of the fact that he could have landed
you in prison, not just for a few weeks, but for years.'

'That's it.' Linda nodded. 'And none of them is
going to admit complicity by coming into court and
giving evidence in my defence, so no judge will believe
that I'm not guilty of knowingly importing weapons for
use by revolutionaries. Now I've told you everything,
I'll get into my clothes and go. You have been terribly
kind to me, so I'm not going to risk the police tracing
me here and involving you in my troubles.'

As she spoke, she meant what she said, and stood up.
But he caught one of her hands and pulled her down
again. 'Wait a minute. If anyone had taken the number
of my car and given it to the police, they would have
been here long before this. You'll be safe here for the
night, anyhow, and I wouldn't be able to look myself
in the face in the mirror tomorrow morning if I turned
a girl like you out into the streets with nowhere to
go.'

She hesitated, then smiled. 'You are out-Galahading
Galahad now. But I'll stay only on one condition. You
must promise me that if the police do catch me here,
you will swear that you had no idea I was wanted
by them—that I told you that I was running away from
a man I had been living with who had gone crackers and
had threatened to kill me if I wouldn't stay with him.'

Colin released her hand, finished his Benedictine and
said, 'O.K. That's a deal, and in the morning we'll talk
about what you'd best do when you leave here. You've
had a long and very tiring day, so now you'd better get
some shut-eye. While you go into the bathroom and
wash your teeth, I'll make up a bed for myself here on
the sofa.'

When, ten minutes later, she came out of the bathroom, he had made up a bed from clean sheets, some rugs and cushions. Smiling at her, he said, 'Anyone could see you are a very nice person, and I'm glad I helped you to get away. You have given me a very happy evening; one I shall long remember. Sleep well, and don't worry too much about tomorrow.'

Linda returned his smile. 'I've enjoyed every moment of it, and you've been very generous to me. I can be generous, too. I'm not really tired, so we needn't call it a day yet. That is, if when you've done your teeth you would like to join me in the bedroom.'

Colin's eyes lit up. 'Oh, bless you! What a wonderful surprise! And how sweet of you. You lovely darling. I must kiss you here and now, otherwise I'd know I was only dreaming.'

He did not prove another Big Bear, but he was a well-built young man and far from inexperienced. Linda, too, had learned a lot about making love since she had gone to Vancouver Island, so it proved a very happy night for both of them.

As was to be expected, they slept late. When they did rouse, he told her that he always cooked his own breakfast, so she found ample supplies in the kitchenette to knock up a meal for them both. Over his second cup of coffee, he said:

'Look, darling, we've got to make a plan. What had you in mind when you left the train yesterday?'

She made a grimace. 'I hadn't an idea, only that I meant to get back to the States if I possibly could. If I can, I don't think they'd go so far as to extradite me. But the trouble is that I had to leave my passport behind, and I dare not apply for another.'

After remaining silent for a while, he said, 'I think

I told you I own a motor launch. Given a bit of luck
and a dark night, I could run you across the lake.'

Her face brightened, then fell. 'That would be marvellous, but I don't think I ought to let you. If we were
caught you would be sent to prison, too.'

'I don't think so. Not if we stuck to the story we
agreed on last night. I wouldn't then be charged with
aiding a wanted criminal to escape, only with having
fallen for a pretty girl who had told me a cock-and-bull
story about trying to get home while running away
from a man she hated. After one look at you, I'd have
the sympathy of the jury, and be let off with a fine.'

'If you really think that, I'll accept your offer.'

'That's settled then. We've got to get through today,
though. I'd give a packet to spend it with you here, but
I'm afraid that would be running too great a risk. You
see, although no-one can have taken the number of my
car, there can't be many like it in Toronto, so by now
the police will be making enquiries of everyone who
owns a scarlet sports model. I ought to have thought of
that before. Anyhow, the sooner we get out of here, the
better.'

'I see. Yes, you're right. But where can we go?'

'Have you ever been to Niagara Falls?'

Linda shook her head.

'Then I'll drive you there. It's less than forty miles,
and the view from the Canadian side is much better
than that from the States. We won't go in my car,
though. Too risky. I'll hire one with my Hertz card.'

They dressed as quickly as they could, and Linda
packed her new possessions in the pigskin case, then they
went down in the lift. The porter was not in evidence,
so they slipped out by a back entrance. Ten minutes'
walk brought them to a garage where Colin was not

known. He produced the Hertz card he used in distant cities, or when abroad, and they were soon on their way south, by by-roads on the outskirts of the city, in order to avoid its well-policed centre.

As it was a pleasant autumn day, instead of heading direct for the Falls after passing through Oakville, Hamilton and St. Catherine's, he made a detour down to the frontier post on the outskirts of Buffalo, so that he could take her along the drive on the Canadian side of the broad river. Well back from the road, there was mile after mile of beautiful homes set in fine gardens, with swimming pools and ornamental trees. Opposite them, on the river bank, there were more lovely trees with here and there pleasant sites arranged for parties to picnic in the summer. Linda thought it one of the loveliest stretches of scenery she had ever seen and, as Colin drove along slowly, they did not arrive at Niagara until after half past one.

In front of the hotel and on both sides of it charming gardens had been laid out. They lunched there in a glassed-in terrace, off fresh trout and another bottle of the Canadian Sauternes, Domain St. Martin, that Linda had so much enjoyed in Vancouver. Before them lay the splendid prospect of the Falls, marred only by the centre being obscured by the great clouds of spray sent up by the millions of tons of water descending from the river over the sheer, horseshoe cliff.

As they were finishing lunch, Colin asked Linda what she meant to do if he succeeded that night in putting her ashore in the States. She told him that when she had come to Canada from Boston, her parents had returned to England; and, in case the Canadian authorities did trace and make trouble for her, she would not risk going to any friends she had made while in America.

So, for the time being, she must find a place for herself, and lie low there.

'You're right,' he nodded. 'But I was thinking of the immediate future. How about my telephoning the Hilton in Buffalo to keep a room for you, and say that you will be arriving tomorrow morning?'

'That's a good idea. I wish you would. But it had better be in another name. What shall it be?'

'Venus,' he suggested with a laugh.

'Hardly, although it's a charming compliment. Let's say . . . let's say, Mrs. Gene Wellard.'

While Colin telephoned, Linda went to the ladies' cloakroom. She had told the woman there that she had been in a car smash, and asked if, while they lunched, something could be done about her fur coat. Scenting a good tip, the attendant had sewn up the tear and removed from the mink most of the smears that Linda had been unable to get out with a brush during her train journey.

Late in the afternoon they drove slowly back to Hamilton. There, at a pleasant restaurant, they lingered over cocktails and dinner. A little after ten o'clock, they set off again. About half-way to Toronto, Colin turned off the highway down a lane that led to a wood. Linda had no reason to be apprehensive, so her voice was quite normal as she asked, 'Where are you taking me?'

He slowed down a little and replied, 'Well, we daren't make a start from the yacht basin until after midnight, and maybe in a few hours we will have parted for good. The back seat of a car is not my favourite place for making love but, well . . . I thought perhaps. But if you'd rather not . . .'

She laid her hand on his and pressed it. 'I'm not

quite such a naughty girl as I may have led you to suppose, so I've never done it in the back seat of a car. But I gather plenty of couples do. I like you a lot, Colin, and this may be our last chance; so let's have fun while we can. There's one thing, though. When you pull up among the trees, give me a few minutes to get ready before you join me.'

Linda had made this stipulation because her briefs were still in ribbons where the lorry-driver had torn them away to get at her. She had not liked to ask Colin to buy her new ones the previous afternoon, and did not want him to find them in such a shocking state. Among the trees, he remained seated at the wheel, while she got into the back, wriggled out of them, stuffed them in a pocket of her coat, then called to him.

To use the phrase of the famous Duke of Marlborough when, on returning from the wars on the Continent, he met his wife at Margate, 'I pleasured her twice while still in my breeches and boots.' So did Colin to Linda in the next hour or so. Then, silent but happy, they slowly drove on to Toronto.

When they reached the yacht harbour no-one was about. Remarking that it was lucky she had not come on the scene a week later, as in a few days he would be making arrangements to have the launch laid up for the winter, he handed her down into it. After a few minutes they were out on the open waters of the lake.

The car had been heated and, while it had been stationary, it had been sheltered by the trees in the little wood. But a sharp wind was blowing, and out on the water it was bitterly cold. Colin set a course south-east and told Linda that he hoped to land her between the small towns of Wilson and Olcott, a trip of about thirty-five miles. In either town she should be able to get a bus that would run her the twenty-five miles into Buffalo.

They were not far out from Toronto when the snow, predicted the day before by the porter at Colin's block of flats, began to fall. Linda, huddled in the cabin, shivered and drew her fur coat more closely about her; but Colin said it was a good thing, because it would give them a better chance of evading the Revenue cutters that patrolled both shores, on the look-out for smugglers. Twice, through the murk, they caught sight of distant searchlights sweeping the water, but were too far off to be picked up, and the launch was forging ahead with her own lights out.

Having fished the lake for years Colin knew it well, and he hoped to land Linda on a stretch of sandy shore not far from Wilson; but without lights, in the darkness and drifting snow he could not make certain of finding it. A denser darkness suddenly looming up warned him that there was land immediately ahead. Quickly he checked the launch, reversed, then steered her at low speed along the coast. Presently he made Linda take the wheel and himself went forward with a boathook to sound the depth and test the type of bottom. For a while he struck rock about four feet down, then came upon sand. Returning to the wheel, he nosed the launch in until she grounded about ten feet from the shore.

Linda looked across the dark stretch of choppy water with dismay, but Colin had thrown out the anchor and was now taking off his shoes. 'Don't worry,' he said. 'I'll carry you.'

'I weigh a ton,' she murmured unhappily, 'and you'll get frozen.'

'I'll manage,' he assured her, getting out of his

trousers. Then he slipped over the side and held out his arms to her. She put hers round his neck and pressed her cold cheek against his. As he took her full weight, he nearly dropped her, but righted himself and staggered with her to the shore. The water was icy and as he set her down his teeth were chattering.

'Oh, darling,' she whispered, 'you're a hero, a real hero.'

He shook his head with a faint smile. 'No, just . . . just an idiot . . . an idiot who has fallen in love with a girl he may never see again.'

Turning away, he waded back and fetched her bag; then they embraced and she tried to thank him for all he had done for her, but found her words quite inadequate.

'You'll . . . you'll write to me, won't you?' he said. 'Let me know how you get on. Promise?'

She nodded, although she knew she would never dare to, any more than she had to Big Bear or her beloved Eric, for fear of letting anyone know where she had gone. She hated herself for all the lies she had told him; but she could not have brought herself to let him know that she was a thief—a real criminal.

They kissed again and he said that when he was next due for a holiday he would come to the States, and they would have a marvellous time together. She agreed, while knowing sadly that could never be. By then, he was shivering in her arms. Reluctantly he let her go, wished her luck and waded back to the launch.

She remained standing on the shore until he had hauled up the anchor, started the motor and the faint outline of the boat had disappeared in the darkness.

Her heart was very heavy. She had got away from the Canadian police and across the frontier into the

United States. The chances of her being traced there seemed very slender, so all the odds were now in favour of her keeping her freedom. But she had no passport, no possibility of getting one, and no hope of getting back any of the jewels she had stolen. Her case was far worse than it had been when she first landed in Canada. Then she had had ample funds; now she had only enough money to keep herself for a few weeks.

The snow was falling faster now, and she did not even know the way to the nearest town. She was alone and friendless in a hostile world. The tears began to trickle down her freezing cheeks.

16

In It Up to the Neck

LINDA had never felt so near to giving way completely,
sitting down there on the ground and crying her heart
out. But even now the courage that had already
brought her through so many difficulties and dangers
did not desert her. In addition to Coastguard launches
on the lake, Colin had warned her that there were
certain to be anti-smuggling patrols on shore, and in
another hour or so first light would herald the dawn.
If a patrol came upon her at this hour near the beach
and carrying a night case, they would cross-examine
her relentlessly, and the fact that she could not produce
a passport would inevitably lead to her being taken into
custody pending further enquiries. She must get away
from the neighbourhood of the lake as swiftly as she could.

Picking up her case, she turned her back on the
lapping water and headed up a dimly-seen slope. The
going was tough, for it was over tufts of coarse, frozen
grass, from which, here and there, sprouted low bushes.
The snow continued to fall. It had lightly covered the
ground, helping her to see her way immediately in front
of her, but obscuring the lie of the land ahead. For a
quarter of an hour she struggled up the slope, then,
panting, reached the crest.

Having rested for a few minutes she plodded on, still

over coarse grass, until she came to a road. Turning left along it, she walked for about a mile. By then the snow had eased, falling in only occasional flurries. Between two of the flurries she caught sight of several lights in the distance, and assumed that they were on the outskirts of either Wilson or Olcott.

For her to go into either of these small towns so early in the morning could have proved dangerous; so she left the road for a nearby haystack and sat down on its lee side, where she was sheltered from the wind. She had not slept since she had woken up in Colin's bed the previous morning, so she was very tired. Soon, in spite of her anxieties, she dropped off.

She was roused by the sound of a traction engine clanking along the nearby road. By then it was full daylight. Looking at her watch, she saw that it was half past eight, so she must have slept between three and four hours. Apart from a nasty taste in her mouth, she felt better, but was still filled with apprehension about the immediate future. It was over forty hours since she had left the train at Toronto. During the past day it was certain that the police there would have traced the owner of every red sports car in the city, so would have called to question them all. They would not have found Colin in his apartment, but might have learned from the porter that he had brought a girl there answering her description. Further questioning might have elicited the fact that Colin owned a motor boat and had not been home the previous night. That could have led them to suspect that he had run her across to the States.

She prayed fervently that, if things had gone like that, he would not get into trouble, then tried to comfort herself with the thought that if he swore he had only put her up for the night and had no idea that the police were after her, there would be nothing with which they could charge him. They could not possibly prove that he had taken her across the lake. Nevertheless, if they suspected that he had, they would by now have got in touch with the American police. So the Americans might be on the look-out for her. If she was caught by them, they would need no warrant of extradition to send her back to Canada. That she had no passport, so could be presumed to have entered the country illegally, would be ample grounds for them to put her back across the frontier.

Only a quarter of a mile down the road lay the buildings among which she had seen lights a few hours earlier. In considerable trepidation, she set off toward them. They proved to be bungalows and a row of small shops on the edge of a town with street lighting along the pavements. Few people were about and, before she had gone far, she came upon a pastry cook's, with marble-topped tables inside. The smell of coffee proved irresistible, so she went in, warmed herself up with two large cups and, although she was not hungry as she had had such good meals the previous day, she enjoyed a newly-baked roll with butter. When it came to paying, she suddenly realised that she had only Canadian money. Being so close to the frontier, with people constantly crossing, the waitress accepted it without question; but it gave Linda a nasty jolt, as if the American police were looking for her in that neighbourhood, it just might lead to their getting on her trail.

Setting off again, she saw from a sign over a garage that she was in Olcott. Near the centre of the little town she found the bus depot and learned that a coach would be leaving for Buffalo in half an hour. Anxious now not to lay a further trail by paying her fare in Canadian money, she went into the only hotel she could see and asked them there to change a twenty-dollar bill for her. To her relief the girl at the desk did so cheerfully and without comment. By ten o'clock she was on her way to Buffalo.

Although the bus stopped at numerous villages *en route*, it did the journey in under an hour. As it stopped in the main square the good-natured conductor, realising that she was a foreigner, pointed to a large monument in its centre and told her it was in commemoration of President McKinley, who had been assassinated there by a fanatic in 1901. It was the only thing of interest that she saw during her short stay in Buffalo, which she found a dreary, dirty city.

The Hilton, which lay on the far side of the square, did not impress her at all favourably. Having booked in as Mrs. Gene Wellard, the name Colin had used when telephoning, she was taken up in a crowded lift to the room he had booked for her. It was quite adequately furnished, but one of the two windows was useless, as it was immediately opposite the windows of another, nearby skyscraper; so, unless the curtains were kept drawn, everything in the room was exposed to view.

By the time Linda had unpacked her few things, had a bath, done her hair and dressed again, it was getting on for one o'clock, so she went down to lunch. The big lounge running from one end of the hotel to the other was a seething mass of people. To her surprise, quite a number of well-dressed, middle-aged and elderly men were wearing fancy hats that, had they not been made of materials such as silk, might have come out of Christmas crackers. On passing a notice board she saw the reason. Three conventions were being held in the hotel, so these headdresses, which made men in

1

ordinary lounge suits look so absurd, indicated that they were Grand Wizards, King Bisons, Chief Druids, etc.

Having now to be very careful of her money, she went into the coffee shop instead of the restaurant. As she had learned in Canada, coffee shops varied from excellent restaurants where one could have a single dish instead of a full *table d'hôte* lunch, to cafeterias in which no-one but the hard-up would have eaten from choice. While she got through a leathery pancake with maple syrup, she debated her next move.

That morning she had counted up her money. When she had arrived at Banff she had had with her a little over four hundred dollars. Her stay at Lake Louise and return from Banff to Toronto, including meals on the trains, had cost her something over one hundred and eighty, so she found that she was down to two hundred and thirty-four dollars—just under one hundred pounds.

Her prime object now was to start yet another new life where any account that she gave of her past would be accepted; so, to avoid becoming noticeable as a stranger with an English accent, she must go to a big city. New York was naturally the first to cross her mind. But there was an objection to it. It was too international. The friends she had made while living with Rowley, and other people they had become acquainted with in big hotels during their trips abroad, were mostly wealthy and travelled a lot. Several of them might have an apartment in, or come on a visit to, New York. It was still less than eight weeks since Rowley had died. The story of her having made off with the jewels must have got into all the papers. Everyone she had known was not likely to forget what she had done. If she settled in New York and good fortune later enabled her to frequent the better restaurants, she might run into

someone who knew about her crime. The chances of
that happening were remote, but Linda had by now
learned never to take an unnecessary risk.

Her next thought was of San Francisco. Everyone
she had ever met who had been there declared it to be
the most delightful city in the United States. But Los
Angeles offered her better prospects. It was imperative
that she get a job within the next week or so and, as a
typist without shorthand, she could expect only a salary
that would barely keep her. On the other hand,
although she could neither dance nor sing professionally,
she had a lovely face and splendid figure. Surely one of
the film companies would take her on as an extra?

The dream had hardly come before it faded. Los
Angeles was getting on for two thousand five hundred
miles away. Cheap as railway and coach fares were in
Canada and the United States compared to Europe,
she knew she could not possibly afford the money for
the journey out of the small capital that remained to her.

Chicago then suggested itself. Few British citizens,
except business men, ever went there. In such a great
city she should be able to find a job, and could live
there without fear of recognition. To go there would
cost her only about a fifth of what it would to reach the
Pacific coast, and it would be well worth that much to
get right away from this area in which her description
might at any time be circulated.

After lunch she went to the Greyhound office and
learned that a coach was leaving for the west at a
quarter past four. Having now developed an instinct to
cover her tracks even when there was little need to do
so, she booked only as far as Cleveland, instead of
taking a ticket to Chicago.

She spent the better part of the next two hours in

buying serviceable but inexpensive underwear, strolling along the main streets of the city, then packing and paying her hotel bill. Refusing to employ a porter, she carried her bag to the coach station and set off on the first stage of the journey. For the whole of the hundred and eighty-odd miles, the highway ran south-west parallel with the shore of Lake Erie, and she enjoyed the vistas in the gradually fading evening light.

Over the long, straight highway the coach made good speed, so it was only a little after half past eight when it set her down in Cleveland. There she put up for the night at a small hotel near the bus depot, and the following morning at ten o'clock took another coach on to Toledo. It got her there in time for an early lunch and at half past one she set off on the last stage of her journey. The highway now left Lake Erie and crossed the neck of land that separates Erie from Lake Michigan, on the south-west corner of which lies the great, sprawling metropolis of Chicago. Traffic and cross-roads slowed down the coach on the last twenty miles into the city, but by seven o'clock Linda was carrying her case to the Sherman House, in the block next to the Greyhound depot, where the hotel had been recommended to her as good, but not too expensive. She registered there as Irma Jameson.

Even the price of a room with a shower on one of the lower, noisy and viewless floors was more than she felt she could afford for long, unless she could find a job; but she could economise by eating out, and a good address might stand her in good stead. She decided to take the room and that evening made do with hamburgers and a Coca-Cola at a delicatessen with a snackbar.

Next morning she gave to exploring the city. She had always imagined Chicago to be a vast, hideous, industrial complex, so she was pleasantly surprised to find that, at least for the rich, it could be a very pleasant place in which to live. The famous stockyards, where thousands of animals were slaughtered and tinned daily, and their grim surroundings of dives and tenements, were a world apart, lying quite a long way from the city centre. On its other side lay the lake shore, along which extended several miles of public gardens varying in depth from one to several hundred yards. Looking out from them across the lake were fine blocks of luxury flats, hotels and skyscrapers. The lake was so broad that the opposite shore could not be seen, so this garden waterfront with its many flower beds gave the impression that it was the sea front of an expensive watering place. The city also had the attraction of a river running through it, with a yacht harbour below two huge, circular skyscrapers, the lower floors of which were garages and the upper ones flats.

Linda found, too, that Randolph Street, on which lay her hotel, had many fine shops, including the famous store of Marshall Field, where Gordon Selfridge had made his name before coming to London. There she bought a pair of shoes and a few other things she needed.

After a three-hour walk she ate a frugal lunch, meanwhile looking through the 'Situations Vacant' in a copy of the *Chicago Tribune* and marking likely possibilities which were only a few blocks distant. During the course of the afternoon she made a dozen calls at offices, but without success. In some cases the vacancies had already been filled, others had no use for a girl who could not take shorthand, and others again turned her down because she was not able to produce any references.

Next morning she again scanned a paper, this time ignoring the 'Secretaries and Typists' column and marking instead those for doctors, dentists and hotel receptionists. After several calls, she found that the medical people preferred women who had trained as nurses, and the hotels required receptionists to have had at least some experience. On the few occasions when there seemed a chance that she might be given a trial, her inability to provide references again caused her to be turned away.

That evening, tired and dispirited, she returned to her hotel and ruminated anxiously on her future. Two of the business men who had interviewed her the previous afternoon had said that if she would like to have a little dinner with them, they could 'talk things over'. But she knew what that meant, and had no intention of going to bed with anyone for a free meal and a dubious chance of getting a job at the lowest rate paid to typists; so she had promptly declined.

The thought that she had had when, had she been able to afford the fare, she would have gone to Los Angeles then recurred to her. Hollywood would undoubtedly have been the most likely place where she could have earned a reasonable living by displaying her face and figure; but there must be a market in every big city for female attractions. There were musical comedies in which expert dancing was not required of the chorus, night clubs with floor shows in which the girls had only to strut about bedizened in diamanté bikinis and ostrich feathers, and striptease joints.

Linda was reluctant to resort to this means of livelihood, not on account of false modesty, as she was justly proud of her beautiful figure, but because it would mean that night after night she would have to be bored by the company often of drunken men, and then annoy them by refusing to go to some sleazy hotel with them in the early hours of the morning. And, as she had once heard it expressed by an actress she had met in the South of France, she was definitely not prepared to take a job in which 'the couch was in the contract'.

But by now she had become unhappily aware that beggars could not be choosers. The only alternative to some form of night life appeared to be to become a sales girl, and the idea of standing behind a counter eight hours a day for a pittance was more than she could bear.

Accordingly, next morning she ran through the papers for the addresses of theatrical agents, took down three, made herself as attractive as possible and went out on her third day's search for employment.

At the first agent's to which she went, the office had only just opened; so, after giving the name under which she had registered at the Sherman House to a pimply youth, he showed her in almost at once to the manager's office. There, a big, bald man sat in his shirt-sleeves behind a large desk littered with papers. In the corner of his mouth there was an unlit cigar, and he eyed her appraisingly out of watery eyes beneath which were heavy black hollows. After a moment he asked:

'Waal, kiddo. What's your line?'

'Modelling,' she lied. 'But I'm sick of undressing and dressing again all day to show clothes off to other women. I thought it would be a change if I could get on the stage or in a floor show.'

'Kin you dance or sing?'

'Both, a little, but not sufficiently well to do solos. With a little practice I feel sure I could pull my weight in a chorus.'

'Pull your weight, eh?' he smiled. 'That's a queer expression. You don' sound to me as if you was an American.'

'I'm not,' she felt compelled to admit. 'I'm Irish.'

'Waal, I've nothing against the Micks. Let's see your work permit.'

'I haven't got one.'

His large mouth turned down at the corners, and he shook his massive head. 'You got the right curves. I could place you easy, and get you plenty. But being a foreigner, not without a work permit. Take your passport round to City Hall and get one. Then come back and see me.'

Endeavouring not to show her disappointment, she thanked him, smiled and left his office.

Out in the street she felt greatly perturbed at this new obstacle which had suddenly arisen as a requisite to her securing employment. As, she now recalled, had been the case in Canada, to be able to produce a passport was essential to getting a work permit. She could only hope that all agents were not so particular about regulations. The second address she had taken down was some way off and when she reached it she found half a dozen people sitting in the waiting-room. Two were men talking together, one very tall and thin, the other very short and fat, so she put them down as a pair of comedians. All four of the women had good figures. In the daylight the three older ones looked slightly blowsy under their make-up. The fourth was a young Negress with a pert little face, but thin, unattractive legs.

Linda had to wait half an hour before her turn came to be shown into the manager's office. He was a small, round-shouldered Jew, wearing heavily-rimmed spectacles, and had an abrupt manner.

Their opening dialogue was very similar to that which had taken place in the first agent's office. He then said to her:

'Pull up your skirt.'

She lifted it several inches.

'Higher,' he said.

Again she obeyed. Getting up from his desk, he came round to her, pinched one of her thighs, then laid a hand on one of her breasts to squeeze it.

Stepping swiftly back, she snapped, 'Stop that! Keep your hands to yourself.'

He grinned, showing a gold tooth. 'Vot you think I'm up to, eh? This is pusiness. I don't lay dames in my office. All I vant is to be certain you ain't padded. I bin had that way before. No, you'll do. But you ain't American, that's for sure. Where's your work permit?'

Again she had to admit that she had not got one.

His dark eyes behind the spectacles suddenly filled with anger, and he snapped, 'Vot the hell you vaste my time for then? Get the hell outa here.'

This second defeat sent her spirits down to zero. Out in the street again, she wondered if it was worth while to go to the third agent whose address she had taken. But it was not far off, so she rallied her courage to try once more, in the hope that the old saying, 'third time lucky' might work and that the agent would be willing to risk placing her without a permit.

The waiting-room was more crowded than at the agent's she had just left. Of the dozen people in it eight were women, ranging from old-stagers to pretty, youngish girls. Three of the four men were middle-aged, the fourth looked to be only about thirty. He was tall, slim, olive-complexioned, well dressed in a rather flashy way and had a black, hairline moustache. Linda put him down as an Italian.

Having given her name to a long-haired youth who was addressing envelopes at a small table, Linda sat down to wait her turn. Every five minutes or so, from a glass-panelled door marked 'Private', people emerged, looking smugly pleased or slightly peeved, and the young man showed others in to be interviewed.

After a while the youngish Italian-looking man came over to Linda, politely tipped the soft hat he was wearing at a rakish angle, and said, 'Hiya, sister. You're new here, ain't you?'

She gave him a brief smile. 'Yes, but how did you guess that? Do I look so unlike the others?'

'You sure do; but it wasn't that. My name is Marco Mancini, and I'm a journalist. I hang round this joint quite a bit to pick up paras about theatrical folk, so I know most of the regulars by sight, and I've never seen you before. Mind if I sit down?'

His manner was pleasant and Linda liked his smile, which displayed even, gleaming-white teeth, so she said, 'By all means do. As I'm new at this sort of thing, perhaps you may be able to give me some useful advice?'

'Sure, I'd be happy to if I can.' As he took the chair next to her, he went on: 'What's your line?'

Linda repeated her story that she had been a model, but was fed-up with changing her clothes twenty times a day and that she had no stage training, but hoped that her face and figure might get her a job in a chorus.

His teeth flashed again. 'You've got what it takes, baby. And if I was you I'd ask plenty. That face and them legs of yours will land you a contract in any city any day.'

'You're wrong about that. I've been turned down by two agents this morning already.'

'You don't say!' His well-marked eyebrows lifted in surprise. 'How come?'

'I gather that anyone who is not an American citizen

has to have a work permit. I'm not, and I don't think I could pass as an American, unless I could produce evidence that I had been naturalised.'

'You certainly could not. The moment you opened your mouth I said to myself, "Marco, this babe is English, or else she was reared there and brought over by some lucky guy." '

'You're right,' Linda conceded, then elaborated on the supposition he had formed. 'But the guy wasn't all that lucky. I had known him in England and came over to marry him. I'd no idea that he was mixed up in a gambling syndicate, but he was. He met me when I arrived in New York, flew me here and took me to his apartment. He told me then that his money came from graft and that he was having trouble with his past associates. Two days later, when I returned from shopping I found him gone. He'd left a note for me saying that he had had to clear out because his life was in danger. He left no address, but I was scared stiff that the men who were after him might think he had, turn up at any moment and take me to pieces in the hope of getting it out of me. So I packed as quickly as I could and moved to an hotel. We were to have been married, at least that's what he'd said; but perhaps he never meant it. As it is, I've been left high and dry.'

Marco shook his head. 'You poor kid. But why didn't you go back to England?'

'I hadn't enough money for the fare. And I know no-one in England whom I could ask to lend me that much. You see, my parents aren't at all well-off, and I left home when I was seventeen. Either to get back or go on living here I've simply got to get a job, but the trouble is that I haven't a work permit.'

'You could get one at City Hall.'

'No. They wouldn't give me one unless I produced my passport, and I haven't got one. It was in my friend's safe. I didn't know the combination, so had to leave it there.'

'You're in a jam, baby; you're in a jam.' Marco jerked his head in the direction of the door marked 'Private'. 'Old man Jutson in there won't give you a job without you got a permit. That's for sure. If he did, and it came out, he'd be liable to lose his licence as an agent. He'll not risk that, so you're just wasting your time sitting here.'

Linda sighed. 'In that case I'd better go back to my hotel. Perhaps I could get a job as a shop assistant, but I'd hate to have to do that. Is there nothing you can suggest?'

Again Marco shook his head. 'Seeing you're a foreigner, you couldn't even get work in a store without a permit. Still, for those who know the ropes, anything is possible. Have you no friends in Chicago?'

'No, I don't know a soul.'

'I'm well-off in that respect. A Press man has to be. I'd like to help, and I just might be able to pull a few strings. How about coming round the corner and having a cup of coffee while we talk it over?'

Linda accepted at once. 'That's very kind of you. I'd be most grateful for anything you can do.'

Ten minutes later they were seated opposite each other at a table in a pâtisserie. As soon as they had been served, the handsome Marco wasted no time in beating about the bush. In a low voice he said:

'Now listen, baby. If you've no friends and not much money, you're up against the wall. But I can put you in the clear if you're prepared to play along. As I've said, I've plenty of friends and some of them can do pretty

well what they like in this little old city, law or no law.
I can get you a passport so you can get a work permit,
and a well-paid job into the bargain. But you've got to
treat me right. I've taken a real fancy to you. We
could have fun together. You've got sex written all over
you, and I'll bet you're a damn' good lay. I'll trade you
a passport against you coming to bed with me cheerful
and willing.'

From the way he had been looking at her Linda was
not very surprised at his making this proposition, but
she did not reply at once. With her eyes cast down she
forced herself to consider his offer dispassionately.

She had got to know Big Bear quite well, and had
come to like him a lot before she had accepted his
invitation to go with him to Victoria Island. Colin's
gallantry and generosity had touched her so deeply that
she had felt a spontaneous urge to repay him in the only
way she could. Both of them had also been of the world
that she had entered on becoming Rowley's mistress.

But this was different. There was nothing repulsive
about Marco physically. In fact, he was good-looking,
although he was not of a type that attracted her, and
he was certainly not of the class to which Rowley had
raised her. His clothes were flashy, his manner slick. She
felt sure that he would never have been accepted into
what was termed 'polite society'. It was quite possible
that he had been brought up in a better home than she
had; but she had acquired new standards and, absurdly
snobbish as it might seem, she knew instinctively that
for a long time past it would never have entered her
head to have an affair with a man of his kind.

Therefore, to do as he suggested would be to lower
herself in her own eyes. To trade the use of her body for
a passport would be selling herself. It would be exactly

the same as going to bed with a man for money. To be honest with herself, she would become a whore.

On the other hand, what if she refused? Her hotel bill at Buffalo, bus trip to Chicago, the things she had bought since, and her expenses during the past few days had reduced her resources to a bare hundred dollars—only just over forty pounds. That would not keep her for long in America, and it was all she had in the world.

Having no passport, she could not get a work permit. Without one it seemed there was no way in which she could earn money. And money she must have, otherwise within a month or less she would find herself destitute. The alternatives then would be starvation or the streets.

At the thought she gave an inward shudder. But she was still loath to take the flashy Italian as a lover, and racked her brains for other means of escape. She still had two thousand dollars in the bank in Vancouver, but could not draw upon it because her cheque book had been in the night case she had abandoned to fight her way through the crowd at the exit to Toronto Station. And she dared not write for another, because she would have to give an address to which to send it, and the bank would pass it on to the Canadian police.

Both Big Bear and Colin were rich men, and she felt sure that the bonds she had forged with them would have induced either to answer an appeal from her for help. But again she would have to give an address for a reply, and that would entail a certain risk. If Colin's call from Niagara to the Hilton at Buffalo had been traced by the Canadian police, they would have alerted their opposite numbers in the States that she had probably got across the frontier, so she would be on their list of wanted persons. Should either of her letters go astray or fall into wrong hands, they would pounce within a matter of hours. Her beloved Eric remained the only possibility. Even though he might wish to have no more to do with her, for old times' sake he would send her enough money to fly down to Mexico, or somewhere in the Caribbean where work permits were not required. But she had no idea where he had gone, and a letter to him care of the Foreign Office would probably not reach him for weeks.

She had remained silent, staring down at her plate for a good two minutes. Her cigarette, unheeded, had burnt down almost to her fingers. As she quickly stubbed it out, Marco spoke:

'Come on, baby. Make up your mind. You give me a good time and I'll see you right. Otherwise you'll soon find yourself pawning that fine mink coat.'

The idea had not occurred to her. It was a way out. She could get enough for it to fly from the States to some other country. But no; she could not. She had no passport and no means of getting one. Fate had played her one scurvy trick after another. But at least she was still free and, having covered her trail from Buffalo, now stood a good chance of remaining so. By selling her coat she could keep herself decently for quite a while, but not indefinitely. A chance was being offered her of starting a new life with little to worry about. The first agent she had seen that morning had said he would have no difficulty in getting her a well-paid job if she had a work permit. Marco could provide her with the means of getting one. Such a chance might not occur again. She simply could not afford not to take it.

Putting the best face on this unattractive situation, she smiled when she at last looked up. 'I'm not accustomed to going to bed with men I've only just met;

that's why I've taken a little time to think it over. But I like you, Marco.'

He laughed. 'Any mutt could see you weren't an easy push-over. That's what got me. Else I wouldn't have propositioned you with that bit of pasteboard. The boys who can get them don't part with them for peanuts; so it's going to cost me plenty. But I'm no meanie. We'll eat tonight at the Lido, a real good Italian restaurant on East Monroe. And afterwards I'll just not be able to wait to sample the goods.'

The smile left Linda's lips and she sat back. 'No, Marco. It's not going to be like that. I like you enough to promise you a good time if you play the game by me. But I'll not so much as kick a shoe off until you've given me that passport.'

'Oh, come on, baby,' he sought to cajole her. 'You sure can trust me. I wouldn't do you down. But I can't get what you want just in an afternoon. Fakin' a passport takes a bit of time. Earliest I could hope my friend to let me have it would be some time tomorrow. Be a sport now and let's seal our deal tonight.'

Linda shook her head. 'No, Marco. Let's face the facts. I've no particular wish to go to bed with you, although I may enjoy it when I do. So this is a business deal in which I'm acting like a tart. I've never done that before, so I don't know much about it, but I've always understood that they don't rely on promises. They require the money on the spot.'

Instinctively he realised that she was speaking the truth about herself, and the thought that she normally slept only with men she had fallen for inflamed his desire for her still further. After fingering his thin black moustache for a moment, he said:

'O.K. then. I'll start the ball rolling this afternoon.

We'll dine together this evening, just to get better acquainted. With luck, tomorrow I'll be able to give you what you're wanting.'

Producing a slim notepad from his pocket, he went on, 'Maybe, though, my friend wouldn't be able to produce a British passport, so we'd best make it American. Despite your accent, with that to show you won't need a work permit.'

On her agreeing, he took down particulars which she gave him about herself. *Name—Irma Catherine Jameson. Unmarried. Place and date of birth—Illinois, 6/7/52. Height, six feet. Colour of eyes—brown. Colour of hair—dark brown.*

When he had paid the bill he took her to a nearby photographer's, where she had a passport photograph taken. Then, having agreed to meet at the Lido at eight o'clock that evening, they parted.

That afternoon Linda rested on her bed at the Sherman House, her mind filled with thoughts about Marco Mancini. She decided that she had been right to put her scruples behind her and do this deal with him. After all, once she had the passport she would not have to see him again. And for a single night he would be quite bearable, because his hands and linen had shown her that he was almost fastidiously clean and he had the cheerful live and let live disposition that usually goes with Latin blood. But she had a strong feeling that he was not to be trusted, and definitely made up her mind that until the promised passport was actually in her hands she would not let him take her to any place where they would be alone together.

That evening, at the Lido, he spared no expense on giving her a good dinner and did not bother her much with questions about her past. Most of the time he talked cheerfully about himself. He was a second-generation American and his family came from Palermo in Sicily. He claimed to be descended from Olympe, one of Cardinal Mazarin's nieces. She did not for one moment believe him, but thought the claim in keeping with his distinctly brash personality. As she knew Venice well, she was able to talk about the city and say how much she liked Italian people.

Toward the end of dinner, he tried to persuade her to go on to a night club with him, but she was adamant in her refusal. As an excuse she said she needed lots of sleep and that, if she stayed up late, she would be much less fun for him the following night.

Eventually he gave in, and took her back to the Sherman in a taxi. No sooner were they in it than he gave free rein to his amorousness. She let him kiss her and returned his kisses with sufficient ardour to let him know that she was not frigid by nature. But when he went further, she fought him off determinedly until he gave up his attempts and laughingly declared that, from her height and strength, he thought she must really be a man dressed as a woman.

The next day she felt restless and depressed and went for a long walk along the lake front, during which she endeavoured to put Marco out of her mind. But he persisted in returning to it and, as the day wore on, she came more and more to dislike the thought of spending the night with the flashy young Italian. Yet she knew that if he produced the passport she must now go through with it.

At eight o'clock they met again at the Lido, as they had arranged. As soon as he had ordered cocktails in the little lounge, her eyes asked him a question. Grinning, he produced the passport, opened it to show her her photograph, then slipped it back into his breast pocket.

The fact that he had really got it for her filled her with mixed emotions: elation and relief that she need no longer worry about how to keep herself in the future, but at the same time a feeling of annoyance and disappointment. Subconsciously she had been hoping that he had been lying and would fail to fulfil his promise, which would free her from having to fulfil hers. But now there was no escape from having to give herself to him.

Now that she must do so her sense of fair play insisted that she should give him as good a time as she could. If she had plenty to drink, that would not be too difficult and, as ever, when she went to bed with a man, she could close her eyes and think of her beloved Eric.

Putting her heart into her part she was as gay as any man could have wished over dinner; but toward the end her laughter became so loud, after the amount of champagne she had drunk, that Marco refused her a liqueur, saying that she had had enough liquor for the moment and that they would have more drinks later. Then he sent for the bill and, immediately he had paid it, took her arm to pilot her out of the restaurant.

In the taxi he did not attempt to kiss her. She leaned back in her corner, taking no notice where they were going, but it seemed a long drive.

When the taxi pulled up she noticed only vaguely that it was in an ill-lit street, and seemed to be in a poor part of the city. He led her up the steps of an old, brownstone house. The door was answered by a huge Negro who grinned a greeting and said, 'Number six is all ready for yo', Mr. Mancini.'

They went up to the first floor. As Linda reached the landing, she glimpsed a blonde girl in a kimono going into one of the rooms. Turning to Marco, she asked, 'What is this place? I thought you were taking me to your apartment.'

His teeth flashed in a grin. 'My landlady is mighty particular. She don't allow fellers to bring dames along to stay the night. This is a rooming house, but quite respectable.'

As he spoke, he opened a door and showed her into a big room. The furniture was old-fashioned, and against one wall there was a large brass bedstead. At its foot was a table, with glasses and bottles. When he had closed the door, she sat down in an armchair. Walking past her to the table, he opened a bottle of champagne.

She lay back and closed her eyes, then opened them again as he said, 'This is what you need, babe,' and held out a full glass to her. Taking it, she smiled up at him.

'Here's to us.' He lifted his glass and they both drank. A moment later Linda felt her head swim. Her limbs suddenly seemed to go limp. She dropped the glass and passed out.

When she came to she was in bed, naked and alone. Her head was aching as though it would split. Raising it painfully, she gave a bleary glance round. Curtains were drawn across a single window, but enough light came through them for her to see by. It was not the room in which she had passed out, but much smaller and had hardly any furniture. Wildly, she looked round for her clothes. They were nowhere to be seen, and the room had no cupboards.

With utter horror, the reason for her being there flashed through her mind. Marco had sold her into a brothel.

17

A Night in a Brothel

WITH every beat of her heart, Linda's head gave a violent throb. She let it fall back on the pillow and shut her eyes again, endeavouring to concentrate in spite of the stabs of pain. It could not be true. She was the victim of an awful nightmare. She lay flat on her back, her arms stretched out limply on either side of her. Raising a trembling hand, she ran it over her stomach, up to her breast and pinched one of her nipples. Yes, she was both naked and awake.

Making an effort, she forced herself to sit up. Her head rolled on her shoulders, but she managed to steady it and got a clearer view of the room. It was only about ten feet by twelve. It had no dressing table or chest of drawers. There was a white-painted wooden wash-stand, with a chipped basin and an enamel jug. Underneath the washstand there was a slop pail and on top two bottles that looked as if they held disinfectant. There was a single chair and a dumb valet, on which a man could hang his clothes. A white-painted bedside table held a lamp with a pink shade, a brass ashtray with two cigarette stubs and a box of matches in it, and a pot of vaseline.

As she lolled back again, she saw that in the ceiling above the bed there was a mirror about five feet by three. Owing to the semi-darkness she had not noticed it before. In it she saw dimly reflected her tousled hair, gaping mouth and naked shoulders. It confirmed her worst fears. Big Bear had told her about his nights out after attending conventions in the United States, and that some of the more expensive brothels had six-sided rooms in which all the walls and the whole ceiling consisted of mirrors, so that copulating couples could see themselves from many angles. The mirror over the bed was obviously a makeshift in a cheaper kind of house.

Closing her eyes again she thought back over how she had let herself be trapped in this ghastly situation. Marco Mancini was obviously a professional pimp. His dark good looks and flashy clothes were just the things to attract girls who came from poor homes. And what better hunting ground could he have chosen to find likely victims? In theatrical agents' waiting-rooms there were always passably good-looking girls, out of a job and willing to be picked up. In most cases she supposed he simply gave them a dinner, made them a little tight and persuaded them to spend the night with him, on the pretext of finding them work. Once he got them to this house, the rest was easy. He simply gave them a Micky Finn and collected his money.

In her case he had had to do more. But no doubt his nefarious activities brought him into contact with many types of criminal, and she had once heard Eric say that in every city forged passports were obtainable if only one knew where to go for them. Evidently Marco had thought it worth the expense of having one made for her, because he could get a very high price for a girl with her looks and figure. Bitterly she wondered how much he had got for her.

For ten minutes she lay, still suffering both physical

and mental misery. Her head continued to ache abominably and she had a foul taste in her mouth. It was this last that rallied her into getting out of bed. As she did so she staggered, but grasped the back of the chair, and so reached the washstand. Having gulped down two glasses of water, she dipped the corner of one of the rough towels into the jug and scrubbed her teeth as well as she could. Then she filled the basin and spent several minutes alternately plunging her face into it and drawing deep breaths. That made her feel a little less awful, but no less desperate about her situation.

She tried the door, but, as she had expected, it was locked. Going to the window, she drew back the cheap cretonne curtains, to find that the room she was in was high up, probably on the fourth floor and at the back of the house. Below was a builder's yard, but no-one was to be seen there. Beyond, the prospect consisted of grimy buildings and a small section of mean street. The window was open a few inches at the top, but when she tried to open the lower half, she found that it was screwed down. Even if she could have got it open she thought it unlikely that anyone passing in the section of street would hear her cries for help, as it was quite a long way off.

As she turned away in despair, her glance fell on a hook at one side of the window, just showing beyond the edge of the curtain. Her eyes dilated with horror. It held a whip.

Turning, she ran to the door and hammered hard on it with her fists, crying, 'Let me out! Let me out of here!' at the top of her voice. For a good five minutes she continued to batter on it until her hands were bruised and sore, but there was no response.

Breathless and shaking, she staggered across to the

bed. As she pulled back the sheets to get in, she saw a corn plaster. Vividly there sprang into her mind Marco in the shop to which he had taken her to get the photographs for her passport. He had stubbed his toe against the counter, giving an 'Ouch' of pain, and exclaimed, 'Jesus! That got my corn.'

A moment later she saw other evidence that he had been in bed with her while she was unconscious. Wrenching open the bedside cupboard she was just in time to grab the chamber pot and be sick in it.

It was a horrid bout, but at length she managed to pull herself together and washed her face again. Then, so shattered that she could not even relieve her agony of mind by tears, she crawled back into bed.

After a while her headache eased and her bout of vomiting had rid her of the bile resulting from the Micky Finn. Yet she racked her brains in vain for a way to escape the ignominy that threatened her. Even if she could have got a message smuggled out by some servant in the place, or by pleading with the first man who paid to make use of her, there was no-one to whom she could send for help; for it was certain that neither a servant nor a customer would take a message to the police, and she had not a single friend in Chicago.

Worn out with misery, she presently fell asleep. When she awoke, it was dusk. Not long afterwards the key turned in the lock, the light was switched on and a middle-aged woman came into the room.

She was pear-shaped, her breasts and stomach sloping off into enormous hips. Her hair was brassy, her face heavily powdered and her cheeks rouged. Between them she had a small, beaky nose and below it a rat-trap mouth and a chin that hardly protruded from her thick throat. Without preamble she said in a deep voice:

'Get up, girl.'

Linda sat up and, holding the sheet across her breasts, angrily demanded her clothes.

The woman ignored her outburst and repeated harshly, 'Get up, I said. I saw you last night, but I want to take another look at you.'

'Fetch me my clothes!' Linda cried again. 'And you'll let me out of here. If you don't, I'll get out somehow, sooner or later and, by God, I'll have the police arrest you for kidnapping.'

'So that's your tone.' The woman's thin mouth curved into an evil smile. With a speed surprising for her bulk, she darted across the room, grabbed the whip that hung beside the curtain and brought it down with a cruel swish across Linda's shoulders.

With a scream of pain, Linda cowered back. The harsh voice came again, 'Now will you get up, you stubborn bitch?'

Sobbing from the searing lash she had received, Linda slithered from the bed and stood up, still holding the sheet round her.

The woman raised the whip again. 'Drop that sheet and walk towards me.'

Petrified, Linda obeyed and came to a halt, naked, in front of her tormentor.

For a good minute the woman remained silent, while walking slowly round Linda, her small, black eyes appraising every feature of the superb body. Then she said in a pleased voice, 'You'll make a splendid cow for my best-paying bulls. Worth every buck I paid for you. Those hips of yours were just made for this business. When the thirty bucks a night boys tire of you and want something fresh, I'll put you on the short-timers at five a go, and rake in still more. You could take ten a night

easy, and fifteen when we've a crowded house Saturdays. Maybe I'll start you with five or six, though, for
a few nights, just to run you in.'

Choking with rage and terror, Linda burst out, 'You
filthy hag! I won't take one. I swear I won't. I'd rather
die.'

The woman chuckled. 'Plenty of them say that at
first, but they soon change their tune. Best be sensible,
dear. You'll enjoy it then, anyhow to start with. My
name's Lottie. I'm the Madam here, and I treat my
girls good as long as there's no complaints from the
customers. I split fifty-fifty with them on what they
bring in. That goes as well for any tips they may give
you in private. And don't you dare try cheating me on
that, or it'll be the worse for you. Of course, you'll have
to earn first what I give for you. Five hundred bucks
that heel Marco screwed out of me. But I couldn't
afford to quarrel with him, otherwise he'd take his
pick-ups to another house. Then there'll be your
clothes and hair-dos. In three or four months, though,
you'll be making good money. Now you've near slept
the clock round you're quite fit enough to make a start.
I'll send old Sal up to you. She'll take you along the
passage to a room where you'll find make-up an' all,
and she'll fit you out with black stockings, mules and a
dandy nightie. Then you'll come back here and in
about an hour I'll send up the first randy gent who's
willing to pay plenty to have a new girl.'

'I won't!' Linda shouted. 'If a man comes here and
tries to take me, I'll tear his eyes out. You can try
your whip on me again, but I'm a damn' sight stronger
than you are, and if you do, I'll choke the life out of
you.'

Lottie shook her head. 'No, dear. I'm not going to

use the whip on you no more. That would spoil your
lovely body for the customers. But I see you've got to
be broke in, so I'll send Bimbo up instead. He'll be real
pleased at the chance to use his weapon on a gorgeous
doll like you.'

For the moment, while Lottie walked out of the room
and locked the door behind her, Linda did not register
the meaning of this new threat. Then, with full force,
it struck her. A brothel, she felt sure, would have on
its staff a strong-arm man to act as a chucker-out if any
of the customers became troublesome. Bimbo must be
the name of the one here, and he was to be sent up to
rape her.

The memory of the lorry-driver came into her mind.
Bimbo was probably just such another coarse and
powerful brute. From being raped in the shack she had
succeeded in defending herself. Then she had at least
been fully clothed and with nothing to prevent her
from running away if she could free herself from her
attacker. But here she was stark naked and a prisoner.

She visualised Bimbo as an ex-pugilist or all-in
wrestler. What possible chance would she have of
defending herself from such a muscular ruffian? For a
few minutes she contemplated surrender. But that
would not save her from what would follow. Lottie had
spoken of ten to fifteen men a night. Linda knew from
having once read a book about an American prostitute
who worked in a house on Hawaii during the Second
World War that it was possible for a woman to accept
that number, night after night, and retain her health.
But the horror, the degradation of it!

A macabre procession of naked men paraded through
her mind. Bald men with enormous bellies, one-armed
and one-legged men, gaunt creatures hawking and

spitting from afflicted lungs, men with rashes, scrofula and only partially-healed sores, men who would wish to be whipped and in turn whip her, perverts who would demand of her unmentionable obscenities, perhaps a homicidal sadist who would try to strangle her, and others with venereal disease from which it would be impossible for her to protect herself from catching sooner or later.

Shudders shook her, but her resolution returned. She would fight them one by one until some brute, infuriated by her resistance, inflicted some injury upon her that would cause her death.

Quickly she looked round the small room for something with which to defend herself. There was nothing having a blade or that could be used as a bludgeon. And the whip was gone; Lottie had walked off with it. It occurred to Linda to barricade the door. Even if she got all the furniture in the room against it, that would not be anything like sufficient to prevent them from forcing it open after a while; but at least it would show that she was determined to thwart them by every means she could.

Getting her hands under the end of the low bed, she raised it a little and began to drag it toward the door. She had moved it no more than a foot when the key turned in the lock and the door opened. Dropping the bed, she swung round and came to her full height. A giant Negro stood there, his white teeth gleaming in a wide smile of anticipation.

She recognised him at once. Bimbo was the doorman who had let her and Marco into the house on the previous evening. Her mouth fell open and her eyes opened to their fullest extent. She had become casually acquainted with several coloured men of the upper class during her trips abroad with Rowley. They had all proved pleasant and intelligent, so she had liked them and had no racial prejudice. But this was different. The thought of his black skin pressed against hers made her flesh creep.

Still grinning, he surveyed her eagerly from head to foot, then rolled a red tongue round his thick lips and said, 'Waal now, if ol' Bimbo ain't the lucky boy. Yo's a real peach, sweetie. Ah could keep on layin' yo' till the cows come home.'

At last she found her voice and croaked, 'Get out! Get out!'

He slowly shook his head. 'Yo' got it all wrong, honey bunch. I'm heah to gi' yo' a real good time. An' I'm not leavin' till yo's as limp as lars' week's washin'.'

He was clad only in a singlet and a pair of shorts. In one swift gesture he pulled the singlet over his head of crisp, black curls and she heard the electricity crackle as he did it. A moment later he had kicked off his shoes, undone his belt and was stepping out of his shorts. As he again came erect, Linda got a full sight of what Lottie had referred to as his 'weapon'. She had seen those of only four men, and had never dreamed that any man could possibly possess such a formidable organ. Horrified but fascinated, she stared at it as he said:

'Jus' look what the very sight o' yo' has done to ol' Bimbo. Now for it, honey. Spread yo'self out on that there bed and thank da good Lord for what he's sent yo'.'

'I won't!' she yelled. 'I won't!' But she was standing with her back to the edge of the bed. He took one stride forward, gave her a push with the flat of his great hand, and she fell backward at full length upon it. Next moment he was on top of her and the Negro stink came sickeningly to her flared nostrils.

As his big, fleshy lips came down on hers, she pulled her mouth away, began to scream with all the strength of her lungs and strove to cross her legs. But the weight of his on top of her made that impossible. Raising one knee, he jabbed it hard down between hers, forcing apart her thighs. His movement as he partly lifted himself gave her her opportunity.

She had never forgotten how, when she had told Rowley about the schoolmaster having raped her when she was sixteen, he had said that no girl who had courage and a fair degree of strength need allow herself to be raped. The lorry-driver had never got his breeches down, but the Negro was naked. As he raised his knee, her right hand shot down and grasped his testicles.

They were as hard as solid rubber balls, but she gripped them with as determined a clutch as a drowning man would have seized the cord of a lifebuoy, then squeezed them with all her might.

Rearing up, he let out a howl of rage and pain. With wild, distended eyes, she saw him lift his fist to bring it crashing down on her face. Just in time she jerked her head aside. He gave another agonised yell, and strove to wrench his body away from hers, but he could not break her vice-like clutch on his testicles. Great beads of sweat had broken out on his forehead and were dripping from his chin. His eyes were bulging, their whites stark against his black skin. Again he raised his fist, but again she was too quick for him and, to protect her face, thrust it up against his neck. Opening her mouth to its fullest extent, she bit him savagely under the ear.

He bellowed, yelled, screamed, but she had him now as firmly as a snake could wrap itself round a large wart-hog that had trodden on it, and with all the venom of an injured cobra. In vain he rolled about the bed, alternately on top of and beneath her. With her hand she crushed his testicles and her strong teeth bit deep into his neck. Blood spurted from the wound, filling her mouth. Choking and half suffocated, she swallowed it rather than let go.

To her this terrible conflict seemed to last an age, but actually it could not have been more than two minutes before his screams subsided to groans and a whining moan, the spasmodic jerking of his limbs lessened to an agonised squirming. She knew then that she had won, relaxed her hold, unclenched her teeth, and lay, half-fainting from exhaustion, beside him.

For several minutes she lay still, drawing her breath in harsh gasps. Then she raised herself on one elbow and looked at him. His great limbs were twisted in an unnatural heap. Blood was still pouring from the wound in his neck, making a crimson pool on the white sheet. She then realised that, by pure chance, her savage bite had torn open his jugular vein. He was still breathing, but his eyes had turned up so that only the whites were showing. She needed no telling that in a matter of minutes he would be dead.

Then it struck her that she had murdered him. She felt no regrets about that, only new fears for herself. But no; as far as the law was concerned, she had no need to worry. No jury would ever give a verdict against a white woman who had killed a Negro while he was attempting to rape her. In any event, the owner of the brothel would never dare bring such a case to court. But that was the least of her anxieties.

It seemed probable that anyone who had heard Bimbo's screams had taken them for a continuation of her own, while still endeavouring to fight him off.

Even so, Lottie might come in at any moment, to see how things were going and to watch the sport. Big Bear had once said that in brothels people often paid to watch erotic spectacles.

Slipping off the bed, Linda stumbled to the door, opened it, took out the key then put it on the inside and locked the door. The house was old, and the door a stout one, so it would take a lot of forcing. That would at least give her more time in which to think.

Yet how could thinking help her? She was no better off than before Lottie had come to the room and said her piece about the life led by girls who had been sold into brothels. In fact, far worse; for when they eventually broke the door in and found that she had killed Bimbo, God alone knew what they would do to her.

Unless they had a crook doctor who would give a certificate that the Negro had died from a heart attack, or something of that kind, they would not dare invite an inquest with her teeth-marks in his neck and his testicles bleeding from where her nails had pierced them. The only course open to them would be to get rid of the body clandestinely. Perhaps by lowering it into the sewers. If so—ghastly thought—they might avenge themselves on her for having killed him by throwing her, too, into the sewers.

Quaking with terror at the thought, she bit her thumb hard to prevent herself from giving way to a fit of hysterics. To unlock the door and venture out into the passage would only precipitate whatever frightfulness was in store for her. From the fourth floor she could not possibly hope to get down several flights of stairs and out of the house undetected. Besides, she was still stark naked.

In both men and women nakedness, more than any

other factor, paralyses action. On an impulse she snatched up Bimbo's shorts, stepped into them, drew the belt tight round her waist, then put on his singlet. Normally she would have been revolted at the idea of wearing a Negro's sweat-stained garments, but now she did not give it a thought. On the contrary; she no sooner had the clothes on than they had the psychological effect of modifying her sense of panic. Even so, she felt certain that she had no chance at all of getting downstairs unseen and escaping from the house.

She ran to the window. It was now pitch dark outside. There were lights on in most of the buildings and in the section of street, but none of them was less than two hundred yards off. On the floor, one of the heavy shoes Bimbo had kicked off lay upside down. The heel was nail-studded. Snatching it up she broke the window-pane with it, then hammered frantically away until she had smashed out all the triangles of glass from the window frame. Leaning out she began to yell for help.

She shouted in vain until she was hoarse. Under an arc light she could see figures moving in the street; but they were either too distant to hear her or, if they did, took her cries for those of some woman involved in a drunken brawl which was no concern of theirs.

Withdrawing her head she stood back breathless, racking her brains for a way to raise the alarm. The very word 'alarm' brought her inspiration—fire alarm!

Running to the bed, she seized the dead Negro by one ankle. Exerting all her strength, she dragged his heavy body towards her till it fell with a thud on the floor. Getting her hands under the end of the bed, she lifted it and, step by step, drew it, with its trailing, blood-soaked clothes, across the door. Taking the lamp, ashtray and matches from the bedside table, she threw

K

the table, chamber pot and all, on to the bed. Throwing aside the still half-full enamel water jug, she heaved the washstand alongside them, then tore down the cretonne curtains and added them to the pile.

Her dishevelled hair had fallen over her sweating face. Shaking it back, she picked up the matches, lit three one after the other and pushed them under folds in the curtains. Within a minute three flames shot up, surrounded by wisps of smoke. Two minutes later three small fires were spreading rapidly. The dry wood of the cheap old furniture caught, then the bed and bedding beneath it. There came a loud crackling, sparks flew, clouds of smoke billowed out.

Satisfied now that no-one could force the door without getting badly burned, Linda ran back to the window, leaned out as far as she dared, and shouted, 'Fire! Help! Fire!' at the top of her voice.

But still no-one in the distant street took any notice. The blaze behind her began to roar. She heard a furious knocking on the door and someone shouting 'Open up! Open up!' But she could not now, even if she had wanted to. The door itself was on fire and smoke must be pouring under it into the passage.

Pulling in her head for a moment, she saw that the room was full of smoke. Had she not known the direction in which the door lay, she could have found it now only by the flames that licked about it. The smoke made her eyes smart and caught her in the throat. She was seized by a bout of violent coughing. Quickly she thrust her head out again to gasp in the cold, fresh air.

It relieved her only temporarily. The room was now so full of smoke that it was billowing past her out of the window. There was still no sign down in the street that anyone had noticed the conflagration. A few more minutes and she could no longer see the lights there. The smoke pouring from the window had become so dense that it blotted everything out.

For some minutes she had felt the heat increasing behind her. Although she leaned out as far as she could, it was beginning to scorch her legs and backside. Panic again seized her. She had feared for her life before and had sought this desperate means of escape. Now it seemed she was to lose it for certain. She had trapped herself and would be burnt to death. There was no way out except by throwing herself from the window. But she was up on the fourth floor of the building, and had long since decided that to jump was certain to prove fatal. She would land in the builder's yard, a heap of mangled flesh and broken bones. Coughing racked her until she thought her lungs would be torn to pieces. Still leaning as far as he dared out of the window, she began to lose consciousness.

Her last thought was that she had failed, and failed miserably. She had counted on the fire brigade arriving on the scene, running up a tall ladder and rescuing her. But if they came now, it would be too late. Either Lottie's people would smash down the burning door, put out the fire and drag her out, then inflict some ghastly death upon her, or she would be roasted alive. Then she fainted.

18

Drugged and Kidnapped

WHEN Linda came to, she was lying on her back and her first sensation was one of movement. An electric bell clanged loudly somewhere above her head. She then realised that she was in an ambulance. The lower part of her back and her legs hurt. The fire and the desperate peril she had been in returned to her. As she opened her eyes, she saw that a man in a white coat was sitting beside her. Seeing that she had come out of her faint, he smiled and said:

'You was born lucky, sister, else you'd been barbecued by this. If you'd fallen back inside that room when you passed out, the smoke were so dense the firemen who went up the ladder wouldn't have seen you. The wood in them old houses burns like tinder. Time they got you down, the whole top floor were a ragin' furnace.'

With the full return of consciousness the pain in her lower limbs increased. In a low voice she asked, 'Am I badly burned?'

He grinned. 'Your pants had caught, so the feller that brought you down had to give you a good spankin' to put the flames out. But not to worry. You'll be all right agin in a while.'

Soon afterwards the ambulance stopped and Linda

was carried into a hospital. In the casualty receiving room she was asked her name, which she gave as Irma Jameson, then she was wheeled to the operating theatre and transferred to a table. A young doctor examined her, a nurse smeared her bottom and calves with a thick, yellow ointment that relieved the pain, a second nurse helped to bandage her, the doctor gave her a shot in the arm and, as she was wheeled away to a lift, she lost consciousness.

Early the following morning she was awoken by a nurse gently shaking her shoulder. She was lying on her stomach and, when she made to turn over, she found that she could not, because a broad bandage had been wound round her middle and the ends tucked in on either side of the bed. The nurse undid it for her, then she saw that she had been lying under a cradle. Screens round the bed told her that she was in a public ward. A doctor and an elderly Sister were standing at the foot of the bed. While the nurse took Linda's temperature, the doctor felt her pulse. The result was apparently satisfactory, as the doctor said:

'O.K. It will do her no harm to move her. Re-dress her burns and we'll get her downstairs.'

As the nurse began to undo the bandages Linda was suddenly seized with panic. She had often heard that hospitals were so crowded that patients were sent home as soon as they were fit to be moved. The thought of again falling into Lottie's hands terrified her, and she gasped:

'Where are you going to send me?'

The doctor shrugged. 'I don't know. But we have had special instructions about you. You're not to be allowed to talk to any reporters and are to be collected by a private ambulance.'

'I won't go!' Linda cried. 'I won't! I won't! I'm not going back to that house. I demand police protection.'

'Quiet, dear, please,' urged the Sister softly. 'You will disturb the other patients.'

'I don't care. I was kidnapped. I'm not going back. Nothing will induce me to. Get the police. Please! Please!' Linda's eyes were wild, and her fury had turned to pleading.

The Sister and the doctor exchanged glances. He nodded. The Sister signed to the nurse and the two women simultaneously flung themselves on Linda, pressing a towel over her mouth and holding her down. Meanwhile the doctor had picked up a syringe from a trolley at the foot of the bed and was filling it. A moment later Linda felt the slight prick of the needle. Almost at once the strength seeped from her limbs and soon afterwards she became unconscious.

When her brain started to function again, she was still in bed, but lying on her side. On opening her eyes she saw that she was no longer in a ward, but in a private room and, instead of the plain, cotton night-dress into which they had put her in the hospital, she was wearing a pretty one of pink chiffon. Her legs and bottom itched but no longer pained her. Sitting up, she looked round and found to her surprise that the room was not only comfortably furnished, but a vase of a dozen big chrysanthemums stood on a table near the window. On another table, beside an armchair, there were a row of neatly laid out magazines and a pile of paperbacks. Pushing back the bedclothes, she ran to the window and looked out. She was in a room on the first floor. Below lay a pleasant garden, but it was enclosed by a ten-foot-high wall.

Profoundly puzzled, she got back into bed. The place

to which she had been brought had nothing remotely suggesting any connection with a brothel. And surely the very last thing that hideous hag Lottie would have done would be to have her removed to a luxurious private sanatorium? Yet who else could possibly be responsible? And the sinister fact remained that the ten-foot-high wall clearly indicated that the place was some sort of prison.

On the bedside table there were two thermos flasks. She found one contained iced milk and the other barley water. Preferring the former, she poured herself a long drink and as she did so noticed that behind the place where the thermos had stood there was a bellpush. Impatient to learn the best or worst about her new situation, she pressed it.

Two minutes later the door opened, and a nurse came into the room. She was thin-faced and had a hard mouth, but she smiled and said, 'So you are awake. How're you feeling?'

'Not too bad, thank you,' Linda replied. 'The places where I was burnt are itching and I've got a slight headache. But otherwise I'm all right.'

The nurse nodded. 'The headache is the result of the injection you were given. It will soon wear off. So will the itching in a day or two. The places will peel, of course, but you were only scorched. You have a very healthy skin and in a fortnight or so there will be no trace of it ever having been damaged.'

'Well, that's a mercy,' Linda smiled. 'And now please where am I, and why was I sent here?'

'You are a few miles outside Chicago. But more than that I cannot tell you. The staff here are strictly forbidden to discuss with the patients any matter other than their ailments. Now, as it is well on in the

afternoon, I expect you must be hungry.' The nurse
produced a menu from her apron pocket and handed
it to Linda. 'There is always someone on duty in
the kitchen, so anything you care to choose from that
can be brought up to you in about half an hour's
time.'

The last meal Linda had eaten had been her dinner
with Marco, well over forty hours earlier, and, as she
ran her eyes down the list, she suddenly realised that
she felt very hungry indeed. From an excellent choice
she decided on omelette Portuguese, stewed turkey and
chocolate soufflé.

'And to drink?' asked the nurse. 'I don't advise
spirits, but you can have any wine or soft drink that
you like.'

'Champagne?' hazarded Linda.

'Certainly. We are giving Pol Roger Non-Vintage at
the moment.'

'Splendid!' Linda laughed. 'As long as I am not
expected to pay the bill. I have no money with me.'

'Oh, no. That's all taken care of. Now I'll go and
order your dinner.'

'Thank you. But there is one other thing. Before I
have it I'd like a bath.'

The nurse shook her head. 'No. Tomorrow perhaps.
It wouldn't do for you to sit in a bath yet. But I'll take
you to the bathroom, and you can wash yourself,
provided you don't wet your bandages.' As she spoke
she opened a wardrobe, took out a prettily-frilled, silk
dressing gown and held it out for Linda.

In the bathroom Linda found everything she could
want neatly laid out. Her hair had been screwed up
into a bun on the top of her head. After washing her
face and as much of her body as she could, she gave her

hair a good brushing, then did it more becomingly. Not long after she was back in bed, her early dinner was wheeled in on a trolley by the nurse, each course being kept hot in a thermos container. It was an excellent meal. Linda enjoyed every morsel of it, and washed it down with two glasses of champagne; but all the while her mind was troubled. What could all this cosseting of her be leading up to? There must be a catch in it somewhere—a price to pay, and perhaps one that she would find hateful. That she was being prepared for something, she felt certain, but what? What? What?

When she had finished her meal the nurse came in again, wheeled out the trolley, then wheeled in another containing bandages, bottles and enamel basins. Having re-dressed and re-bandaged Linda's burns, she went to the wardrobe and produced an expensive bed-jacket. As she put it round Linda's shoulders, she said:

'You needn't wear this now, if you find it too warm; but you'll need it later. I telephoned while you were in the bathroom, to say that you are sufficiently recovered to receive a visitor, and in about an hour a gentleman will be coming to see you.'

Linda sat up with a jerk. Her brown eyes blazing, she cried, 'Then this *is* a brothel! But a really expensive one.'

'A brothel!' the nurse repeated, staring at her in surprise. 'Certainly not. Whatever gave you such an extraordinary idea?'

'I escaped from one last night,' Linda burst out. 'Surely you know that? Then the people who ran it had me drugged in the hospital and brought here. They must have. Who else could have? I don't know a soul in Chicago.'

The nurse shook her head. 'You must be imagining

things. I know nothing about you. Perhaps this is delayed shock. When I was told that you had been in a fire I expected you to show symptoms of shock; but you are a very strong young woman physically and—it seemed to me—mentally, so . . .'

'I'm not suffering from shock,' Linda cut her short. 'I tell you I was drugged and sold into a brothel. Then, at the hospital, I was drugged again and kidnapped. If any man tries to touch me, I'll kill him, just as I . . .' She suddenly faltered, fearing to admit that she had killed Bimbo.

Taking advantage of her pause, the nurse said sharply, 'You may be telling the truth. But it is none of my business. I've already told you that the staff here are forbidden to discuss the patients' private affairs with them.' Then she walked out of the room.

Linda was breathing heavily. Again her mind was in a turmoil. Her recent terrible experiences, and the lack of any possible explanation about how she came to be where she was, other than that old Lottie had arranged for her to be sent there, led her to conclude that there could be only one reason why a man was coming to see her.

Immediately the thought of trying to escape sprang into her mind. But could she possibly get out of the house without someone seeing and preventing her? There was the window, and it was only about twelve feet up from the garden. She could hang from the sill and let herself drop, but she would probably break an ankle. Anyhow, she would never be able to get over the ten-foot wall. And she would have on only a dressing gown. Any attempt to get away from the place was stymied by the wall and the fact that she was in her night clothes.

Her headache was gone. The soothing ointment with which her burns had been dressed had reduced their irritation to a degree that made it almost imperceptible. The good dinner and champagne had restored her strength and courage. If need be, she would again fight off any man who attempted to take her by force. Her glance fell on the empty pint champagne bottle. The nurse had left it on her bedside table. Used as a club, it would make a formidable weapon.

In spite of her renewed resolution the hour that followed was one of the most trying that Linda had ever endured. Greatly as she dreaded the coming of this unknown man, with half her mind she was eager for his arrival; for, through him, she hoped to learn the answer to the mystery that surrounded her transfer from a third-rate brothel to this luxurious prison.

The hour seemed never-ending, but at last there came a knock at the door. Linda called 'Come in.' The door opened. She caught a glimpse of the nurse in the passage, then the door closed again as her visitor stepped briskly into the room.

He was a tall, thin man, probably about forty, Linda thought, as his face looked youngish although his hair was grey and thinning. His forehead was high, his nose prominent. Perched on it was a pair of steel-rimmed spectacles. The lower features completed a strong, intellectual face and his clothes were in keeping with it: a well-cut, grey lounge suit, a scrupulously clean, faintly-patterned collar and shirt and, one splash of colour, a royal-blue silk tie.

For a moment he studied Linda, his face expressionless. Her face and voice were equally so as she asked, 'What do you want with me?'

He smiled then, and it was a pleasant smile. 'I am

here on behalf of a person of considerable importance who has become interested in you.'

'Indeed!' She raised her eyebrows. 'Are you that person?'

'Dear me, no. I'm only a fairly high-up cog in his machine. Nobody even knows his real name. He is spoken of simply as "The Top".'

Reassured now that her visitor's intentions were not of the kind she had feared, Linda smiled. 'This all sounds very mysterious.'

'It would to you, so perhaps I'd better explain. No doubt you have heard of Al Capone?'

'Vaguely. Wasn't he a big-time gang leader? But years ago. Long before I was born.'

'That's so. For years he controlled all the rackets here in Chicago. Well, The Top is the modern equivalent of Al Capone, although, of course, he is a very different type of person. Capone was a lower-class Italian born in Brooklyn. The Top is a highly-cultured gentleman. It is said that way back in the war he was a big shot in either our C.I.A. or the British M.I.6. Anyhow, there is little he doesn't know about the workings of the F.B.I. and Security Services. You may have heard the expression "Top Secret". That's why he's called "The Top". After the war he devoted his talents to what, as a lawyer, I would term "illegal activities". And he has built an empire out of the criminal elements in a great part of the United States. Very few people actually know him, but thousands of dope pedlars, brothel-keepers, bank robbers and every sort of hoodlum pay him tribute; so he is immensely rich and his word is law. Now, may I sit down?'

'Of course, please do. I should have asked you to before.' As the lawyer lowered himself into the arm-

chair and crossed his long legs, Linda went on, 'All this
sounds frightfully like a "thriller"; but lots of people do
seem to think that modern crime is organised by a few
big brains that no-one would even dream were connected with that sort of thing. All the same, I can't
think why this Mr. Top should have become interested
in me.'

'It is your good fortune that he happened to see you.'

'When did he do that?'

'He chanced to be dining at the Lido the night before
last, when you dined there with Marco Mancini before
he took you to that house.'

'Marco! That little swine! I'd give a lot for the
chance to pay him out for having sold me into that
ghastly place.'

'You needn't worry. He's been rapped, and hard, for
acting contrary to standing orders. The job of these
dirty little ponces is to pick up lower-class girls who are
more or less on the rocks. Most of them have run away
to the big city from homes in small towns, so they have
no family or rich friends to worry about what has
become of them. They may create a scene or two to
start with, but they soon resign themselves to life in a
brothel. Women like yourself are different. They nearly
always make trouble. In your case you caused thousands
of dollars' worth of damage and, still worse, led to a
house that was paying well having to be written off.
Marco knew damn' well that you were not the type
that he could sell down the river without the risk of
burning his fingers; but I suppose he was tempted by
the big money he could get for a girl with your looks.'

'I see.' Linda smiled. 'Well, it's good to know that
little rat is now paying for his mistake, but . . .' Linda's
smile changed to a frown. 'What about your Mr. Top?

Having seen me, I suppose he took a fancy to me and has sent you to collect me for his harem.'

The lawyer laughed. 'Oh no, nothing like that. I take it you have heard of Cherril Chanel?'

'The film star? Yes, of course.'

'Has it ever struck you that you are very like her?'

Linda hesitated. 'Well, I suppose I am in a way. But she is blonde, whereas I am a brunette.'

'That is easily remedied. Anyway, when The Top saw you at the Lido, he was immediately struck by the resemblance. At the moment, Cherril is on vacation with her latest boy friend in the Fijis. But she might quite well suddenly have had enough of him and fly in to Chicago. For a few days you are going to impersonate her. At least, I hope so.'

'Why does this man Top wish me to do that?'

'It is a matter of getting some highly secret documents over the border into Canada. The Top has a big organisation there as well as in the States; but for a year or more he has been having a lot of trouble with a rival group there, and he has decided that it would pay him better to sell out than start a really bloody gang war. These documents are leases of many properties, lists of sources of income and pay rolls of his people, which he is turning over to the other side. The Feds know that this deal is about to take place, so they are watching like hawks everyone here who has either a criminal record or is suspect. If these papers fell into wrong hands, not only could Canadian police smash the biggest crime ring in Canada, but the Feds would have leads to many people back here; perhaps even to The Top himself. So you see they have got to be taken through by somebody who is absolutely above suspicion.'

'Why can't you smuggle them across the lake by night in a fast motor launch?'

'That has been considered. But it is too risky. If the launch was caught by a patrol boat, the game would be up. No, they've got to be carried through Customs by some well-known person who will be bowed through with smiles, while the Press boys take photographs. Cherril Chanel could do it and, posing as her, so could you.'

'What happens if something went wrong and I was caught?'

The lawyer smiled a little wryly. 'That would be just too bad. You could swear that the stuff had been planted on you without your knowledge. But it would be bound to come out that you weren't the real Cherril Chanel. So they wouldn't believe you, and the odds are you would be sent down for a term of years.'

'Then why should I take that risk?'

'Because for you it is the better alternative.'

'What do you mean by that?'

'Exactly what happened in that house run by old Lottie Finkestein no-one will ever know—unless you tell them. When the Negro's body was recovered, it was simply a charred corpse. How you succeeded in knocking him out I just can't think. But I take my hat off to you for it, and when The Top was told he thought it one of the best jokes he'd ever heard. He doesn't even hold against you what the fire has cost him. But the Negro's death is neither here nor there. The thing that does concern you is a matter of arson.'

The lawyer paused and lit a cigarette. Then he went on in a very level, quiet voice, 'If Lottie hadn't been so impatient to get back some of the dough she had paid for you and sent the Negro up to break you in last night, The Top would have had you out of her place and brought here this morning, because he had already made up his mind to make use of you.

'This sanatorium, of course, is owned by him. It has a variety of uses. If any of his people are wounded in a gun battle, they are brought here and taken good care of until they are well again. There are cases when it is desirable to take certain people out of circulation for a while. They are brought here to relax pleasantly in rooms on the upper floor that have barred windows. Hence, too, the high wall that you may have noticed surrounding the property. Anyway, as Marco could not be found and questioned about who you were until too late, we had to have you collected from the hospital. But we can send you back there and no questions will be asked.'

'And what would happen then?' Linda enquired.

'Now that you are well enough, the police would take you into custody and you would be charged with arson. Officially, as far as the police are concerned, Lottie's place is a respectable rooming house. Marco would give evidence that he took you there at your own request because you were looking for a cheaper lodging. That he called on you the second evening you were there and found you quarrelling with old Lottie. You accused her of having stolen some money that you had left under your mattress when you went out that afternoon. She, of course, would give evidence to that effect. Both of them will say that you were drunk and swore you would get even with her. A few hours later a fire starts in your room. Presumably you started it and meant to get out; but you were drunk, made a mess of things and the flames spread so quickly that they reached the door before you could get to it. I won't go into all the details, but plenty of supporting evidence will be given. When The Top gives orders for a case to be brought against anyone who has crossed him, the verdict is a foregone conclusion. You may bet your last buck that you'll get at least two years in the can.'

'Then it looks as though I'm likely to be sent to prison anyway.'

'Oh, no! You certainly will be if you refuse to do as you are told. But, if you play along, the odds are a thousand to one against it. By the time it's emerged that Cherril Chanel has never left Fiji, you will have disappeared. You will have a brand-new wardrobe, and The Top is no penny-pincher to people he employs. On completion of the job you will be given two thousand bucks with which to make your get-away, and as a sweetener towards forgetting that you had ever heard of The Top. If it ever came to his ears that you had talked about your very temporary association with his affairs, although you don't know enough to do him any harm I wouldn't give you more than a month to live.'

'I see. And whereabouts in Canada would I have to go?'

'To the capital, Ottawa.'

Linda considered the matter, but it did not take her long. She knew that she would not stand an earthly chance in the sort of case that a man like The Top could bring against her. She had never been in Ottawa, and golden hair would greatly alter her appearance. Two thousand dollars was over eight hundred pounds, and she was to get a new wardrobe of expensive clothes into the bargain. The risk was small, and it meant a new start, with enough money to keep her comfortably for several months.

'All right,' she said. 'I'll take those papers through for you.'

'Fine,' he smiled. 'Marco told us you were staying at the Sherman House, so we've paid your bill there and sent a forged note authorising us to collect your things. I'll have the nurse measure you for others, then tomorrow I'll come out here with them and give you your instructions.'

Without wasting further words, he stood up, wished her a pleasant 'good night' and walked out of the room.

Shortly afterwards the nurse came in and took her measurements, brought her, at her request, another half-bottle of champagne, then left her to her own devices. While drinking the champagne, Linda conned over this extraordinary new development which, unless she was very unlucky, would rescue her from poverty and anxiety and set her on her feet again. At ten o'clock she was still wondering if it would be best for her to endeavour to find a steady job in Ottawa and go to earth there, or try to get out of Canada, perhaps down to South America, when the nurse came in once more and gave her a 'sleeper'. She fell asleep more relaxed in mind than she had been for a long time past.

Next morning she was allowed to have a bath. Her calves and backside were red and tender, but had ceased itching. She lunched in bed and, not long after she had finished, the lawyer arrived. With him he brought a dressmaker and a hairdresser.

The latter flattened Linda's hair on top of her head with some glutinous substance which he said would easily wash off, then fitted her with a pale-gold wig dressed in the same style as Cherill Chanel was wearing her hair in a recent photograph. He next partially shaved her eyebrows, added tiny pieces to them which gave them a slightly different slant, tinted them and her eyelashes; then, satisfied with his work, handed her over to the dressmaker.

Meanwhile the lawyer had brought in four expensive air-travel suitcases, bearing the initials C.C. One of them, to Linda's relief, contained her mink coat and few possessions. The others held a variety of dresses, shoes and lingerie. Over another hour went by while the ready-made clothes were fitted, then the dress-maker took them away to make the necessary minor alterations. Linda got into bed again and the lawyer came back into the room.

Sitting down in the armchair, he said, 'Now I must make it clear that in our business we take no chances. Everyone is suspect and a check kept on them by someone else. Cherril would naturally have a personal maid with her. So will you. Her name is Gerta Hoffman. She is unknown in Chicago and we've brought her up from New York specially for this job.

'Presently I shall take you to the airport. Gerta will have the tickets and it will appear that you are only changing planes here, having both just flown in from San Francisco. There would be an hour and a half's wait between planes. One of our people at the airport will put you in the V.I.P. waiting-room. The time between planes is enough for the Press to learn that you are passing through Chicago. We shall leak it, anyway. So, as you go on board, you will have to face the Press photographers. Smile at them, but you are not to say one word. Gerta will do any talking that is necessary.

'At Ottawa the Press photographers will be waiting for you. Again you will keep your mouth shut. A suite has been booked for you at the Château Laurier. You will drive straight there and have supper for both of you sent up to your sitting-room; and so to bed.

'The following morning a gentleman will call you from the lobby, and ask if he may come up. You will say yes, and Gerta will go out into the corridor. She will remain within call, and within call of her there will be two of our men in Ottawa; one by the lift and the other by the stairs.

'When your visitor comes in, you will ask him for the password. It is "Peace Pledge". Remember that— "Peace Pledge". You will then place on a table the packet of documents that I shall give you before we part. He will also place a packet on the table. You will then swap packets. His should contain two hundred and thirty thousand dollars in U.S. currency. You will count them through carefully while he is examining the documents. If all goes satisfactorily, he will go out and Gerta will come in. You will hand her the money and she will give you your two grand. You should, of course, have packed beforehand. You can then leave the hotel as soon as you like.

'Should anything go wrong, or your visitor try any funny business, you will step on a small mechanism that Gerta will have fixed under the table, within easy reach of your foot. It will set going an electric siren which Gerta can't fail to hear. She will alert our two gunmen and they will tackle your visitor before he can get away.

'But remember, the papers you will be carrying are immensely important. You will be under surveillance the whole time. Should you get cold feet at the airport and decide to quit, we have people there who'll gun you down in order to get those papers back at once. And when you reach Ottawa the same applies. Is that clear?'

Linda gave a wry smile. 'Perfectly clear. When am I to start?'

He glanced at his watch. 'In about an hour's time. I'm afraid you will have to miss your dinner, but I'll have some sandwiches and champagne sent up to keep you going.' With a light wave of his hand, he left her.

The dressmaker had laid out the clothes Linda was to wear. The suitcases and all her other things had been taken downstairs to be packed there. The nurse brought her the wine, sandwiches and a plate of cakes. When she had eaten as much as she wanted, she went to the bathroom, made up her face very carefully, then returned to the bedroom and dressed.

At six o'clock the lawyer came for her. He was carrying a blue leather beauty box, with the silver initials C.C. on it. 'This,' he said, 'contains the goods. It has a simple combination lock. The letter C is equivalent to the number 3. So I've set it with your initials, plus an extra C. You can't possibly forget that. Turn the knob left three times to 3, right twice to 3, then once back to 3, and it will open. You had better try it.'

She did as he bade her and saw that inside the box there was nothing but a thick, sealed envelope. Shutting the box, she twirled the knob, locking it again.

'We'll go now,' he said. The nurse was standing outside in the passage. Linda thanked her and shook hands, then accompanied the lawyer downstairs. A chauffeur-driven limousine was drawn up outside the front door. They got into it and drove a hundred yards, halted for two minutes while the gates in the tall wall were opened, then drove on along a road. After covering about three miles, the car drew up again. The lawyer signed to Linda to get out. Surprised and slightly apprehensive, she did so. He pointed to another car standing at the roadside twenty yards ahead. As they walked toward it he told her that it was the car that would take her to the airport, and that Gerta Hoffman would accompany her. Then he added:

'You will just say "Good evening" to Gerta as though you know her well. Then you will refrain from talking to her during the drive, and at the airport only as far as is absolutely necessary. Remember, although she is actually our watchdog on you, she is playing the part of your maid.'

Beside the car ahead a dumpy female figure was standing. In the faint light Linda could only guess that the hard-featured woman was about thirty. She made a slight bob and said with a heavy German accent, 'Goot evening, Madame.'

Linda returned the greeting. The chauffeur from the first car was bringing along Linda's luggage. When it had all been transferred to the boot of the other, the lawyer held out his hand to her and said, 'It's been a great pleasure to be of service to you, Miss Chanel.'

She replied, 'Not at all. I'm happy to have met you.' Then she got into the car, Gerta followed her, and it drove off.

A few minutes later they were in the outlying suburbs of Chicago. For half an hour they skirted the great city, then the car pulled up outside the airport—but not at the front entrance. Evidently The Top's people had made special arrangements. An official met them on the far side of the building. With him there was a porter with a trolley, on to which the luggage was loaded. They followed the official for some distance to the entrance of a covered ramp. There he asked for their tickets. Gerta produced them from a heavy bag

she was carrying and they were given to the porter, who
went off with the luggage while the others walked up the
ramp into the glaring lights of the airport terminal.

Before leaving the sanatorium Linda had been quite
satisfied with her appearance, but now she felt distinctly
nervous. She half expected that everyone would recognise her as the famous film star, and feared that someone who knew Cherril might stop and speak to her. But
she was wearing a scarf over the *blonde-cendré* wig and,
except for a few men who looked after her in admiration,
to which she was used, no-one gave her a second
glance.

It was not until they were ushered into the V.I.P.
waiting-room that anyone took any special notice of
her. The air hostess on duty stared at her for a moment,
then exclaimed in a voice of awe:

'Why, surely you are Miss Cherril Chanel?'

Linda smiled and nodded. The girl hurriedly led
them to comfortable armchairs in a corner and asked
what they would like to drink. Linda asked for rum and
coke, Gerta for coffee.

While the drinks were being brought, Linda had her
first chance to take a good look at her personal maid,
and she was not favourably impressed. Apart from
being physically unattractive, there was something
mean about Gerta's face. She was a blonde, with pale
blue eyes and a small, pursed-up mouth. Her neck was
short and thick where it merged into her heavy body.
But she was dressed appropriately for her part, in a
dark-blue coat and skirt, good but heavy shoes, a white
blouse with a modest gold brooch, and had her dull fair
hair drawn flatly back into a bun.

Bowing his excuses, the official said he must leave
them for a few minutes. To account for her silence, as

soon as the drinks were brought Linda picked up a magazine and pretended to read it. Covertly, she saw that two other air hostesses had been brought in by the first, to gaze at her from a distance.

The official returned with the baggage checks clipped to the tickets. Gerta took them and put them in her capacious bag. A few other people came in. One couple evidently thought they recognised Linda, and could not take their eyes off her. Presently the air hostess came over and said:

'Miss Chanel, there are some Press men outside. They are anxious to have a word with you.'

Gerta spoke at once in her heavy German accent. 'No interviews. You say Madame iss too tired after her journey.'

A quarter of an hour later their wait was over. The official led them out. A group of about eight, mostly young, men were outside. Several had cameras. Linda was assailed with a barrage of questions:

'How was Fiji, Miss Chanel?'

'Why you goin' to Canada?'

'How d'you leave Ricky Maloney?'

'Give us a line on your next film, do.'

Linda remained silent and shook her head, but she gave a sweet smile and halted for a moment while the cameras took her. Between them, the official and Gerta pushed a way for Linda through the little crowd. Ten minutes later she was welcomed into the aircraft by a broadly-grinning steward, who led them to bulkhead seats. Everything had gone without a hitch and Linda was rather enjoying playing the part of a celebrity.

During the six-hundred-mile flight she had plenty to think about. With luck, by this time tomorrow the end of this dangerous mission would be several hours

behind her. She would be on her own again, but with
ample money. But where should she make for? Even if
she got rid of the blonde wig, it would be too big a risk
for her to stay in Ottawa because she bore such a strong
resemblance to Cherril Chanel. Somehow she must try
to get out of Canada. Suddenly she remembered the
U.S. passport that Marco Mancini had procured for
her. She had never seen it again after he had shown it
to her in the Lido. What a fool she had been. If only
she had asked the lawyer to get it for her, or another
similar, she could have returned to the States and had
it visaed for any country she liked. But it was too late to
think about that now.

Dinner was served, which made the flight pass
swiftly. By the time the aircraft began to come down,
she had decided that she would go to Quebec. No-one
knew her there and, as she had money, she might somehow manage to get herself smuggled aboard a ship.

At the Ottawa airport Gerta produced two passports
and, as soon as the Immigration officer opened
Linda's, he gave her a broad smile. In the Customs hall
she was recognised. A chubby young officer asked her
casually, 'Anything to declare, Miss Chanel?' When
she said, 'No, nothing,' he chalked all her bags, touched
his cap and wished her a good time in Canada.

Outside the hall they were awaited by a group of
reporters. Again the barrage of questions. Linda
refused to speak, but posed smiling for her photograph.
A uniformed chauffeur had come up and led them,
with their luggage, to a limousine. Linda noticed that
he was a very broad-shouldered man with an aggressive
but boyish face. He drove them straight to the hotel
and, while the bags were being unloaded, Linda heard
him say in a low voice to Gerta, 'If any trouble blows

up, call Room seven-seventeen.' So she knew that he must be one of The Top's watchdogs. At the Château Laurier they were given a two-bedroom suite on the seventh floor. In all the rooms there were flowers with the Manager's compliments. Gerta tipped the porter, and as the man left the room Linda picked up the telephone.

In an instant Gerta was beside her, grabbed her arm and asked throatily, 'Who you gointa call?'

Linda shook her hand off and replied, 'I'm going to order myself a nightcap. Would you like anything?'

'No. I nefer trink. It is not goot for pusiness. But I will order; not you.'

When a brandy and soda arrived, Linda took it into her bedroom. There she found that, with German thoroughness in playing personal maid, Gerta had unpacked for her the few things she would require for the night. When Linda had thanked her, she said:

'You make use off bathroom soon, please. After, I haf to lock your door. It is an order.'

Linda shrugged. Evidently, just on the remote chance that she had been got at, The Top's people were taking no chances. For fun she decided to take her time, and ran herself a bath. Gerta looked sullenly angry, but discipline restrained her from any protest at being kept out of bed for another hour.

Quite early in the morning Linda was woken by the sound of Gerta unlocking the bedroom door, but she turned over to doze again, then, at half past eight, had Gerta telephone down for breakfast. When she had finished she dressed again in her travelling clothes and did her own packing. When she went into the sitting-room carrying the precious beauty box, which she had never let out of her reach, she found Gerta reading a heavy-looking book. The manager had sent up more flowers and a pile of newspapers. Linda tried to read one of them, but found it impossible to concentrate. Now that the time for the big deal was approaching, she could not keep her mind off it.

It was close on midday before the telephone rang. Gerta answered it. After a moment she put her hand over the receiver and turned, frowning, to Linda. 'It is not a man who asks for you, but a woman. What you wish I say?'

Linda shrugged. 'Tell her to come up. If she is a reporter you can send her away. If she is the person we are expecting she will be able to give the password, and we'll know things are all right.'

Having given the message, Gerta rang Room seven-seventeen, and said, 'Someone comes. Make ready.'

Two minutes later a bell-boy showed the visitor into the room. She was a large, fair woman, with an oval face and blue eyes. To Linda's surprise she was wearing a black cloak, below which showed a chauffeur's uniform and long, shiny, black boots. She was carrying an attaché case and a chauffeur's cap. As the door closed behind her, she gave a jerky bow and said, unsmiling, with a heavy accent, 'Greetings, lady. I come as arranged. Peace Pledge.'

'You are welcome, Madame,' Linda replied. Walking over to the table, she laid the beauty box on it and took up a position where she could immediately put her foot on the small alarm device, which looked rather like a mouse-trap, that Gerta had placed there in position. Then she signed to Gerta, who walked out into the corridor and closed the door behind her.

The visitor placed her attaché case on the other side of the table. With a cautious glance at each other they

unlocked their cases. Each of them took out a thick
envelope and pushed it across to the other. Linda
opened the one passed to her. It contained a two-inch-
thick wad of thousand-dollar notes. She began to count
them. Having got to one hundred, she placed that wad
aside. As she did so her glance fell on the papers that
the woman opposite her was examining.

For a moment she remained quite still. Her eyes
lifted to the big bust and pink face of the powerful
woman on the other side of the table. She felt sure the
woman was a Russian.

When her glance had fallen on the documents she
had seen at once that they were not leases or lists of
names with figures in dollars opposite them. They were
complicated algebraical calculations.

Although she had not understood them, she had
many times seen similar arrangements of symbols made
by Rowley while she had acted as his secretary. This
was not a transfer of interests from one gang leader to
another, but something very different. She was assisting
in selling nuclear secrets to an enemy of the Western
Powers.

19

Top-secret Documents

LINDA's brain began to work overtime. She had fully
realised that by acting as The Top's representative and
collecting money on his behalf, she was performing a
criminal act. The lawyer had made that quite plain.
Although she was only too well aware that she was a
jewel thief wanted by the police, all her instincts were
those of an honest, law-abiding citizen. In normal circumstances she would have rejected indignantly any
proposal that she should handle the assets of an organisation built up by robbery, prostitution and peddling
dope. But, short of being framed and sent to prison, she
had had no option. She had not been required to take
any part in The Top's criminal activities. She had
been picked on by him only by chance to act as his
courier, because she happened to resemble a famous
film star. Had she refused, it was certain that he would
have found someone else, who would appear to be
equally above suspicion, to get these papers across the
frontier. She did not feel that any fair-minded person,
knowing the circumstances as they had been presented
to her, and her own at that time, could possibly blame
her for seizing on this chance both to avoid being sent
to prison and once again to escape the anxieties of
being on the borderline of destitution.

But the true circumstances had not been presented to her. The lawyer's story about The Top selling out his Canadian interests to a rival group there had been thought up in case she had scruples if she were told the truth.

And she had scruples. Her two-year association with Rowley had been more than enough to bring home to her the immense importance of the Western Powers keeping ahead of Russia and the increasing menace of China, in know-how about the development of nuclear power. Those papers that the blonde woman on the far side of the table was scrutinising so carefully had obviously been stolen from one of America's secret research centres, and their possession might well give Russia the lead which would enable her to impose her will on the free nations of the world.

Linda made a pretence of resuming the counting of the pile of banknotes in front of her. But she was not even attempting to do so. She was thinking how fortunate it was that a woman should have been sent to carry out the exchange—for somehow she must get back those papers, and she would stand a better chance against a woman than a man.

That a woman should have been sent dressed in the uniform of a chauffeur did not now surprise her. Although Eric had never let drop a word about his own job, he had often talked to her and Rowley in general terms about the Russians. She recalled his once saying that, in the majority of cases, Russian Ambassadors were only puppets. In every Embassy there was a secret nominee of the Politbureau, generally posing as a junior clerk, the butler or some other servant; and it was he, or sometimes she, as the Russians had a high regard for the abilities of women, who dictated all matters of major policy. Greta Garbo's film *Ninochka* flashed through Linda's mind. Possibly this woman was the key figure at the Soviet Embassy in Ottawa or, more probably, a nuclear scientist who had been sent over specially to collect these papers.

For a moment Linda considered stepping on the siren device that lay near her foot under the table. The loud wail would result in Gerta's alerting the two strong-arm men outside and herself running into the room with them behind her. But what good would that do? When they learned the reason why she had refused to go through with the transaction, they would knock her out, bind and gag her, lock her up in her bedroom, complete the business themselves and make off as quickly as they could.

No. Some way she had to get the better of the woman by herself. But if she snatched the papers back, a fight would ensue. The woman might be armed and, perhaps, shoot her. Anyway, if she was attacked she would almost certainly shout. That would bring Gerta into the room and Linda could not possibly overcome the Russian, Gerta and the two gunmen who would probably follow her in.

To give herself more time to think, Linda exclaimed, 'Oh, damn!' and, as though she had miscounted, began to count the notes all over again. By the time she had done the Russian had finished examining the papers and had put them in her attaché case. By then Linda had decided what she must do. Putting the pile of notes into her beauty box, she expressed herself satisfied.

The woman gave an abrupt bow and said, 'I also. Now I will go.'

Linda did not attempt to show her visitor out, but followed her toward the door. On the far side of the table stood a chair. As the woman walked past it,

Linda grasped its top rail, swung it sideways and up, then brought it crashing down on the Russian's head.

One of the chair legs hit her above the left ear. She gave a gasp, fell to the floor and rolled over, her blue eyes glaring upward. Dropping the chair, Linda launched herself upon her and, before she could shout, seized her by the throat. The Russian was already only half-conscious from the blow, so the struggle was brief. In less than a minute she had been choked into insensibility.

Coming to her feet, Linda quickly locked the door, to prevent Gerta from coming in should she think the transaction was taking unnecessarily long and that something had gone wrong. Turning back, Linda saw that her victim's cloak had fallen open, revealing a black leather belt that carried a pistol holster on her left hip. Kneeling down, she undid the flap and took out the weapon.

Linda had not ever handled a pistol, so she held it carefully. It was of a type she had never seen, small and stubby, with an unusually short, very wide barrel. It occurred to her that this might be a silencer, but it was only about a third of the length of silencers she had seen in gangster films. Gingerly she took out the magazine to make certain that it was loaded. It was, but not with the sort of bullets she had expected. They were transparent capsules, three-quarters full of a yellow liquid. Clearly, the gun fired some kind of chemical which would become gas and temporarily blind or paralyse anyone whose face was within a few feet of the muzzle.

Laying the gun down on the table, she took the unconscious Russian by the ankles and dragged her into the bathroom. As quickly as she could she shed her own clothes, then took off the woman's cloak, uniform and long, black boots, and put them on. The tunic and skirt were too full for her, and the boots were on the tight side; but the cloak would hide the looseness of the tunic, and the boots gave a little when she flexed her toes.

Meanwhile, the Russian had been breathing stertorously and now showed signs of coming round. Seizing a towel, Linda gagged her with it and used another to tie her feet together. To secure her hands Linda cut off the blind cord with a pair of scissors.

Running back to the sitting-room, she picked up the attaché case which the Russian had dropped when struck down. It had not got a combination, but two separate locks. While putting the notes in her beauty box Linda, out of the corner of her eye, had seen the woman lock the case and slip the key into her left breast pocket. As she fished for it, she could not get her fingers to the bottom of the pocket on account of what felt like a hard piece of cardboard. Pulling it out, she found it to be a Russian passport in the name of Anna Zubarova.

There was also something in the right breast pocket. It proved to be a notecase holding a wad of Russian notes and three Canadian dollar bills. Folded flat inside it was an air ticket in Anna's name. It bore that day's date and was for Moscow via Oslo. The time of departure was 22.15 hours. Evidently the Russians had sent Anna over specially to vet the nuclear papers and meant to lose no time in getting her back with their haul.

Linda's heart leapt. If only she could reach the airport and pass herself off as Anna she would be out of Canada, could leave the plane in Oslo and be safe in Norway with a fortune that would last her a lifetime.

L

Again dipping her fingers in the pocket she found the key, unlocked the attaché case, took out the precious packet, threw it into her still open beauty box and slammed down the lid.

Quick as she had been in dealing with the Russian, changing into her clothes and tying her up, considerably more time had elapsed than should have been taken to count two hundred and thirty banknotes, so she dared not delay in tackling Gerta. Righting the chair, she pulled it behind the door and put on it both the beauty box and Anna's peaked cap. Picking up the pistol, she held it in her right hand behind her back. With her left she unlocked the door, opened it a few inches and called to Gerta:

'Will you come in? There has been a misunderstanding.'

As Gerta, all unsuspecting, pushed the door open, Linda stepped back behind it; then, the moment Gerta was in the room, gave it a swift push that shut it again.

A second later, they stood face to face. One look at Linda dressed in the Russian's uniform and Gerta realised that she had fallen into a trap; but before her face even had time to register surprise and anger, Linda had the pistol levelled at it. She pressed the trigger. Nothing happened.

Instantly Gerta's hand went down to a pocket in her skirt. There was a pistol in it. She pulled at it and her hand, clasping the butt, came out. The awful bitterness of defeat seared Linda's mind. She had overcome the Russian, got possession of the scientific secret that might even give the Communists the power to dominate the world, secured a passport that could get her out of Canada, and a fortune for herself. Now, at only the second hurdle, she had failed. Under the threat of

Gerta's gun she would be despoiled of everything—
even her fine collection of new clothes and the two
thousand dollars with which she was to have been paid
off.

During the past few months fate had played Linda
many scurvy tricks, but now it suddenly turned in her
favour. Some part of Gerta's pistol had caught in the
lining of her pocket. Wrench at it as she would,
clutching at her skirt with her free hand, she could not
get it out. That hitch proved Linda's salvation. It
flashed upon her that, being unused to weapons, she
had neglected to put the safety catch off.

Still unable to get her pistol free, Gerta turned
toward the door, and opened her mouth to shout for
help to the gunmen out in the passage. At that instant
Linda flicked up the safety catch on the Russian's pistol,
and again pressed the trigger.

The gun gave a faint plop, a jet of liquid spurted
from the wide muzzle, dissolving almost instantly into a
white mist that entirely enveloped Gerta's head and
face. She gave one gasping cough and slumped to the
ground. As the mist dissolved, Linda saw that she was
out cold.

For a moment, breathing heavily from the emotions
that had racked her, Linda stood there staring down at
her second victim. Then she pulled herself together.
She had no idea how long the effect of the gas would last.
If Gerta came to within a few minutes she might
succeed in preventing her from getting away from the
hotel. As she had done with the Russian, she took
Gerta by the ankles and dragged her squat, ungainly
body across the sitting-room and into the bathroom,
alongside Anna. Gerta looked completely out, and if
she came round fairly soon and shouted, it was unlikely

that she would be heard out in the passage; but Linda tied her wrists and ankles with two more towels, and gagged her.

Locking the door of the bathroom behind her, Linda spent a couple of minutes arranging most of the hair in her fair wig so that it would be hidden by Anna's peaked cap. She then picked up the beauty box. But, just as she was about to leave the room, she suddenly remembered that, apart from the huge sum it contained, she had no Canadian money, except the three dollars in the Russian's notecase. She would require more than that and restaurants or taxi-drivers are in no position to cash thousand-dollar bills.

Gerta had left her bag on a chair. Linda knew there was a billfold in it, because she had seen Gerta tip the porters. Opening it she took out the billfold. It contained a fifty and several fives and ones. Slipping it into her own bag, she thrust her arm through the strap and pushed it right up under the cloak until it fitted tightly over her shoulder so that she would have both hands free. Opening the door, she picked up the beauty box with her left hand. In her right, under cover of the cloak, she clutched the gas pistol.

As she stepped out into the corridor, she glanced swiftly to left and right. Seventy feet away, a man was standing at the top of the stairs. Although he was now wearing a checked suit, she recognised him by his broad shoulders as being the boyish-faced chauffeur who had driven them from the airport the previous evening. In the other direction, only thirty feet off, a thick-set, bearded man, smoking a cigarette, was lounging near the lift. With a firm stride she walked toward him, praying that he either had not seen Anna Zubarova come up in the lift or had caught only a glimpse of her so that, with the peak of her cap pulled well down, her own impersonation would not be detected.

When she reached the lift, the man stood aside for her. With the thumb of the hand that was holding the beauty box she pressed the bell. She now had her back to the man, but it seemed to her an age before the lift came up, and she tried to keep her breathing steady. The moment the lift stopped, she pushed back the gate and stepped into it. On the opposite wall there was a mirror. In it she found herself staring straight into the eyes of the bearded man behind her. His face showed sudden surprise, and he exclaimed:

'Cherril Chanel! Where are you off to in that uniform?' At the same moment he thrust his foot forward, so that she could not close the lift gate. Her right hand came out from under the cloak. Raising the pistol she fired it at his face.

He took a quick step back, staggered about wildly for a moment, then collapsed. She closed the gate and pressed the button, sending the lift up instead of down; for she had realised in time that the boyish-faced man must have seen what had happened and by now be dashing down the stairs to intercept her.

Two floors higher up she got out and, brushing past a couple who were waiting for the lift, ran the whole length of the corridor to another lift she knew to be there, because she and Gerta had been brought up in it on their arrival. As she waited for it to come up, she put the safety catch down on the pistol and thrust it into the side pocket of her tunic.

She took the lift down to the ground floor and found to her relief that the big lobby was so crowded that she could not be seen from the further end where, by now, the boyish-faced thug would be waiting for her at the other lift. Pushing her way past a batch of new arrivals, she left the hotel. Inside it had been beautifully warm; outside it was freezing and a bitter wind was blowing. Hurriedly she looked about for a taxi. Seeing one about fifty yards away just being paid off by a woman, she began to walk quickly toward it. Then she heard a voice crying behind her:

'Anna. Anna,' followed by some words in a foreign language, which she had no doubt was Russian.

Turning her head, she saw a bulky man wearing a coat with an astrakhan collar and a hat to match, standing beside a stationary car which had the C.D. of the Diplomatic Corps next its number plate. Clearly, he was from the Russian Embassy. No doubt, although Anna was actually his superior, she had driven him to the hotel, then had gone in as though sent by him on some errand, and he was waiting for her to come out. Thinking she had taken the wrong direction by mistake, he was shouting to catch her attention.

Ignoring him, Linda ran to the taxi. The driver was slow in giving change to the woman who had just paid him off. Linda threw an anxious glance at the Russian. He was fifty yards away, but had started to run after her.

The moment the woman had her change Linda jumped into the taxi and called to the driver, 'Take me to the British Embassy as quickly as you can.'

The driver turned his head and stared at her. 'There isn't one, Miss; not in Ottawa.'

'Drive off anyhow!' Linda cried desperately. 'Go on! For God's sake! Take me to the Governor General, or the High Commissioner.'

A glance through the back window of the cab showed her that the Russian was now within twenty yards of it. The taxi began to move. Seeing that it was too late to catch it, the Russian pulled up with a jerk, faced about and started to run back to his car.

Linda sat back and breathed again. The taxi-driver turned his head and called, 'I'd best take you to the High Commissioner's. That's in Elgin Street.'

'Yes, please do,' she called back. Although she had little doubt that the nuclear calculations had been stolen from an American scientist, immediately she had seen them she had determined that, if she could get hold of them, she would take them to some British authority. Britain was America's ally and, after all, it was the British who had started all this atomic business, so she reasoned that her own country had first right on any new developments that might have been discovered. With luck now she would have the packet in the hands of some responsible British official within the next twenty minutes, or half an hour at the most.

At a cross-roads, red lights caused the taxi to pull up. Turning to get a second look through the back window at an ornate building they had just passed, she got a horrid shock. There was not a great deal of traffic in the street and, two cars behind, she caught a glimpse of the Russian. He was leaning out and she instantly recognised him by the round shape of his astrakhan *papenka*.

The taxi ran down a long, broad street. When lights again brought it to a halt at another cross-roads, the Russian was separated from it by only one car. Two minutes later the taxi turned left. Linda had no idea that they were in Elgin Street, but two hundred yards further on it pulled up in front of an imposing building. Having arrived at her destination un-expectedly, she had not got the money ready to pay her fare. Hastily, she wriggled her bag down from where she had been clutching it under her arm, and got it free of her wrist. As she opened the bag to take out Gerta's billfold, she saw the Russian's car shoot past and pull up with a squeal of brakes fifteen yards ahead of the taxi. Jerking two dollar notes out of the billfold she thrust them through the opening of the partition window at the driver, opened the door and jumped out. At the same moment the Russian jumped out of his car.

To open her bag she had had to put the beauty case down on the floor of the taxi. Now, having shut her bag, she had to turn round to pick up the beauty case. As she did so, she saw another taxi brake and pull up with a jerk immediately behind the one she had just paid off. Out of it jumped the broad-shouldered, boy-faced thug.

Evidently he had known that the Russian was waiting outside the hotel for his female associate. Having seen her knock out his bearded friend by the lift with her gas gun, he had realised something had gone wrong, dashed downstairs and out of the hotel, just in time to see the Russian drive off, then followed his car under the impression that the woman was with him.

As Linda snatched up the beauty case, her back was turned to the Russian, but she heard him shout, 'Anna! Anna Zubarova!' followed by a spate of Russian. From his angry tone she guessed that he had not yet realised that she was not Anna, and had jumped to the conclusion that Anna was attempting to defect and sell to the British the papers for which they had paid such a high price.

He and The Top's thug came charging toward her at the same minute. Each believed his principals to have been cheated. Dashing toward each other, glaring with malignant rage, they momentarily ignored Linda. The two taxis and the Russian's car had come to a halt within a minute of one another. Outside the High Commissioner's a fur-clad commissionaire was standing. Linda realised that he was her only hope and shouted to him, 'Help! Help!'

As she did so, the two men met in front of her. The thug's fist shot out, caught the Russian in the face and knocked him to his knees. He gave a quick shake of his head, swung his body round and made a grab at Linda's beauty box. But she was too quick for him and jumped aside. The young thug had not paid off his taxi. The driver now came up, grabbed him by the arm and demanded his fare.

Linda seized the opportunity to thrust the beauty box at the commissionaire, crying, 'Here! Take it! Take it to the High Commissioner! It's terribly important.'

He took it, but held it only for a moment. The thug lashed out. His fist caught the man on the side of the jaw. His knees buckled, he fell back, measuring his length on the ground. He had dropped the case and it slithered across the pavement.

The thug and Linda dived for it at the same instant. The Russian had come to his feet. Thrusting out his leg, he tripped the thug, who fell headlong into the gutter. Linda snatched at the box, but missed it. The thug had jerked himself up in time to intercept her. The Russian's hand darted between them, at the box. Linda kicked out hard. Her toe caught him on the thigh and he staggered back.

A little crowd was gathering. Boyface, evidently a trained athlete, had picked himself up in a second. His mouth set grimly, he dashed past Linda. But the Russian caught him by the collar and swung him round. He wrenched himself free. The box lay on the edge of the pavement. Both of them grabbed at it simultaneously. Their hands locked and they began to wrestle. The commissionaire was now blowing his police whistle.

Linda saw her chance and grabbed the box. The two men suddenly thrust each other off and came at her. The commissionaire was by then on his feet, but they were between him and Linda. Had she attempted to throw the case, one of them would have got it. Turning, in spite of the oncoming traffic which had just been released by the lights going green, she started to dash across the road.

If she could get across safely it would cut them off and give her a chance to disappear in the crowd on the opposite pavement. A big lorry braked hard, the driver cursing as she skimmed past the bonnet. Hidden beyond it was a small car. The driver did not see her in time and braked too late. The mudguard hit her hard on her left leg. She was thrown sideways. The beauty box she was clutching struck the road with a thud and flew open. When she had shut it, she had been so pre-occupied about dealing with Gerta that she had forgotten to turn the knob of the combination which would have relocked it.

Out came the packet and the pile of thousand-dollar notes beneath them. The bitter wind was blowing half a gale. The banknotes sailed up into the air like a flight of startled birds, scattered in all directions, then fluttered down on the traffic, on the road and on the pavements on both sides of it. Pandemonium broke loose. Everyone within half a mile seemed to be shouting as they scrambled and fought for this manna from heaven which had suddenly fallen amongst them. Only half-conscious, Linda lay in front of the car that had knocked her down.

20

Full Circle

LINDA remained where she had fallen for less than half a minute. The beauty box lay open upside down only a yard away from her. Beside it, too heavy to be blown away, lay the packet; but the high wind was causing the notes to spiral up into the air like a fountain of paper. To her, it was the packet that mattered beyond all else. Scrambling to her knees, she reached for and seized it.

The driver of the little car was a young girl. Immediately it had struck Linda and jerked to a halt she opened the door and jumped out. Her face white with fright at having run down a woman, she grasped Linda's arm and helped her to her feet, while gasping:

'I . . . I'm terribly sorry. Are you hurt?'

'My leg,' Linda murmured. 'Your buffer caught it an awful blow. It's not broken though.' But as she spoke she was not looking at the girl. She was staring anxiously across at the High Commission building. The stream of traffic was running on. Between passing vans and cars she caught glimpses of a struggle taking place on the pavement. The Russian had disappeared, but a policeman had come on the scene. Between them, he and the commissionaire were struggling to hold on to the big, boyish-looking thug. But the little crowd that had gathered in the early stages of the rumpus had now dispersed. Men, women and children were scrambling wildly for the fluttering notes.

The girl picked up Linda's beauty box, shut it and held it out to her. United States banknotes are all the same size and colour. They vary only in the portraits of various past Presidents and the value on them, so the girl had no idea that the best part of a quarter of a million dollars had been scattered by the wind. But even had they been one-dollar bills their total value would have been considerable, and she said:

'I'm afraid you've lost an awful lot of money.'

Turning, for the first time Linda got a full view of the girl. She was a pretty little thing of about eighteen, with blue eyes and long, flaxen hair. 'Thank you.' Linda took the box and added lamely, 'I . . . I was taking it to the bank.'

'I'm sorry about your leg.'

Impatiently Linda shook her head. 'Don't worry. I think it's only bruised and the pain will wear off. Anyway, it wasn't your fault.'

Meanwhile, she was wondering desperately what she had better do. Dared she recross the road and try to get the precious packet to the High Commissioner? No. There were now two policemen there, holding the thug and talking with the commissionaire. If she crossed to them, it was certain he would tell the policemen that it was her arrival that had started all the trouble. They would insist on her coming to the station to make a statement, and she was still 'wanted' by the police in Canada. The fact that she could give no address or particulars about herself was certain to make them suspicious. They would go through their books of photographs and, in spite of her blonde wig, might identify her. At all costs she must keep away from the police. She must try to get the papers to tne Governor General or the British Consul.

The girl was speaking again. 'Apart from losing all that money, you had a nasty fall. You really ought to go to a doctor and have your leg looked at; or, any-way, to your home so that you can lie down for a while.' She held open the door of the car. 'Please get in. Tell me where you'd like me to take you, and I'll run you there.'

It was at that moment that Linda caught sight of the Russian again. Evidently he had run down the street for a hundred yards or more, then crossed to an island. He had seen her and was now about eighty yards off, hurrying toward her between the two lanes of traffic and shouting, 'Anna! Anna!'

Even if the girl had been willing to become involved in the affair and help Linda get away, there was no time to explain the situation to her before the Russian was upon them. Linda threw the beauty box and packet on the back seat of the car, got quickly into the passenger seat and pulled shut the door. As the girl walked round the bonnet to get in on the other side, Linda slid across into the driver's seat. She had only to push the gear lever and the car shot forward, leaving the astonished owner staring after it.

A main cross-roads lay two hundred yards ahead. By the time Linda was half-way there, the lights turned orange. She swore and looked in the driving mirror. The Russian had reached the place where she had been knocked down and, with the girl beside him, was giving chase. The girl was shouting as she ran, 'Stop! Stop! Stop thief!'

The light went red just as Linda reached the cross-roads. If she pulled up it was certain they would catch her. Ignoring the policeman on point duty, she drove on. He yelled at her and blew his whistle, but she was aided by the confusion which still reigned owing to the shower of notes. Several drivers of cars and lorries had left their vehicles to secure a share in this incredibly lucky windfall. Some of the people were looking dubiously at the notes they held, evidently wondering if they ought not to hand them over to the police, but the majority were slapping one another on the back and shouting with joy, or furtively hurrying off down side turnings.

Linda's heart lurched as she missed by inches an old, blind man carrying a white stick, who had started to cross the road. Then she was round the corner. With a clear run ahead now, she jammed down her foot on the accelerator. As the car leapt forward pain shot up through her left thigh, but she gritted her teeth and maintained the pressure.

Another cross-roads loomed ahead. She slowed down, but the lights were green. Having crossed it she took the first turning to the right, the next to the left, then she caught a glimpse of the Ottawa river. Two hundred yards further on, she came abreast of the entrance to a bridge. Turning, she crossed it, and ran on for a mile or more through streets of shops and blocks of dwellings. Gradually they thinned out and she was passing pleasant homes with private gardens. Twenty minutes after having stolen the car she was out in open country. Reducing speed, she turned into a by-lane, pulled up, took her hands off the wheel, lay back and closed her eyes.

For a good ten minutes she remained slumped in her seat. Then, fully recovered from her nerve-racking drive, she sat up, reached over for the packet and the beauty box to put it in. When she opened the box, to her surprise and delight she found that there were still some of the bills in it. Quickly she counted them. There were four—four thousand dollars—nearly one thousand, seven hundred pounds.

It was salvation. With such a sum she could keep herself in reasonable comfort for a long time. But those accursed nuclear calculations? What was she to do about them? Most of the personnel of the Russian Embassy and all The Top's men in Ottawa would be looking for her. By now they would have picketed the Governor General's residence, the American Embassy, the American and British Consulates and every other place at which a defector might try to hand over documents.

Could she possibly carry out the plan that had flitted through her mind when she had first come upon Anna Zubarova's passport? If only she could get to Oslo she could hand over the papers to the British Ambassador there.

Besides, as long as she remained in Canada she would never feel really safe. After Sid's act of idiocy had put the police on to her, it was certain that her story would have got into the Press under some awful heading such as '*Young mistress of elderly scientist steals fortune in jewels*', and her photograph would have been published. There had been several of her that she had left behind at the house in Park Side West. Elsie would have given them to the police, and they would have sent copies to Canada.

That she would now be recognised from one was unlikely. But from the time the hunt had been up for her in Canada, most of the people she had met while there would have read about and remembered her.

There were the residents at the Astley, people who had seen her with Big Bear in the restaurants in Vancouver, at the Empress on Victoria Island, and many more she had met with him in Montreal. In addition there were the people up at Lake Louise, shop assistants from whom she had bought things to be sent round for her to the Ritz-Carlton, chambermaids, waiters and porters there and at other hotels at which she had stayed, taxi-drivers and attendants on trains. People were always moving from city to city. One way and another, there must be hundreds who would know her again if they saw her in the street. Ruefully she realised that this was a penalty of being both unusually tall and beautiful. With the added interest of crime, her face must have stuck in the memories of innumerable men and women.

Getting out the passport and air ticket again, she examined them more carefully. The flight was definitely for that day, and due to take off from Ottawa at 10.40 hours. The passport was made out in both Russian and English. She learned from it that Anna was seven years older than herself. Her height was five foot nine. Fortunately, she had a broad forehead and oval face. Her mouth was fuller than Linda's and her eyes green. Her nose Linda knew to be flatter, but that did not show in the photograph. Except for the shape of the two faces there was not much likeness. Still, if she altered her appearance in certain ways, Linda felt there was a sporting chance that she might pass for her.

Although she had been flown in to Ottawa, as it had been dark when the aircraft landed she had no idea on which side of the city the airport lay. But in a pocket of the car she found a map. It showed her that, having crossed the river to the western side, she had driven through a considerable suburb called Hull, and must now be out in the country beyond it. By far the greater part of the city was east of the river. To the north there was a large area marked Rockcliffe Park, and to the east of it was the airport.

For a long while she sat in the car, trying to decide what to do. One thing was certain—she must procure a change of clothes. Anna's chauffeur's uniform: cloak, black, shiny top-boots and peaked cap were identifiable at a considerable distance. Gerta and the two thugs had all seen her in them, so had the girl who owned the car and the policeman at the cross-roads. The Russian, too, still believing her to be Anna, would have all his people out looking for her dressed as she was.

If she was to attempt to get out of Canada, she would have to effect a difficult compromise—become unlike Anna in general appearance, yet retain such blonde likeness as she could in order to bluff her way past the Immigration officials. Another half-hour passed while she made a mental list of all the things she must buy to give herself the best chance of succeeding in her plan.

All this while her leg had been paining her badly. The engine was shut off, so it had become very cold. Anna's cloak was a poor substitute for her own mink, which she had been forced to abandon at the Château Laurier; and, having counted the money in the billfold she had taken from Gerta's bag, she found she had only eighty-seven dollars—not enough to buy a really good-quality cloth coat in addition to all the other things she needed.

Starting up the car, she drove back to Hull. By the time she found a car park off one of the main streets, it was three o'clock. Loath as she was to leave the precious beauty box, she knew she would need both hands for her shopping, so she locked it up in the boot. It was long past lunchtime, so she limped along to a delicatessen she had noticed. There she warmed herself up with two cups of steaming coffee, and made a meal off hamburgers and apple pie. She also bought some ham rolls, biscuits, chocolate and a tin of Coca-Cola, so that she could picnic in the car that evening instead of having to go to a restaurant.

Further along the street there was a good-sized store. Her first purchase there was a cheap suitcase. Next she went to the shoe department. Getting her left leg out of Anna's long boot was painful, but the easing of its pressure brought her relief, and she left the department in a pair of low-heeled brown shoes. During the following half-hour she bought the thickest woollen pullover she could find, a muffler, a raincoat, a rainproof hat with a brim that turned down all round, a nightdress, dressing gown and slippers, a modest selection of washing and make-up things, a pair of semi-dark glasses, a walking stick with a crook, a pair of scissors, a packet of labels and a Biro.

With the black boots and the things she had bought in the suitcase, she walked back to the car, then drove out again to the country lane where she had first pulled up.

Being unable to afford a thick coat, she had decided to continue wearing Anna's tunic; but, hidden under the long pullover and with the raincoat over it, she would at least be protected from the wind. Anna's cloak and cap she put with the boots in the suitcase, then wrote a label for it, giving the flight number and adding, in large letters, OSLO.

Her next concern was her wig. Being blonde, the difference in colour from that in the passport photograph would not show, but it was elaborately dressed in the style favoured by Cherril Chanel, whereas Anna's hair was straight and cut short in an untidy bob. Taking off the wig, Linda cut off two-thirds of the long hair with the scissors, and tried it several times on her head until she was satisfied from her reflection in the driving mirror that, under the rim of the rain-hat, it looked much as Anna's hair would have done. Lastly, she touched up her eyebrows and used the lipstick to give her mouth a squarer appearance.

By the time she was finished it was past five o'clock, but she still had over four hours to go until reporting time for her flight and, as the number and description of the stolen car would have been given by the girl to the police, she felt she would stand less risk of the car being spotted if she did not drive through the city until after dark, so she shut her eyes and tried to sleep.

Her mind was much too active with apprehension for her to drop off properly, but she managed to doze at intervals for a couple of hours. By then darkness had fallen, and she was again feeling the cold so badly that she made up her mind to run the gauntlet of the city.

Driving very carefully, for an accident would have been disastrous for her, she passed through Hull, seeing now in front of her the heights of East Ottawa, on which stood the square gothic towers of the Parliament buildings and, rising from them, lofty and narrow against the darkening evening sky, the Peace Tower. Crossing the river she turned left, along a broad highway which she hoped, from her study of the map, was Rideau Street. After a short distance her hope was confirmed, as it curved north-east. Further on it crossed another, smaller river and eventually brought her to Rockcliffe Park. After driving for half a mile through the park, which at that hour was almost deserted, she drove off the road and pulled up among a group of tall trees.

There she slowly ate her supper and drank the Coke, while wishing longingly that she had with her something stronger to fortify her for the big risk she must soon run. But, although she had spun out her picnic meal as long as possible, there was still over an hour to go before reporting time at the airport. The waiting seemed to drag as though every minute were ten and, even when she could have started, she forced herself to wait another twenty minutes, in order to cut the time she would have to hang about the airport as short as possible. At last she made up her mind to start and face whatever fate had in store for her. Ten minutes later, she pulled up in the airport car park.

Before leaving the car, she scribbled with the Biro on the back of the map: *So sorry to have deprived you of your car for a few hours, but it was a case of real necessity*, then put the map back in the side pocket where the girl would, sooner or later, find it.

Carrying the suitcase in one hand and her beauty box in the other, she walked across to the airport building and entered the great central hall. She had the brim of the rain-hat pulled well down, so that tufts of fair hair showed only covering her ears. Tucked into the raincoat the woollen muffler hid the lower part of her chin—for which the bitter cold was an adequate reason—and she was wearing the tinted glasses which, without being dark enough to arouse suspicion, obscured the colour of her eyes. In the hand that held the beauty box she also carried the stick, leaning heavily upon it with every step she took. That, and her low-heeled shoes, disguised her height, so that at a casual glance she appeared to be no more than Anna's five foot nine.

On reaching the desk for her flight, she produced

both the passport and the ticket. It was, she had noticed, economy class, so evidently, if distinguished Russian scientists went about dressed as chauffeurs, they had to travel in accordance with the role they were playing.

The woman behind the desk checked the ticket with her list, then handed it back with the passport and a boarding card. Linda's suitcase was well under the allowed weight, but the label caught the woman's eye and she said, 'You change aircraft at Oslo, but this will not be transferred to the other plane unless you label it MOSCOW.'

Making her voice as husky as she could, Linda replied, 'Et is all right. I break journey two night in Oslo.'

An official led her to another counter where she was screened as a precaution against her being a hijacker. Knowing this would happen, she had left the little gas pistol in the car; but, as the beauty box was steel under the blue leather covering, she had to open it. Since it contained only papers and banknotes, she was passed through.

So far, so good. But now she must face the really big hurdle: the Immigration people. At the gate there was a short queue. When she was within thirty feet of the end of it, she halted abruptly and turned about. Standing near the gate were the Russian, another well-dressed man wearing glasses, and a hospital nurse. As the women were passing through the gate the Russian, his head thrust forward, was scrutinising their profiles.

The blood drained from Linda's face and her pulse was racing. She had failed to take into account the fact that the Russian would know that Anna was booked on the plane leaving for Oslo that night. Naturally he had come there to stop her.

That he had a nurse with him strongly suggested that the other man was a doctor. She had heard of cases of people being carried off against their wills by someone, accompanied by others posing as a doctor and a nurse, who declared that he was a relative of the person they wanted to get hold of and that he, or she, was a mental case escaped from an asylum. The Russian, as an official of the Soviet Embassy, would state that he was responsible for her and insist on her showing Anna's passport.

He would get a shock when he realised that she was not Anna. But he would immediately assume that Anna, having given her the passport and ticket, had also passed the papers on to her. As she could produce no proof that she was not Anna, he would swear that she was and, just the same, carry her off to the Russian Embassy where she could be searched and 'grilled'.

Linda cast a quick glance over her shoulder. The Russian was so close to the queue that, even if she kept her face averted, he could not fail to recognise the tuft of blonde hair over her ear, which she had taken such pains to make look like Anna's.

Perhaps she could pass by staring him straight in the face, so that he would at once realise that she was not Anna. But no! That would not do. She was carrying the blue beauty box. It was too large to conceal under her raincoat. He would recognise it instantly as the one he had fought to get hold of outside the High Commissioner's that morning.

What could she do? How, in heaven's name, could she get past him? Beyond the barrier lay Norway, final escape from the Canadian police, those nuclear calculations safe in the hands of the British Ambassador there, and a new life with sixteen hundred pounds in her purse.

For a good three minutes she stood with her back turned to the queue, striving with all her wits to devise a means of getting past the Russian. At last one came to her. But it entailed another risk—that she might not be allowed to board the plane. Should she take it, or leave the airport while the going was good, and try to find a hide-out, or get away from Ottawa?

But, apart from thousand-dollar notes, the things she had bought that afternoon had reduced her ready money from eighty-seven dollars to five. Nowhere, except at a bank, could she change a thousand-dollar note; and by now the Russian might have sent in the numbers of the notes that Anna had taken to the Château Laurier and asked that anyone who tried to change one of them should be detained.

Now she was wanted by the police not only on account of the jewels, but also for having stolen a car. It was certain that the Russians would have their people watching for her at the railway and bus stations. Still worse, there was Gerta, her two thugs and probably a score of other men under The Top's orders in Ottawa searching hotels and eating-places for her. And if they got her, it would be not prison, but death.

She could not possibly hope to escape for more than a few hours from being recognised and caught by the police, the Russians or the gangsters. She must take the gamble she had thought of. It was the only conceivable chance.

With swift steps she walked back to the bookstall and bought a paper. Then she asked the woman who had served her if she could give her a piece of string. The woman willingly produced a piece that had tied up a bundle of newspapers. Thanking her, Linda hurried across to the women's lavatories. Shutting herself into one, she wrapped the tell-tale beauty box in the paper, tied it up with the string and made a handle to carry it by. Next, she took off her hat, folded it and pushed it into the pocket of her raincoat. Then she took off what remained of the wig and threw it down the lavatory. Her own brown hair had been firmly plastered down. It took her several minutes to pull it free into rats'-tails, then comb it through again and again until the curls had reappeared. Then she fluffed it out in a great, light bronze halo that framed her head and hung down all round to her shoulders.

She feared that the woman attendant might notice her metamorphosis and, believing her to be a crook, start asking questions. But the woman was talking to a girl who was making up her face, and did not even glance in Linda's direction as she left the lavatory.

Carrying her parcel in her left hand, she returned to the gate where the queue had been. Everyone had now gone through except a woman with a child. Linda stood behind them for a minute and, turning her head, looked the Russian straight in the face. As he returned her glance he saw only a very pretty girl leaning on a stick who, with her wildly disordered fuzzy hair, looked like a hippie. No flicker of interest came into his eyes. The woman and child moved on. Linda followed and the man on the gate waved her toward the desks of the Immigration officers fifty feet further on.

Her ruse for getting past the Russian had succeeded. But what now? By so drastically altering her appearance she had greatly reduced any likeness she had had to Anna. When she showed the photograph in the passport, they could not help seeing the difference. All the odds seemed against their letting her through.

Mustering all her self-control, with an air of assurance

she handed her passport to a youngish officer, then looked away as though the matter hardly concerned her. Having turned two pages of the passport, he suddenly frowned and said:

'This passport belongs to someone else. The photo is not of you.'

On the door to the lavatories there had been a dual-language notice: *Ladies—Dames*. That had given Linda an idea. She had not a notion what a Russian's accent sounded like when speaking English. But on trips abroad with Rowley, she had picked up colloquial French. And when a person who is not French speaks that language, it is far from easy for anyone to detect to what nation he belongs. Knowing that all Canadian officials speak at least some French, Linda stared at him in simulated annoyance and surprise and demanded:

'*Qu'est-ce que vous voulez dire, Monsieur? C'est une photographie de moi-même.*'

'It is not, Mademoiselle,' he insisted. 'The hair of this woman is blonde. Your hair is brown.'

Continuing to use French, Linda replied, 'But that was taken in Moscow. Since I come here I grow my hair long and have it dyed. You see, in Russia nearly all girls are blonde. As a brunette I shall be a sensation.'

'But the face is not like yours, Mademoiselle. It is much fatter, and coarser.'

'Ah!' Linda laughed. 'That is how I used to look when I worked on the farm. But since I come to your lovely Canada I work hard to make myself different. In Russia beauty treatment is unknown. But here, yes. I diet. I have the massage. There are the skin lotions. I make myself a lovely girl. When I get home every man wish to sleep with me.'

The young officer suppressed a smile, and Linda

hurried on, 'Do you not agree? Even in Canada I now receive much admiration. Ask yourself, Monsieur. Had we met in night club, would you not have been tempted to make naughty propositions to me?'

'Er . . . well, Mademoiselle . . .' He went a little pink about the gills. 'I wouldn't like to seem rude by saying "no" to that. But, all the same, I don't believe this passport was issued to you.'

Linda's heart sank. In desperation she took another line and pretended sudden anger. 'Monsieur is being obstructive without reason. It is because you are a bourgeois capitalist. You wish to put spokes in my wheels because I am a citizen of the Soviet Union of Socialist Republics. That I will not tolerate. I am a diplomat and I go to my country on urgent business. You will let me go to my plane or I will report you.'

It was the wrong line. The young man's expression became stony and he said, 'There is nothing political in this. I am simply doing what I am paid for, and I'm not letting anyone out of this country whose credentials I regard as suspect. Now I'm going to fetch my chief, and you can abuse me to him to your heart's content.'

As he left her, Linda gave an inward groan. If she could not win over an impressionable young man, it was certain that she would stand little chance with an older one. She glanced toward the gate fifty feet away. The Russian, the nurse and the man who looked like a doctor were still standing there. A man in a loud checked overcoat and with a brightly-coloured band round his hat, looking like an American tourist, came past them at a run and halted, puffing, behind Linda.

At that moment the young officer returned with his grey-haired senior. The latter was holding Anna's passport. He gave Linda a quick scrutiny and said, 'I can't believe this is a photograph of you, Miss.'

'It is,' Linda insisted angrily in French. 'I know I have changed a lot since it was issued to me in Moscow. But that is as I used to look before I slimmed, let my hair grow and dyed it. As I have said, I've been attached to the Soviet Embassy here, and I'm being sent home on an important mission. It's very urgent. You must let me through.'

The grey-haired man shook his head.

Linda played her last card. It was a desperate bluff. 'If you don't believe me, telephone the Soviet Embassy. Describe me as you see me now, and they will confirm that I am Anna Zubarova.'

'Fur Jesus' sake!' exclaimed the man behind Linda. 'Don't hold me up while you argue with this woman, or I'll miss my plane.'

'And so will I,' added Linda wrathfully. 'Telephone my Embassy if you like. But, by the time you have, the flight will have left. Then there will be great hell to pay. If you want a diplomatic incident, you will get it. You are asking for one.'

'O.K., O.K.!' said the senior officer, giving Linda a sour look. 'I won't hold you here. You can go aboard. Meanwhile, there'll be time for me to call your Embassy before take-off.' Then he stamped her passport and that of the man behind her.

Side by side they hurried down the long corridor, the man a few feet ahead, as Linda was still a little lame and, for appearances' sake, had to continue to use her stick. But he waited a moment to allow her to precede him on to the plane.

The economy class had three seats in a row on one side and two on the other. The gangway seat of the

last pair at the rear of the aircraft was vacant, so Linda
decided to take it. The other seat was occupied by a
tall, blue-eyed man with neatly-brushed grey hair, who
looked to be about sixty. As she was taking off her
raincoat and muffler to put them up on the rack, he
stood up, smiled at her and said:

'Wouldn't you prefer the window seat? It doesn't
make any difference to me. I've flown the Atlantic so
often.'

Her mind was in a turmoil. She had got past the
Russian and through Immigration. She was actually on
the plane that was due in a few minutes to take off for
Europe. But by now the surly senior official would be
telephoning her description to the Soviet Embassy. It
was beyond all doubt that they would say she was not
Anna Zubarova. Linda's vivid imagination conjured
up a picture of herself within a few minutes being
ignominiously escorted off the plane. She would
probably also be charged with attempting to leave the
country under false pretences. In any event, she would
still be in Ottawa, with the police, the Russians and
The Top's men all after her.

Only vaguely taking in what the nice-looking, grey-
haired man had said, she murmured, 'Thank you,'
collapsed into the window seat and shut her eyes.

Minutes passed. She heard a slam nearby and
opened her eyes. The steward had shut the rear door of
the aircraft and was bolting it, but it could easily be
opened again. The plane remained stationary. Another
five minutes dragged by, then the plane began to move.
Slowly it turned out into the runway. There it came to
a halt. It could still be detained by a signal from the
control tower, and a jeep sent out to take her off.
Clenching her hands, her eyes again closed, Linda lay

back, hardly breathing, while suffering agonies. Her mind went back to the awful suspense she had endured in similar circumstances at Heathrow. She had got away then. Would she now? Suddenly the jets roared. The great aircraft rushed forward, lifted and was airborne.

Linda gave a long, deep sigh of relief and sat up. She had won. They would not recall the plane now that it was on its way. The elderly official must have failed to get through to the Soviet Embassy in the limited time at his disposal. She was out of Canada, on her way to Norway. And she had both the papers and plenty of money.

Her companion turned toward her and asked, 'Are you all right? I was afraid you were feeling ill.'

'No . . . no,' Linda smiled. 'I'm feeling fine. I could do with a drink, though.'

'We'll get one in a minute. They always start at the rear of the aircraft.' As he spoke, an air hostess came up beside them with her order sheet.

'Champagne for me,' he said promptly. Linda nodded. 'For me, too, please.'

'Getting served first is not the only good thing about being in a rear seat,' he went on. 'If the kite crashes, you stand a better chance of getting out alive. Tail usually breaks off, so you don't get fried. All the same, I travel first most of the time.'

'You fly a lot, then?' Linda asked.

He grinned. 'I like it, and I can afford to. Part of my pension, you see. I'm a senior B.O.A.C. pilot, recently retired. On all B.O.A.C. routes throughout the world I can fly for only ten per cent of the ordinary fare.'

'How lovely for you. But this isn't a B.O.A.C. plane, is it?'

'No. That's why I'm flying economy. Got to get to Olso in a hurry. My wife is Norwegian. She has been there on a visit to her family, while I've been renewing my memories of Canada. Had a cable this morning to say she'd been in a car smash. Not in danger, thank God; but I am naturally anxious to join the old girl as soon as I can.'

'I do hope you'll find that it's nothing serious.'

'Thanks. By the way, my name's Matthew Jackson. But people always call me Captain Jacko.'

'Mine's . . .' Linda hesitated. 'Mine's Anna Zubarova.'

He raised his bushy grey eyebrows. 'That sounds Russian; but surely you're English, aren't you?'

'Yes,' Linda admitted, seeing no reason why she should any longer conceal the fact.

Their drinks arrived. Linda had forgotten that, as she was not travelling first class, she would have to pay for hers, but Captain Jacko would not let her. With more enthusiasm and happiness than she had felt for weeks, she drank the old toast he gave her, 'Happy landings.'

Shortly afterwards another air hostess came through the distant curtains separating the first from the economy-class passengers. As she approached, Linda caught her words. She was calling out, 'Miss Zubarova. Miss Zubarova.'

Linda paled, wondering who could have sent her a message. Perhaps back in Ottawa they had verified the fact that she was travelling on a passport that did not belong to her and radioed the pilot. But surely the plane would not turn back, so what could they do to her? Suddenly the awful thought came into her mind that they might prevent her landing in Oslo and bring her back to Canada. But there was no alternative to accepting the message. Reluctantly she held up her hand.

The air hostess gave her an airmail letter card, with the name she was passing under scrawled on it, and said, 'This was handed in up forward just before take-off. We always have so many things to see to then that I forgot it temporarily. I'm sorry about the delay.'

Acknowledging the apology with a faint smile, Linda took the flimsy, folded paper and tore it open. One glance told her that it must be written in Russian. She stared at it, put it down, then stared at it again. To know what the message was might be terribly important to her. Seeing her worried look, Captain Jacko said:

'Not bad news, I hope.'

'I don't know,' she admitted. 'It is in Russian, and I don't know that language.'

'Perhaps I can help,' he offered. 'In the war we not only sent tanks and guns to Joe Stalin, but also aircraft. That was before I became a pilot. I was a young engineer flight sergeant, and one of the lads sent out to help the Russians assemble our machines after we'd got them uncrated. I was the best part of a year in Murmansk. Had a Russian girl friend. Pretty little piece, and that's the best way to learn a language. I picked up quite a lot from her.'

Linda hesitated only a moment. Nothing could stop her now from reaching Oslo, but her future safety might depend on how she acted when she got there. Handing over the letter, she said, 'If you can translate it, I'd be very grateful.'

Getting out a pair of spectacles, he pored over the letter for several minutes, then he muttered, 'I'm afraid my Russian is pretty rusty, but from what I make of this it seems that you're in a spot of trouble.'

'Don't I know it!' Linda heaved a sigh. 'I may as well tell you at once that I got out of Canada on another woman's passport, pretending I was a Russian, and I'm very anxious to know what they can do about it.'

He gave her an appraising look. 'The devil you did! Well, this is more or less what the letter says: *Comrade Zubarova. We know you to have succeeded in boarding the air-craft. Your defection puzzles and distresses us all. Soviet Ambassador will be radioed to meet aircraft at Oslo. You are ordered to hand him papers you carry. Failure to do so will result in disciplining. Sergei Petrovitch, on behalf of Ambassador Chernicov.*

After a short pause, Captain Jacko added, 'There are some words before "disciplining" that have been partly scratched out. They look like the Russian for your being "liquidated". I suppose the chappie who wrote this felt that if anyone other than you read this, he might think a threat of murder went a bit too far.'

'That's what they mean to do to me, though,' Linda said in a strained voice. A few moments before she had been feeling on top of the world. This sudden know-ledge that she had not got away, after all, had, like a bombshell, blown the earth from beneath her feet. From the set-up at the Ottawa airport, she could guess what would happen when they landed at Oslo. As she left the aircraft she would be met by several Russians, including a doctor and a nurse. They would have an ambulance standing by. Despite her protests, she would be hustled into it. The louder she screamed, the more convinced onlookers would be that she was a mental case, the fact that she was carrying a Russian passport being evidence enough that it was her own people who were taking her away. They would take her to the

Soviet Embassy and, in a cellar there, either shoot or strangle her.

She wondered what had happened to the real Anna Zubarova. The battering she had received must have inflicted a serious injury to her head. Bad enough for her to be carted off to hospital, and the probability was that she was still lying unconscious there. In any case, it was clear that she had been unable to communicate with her friends, otherwise they would not still be under the impression that she had defected. And it was certain that The Top's people would not have told the Russians what had really happened. They had nothing to gain by doing so; on the contrary, the less the Russians knew the better chance they would have reckoned they had of getting back the papers themselves and selling them for another fat wad of thousand-dollar bills.

These thoughts had hardly rushed through Linda's mind when Captain Jacko leaned over and whispered to her, 'It's none of my business, but it seems to me that if these Ruskies get you you'll be for the high jump. I take it you are one of "C" 's people. If so, I'm willing to do anything I can to help.'

She turned and stared at him. 'What do you mean by "C"? Who is he?'

The elderly man's face froze. 'Oh, well, if you are working for a foreign power, you must count me out.'

'I'm not,' Linda replied. 'I'm on my own.'

He shrugged. 'You can hardly expect me to believe that. Young girls like you don't carry round documents that might cost them their lives, unless they are paid jolly well by somebody to do it.'

At that moment the air hostess began to hand out the plastic supper trays. As it was after midnight, the meal was a cold one, consisting of snacks, sandwiches,

M

pastries, cake and fruit on a trolley, from which the passengers took their choice. For once Linda had no appetite, so she asked only for a piece of fruit cake. Captain Jacko took two sandwiches and a banana.

While they were eating, Linda was thinking hard. There was now no getting away from the fact that when they reached Oslo she would be lucky if within a few hours she was not dead. There might be some way in which Captain Jacko could save her. But, apart from admitting to having stolen the jewels, she would have to tell him her whole story, from the time she had arrived in Chicago. As she looked back on it, the way in which she had become involved in The Top's affairs seemed so fantastic that she felt sure the Captain would not believe her. But there was one thing she could do. She could tell him that the nuclear calculations had come into her possession by pure chance, then hand them over to him. That, at least, would prevent the Russians from getting hold of them, and might induce him somehow to keep her out of their clutches.

He had finished his sandwiches and she was still thinking of the best way to reopen the subject when the air hostess from the first-class compartment came through, stopped beside him, smiled and said, 'Captain Fisher's compliments, sir, and would you care to come up to the flight deck for a while?'

It was the invitation normally extended during flights to any V.I.P.s or senior ex-pilots who happened to be in an aircraft. Captain Jacko promptly stood up, wiped his mouth on the paper napkin, left the banana on his plate and replied, 'Delighted, my dear,' then followed the girl down the gangway.

Linda sat on, continuing to envisage the awful things that might happen to her after she landed in Oslo. But she had definitely decided by then that, immediately Captain Jacko returned, she would give him the papers and ask for his help.

She refused coffee and ordered another glass of champagne. Captain Jacko seemed to be away for a long time. She could only suppose that he had taken the co-pilot's seat and was happily gossiping with the captain of the aircraft. The plastic plates were collected and the lights dimmed. The air hostess returned to her galley. A few minutes later a single blast from a shrill whistle sounded from the first-class compartment. A Negress, who had been sitting in the outer seat of the row of three on the opposite side of the gangway to Linda, stood up. In her right hand she held something that looked like a small, square box. Raising it above her head, she shouted in a loud, shrill voice:

'This is a hijack! All of youse keep youse seats. I's gotten here a plastic bomb. Make one move, any of youse, an' I drops it. Blow you all to hell.'

In spite of the threat nearly everyone turned his head to stare at her, but no-one stood up. A bald man a few rows in front of her asked angrily, 'Where are you hijacking us to?'

The Negress showed her gleaming white teeth between thick red lips in a grin. 'To Algeria. De land of de free peoples, where they have kill all de rich whitey pigs.'

'God damn you!' said the man. Then there fell a sudden hush, broken only by the anxious whispering of neighbours.

Following her momentary shock, Linda suddenly realised what this meant to her. Unless the hijackers were willing to commit suicide, they would not blow the plane up. For the others, being flown to Algeria and perhaps having to spend several days there before they could get to Europe would be an infuriating thing to happen. But the aircraft was not going to land at Oslo, after all. The team of would-be murderers waiting there to carry her off would now wait in vain. It was unlikely that the Algerians would rob the passengers of their possessions, as the Algerian Government would be held responsible for that; so she would still have her four thousand dollars and the papers. When the passengers were allowed to leave, all the odds were that the aircraft's first stop would be Marseilles, as it was the nearest European airport. She could destroy Anna's passport and say that the Algerians had taken hers from her; then she could leave the plane at Marseilles. There would be no one there to stop her from taking the papers to the British Consul, and she would be free to start a new life in her beloved South of France. What could possibly have suited her better?

Elated beyond measure by this stroke of, for her, undreamed of good fortune, Linda looked round to ask the air hostess to bring her a third glass of champagne. But the girl was sitting on a tip-up seat about ten feet behind the Negress, her eyes riveted in terror on the plastic bomb.

About five minutes elapsed. During this time the massed feeling of apprehension generated by the passengers, who had now fallen silent, could be felt. Then Captain Jacko appeared between the curtains leading to the first-class compartment. Halting there, he addressed the passengers in a loud, calm voice:

'Ladies and gentlemen. You are obviously already aware that this aircraft has been hijacked. Your captain has sent me to tell you that, provided you all keep your seats and do not lift a hand above your shoulders, there is no need for alarm. The hijackers are Black Panthers who succeeded in getting over the frontier from the United States into Canada. They have ordered the pilot to fly the aircraft to Algiers. Once the hijackers have left her, the aircraft will be refuelled and reprovisioned. After the captain and his crew have had a few hours' rest, it will then be allowed to take off again for our original destination—Oslo.'

'Oh God!' Linda breathed, almost silently. She was, after all, to be delivered into the hands of her enemies. Perhaps, though, she could persuade the hijackers to let her get off the plane with them in Algiers. But what then? Algiers was an Arab country, and well disposed toward Russia. If the Russians learned that she was in Algeria, they would ask the Algerians to arrest her, and send somebody to take her back to Moscow. Even if she escaped that, how would she, a white woman, fare among Arabs and Negroes? How long could she hope to keep her money before it was stolen? Besides, the eyes of every man in the street would be stripping the clothes off a pretty white girl on her own. The memory of the giant Negro in the Chicago brothel came back to her, and she shuddered.

Captain Jacko had paused to answer some questions from a passenger in a seat near him. Now he resumed in a louder voice, again addressing the whole company, 'Ladies and gentlemen. I was about to add that, for the convenience of those passengers who may have been flying on from Oslo to other parts of Europe, on her flight north the aircraft will put down at Marseilles, Berne, Cologne and Bremen.'

Linda let her head fall forward. She was nearly crying with relief. She had been granted a reprieve. She would be able to get off at Marseilles, see the British

Consul there, then go on to Nice. There were scores of boutiques there in which an English-speaking girl could easily get taken on. There would be sunshine in the approaching winter, the flower market, with its great bunches of carnations, iced vermouth-cassis in the cafés and leisurely strolls along the Promenade des Anglais.

Captain Jacko walked down the gangway and took his seat beside her again. Having glanced at the Negress who was standing only a few feet away, he said, 'Damned annoying, this. Still, it's a bit of luck for you. Your Russian committee of welcome at Oslo will have their wait for nothing.'

'Yes,' Linda agreed cheerfully. 'I'm sorry for the other passengers, though.'

He shrugged philosophically. 'Oh, well; can't be helped. These things happen. We may as well get some sleep.' Then he lay back as far as possible in his seat.

Linda closed her eyes, but could not sleep. While the aircraft roared on through the night, she was busily planning a happy future on the Riviera. She would take a small apartment overlooking the sea with, if she could afford it, a *bonne à tout faire*, to do her chores while she worked. A job in a boutique would enable her to buy good clothes at reduced prices. There would be concerts to go to, and now and then she might even gamble a little at the Casino.

Dawn came. Captain Jacko was snoring. An hour or so later he suddenly woke up and looked round for the Negress. Standing there for hours had tired her, so she had made the air hostess leave her tip-up seat some distance away and was sitting on it, while the girl squatted on the floor.

Seeing that Linda was awake, he leaned over and said in a low voice, 'We are not going to Algiers—not yet, anyway.'

'Why not?' Linda whispered back.

'Not enough petrol to fly us there. We'll have to come down somewhere on the way to refuel.'

'Where?' asked Linda anxiously.

'Don't know. Depends on Captain Fisher and the strength of the head wind we're flying against. Lisbon perhaps; but maybe we won't be able to get that far, and have to land at Bordeaux.'

'Will . . . will there be any chance of our getting off?'

'There may be. It all depends on what sort of precautions the ground staff at the place we come down are taking about this sort of thing. And, of course, on how tough these bloody Black Panthers are. If I had my way I'd hang every blasted hijacker that was caught. As they imperil hundreds of people's lives, there ought to be an international law to that effect.'

He fell silent, and Linda was left to ponder on this new possibility. If she was able to leave the plane at Lisbon, or, even better, Bordeaux, she would escape any unpleasantness at Algiers. From the latter she could make her way overnight to the South of France.

Another hour and a half drifted by. Linda was now hungry and would have given a lot even for a cup of coffee. But there was no possibility of breakfast being served.

There came a break in the clouds. Looking out of the window, she could see land beneath them. Captain Jacko leaned across her and peered down. He drew a sharp breath and exclaimed, 'By Jove! We're over Ireland. I'd know it anywhere by the green of the fields.

Fisher couldn't make the Continent, or said he couldn't.
Well done, him! He's heading for Heathrow.'

'Heathrow!' Linda exclaimed in consternation.

He gave her a surprised look. 'What's wrong with
that? Our people there know their stuff. They keep a
guard there now, armed with rifles, to deal with
hijackers. They'll shoot the tyres to pieces so that the
aircraft can't take off again. We're as good as home and
dry.'

'I . . . I was only surprised,' Linda said lamely. But
her mind was seething with agitation. Like it or not,
unless the hijackers were fanatics and blew up the plane
with everyone in it, she would be forced to land in
England. Her passport was Anna's and she could not
speak a word of Russian. Even if she destroyed it, she
would be no better off. It was certain that the Immigration people would hold her until they had checked up
on whatever story she told them. And, of course, they
would cable Ottawa, to find out how she had got
aboard the plane, and what was known about her there.
The police in Ottawa would report that she had stolen
a car. And—a new and terrible thought—perhaps she
had choked the half-conscious Anna to death. If so,
they would want her for murder!

In any case, she was on the books of the British police
for the jewel robbery. That had been only two and a
half months ago. Two and a half months! She had gone
through so much since then that it seemed a lifetime.
And the police had long memories. Ten weeks were
nothing to them. Her photograph among those of
wanted criminals must still be in the memories of scores
of policemen; and her height made her so conspicuous.
She had no wig now, and her hair was not straight as
it had been when she left Heathrow; but again its old

halo of curls. What possible chance did she stand of
remaining unidentified for long?

Could she somehow induce Captain Jacko to get her
past the barriers, so that officially it would not be known
that she was back in England? Then she would stand
a chance of going to earth in some London suburb.

The aircraft had passed over the Irish Channel and
began its long descent. Madly she sought a way that
might persuade him to serve her purpose. At length she
said huskily:

'Captain. These papers I've got. They are important,
terribly important. I stole them from the Russians. I
tried to get them to our High Commissioner in Canada.
But I failed. That's why I took this aircraft. I thought
I would be able to give them to the British Ambassador
in Oslo. That is impossible now. But I must hand them
to somebody who is really high up. They are secret,
top secret. Even a British Customs man must not be
allowed to see them. Could you possibly vouch for me?
Take me through and to the Foreign Office in London?
You can remain with me and see me hand them over.'

His blue eyes were fixed steadily on hers. 'So you are
one of "C" 's people, after all.'

'No. I'm just a private individual. This happened by
pure chance. I was once the secretary to a nuclear
scientist; I realised what these papers meant, so I stole
them. But I'm not giving them up to anyone who
would not realise their vital importance.'

He considered for a moment, then smiled, 'You are
quite a girl, aren't you? In fact, it makes me pretty
proud to have met you. Well, everyone at Heathrow
knows me. I think they'll let you through with me, if I
vouch for you. Anyway, for time enough for you to do
your business with no questions asked.'

'Oh, bless you.' Linda breathed again, then added quickly, 'I've only this Russian passport, remember. And I daren't show that, as it would lead to all sorts of complications.'

'Don't worry. I can fix that, too. If only these bloody anarchists don't blow us up before we can get off the aircraft.'

The plane was now circling over the English country-side. Linda caught a glimpse of Windsor Castle and the Thames, then, a few minutes later, of the long Heath-row runways. Given that the hijackers could be dealt with, and provided her luck held, she would be at the Foreign Office within about an hour. Once she had delivered the goods she could say good-bye to Captain Jacko and fade away among London's seven million inhabitants.

Slowly the aircraft came down. It bumped twice lightly on the tarmac. The pilot reversed the jets. It braked to a halt, then taxied along to the great com-plex of airport buildings.

Captain Fisher had sent out the secret radio signal that he had hijackers aboard. Preparations had been made for their reception. There came a crash of rifle fire from men concealed under jeeps and cars. The aircraft lurched as its big tyres flattened.

Linda looked apprehensively at the Negress. Her eyes were wild and she again held up her bomb, ready to drop it. The air hostess bravely stood up and unbolted the rear door. Two minutes later a police inspector came on board, a revolver ready in his hand. The Negress stepped back and lowered her arm. The inspector grabbed it and jabbed the muzzle of his weapon hard into her ribs.

Captain Jacko and Linda were first off the aircraft.

He took her up the sloping passage to Immigration, walked her over to an elderly man at one of the desks and said, 'Hullo, John.' Then he held up his hand to screen his mouth and whispered, 'No passport,' then added a reassuring lie, 'One of "C" 's people. I'm seeing her through.'

The elderly man smiled and nodded. They walked on and down to the Customs hall. There Captain Jacko waved to a ginger-haired officer. Pointing to Linda's newspaper-wrapped beauty box, he called, 'Wotcher, Dicky. Nothing to declare. The lady will see her luggage through later.'

Linda breathed again as they walked through the automatic swing door of the exit on to the pavement, and asked, 'Can we get a taxi?'

'No need,' replied Captain Jacko cheerfully. 'The Chief Security Officer's office is only a couple of hundred yards away, and we'll walk over. He's the liaison between Special Branch and the Foreign Office. Quite a big shot. Has to be with all the queer fish constantly coming and going from Britain's biggest airport. You can hand your atom bomb, or whatever you've got, over to him with perfect confidence.'

It was raining, but not hard. They walked the two hundred yards and entered the other building. Linda had no fears now. She had only to get rid of the packet of papers, thank Captain Jacko and be on her way to London.

Inside the building they were taken up in the lift to the top floor. There, a secretary took Captain Jacko's name and they were kept waiting for a few minutes. Then they were shown into a spacious, well-furnished office.

Alone at a large desk covered with papers sat a man

busily writing. Captain Jacko led Linda forward and said, ' 'Morning, old boy. I've brought a lady to see you.'

The man at the desk looked up and Linda found herself face to face with Eric Dutton.

21

Flight or Prison?

ERIC'S face remained expressionless. Only an almost imperceptible flicker of the eyes told Linda that he recognised her. He stood up, smiled politely and waved her to a chair; then he turned to her companion.

'Jacko, old boy; I think this lady and I have met before. Would you mind leaving us alone for ten minutes or so, then coming back?'

'By all means. I'll go and clear my bags.' He glanced at Linda and grinned. 'It seems I was right about you, after all. Still, mum's the word. Like me to clear your luggage as well, while I'm at it?'

'Thank you. I'd be grateful if you would.' Linda produced her ticket, tore off the baggage check stapled to it, and handed it to him.

The moment the door shut behind Jacko, Eric turned on Linda and snapped, 'Why the hell have you come back here?'

She shrugged. 'I had no choice. The aircraft was hijacked.'

'Of course. For the moment I'd forgotten that. And now you're properly up against it.' He gestured toward a filing cabinet. 'There's a book in that with scores of photographs in it, and yours is among them. It's my duty to hand you over to the police.'

'Oh, well!' She gave a heavy sigh. 'I suppose I've had a run for my money, and was bound to be caught sooner or later. Let's not prolong the agony, but get it over with.'

'Linda, Linda,' he shook his head reproachfully, 'how can you possibly imagine that I'd do that after all we were to each other?'

She smiled then. 'So you mean to give me another chance to keep my freedom? That's very sweet of you.'

He shook his head. 'No; it's simply that I place some things above the law of the land. In this case it is my own conscience. If I sent for the police to arrest you, for all my life afterwards I'd think of myself as another Judas Iscariot.' He paused for a moment, then went on with sudden anger: 'The aircraft you were on was to have flown to Oslo. Why, in God's name, did you decide to return to Europe?'

Tapping the newspaper-wrapped beauty box, which she had put on his desk, she replied, 'This. I had hoped to hand it over to the British Ambassador in Norway.'

'What's in it?'

'Some documents. I believe them to be nuclear calculations, and I stole them from the Russians.'

'Stole them from the Russians?' he echoed. 'Good God alive! You can't mean that! You're pulling my leg.'

'I'm not,' she assured him. 'Undo it, and you'll see.'

Picking up a penknife from a tray on his desk, he cut the string, then ripped off the paper. She operated the combination lock and opened the box. As he took out the thick packet of papers, he exclaimed:

'By Jove! There are some thousand-dollar notes here as well.'

'Yes. Four of them. I stole those, too. Originally there

was a wad with nearly a quarter of a million dollars, but I lost most of them. They blew away in the street.'

'No, Linda!' he protested. 'You really can't expect me . . .'

'To believe that?' she finished for him angrily. 'I do. I've never told you a lie in my life, and I'm not lying now.'

'I'm sorry,' he apologised, 'I shouldn't have doubted your word. But all this sounds utterly fantastic.' As he spoke, he took the papers from their envelope, scanned the few top sheets quickly and went on: 'I'm afraid all these algebraic calculations are gibberish to me. Are you really certain that they are nuclear formulae?'

'No. I can only say that they look to me very like the sort of hieroglyphics that I saw our dear old Rowley working on scores of times. For all I know they may be children's homework. But it seems hardly likely that the Russians would have been willing to pay two hundred and thirty thousand dollars for a set of O-level exercises.'

'Damn it; of course you're right. What a wonderful coup you've pulled off. You deserve a D.B.E. But these things are real hot potatoes. I'm going to lock them in my safe until the experts on this stuff can send a security van with an armed guard to collect them.'

While he was locking away the papers, Linda re-locked the box with the notes in it. When he returned to his desk, he asked, 'But why Norway? You could have saved yourself a flight over the Atlantic by handing them over to our High Commissioner in Ottawa.'

'I tried to, but was prevented. Besides, Canada had become too hot to hold me, and it was a chance to get out of the country. I'd been arrested there once already.'

'What, by the police? And you managed to get away?'

'Yes. I was caught in an hotel up in the Rockies, but I got out of the window and ran off into the forest. Then I got lost in it and had to sleep all night in the snow.'

His eyes beamed admiration. 'What guts. Linda, you're a girl in a million.'

She gave a rueful smile. 'That was nothing to what I went through the following day, or later in Chicago.'

'Tell me about it.'

'It's far too long a story to tell before Captain Jacko comes back with my suitcase. And, if you are going to let me go, I must think about what it would be best to do. You see, I bluffed my way on to that plane by using the passport of the Russian woman from whom I stole the papers. But the photograph of her in it is not remotely like me; so I couldn't bluff your people here with it, get back on a plane and fly off anywhere else. Now I'm here in England, I've got to stay.'

Eric thought hard for a minute, then he said, 'If it's ever found out that, knowing there is a warrant out for you, I didn't have you arrested, I'll be in trouble anyhow. So I might as well be hung for a sheep as a lamb.'

'No, please!' She shook her head. 'I don't want you to risk getting into trouble because of me.'

He waved aside her protest. 'I can't leave the office for the time being; but I'll send you somewhere where we can meet and dine together this evening. Then we can talk matters over and decide what is best to be done.'

As he finished speaking, he walked to the door and opened it. Jacko was sitting in the outer office with his luggage and Linda's case beside him. Eric called him in and said, 'Jacko, will you do me a favour?'

'Of course, old boy,' came the prompt response.

'Thanks a lot. I want you to take this lady over to the Excelsior Hotel. She had better register as . . . Mrs. Diana Sutherland, British, address in London—Brown's Hotel. Pull your weight and, if you can, get her a suite. Tell them she will be staying as my guest. O.K.?'

'Roger!' said Jacko. As he had his back to Linda he gave Eric a broad wink and added, 'I wish I wasn't too old to apply for your sort of job.'

Twenty minutes later Linda had been installed in a comfortable bedroom in a suite that was usually reserved for visiting V.I.P.s or American millionaires who, for one reason or another, were forced to stay overnight at Heathrow. She was very tired, so undressed and went to bed right away.

It had been wonderful to see Eric again, but she still hadn't a clue about how he felt toward her. He had shown admiration for her exploit, but she was now proud of that herself; and any man might have been expected to praise a girl who had retrieved papers obviously stolen from the Americans, and got away from the Russians with them. He had made no reference to her theft of the jewels, except that there was a warrant out for her. And she could not attribute to love the fact that he had refrained from handing her over to the police. He had made it quite plain that to do so would have been contrary to his personal code of honour.

For a while she worried over what the outcome of her landing back in England would be, then she drifted off to sleep.

Ever since she had woken in Ottawa the previous day she had had a terribly exhausting time, so she did not wake until four o'clock. She felt hungry, but did not want to spoil her dinner. As she had in her bag some of the biscuits and chocolate she had bought in Hull she made do with the remainder of them, then got up and had a bath. Afterwards she spent quite a while getting her still fluffed-out hair back into good shape and doing her face. When it came to dressing, she was in a sad plight, as she had only Anna's ill-fitting uniform in which she had got away, and she would have given anything for a pretty frock in which to dine with Eric. Eventually she decided that, rather than wear the ugly chauffeur's tunic, she would stay in bed.

Shortly after six o'clock there came a knock at the door which led to the sitting-room of the suite. When she called, 'Come in,' Eric appeared, looked at her with a frown, and said:

'I expected to find you up and dressed.'

'Don't worry,' she replied, nettled into sarcasm by his tone. 'This is not another attempt to seduce you.'

'Sorry if I got the wrong impression,' he apologised. 'I'm sorry, too, about that night when you came to my room in Park Side West. If I hadn't behaved like a prude, we would have become lovers, instead of my clearing out. Then, when Rowley died, you would never have stolen those jewels, and got yourself in this awful mess. So in a way it's I who am to blame for your becoming a criminal.'

She shook her head. 'No. You did the right thing. We couldn't have concealed our . . . our fondness for each other for long. And if you had become my lover, I don't think I could have brought myself to continue being Rowley's mistress. I'd have had to leave him; and, after all he had done for me, that would have been a terrible thing to do. I'd have had it on my conscience for the rest of my life.'

'Yes, I'm sure you would. But why haven't you got up and dressed?'

'Because I'm too vain.' She pointed to the tunic which was hanging over the back of a chair. 'To get those papers I had to knock out the Russian woman who was sent to buy them, and I got away by dressing in her awful clothes. They are the only ones I've got, and I just couldn't bear the thought of shaming you by wearing those while dining with you in the restaurant.'

'Oh, we can have dinner sent up here to the sitting-room.'

'That's what I'd hoped you'd say. But I'd still hate you to see me in them. Would you mind very much if I wore my dressing gown?'

He smiled. 'It's O.K. by me. But the waiter will think the worst.'

'Let him, as far as I am concerned. It might not do you any good though, as you are a big shot in the set-up here. Still, I can make things all right by sitting at the table with one leg on a stool, and when you order you can tell the man that I must dine up here because I've been disabled by an accident.'

'Have you?' Eric's face expressed concern. 'I noticed this morning that you were lame and using a stick, but I thought that probably had something to do with the role you were playing.'

Linda pushed back a corner of the bedclothes, drew out her bad leg, pulled her nightdress up to her knee and showed him her bruised calf. It was now a hideous blotch of blue and purple.

'I say, that's a nasty one!' he exclaimed. 'Did you get it in your fight with the Russian woman?'

'No. I was knocked down by a car. It was my own fault, and I really treated the driver rather shabbily. I stole her car.'

He roared with laughter. 'Really, Linda! Those lovelies who appear in the James Bond films couldn't hold a candle to you.'

'Oh, you haven't heard the half of it,' she smiled. 'When I was shown in here, I simply had to get some sleep. But now I suppose I ought to do something about my leg.'

'Yes, you must. When I order dinner, I'll tell the waiter to get hold of some witch-hazel and a bandage. Is there anything special you would like to eat?'

'No. You know all my favourite dishes of old. I'm happy to leave it to you.'

Three-quarters of an hour later they had had their cocktails and were sitting down to dinner. When the waiter had left the room, Eric said, 'There's one thing which has always puzzled me. When Rowley died, why on earth did you steal those jewels?'

'Because he had never made a new will as he had promised he would, making provison for me. Everything went to Elsie. I had only about one hundred and eighty pounds in the bank, and no proper qualifications for any sort of decent job. In a few months I should have been living in some squalid boarding house, on a wage that would barely feed me, let alone buy any clothes. After the sort of life I had been leading, I couldn't face the thought of poverty, and I knew the combination of the safe. It was as simple as that.'

'Yes. That I understand. But what I don't, is why you didn't get in touch with me.'

'I should have, and I know you would have looked after me. I realised that afterwards, when it was too late. But you had gone abroad, and refused to leave your address with the idea that if I could not write to you I would the sooner forget you. And I thought a letter addressed simply care of the Foreign Office would probably take months to reach you.'

Eric shook his head. 'What a tragedy. I told you that I'd applied for a job abroad only because I knew that if we kept on seeing each other it would prove too much of a strain and things would be bound to blow up. Actually I was here all the time. I've been in this job for the past nine months.'

'Oh, if only I'd known! But I had so little time to think. To me, then, it seemed a choice of stealing the jewels within an hour, or facing the future almost penniless.'

'Yes, I see that; and, of course, your mind was not working normally. Rowley's death must have been an awful shock to you.'

'It was terrible. Absolutely horrifying. Far worse than you could know. He actually died on me.'

'Good God! But I thought that because of his heart you weren't going to let . . .'

'Well, I did. I know it was crazy of me. But we'd been out to dinner and had quite a lot to drink. When we got home he tried to persuade me, but I refused and went up to bed. He stayed downstairs for quite a while, knocking back more brandies. Then he came to my room, knelt down beside the bed and pleaded. He wept like a child. It was heartbreaking. I simply couldn't stand it and, in the end, gave way.'

'How ghastly! Neither Arthur nor Elsie told me a word about that.'

'They couldn't, because they didn't know. Nobody does. You see, if his dead body had been found in my bed, the Lucheni couple might have talked. I wasn't going to risk it getting round that a highly respected man like dear Rowley had died that way, and with a girl who was young enough to be his daughter. So I carried him down to his own room.'

Eric gazed at her in admiration. 'God alone knows how you managed it. But it was splendid of you.'

'I owed him that. After all he did for me, it was the least I could do.'

When the waiter had cleared away the dinner things, they settled themselves side by side on the sofa. She told him about how she had escaped from England and of the places she had been to in Canada, but nothing of her personal life. She did not feel like doing that unless the future held some hope of their seeing more of each other. In due course they got on to the subject of how she had succeeded in getting away from Ottawa, and she said:

'It was only by threatening to make a diplomatic incident of it, if they held me up, that I managed to bluff my way through Immigration on the Russian woman's passport. But I'd stand no chance of bluffing my way out of England with it, and I don't suppose that, without references, I could get a British one.'

He shook his head. 'Not a hope. Whatever name you used to apply for one, you would have to send in a photograph of yourself; and that would be as good as asking to be sent to gaol. You see, the department that issues passports has books of photographs of everyone wanted by the police, and the people there go through those books so often that it's at least twenty to one that the likeness would be spotted and you would be pulled in.'

'Then I'm stuck in England for good. What chance do you think I've got of keeping out of the clutches of the police?'

'That depends on where you live, and what sort of life you lead. London would be out of the question. There are so many people there: friends of Rowley's, waiters in restaurants, shop assistants and so on, who used to know you, that within a few months you would be certain to be recognised by someone; and that bitch, Elsie, has offered five hundred pounds reward for anyone supplying information that would lead to your arrest.'

Linda frowned. 'How typical of her. And, naturally, that would be a big temptation to many people if they recognised me.'

'It would. Again, a village would be almost as dangerous, because you are terribly handicapped by the fact that you are a very beautiful girl, and villagers are always curious about newcomers who have no obvious background. Remember, it's less than ten weeks since your photograph was in all the papers, and that makes you very vulnerable to people who have little to do but speculate about their neighbours.'

'I'd stand a better chance then in some provincial city?'

'Yes. Somewhere in the Midlands would be best. Not Scotland or Wales, because in either you would be, in a sense, a foreigner, so again a subject for speculation. But, wherever you settle, you will have to lead a very quiet life. Almost become a recluse in fact, because the more people you get to know, the greater the danger. The trouble is that, after a while, you will feel so secure that you will begin to take risks. That is why nearly all criminals are caught in the long run. Out of boredom,

you will be tempted to join a tennis club, go to sub-
scription dances or even take up charity work. Then,
sooner or later, you will run into someone who used to
know you in London.'

'Oh dear, oh dear!' Linda gave a heavy sigh. 'It
sounds too awful. I'm not yet twenty-one, and to be
condemned never to have any fun any more just
doesn't bear thinking about.'

He lit another cigarette, then said quietly: 'Of course,
there is an alternative. You can give yourself up.'

'But then I'll be sent to prison.'

'Yes, there would be no escaping that.'

Again there ran through Linda's mind the thoughts
she had had so often of all the grim discomforts and
privations she would have to suffer. At length she asked
in a low voice, 'How long do you think they'd give
me?'

Eric gave an unhappy shrug. 'It's difficult to say.
A great deal would depend on the mentality of the
judge who tried you. If he is broad-minded he might
let you off fairly lightly. If not, to put it frankly it
would weigh against you that you virtually prostituted
yourself to a man old enough to be your father, in
order to lead a life of luxury, then unscrupulously
robbed his heirs. He might send you down for three
years.'

'Three years!'

'Yes. But I don't think it would be as long as that,
because there is one good card we can play for you. This
remarkable coup that you've pulled off against the
Russians. Of course, that can't affect the fact that you
will be tried for having stolen the jewels, and the law
must take its course. The judge must pass sentence on
you. But you have rendered your country a very

valuable service. It can also be argued that you could have got away on the Russian's passport to South America. Instead, from entirely patriotic motives, you took an aircraft to Europe. Then, fate having brought you to England, you decided to give yourself up; and surrendering to justice will get you another good mark. So, with luck, you might be given only a year.'

'Even that is twelve months—three hundred and sixty-five days of scrubbing floors, porridge, cabbage, greasy stew, coarse clothes, only one bath a week, and the other women. No, I don't think I could. Anyhow, I must have time to think.'

'How long do you need?'

'Could I . . . could I take a week?'

'I suppose so. But I don't like it. You can hardly stay up here all the time, and down in the public rooms someone might well spot you.'

'No, I didn't mean here. I'd go to some quiet hotel in the country.' Linda paused for a moment, then added in a rush of words, 'Eric, you were in love with me. You told me so that night. Has my being a thief quite killed it? Or . . . or do you still love me a little?'

He took her hand and kissed it, 'My dear, what you did doesn't make the least difference, because I understand why you did it. Anyway, I've never ceased to love you. And you are the only woman I've ever really cared for since I fell out of love with my late wife.'

Her big eyes smiled her delight into his. 'Then couldn't we go away together? I don't mean for good, but just for the week, while I'm making up my mind. I haven't been altogether a good girl since I ran away, because, you see, I didn't expect that we would ever meet again. But I haven't been a very bad one. I've not done anything I am ashamed of. And an unofficial honeymoon with you would mean so very much to me. Whether I give myself up or not, I'd have that to look back on. It would be a memory to treasure all my life.'

Eric put his arms round her and kissed her very gently on the little mole behind her ear. 'Bless you, darling. You couldn't have thought of anything more wonderful. I'm due for some leave. But I'll have to spend tomorrow clearing up.'

She nodded. 'Yes. I'll need tomorrow, too, to buy myself some clothes.'

'Not on your life!' he said quickly. 'I'm not letting you risk arrest in London, even for an hour. If I work all-out in the morning, I can spend most of the after-noon in the West End. But, wait a minute. It's Satur-day, so it will have to be the other way round; and you'll have to make do with things off the peg; but give me your measurements and I'll get you everything you're likely to need.'

'That's it! You shall buy me a trousseau,' she laughed. 'All the pretty things you think I would look nicest in. And I've got lots of money for you to pay for them. That is, if it would be all right for you to change one of my thousand-dollar bills?'

He thought for a moment. 'Yes, why not? I don't think there can be any come-back about my doing that. As the Russians had used them to pay for stolen docu-ments, they can't claim that the notes were stolen from them, and the people who were selling the documents certainly dare not claim them.'

'Splendid, darling, splendid! Then I'll give you one of them and my measurements for everything. My leg is excuse enough for me to stay up here all day to-morrow. You'll come and dine with me again in the evening, and I'll try on all the pretty things you get for

me. Then Sunday morning we'll set off. But where shall
we go?'

'Devonshire,' he replied promptly. 'I know just the
place there where we will be as snug as bugs in a rug
and feed off the fat of the land. It's called the Gypsy
Hill Hotel, and it's at a little place called Pinhoe, near
Exeter. It is run by two old friends of mine: a Mr. and
Mrs. Jack Grout. For many years he was the manager
at Brown's in Dover Street, where foreign royalties and
good old county families often stay. But he left and
bought this place in Devonshire at least a year before
you came to London; so, even if you dined at Brown's
now and then with Rowley, the Grouts wouldn't
know you.'

Twenty-four hours later, in an ecstasy of happiness,
Linda had tried on all the clothes Eric had bought
for her, and had packed them in two new suitcases.

Early next morning, with Eric at the wheel of his
car, as light-hearted as a schoolboy starting his holiday,
they set off for Devonshire. He had telephoned for
rooms the previous day, and when they arrived at the
hotel the Grouts gave them the warmest possible
welcome.

For the five days and nights that followed Linda
determinedly put the future out of her mind. Brief as it
had to be, this was the honeymoon she had so often
longed for; and, when Eric made love to her, she
no longer had to shut her eyes and just imagine that it
was him. She could keep them open and smile into his
adored face while he smiled back his adoration of her.

Every day they drove out in the car or went for long
walks over the moors or through the woods. The
weather was now cold, and at times it rained, but they
were so blissfully happy that they hardly noticed.

During their long walks and in the evenings, seated beside a cheerful log fire, she told him all that had happened to her while she was abroad, concealing nothing. About Vancouver and Big Bear, about the happy fortnight she had spent in Montreal, of her disastrous encounter with Sid and how he had robbed her, then by his folly forced her to take to flight again, of Lake Louise and The Fisherman's Paradise, where she had felt herself safe. She told how, to amuse herself there, she had started to write a novel based on her own life, except that the heroine had stolen bearer bonds instead of jewels, and that it was to have a happy ending because it turned out that her middle-aged lover had made a new will after all, leaving her the bonds, of her arrest and escape, of her night in the forest and terrible experience the following day with the brutal lorry-driver, about her narrow escape from the police on arriving in Toronto and how Sir Colin Galahad had got her across Lake Ontario into the States. She continued with her few days in Chicago, telling of Marco and the horror from which she had saved herself after he had sold her into a brothel, about The Top and how she had bought her freedom by posing as Cherril Chanel and, unaware of what the documents really were, taken them across the frontier to Ottawa. And, finally, how she had overcome both Anna and Gerta, failed to get the papers to the High Commissioner but succeeded in fooling the Russians and getting away on the plane flying to Norway.

Inevitably there came their last night at Gypsy Hill. The halcyon days were over. Linda could no longer delay her fateful decision. At breakfast next morning she said to Eric:

'While I was in Canada, in spite of my being hunted

like a hare, there were at least some bright spots. But
here, if I go on the run again, I'll still be hunted yet
never dare mix with the sort of people I should like to
know. Only some dreary job, boredom and the never-
ending fear of being caught would lie ahead for me. So
I've decided to give myself up.'

'I'm glad, darling,' Eric said quietly. 'I haven't
sought to influence you, but I'm sure that will prove
best for you in the long run. And I'll be waiting for you
when you come out.'

'That's sweet of you,' she smiled. 'Knowing that, I
can stand up to anything. The only sad thing is that we
won't be able to marry.'

'Dearest, of course we shall get married.'

She shook her head. 'No, no! We'd never do that.
I couldn't possibly allow you to marry an ex-gaolbird.'

He laughed. 'Nonsense. You will have paid your
penalty for what I know to be only a moment of folly.
I'll be proud to have for my wife, not only the most
lovely but the most courageous woman in the world.'

They spoke little on the way back to London. That
night Linda slept in a cell. The next morning she was
brought before a magistrate and sent for trial. She
found the remand prison not uncomfortable, and the
wardresses were kind. Eric secured for her a leading
criminal barrister to whom, during several sessions, she
told everything.

A fortnight later she appeared at the Old Bailey. The
judge gave the impression of being severe. The men on
the jury eyed her with admiration, but there were five
women on it and only one of them looked at her with
sympathy. In any case she had pleaded guilty. The
counsel for the prosecution described her as a cynical,
unprincipled young woman. Elsie was in court,

gloating; but not Arthur. And, to Linda's surprise and
dismay, neither was Eric, for she had counted on his
presence for moral support through her ordeal.

The trial was well under way when Eric did arrive.
He was carrying a long, thick paper. Hurrying over
to Linda's counsel, he held a whispered conversation
with him. Together they looked at the document.
When the prosecutor finished his opening speech,
Linda's man stood up and addressed the judge:

'M'Lud. Most opportunely, new evidence has just
come to hand. The late Mr. Frobisher did make a later
will. I have it here. By its terms he left my client all his
jewels and capital sufficient to bring her in an income
of approximately one thousand pounds a year. I submit that there is no longer a case to answer.'

The will was handed up to the judge. He studied it
for a few minutes, then said, 'The case is dismissed.
Release the accused.' The woman on the jury who had
looked kindly at Linda smiled at her and waved her
hand. Linda burst into tears.

Ten minutes later she was in a taxi with Eric, on
their way to the Savoy. With her head on his shoulder,
she whispered, 'Oh, darling, how did you do it? How
did you do it?'

He laughed. 'You did it yourself, my sweet. You
remember the novel you started to write when you were
up at Lake Louise? Last night, when I was thinking
about you, that came back to me and I wondered if
there could be anything in it. A sort of second sight.
Anyhow, I decided to take a chance. In my job, it is
easy to get a search warrant, although one can get into
serious trouble if one does that without any justifica-
tion. First thing this morning I made up a story and got
one entitling me to search Arthur's office. I made him

open Rowley's deed box, and there was the will. I don't doubt that Elsie had persuaded him to suppress it. But the idiot had neglected to destroy it.'

'How wonderful. How absolutely wonderful.'

He laughed. 'I'm the lucky one. I'm getting a lovely wife with a private income and lots of jewels.'

'No. I've lost the jewels, darling. As I told you, I had to leave them in the bank in Vancouver. The police must have found out about that. Elsie would have been notified and she's probably sold most of them by now.'

'Oh no, she hasn't. They are still in Vancouver. The bank would never release them until you had been tried and found guilty, and it had been proved that they were Elsie's property.'

And so there came about the happy ending of *The Strange Story of Linda Lee*.

Dennis Wheatley's work has been published in:

BELGIUM

BRAZIL

CZECHOSLOVAKIA

DENMARK

FINLAND

FRANCE

GERMANY

GREECE

HOLLAND

HUNGARY

ITALY

MEXICO

NORWAY

POLAND

PORTUGAL

RUMANIA

SPAIN

SWEDEN

SWITZERLAND

TURKEY

THE UNITED STATES

YUGOSLAVIA

also in

ARABIC

ARMENIAN

FLEMISH

HINDI

MALTESE

RUSSIAN

SERBIAN

SLOVENE

THULU